Heart's Delight

~~~~~~~~

NEW YORK TIMES BESTSELLING AUTHOR
CHERYL HOLT

PRAISE FOR *NEW YORK TIMES* BESTSELLING AUTHOR CHERYL HOLT

"Best storyteller of the year..."
Romantic Times Magazine

"A master writer..."
Fallen Angel Reviews

"The Queen of Erotic Romance..."
Book Cover Reviews

"Cheryl Holt is magnificent..."
Reader to Reader Reviews

"From cover to cover, I was spellbound. Truly outstanding..."
Romance Junkies

"A classic love story with hot, fiery passion dripping from every page. There's nothing better than curling up with a great book and this one totally qualifies."
Fresh Fiction

"This is a masterpiece of storytelling. A sensual delight scattered with rose petals that are divinely arousing. Oh my, yes indeedy!"
Reader to Reader Reviews

Praise for Cheryl Holt's "Lord Trent" trilogy:

"A true guilty pleasure!"
Novels Alive TV

"LOVE'S PROMISE can't take the number one spot as my favorite by Ms. Holt—that belongs to her book NICHOLAS—but it's currently running a close second."
Manic Readers

"The book was brilliant...can't wait for Book #2."
Harlie's Book Reviews

"I guarantee you won't want to put this one down. Holt's fast-paced dialogue, paired with the emotional turmoil, will keep you turning the pages all the way to the end."
Susana's Parlour

"...A great love story populated with many flawed characters. Highly recommend it."
Bookworm 2 Bookworm Reviews

BOOKS BY CHERYL HOLT

HEART'S DEBT
SCOUNDREL
HEART'S DEMAND
HEART'S DESIRE
HEART'S DELIGHT
WONDERFUL
WANTON
WICKED
SEDUCING THE GROOM
LOVE'S PERIL
LOVE'S PRICE
LOVE'S PROMISE
SWEET SURRENDER
THE WEDDING
MUD CREEK
MARRY ME
LOVE ME
KISS ME
SEDUCE ME
KNIGHT OF SEDUCTION
NICHOLAS
DREAMS OF DESIRE
TASTE OF TEMPTATION
PROMISE OF PLEASURE
SLEEPING WITH THE DEVIL
DOUBLE FANTASY
FORBIDDEN FANTASY
SECRET FANTASY
TOO WICKED TO WED
TOO TEMPTING TO TOUCH
TOO HOT TO HANDLE
FURTHER THAN PASSION
DEEPER THAN DESIRE
MORE THAN SEDUCTION
COMPLETE ABANDON
ABSOLUTE PLEASURE
TOTAL SURRENDER
LOVE LESSONS
MOUNTAIN DREAMS
MY TRUE LOVE
MY ONLY LOVE
MEG'S SECRET ADMIRER
THE WAY OF THE HEART

ISBN: 9781483553016 (E-version)
ISBN: 9781508740049 (Print version)

Copyright 2016 by Cheryl Holt

All rights reserved under International and Pan-American Copyright Conventions.

By payment of required fees, you have been granted the *non*-exclusive, *non*-transferrable right to access and read the text of this book. No part of this text may be reproduced, transmitted, downloaded, decompiled, reverse engineered, stored in, or introduced into any information storage and retrieval system, in any form or by any means, whether electronic or mechanical, now known or invented in the future, without the express written permission or the copyright holder.

Please Note

The reverse engineering, uploading, and/or distributing of this book via the internet or via any other means without the permission of the copyright owner is illegal and punishable by law. Please purchase only authorized editions, and do not participate in or encourage the piracy of copyrighted materials. Your support of the author's rights is appreciated.

No part of this book may be reproduced or transmitted in any form or by any electronic or mechanical means, including photocopying, recording, or by any information storage and retrieval system, without the written permission of the author, except where permitted by law.

Thank you.

Cover Design Angela Waters
Interior e-format by Dayna Linton with Day Agency

Heart's Delight

PROLOGUE

"Give us another minute," Anne Blair begged. "Please?"

There was a sailor guarding the gangplank, and Etherton stoically tarried as the man glared at Anne in exasperation. He'd already given her five minutes to say goodbye to her children and was unmoved by her plea.

"I've been more than accommodating," the sailor told her. "If the captain looks down and sees us, he'll have my head. We have to make the tide."

He grabbed her arm to pull her away, and she beseeched, "One more minute! How can it hurt?"

Etherton tried to intervene, but the sailor wouldn't be deterred.

"I shouldn't have allowed this much, Mrs. Blair. You're pushing your luck."

Anne ignored him and spun to her oldest son, Bryce, who was five. He was a smart boy, a shrewd boy, and she leaned down so they were eye to eye.

"You'll be in charge of your siblings," she said. "Take care of them for me."

"I will, Mother," Bryce somberly declared, "but...but...you'll be back soon, won't you?"

Anne glanced at Etherton, shame in her gaze. They'd explained that it would be permanent, that her felony conviction and banishment to the penal colonies in Australia meant she couldn't return. But her children were very young, just five, three, and two years old. How could they be expected to grasp the concept of *forever*?

"I won't be back, Bryce." Anne sighed with regret. "We talked about this, remember?"

"Yes, but you know I don't understand. Why must you go away? Why can't we go with you?"

There was no time remaining for further clarification or debate. There were only these last poignant seconds of farewell.

"You must be strong for me, Bryce," she murmured. "While I'm away, I want to always recollect how strong you are. Make your father proud." At the mention of her beloved, deceased husband, Julian, she shuddered and nearly collapsed.

"I will make Father proud," Bryce said. "I will, but he left, and now you're leaving too."

"Watch over Sissy, especially. The world is hard for girls, harder than it is for boys."

As if recognizing the import of her mother's words, the smallest child, Annie, whom they all called Sissy, slipped her hand into Bryce's. She was blond and blue-eyed, like a porcelain doll, and her sad expression broke Etherton's heart. How did Anne bear it?

She turned to her twin sons, Michael and Matthew, and she held out her arms. Her wrists were shackled, but she reached out anyway. The twins, being rough-and-tumble scalawags, looked at each other, nodded in agreement that they wished to be hugged, then they let her draw them to her bosom.

Shortly they squirmed away and stared at her, appearing concerned and very solemn. They seemed to fathom—better than Bryce or Sissy—that something very bad had happened that could never be repaired.

Sissy was next. She leaned into her mother, and Anne kissed her hair and rumpled her golden curls.

"My little angel. How will I continue on without you?"

Then she reached for Bryce, but he refused her final embrace.

"Don't leave us!" he furiously said. "I can't watch over them."

"Etherton will help you."

"I don't want Etherton. I want you. And Father. I want to go home."

Anne and Etherton exchanged a tormented glance. Their home was forfeit, their secure existence was forfeit, the life they'd known was forfeit. There was no home for them any longer, no parents or stability or family. From this moment on, there would only be chaos and uncertainty.

Up on the deck, a whistle blew, and suddenly the crew was running and yelling to each other. Ropes were pulled and doors slammed.

"We're out of time," the sailor muttered, and Anne had arrived at the end.

She was yanked to her feet, and though she resisted, she was dragged to the gangplank.

She'd promised Etherton she would be composed and circumspect so she wouldn't frighten the children more than they already had been. Yet she wailed with dismay, and her obvious distress terrified the children.

Sissy began to cry, while the twins scowled and grabbed for her. Bryce called out for all of them, "Mother! Mother!"

He tried to race after her to stop the sailor who was taking her away, but Etherton held onto him, fighting to subdue the boy as he lashed out in a futile attempt to rescue his mother.

In the flit of an instant she vanished onto the ship, and a dangerous silence settled on the dock as they all gaped at the spot where she'd been. They dawdled, waiting for something to transpire, perhaps for someone to speak up and clarify how a mother could be sent away and her children left behind as if they were excess baggage. But there was no rationalization that could justify it.

Down the block, Etherton's driver cleared his throat, the carriage horses shifting impatiently, rattling the harness.

"Let's go, children," Etherton mumbled.

"No," Bryce insisted. "Not yet. She might…might…"

"Might what?" Etherton barked more angrily than he'd intended.

Their father, Julian, was dead in a suspicious hunting accident that Etherton didn't believe had been an accident at all. Their mother, Anne, was being transported as a convicted felon, and Etherton was left behind to clean up the mess. He didn't have children of his own and hadn't wanted the responsibility thrust on him.

But he'd loved their father, would have died for him, would have killed for him, and he would keep Julian's children safe. He would keep them safe or he would perish in the trying.

"Bryce," he stated more calmly, "she won't be back down. They won't let her off the ship. I realize it's difficult to understand, but we must be away."

Nervously he peered around. He didn't suppose Julian's kin would show up at the docks, didn't suppose they cared enough about Anne's children to harm them. However he wasn't taking any chances, and with such fortunes at stake, there was no telling how a greedy person might behave.

"Where are we to go?" Bryce asked. He was blond and blue-eyed like Anne, but he was tough and tenacious too, like Julian. He'd inherited all his parents' best traits.

"I'll explain in the carriage," Etherton vaguely said.

He motioned to two of his servants, and they bustled over. It was a husband and wife, Mr. and Mrs. Wilson, a loyal older couple who could keep secrets. They were accompanied by their adult daughter. Etherton had arranged for the siblings to be separated and sent to boarding schools. It seemed a good way to hide them, and he didn't know what else to do.

Under the circumstances, they had no relatives he could trust, and he was a bachelor without the means to raise four children.

As Mr. and Mrs. Wilson approached, he tamped down his spurt of conscience. He hadn't provided any details to Anne about the children's fate. She'd had enough to worry about, and she'd been too beaten down by events to question his plans.

It was rare for such youngsters to attend school, but the right sort of bribe could open any door, and Anne had given him the last of her money—a substantial amount—and advised him to use it for expenses. The children would be reared in stable situations. They'd be fed and sheltered and educated. They'd be fine.

Wouldn't they?

Etherton pointed to Sissy and told the Wilsons' daughter, "You take her." Then he pointed at the twins and told Mr. Wilson, "And you and your wife take them. You have your instructions, yes?"

The three Wilsons nodded as Bryce frowned and asked, "Where are they going?"

"They're going with Mr. and Mrs. Wilson for a bit," Etherton claimed. "You'll come with me."

"No, I can't allow it." Bryce sounded very much like the little lord he was. "Mother wants me to watch over them. How can I if we're separated?"

"You'll see them again very soon." Etherton hoped the statement was true, but figured it probably wasn't.

It had all happened so fast—Julian's death, Anne's arrest and trial—almost as if Julian's father had orchestrated the swift resolution. Matters were still unsettled, and Etherton couldn't guess when they would calm, when he could stop peeking over his shoulder.

"When will I see them?" Bryce sternly demanded. "When?"

"Tomorrow," Etherton lied.

The entire morning had been too awful, and he gestured to the Wilsons to hurry away, desperate for the horrid interval to be over. He had no idea how to deal with such misery, with shrieking, fretful children who were too young to comprehend what had destroyed them. Would they ever comprehend it?

Mrs. Wilson's daughter picked up Sissy, and she started to scream and weep. She reached out to Bryce, her plump hands beseeching. Bryce clasped hold and shouted for the woman to put Sissy down, but Sissy was yanked away.

Mr. Wilson seized the twins, but they kicked and struggled, so he looped an arm around each one, hoisted them off the ground, and marched away.

The last Etherton ever saw of the twins, they were peering back, stubbornly and silently staring at their brother and sister. Their blue eyes—their father's magnificent blue eyes—shifted to Etherton. They were disdainful and condemning, as if they blamed Etherton for what had transpired.

How could two such small boys be so resolute and contemptuous? They rarely spoke except to each other, and they talked in a secret language only they understood. Perhaps they were brighter than they seemed. Perhaps they grasped much more about the debacle than Etherton had realized.

They were little lords too, just like Bryce, but they were all lost lords now.

Their sneering, scornful gazes dug into Etherton as if to say, *We'll get even for this. We'll get even—and everyone will pay for what they've done to our family.*

CHAPTER ONE

"I'M HERE TO SEE the notorious gambler and criminal, Mr. Michael Scott."

Magdalena Wells, known as Maggie to her friends and family, glared at the oaf guarding the door. He'd just refused her entrance to Mr. Scott's disreputable gambling club, but she was angry and aggrieved and had no time for posturing or nonsense.

The man studied her gray dress, her stern manner, her imperious deportment. "Who shall I say is calling? The bloody Queen of England?"

Maggie didn't care for his attitude or his foul language, and her fury soared.

"There's no need to be rude or crude," she said.

"If you don't like my language, you don't have to stay."

She had no patience for fools and nearly stomped out, but her quest was important, and she wouldn't leave until she'd spoken in person to the exalted, obnoxious Mr. Scott.

"In your line of employment," she told him, "I'm certain you don't often cross paths with a lady, but I assure you I am one. Behave yourself."

Her steely tone garnered his attention, and he flushed with chagrin.

"Yes, ma'am."

"Now then, take me to Michael Scott and be quick about it. Tell him I am proprietress of the Vicar Sterns Rescue Mission."

"Are you hoping to rescue him?"

"No, I've come to give him a piece of my mind."

"That'll send him into a swoon," the man muttered, but he stepped back and motioned her in. Outside it was a bright, sunny June afternoon, so it took a minute for her vision to adjust.

The foyer of Mr. Scott's establishment—hailed far and wide simply as *Scotts*—was dark and dank, and it smelled of stale liquor, tobacco, and wanton habits. In the main room there were tables and chairs arranged in haphazard rows, and she could imagine it on a busy Saturday evening when it would be packed with inebriated men who would wager away their money.

One wall was lined with shelves holding wine bottles and liquor decanters. The other three were covered with large, garish paintings of nude women. Their bared breasts were most prominent, the reddened nipples seeming to leap off the canvas.

The portraits were extremely disturbing, and she was offended by them, but she kept her expression blank, not wishing to provide any hint that she was unnerved by the risqué sight. And she wasn't. Not really.

Over the past few years, she'd grown practical and rational, the calm port in any storm. It would take more than the picture of a naked female to fluster her or deter her from the conversation she was intent on having.

"Mr. Scott, please," she said. "If you'll show me to him?"

"Follow me."

The guard led her in, and though it was only two o'clock, there were men lurking in the corners, drinking hard spirits and numbly watching her pass. Their gazes were curious and prurient.

She experienced a stab of compassion for them, wondering about the sorry state of their lives that they would dawdle in such a seedy place. She wanted to speak to each of them, wanted to discuss what had brought them there, what kept them from departing.

But she didn't. She had no business visiting as she had and wouldn't remain a second longer than necessary.

They continued on, climbed a narrow staircase, and walked down a hall to the end. They stopped at a closed door, and her escort knocked briskly, waited for a reply, didn't receive one, then knocked again.

"What?" a surly male bellowed from inside.

"You have a visitor, Mr. Scott."

"I asked not to be disturbed. Were you confused by my order? Wasn't I clear?"

"You were clear, sir, but she insisted on talking to you. She wouldn't go away."

"She? It's a woman?"

"Yes."

"If you couldn't get rid of a measly woman, what good are you at guarding the door?"

"She's a wee sprite," the man responded, "but she seems ferocious. I didn't think I should rile her."

"She might bite?"

"Maybe."

"Is she pretty?"

There was the most awkward pause as she was thoroughly evaluated.

Maggie could have answered the idiotic question herself. At the moment, she was attired in a drab gray dress, white fabric at the collar and cuffs, and buttoned up from chin to toes as any proper British woman should be. Her hair was pulled into a tight chignon, her gray bonnet shielding the vibrant red color and washing out her features.

She might have been a fussy governess, but in light of the dreary, poverty-filled world in which she existed, she deliberately strove to appear nondescript.

But she had a mirror in her bedchamber, and she could see herself in it. With her auburn hair and merry blue eyes, she was very fetching. She was too thin though, work and worry leaving scant time for leisure pursuits, and there was no overabundance of food at the mission, so her diet was rather sparse. Yet despite being slender, she was femininely curved in all the right spots.

While she wasn't inclined to vanity, she recognized that she'd be incensed if she was described as plain or ordinary, and she snapped, "Oh, for pity's sake. Just open the blasted door."

"I wouldn't dare to."

Previously in her life she'd been a courteous young lady of good family and good reputation, but seven years spent interacting with street urchins had toughened her. Having shed many of her prior virtues, she reached for the knob and blustered in without considering whether she should.

"Mr. Scott, I presume?" She'd been prepared to march over in a huff, but she stumbled to a halt.

"Who the hell are you?" he barked.

She stood very still, determined not to exhibit by so much as the flicker of a brow that she was shocked or dismayed. Why, oh why, had she barged in? What was she thinking?

Michael Scott was seated in a chair behind his desk. Unfortunately, there was a trollop seated with him, balanced on his thigh and doing things Maggie could only guess at. The front of the trollop's dress was unbuttoned, the fabric pushed to her waist, her bosom exposed. Her blond hair hung down her back in a curly wave, her combs scattered on the desktop.

On seeing Maggie, the girl squealed with dismay and leapt to her feet. She struggled with her clothes to shield what should never have been on full display.

Maggie ignored the girl and focused on Mr. Scott, being desperate to learn if any of the wild rumors swirling through the neighborhood about him might be true.

There was an air of danger about him, so she couldn't show any fear or vacillation. He was like a hawk circling in the sky, and at the slightest sign of weakness he'd rip her to shreds.

She hadn't expected him to be extremely handsome, but he was. His hair was black, worn too long and tied into a ponytail with a strip of ribbon. Though he was sitting down, she predicted he'd be very tall, six feet at least. His shoulders were very wide, his arms muscled, his body physically fit. He appeared tough and strong, as if he fenced or boxed to keep himself in shape.

But it was his eyes that most intrigued her. They were very blue, alert and searching, probing every detail of her dull gown, her severe countenance. He was taking her measure, trying to figure her out, and she wanted to say, You'll never unravel my secrets. Not in a thousand years, but she held her tongue.

The trollop had finished buttoning her dress. She nervously peeked at him, and he shooed her out. She scooted by Maggie, the sound of her strides swiftly fading down the hall.

Mr. Scott leaned back in his chair and asked her escort, "Who is this?"

Her escort answered, "She claims to be Miss Magdalena Wells, from the Vicar Sterns Rescue Mission."

"The Rescue Mission?"

"Yes."

Mr. Scott snorted with derision. "I'd have thought such a do-gooder would have better manners."

"As I mentioned, sir," the guard replied, "she's a tad ferocious."

"That she is," Mr. Scott agreed.

Maggie scoffed and stepped to the desk. "Don't talk about me as if I'm not here."

She was having the devil of a time deciding where to look, whether she should stare at Mr. Scott's face or at his person. His blue eyes were riveting and disquieting, but his shirt was open to the waist, so quite a bit of male flesh was exposed, and he'd made no effort to conceal it.

Maggie had had limited experiences with men, and in a society where people completely concealed themselves with clothing in all situations, she didn't think she'd ever seen a man's bare chest before. She was surprised to note a dusting of hair across the top, and the sight of that hair, dark as the hair on his head, tickled her innards.

Her cheeks heated, and she flushed, which he noticed immediately, and he smirked.

"What brings you by, Miss Wells?" he asked. "What can I do for you? Is there something *special* you were hoping to accomplish with me?"

He was scrutinizing her bosom, so it didn't take more than a moment to realize his question was impertinent.

"Stop it," she fumed.

"Stop what?" He appeared innocent as a choirboy.

"Stop being rude."

"Was I being rude?" His tone dripped with sarcasm. "Then I most humbly apologize." He pointed to a chair. "Would you like to sit?"

"I prefer to stand."

"As you wish, but I have no desire to stand with you, so I'll remain seated. Is that all right with you?"

"Yes, that's fine."

"May I offer you a refreshment?"

She shuddered to imagine what sort of *refreshment* might be provided in such a place. "No, thank you."

"Suit yourself." He gestured to her escort. "May he leave us and return to his duties? Or are you frightened to be in here alone with me? Will your reputation be shredded if we don't have a chaperone?"

"I'm twenty-five, and I've been on my own for seven years. I hardly need a chaperone, and I'm not afraid of you."

"You're not?"

"No, so don't act the bully. You can't scare me."

"Well then, I won't even try."

He waved his employee away, and the man slinked out and closed the door. The quiet settled, and very quickly Maggie grasped she should have had the guard stay.

She'd been truthful when she said she wasn't afraid of Mr. Scott. He oozed virility and stamina in a manner no other male of her acquaintance ever had, but she sensed no menace from him. He might preen and posture, and she'd heard he could be deadly if provoked, but she didn't feel he would harm *her*.

Still though, she hated having the door shut. The room was small, and he simply took up too much space in it. She wanted to walk over and yank the door open, but she'd insisted he didn't scare her, and she wouldn't give him the satisfaction of thinking that she might have been lying.

He stared, waiting for her to start, and it occurred to her that this would be much more difficult than she'd assumed. On the way over she'd drafted a pretty speech in her head, but now that they were face to face, she couldn't begin.

He wasn't what she'd been expecting at all.

Terrible tales constantly swirled about him and his antics. He'd grown up on the streets of London, an orphan who was brilliant and dangerous and amoral. He would cheat and steal and rob or kill without a ripple in his conscience—if it increased his personal wealth.

He owned the gambling club and was a gambler himself, but he also loaned money at exorbitant interest rates, and he owned buildings and property and ships. He smuggled and blackmailed and purportedly engaged in every unsavory business practice ever devised.

He had a penchant for violence too, and because of the gossip she'd always pictured him as an ogre, the kind who huddled under bridges and devoured unsuspecting travelers.

But he wasn't horrid. He was handsome and clean-shaven and obviously rich. Dressed casually in a flowing white shirt and tan trousers, his clothes were exquisitely tailored and sewn from expensive fabrics.

He was much younger than she'd expected too. She'd envisioned him as being grim and elderly, but he wasn't much older than she was. She was twenty-five, and he was probably thirty. There was a rough edge to him though, as if he'd struggled and persevered through difficulties she'd never had to experience.

"I'm busy, Miss Wells, so get on with it, would you? Are you here to scold me, evangelize, or beg me for a donation?"

His snide tone jolted her out of her stupor. "I hadn't thought of asking you for a donation, but I'd love you to contribute to the mission."

"You're not too proud to take ill-gotten gains?"

She scoffed. "No. Ill-gotten gains and virtuous gains buy the same kinds of food for the hungry."

"That they do."

His intense scrutiny was disturbing, and she was perplexed by the offer of charitable money. She'd believed him to be cruel and vicious and was disconcerted by the evident disparities in his character. Perhaps there was some hope for success.

"Have you heard of the Rescue Mission?" she inquired.

"Of course. In this neighborhood, who hasn't?"

"Vicar Sterns and his wife purchased it several years ago. They've passed on, and I run it now."

"You?"

"Yes. Why are you so surprised?"

"A stiff wind would blow you over."

"What has that to do with anything?"

"You just don't seem the type."

She snorted with disgust. "What *type* is that?"

"You're too pretty to dabble with the less fortunate, and since you're a *miss*, you're not married. Why aren't you? You should be home tending a dozen brats instead of trying to aid desperate people who couldn't care less."

His comment required so many retorts that she was dizzy with figuring out which she should address first.

He thought she was pretty! How thrilling!

Yet she shoved away the remark, refusing to linger over it like a dog at a bone. No, she wasn't married, and the reason was too humiliating to reveal and she never discussed it. As to her helping others, how dare he denigrate her efforts!

"You grew up on the streets, Mr. Scott."

He nodded. "I did."

"You had to have been provided assistance. When you were, weren't you grateful?"

"No one ever helped me. I helped myself." He stared at her, those cool, riveting blue eyes showing no emotion. "You still haven't answered my question. Why aren't you married? You're not getting any younger. Why waste time on nonsense?"

"Nonsense!" she huffed. "You're being ridiculous."

"Am I?"

"Yes, let's get back to business."

"You haven't told me what it is. I've said I'll donate, but you haven't departed, so you're either about to evangelize or scold. Which is it?"

Despite her owning a Christian mission, she wasn't very religious, and she'd learned practical wisdom from Vicar Sterns. He hadn't been overly concerned with sin and damnation. His worries had run to more mundane issues, to the hordes of homeless waifs who were starving and unclothed. If that was the focus, a lot of sin could be overlooked.

Maggie had adopted his pragmatic attitude, and the idea of her preaching was humorous. "I'm not about to sermonize."

"Praise be. What is it then? I'm to be scolded? As we haven't previously met, I can't imagine how I could have upset you."

"Your reputation precedes you, Mr. Scott. You've done plenty."

"I stand corrected. I have been known to misbehave on occasion. What has spurred your visit? Did I spit on the sidewalk? Kick a dog? Curse in front of a female? What?"

"A boy has been employed here."

"Yes, I employ many boys."

"He ate regularly at the mission. He was a good boy, a sweet boy."

Mr. Scott's beautiful, seductive mouth curled into a smile, and she was taken aback by it. She'd already admitted he was handsome. How could he become even more striking? It didn't seem possible.

"This boy was living on the streets," he said, "and eating at your mission and you describe him as *sweet*?"

"Just because a person is poor, it doesn't mean he's corrupt. I'm sure this is a very fine establishment—"

"Oh, it's the very height of posh and opulence."

She ignored his sarcasm. "I refuse to have him working for you."

"*You* refuse."

"Yes."

"Are you his mother? His sister? What?"

"I'm merely worried about his future under your tutelage. May I be blunt, Mr. Scott?"

"Yes, please be blunt."

"I've heard terrible stories about you."

He chuckled. "I'm certain they're all true."

"I want to take him with me when I leave."

"Are you positive he wishes to go?"

"No, but if I could speak with him…?"

He narrowed his gaze, clearly trying to figure out what drove her. Ultimately he asked, "What's his name?"

"Tim. He's ten or so. Brown hair. Very thin."

"Aren't they all?"

He stood and went to the door, and he opened it and hollered down the hall. "Ramsey, I need you."

He came back to the desk, and they listened as heavy boot steps pounded up the stairs. A man loomed in the doorway. He was broader and taller than Mr. Scott, handsome too, and dressed in black clothes, so he appeared menacing in a way Mr. Scott didn't seem to be.

"What?" he inquired of Mr. Scott.

"Have we hired a new boy named Tim?"

"I believe we have."

"What are his duties?"

"This and that." Mr. Ramsey made a waffling motion with his hand, the phrase *this and that* obviously intended to hide what Tim had been hired to do.

There were rumors he was training as a pickpocket. A pickpocket! As if a boy should be trained at such a task! Her temper flared.

"This and that?" Maggie was incredulous. "What precisely would that position entail?"

Both men ignored her, and Mr. Scott said, "Fetch him."

Ramsey left, and as she and Mr. Scott waited for Tim to arrive, she noted that her knees were quaking.

She peeked at the chair he'd offered earlier, anxious to walk over and slide down onto it, but she didn't know how to pull it off with any aplomb. She'd been too snotty in her insistence that she'd remain standing.

The quiet interval was fraught with distress that she hadn't realized she was harboring. For idiotic reasons she couldn't fathom, she couldn't bear to have Mr. Scott deem her a ninny or a fool. She craved his good opinion and yearned for him to view her as being worthy of esteem, but why would it matter? He was a brigand. Who cared what his opinion might be?

To her relief, footsteps sounded on the stairs, ending the tense, awkward moment.

Mr. Scott murmured, "You can't save the whole world, Miss Wells."

"I can try."

"You can, but doesn't it seem pointless sometimes?"

Ramsey entered, and Tim followed. He looked different, clean and tidied, and he was wearing new clothes, his previously-pale cheeks rosy with color.

"You sent for me, Mr. Scott?" He neared the desk, but blanched when he saw Maggie. "Miss Wells? What are you doing here?"

"I heard you're working for Mr. Scott," Maggie said.

Tim blushed. "Ah...yes, I am."

"You can't want to."

"I *do* want to," Tim asserted. "I've been hoping for years that Mr. Scott would notice me."

"Why?"

"A boy can rise very high in his employ—if he's loyal and learns his craft. Everyone knows it."

Mr. Scott smirked. "See, Miss Wells? Tim is fine."

Maggie stared at Tim. "Will you leave with me? Please?"

"Why would I?" Tim replied. "I like it here."

"You can't mean it."

"I mean it, Miss Wells. Really." He peered over at Mr. Scott. "Will that be all, sir?"

"Yes."

Mr. Scott waved Tim out, and Ramsey led him away.

Maggie gaped at Mr. Scott, and to her horror, she was on the verge of bursting into tears.

He'd said she couldn't save the whole world, but why couldn't she save her little corner of it? Did every boy have to meet a bad end? Did every child have to struggle and toil and degrade himself? There was so much poverty and strife, and for just a second the weight of all those desperate souls seemed balanced on her slender shoulders, and the burden was much too heavy to carry.

He shrugged. "You were fretting over nothing."

"You'll train him in petty crime. He'll become a criminal, and it will be all your fault."

"He'll have a few coins in his pocket and a dry, warm bed to sleep in. It beats starving out in the rain and the cold."

"He'll likely be hanged before you're through with him."

"There are worse endings for a boy."

"Name one," she fumed.

He didn't reply, but scowled, his expression telling her she was an idiot. He gestured to the door, indicating her appointment was over.

"Are we finished?" he inquired. "I've been more than patient."

"I want the donation you promised me," she petulantly said. "I demand it as reparation for all the ways you'll eventually damage Tim."

"I've changed my mind about it. I can't stand people who ride their moral high-horse. You're too persnickety, and I don't like you."

"You don't *like* me?"

"No."

"We're scarcely acquainted. How could you have received sufficient details to have formed an opinion?"

"I'm an excellent judge of character."

"And in your infinite wisdom, what sort of person have you *judged* me to be?"

"You think you're a saint."

"I do not!"

"But you ought to see the world as the dangerous, hard place it actually is."

"I don't need a lecture from you on what the world is like."

"Don't you?"

Because she'd spent years helping the needy, she was regularly thanked and lauded and praised. She couldn't remember the last time she'd been insulted or disparaged. Well, except by her family, but they didn't count.

She was furious and aggrieved and feeling greatly maligned. She'd like to castigate him, to list all the reasons he was wrong about her, but for once she was tongue-tied and couldn't conceive of a single remark worth sharing.

He rose and came over, and he towered over her, glaring as if she was young and foolish and out of her element.

He dragged her over to the door and pushed her into the hall. It was a gentle push, but a push nonetheless.

"Goodbye, Miss Wells. Don't darken my door again with your nonsense."

"I wouldn't lower myself," she huffed.

"Good." He shouted, "Ramsey!"

In a trice, Ramsey appeared. "What now?"

"Miss Wells is leaving. Escort her out, and tell the footmen if she shows up again and they let her in, heads will roll."

"Heads will *roll?*" she scoffed. "Oh, you are by far and away the most exasperating man I've ever had the displeasure to meet."

"I try," he smugly retorted, and he motioned to Ramsey.

Ramsey reached for her arm, but she shook him away and stomped off. She was about to start down the stairs when she peered around at Mr. Scott. He was watching her, looking amused and elegant and maddening beyond measure.

"You haven't heard the last of me," she absurdly warned.

"I'm trembling in my boots, Miss Wells."

"I'll speak with the authorities about Tim. I'll inform them of how you abuse boys in this neighborhood."

His laugh was cruel and snide. "Don't you know, Miss Wells? I *am* the authority in this neighborhood. My word is law. Now go away and don't come back."

He vanished into his office.

She hovered on the top step, yearning to march back to him, to apprise him of what she truly thought, but she wasn't a fighter. She was a problem solver and helper who never argued over any issue, which was why her personal life was such a mess.

She whipped away and kept on down the stairs.

CHAPTER TWO

"What happened to the furniture in the blue salon?"

"Whatever do you mean?"

Maggie glared at her sister, Pamela, and from how Pamela glanced away, it was clear she was about to lie. Pamela was two years older than Maggie, and at age twenty-seven she was no better at fibbing than she'd been as a young girl.

"We've been redecorating," Pamela claimed.

"Redecorating?"

"I'm sure you've heard of it, Magdalena. It's when you spruce up the décor."

"Very funny."

They were in the front parlor at Cliffside, the beautiful country mansion that had been in her family for two centuries. It was a lovely June evening, and the house was full of guests. Mostly they were neighbors, but there were also many people who'd traveled from London.

Her other sister, Rebecca, had just turned twenty-two, and she and Pamela had arranged a weeklong house party to celebrate Rebecca's birthday. Normally Maggie would rather have gone to the barber to have a tooth pulled than visit Cliffside, but despite how she tried to distance herself, she couldn't stay away entirely. Cliffside was home, and Rebecca and Pamela her only relatives in the world.

"I went to the bank the other day," she said.

"How nice," Pamela cooed, not really paying attention.

"I learned the oddest thing."

"What was it?"

"My monthly stipend never arrived. I don't suppose you have any information about it?"

Maggie had once had a fine dowry, but she hadn't married, and the money was still sitting in a trust. Because of what had happened with Pamela—what their father had permitted to happen—her father had let Maggie draw the interest as an allowance.

During her seven years of living in London, she'd had funds to see her through the lean times at the mission. But suddenly there was no money. She wanted to believe it was a mistake, but she suspected that the truth was much grimmer than that.

When she was seventeen, she'd met Gaylord Farrow, a dashing rogue who had flirted and charmed her until she'd fallen madly in love. He'd proposed very quickly, and she hadn't hesitated to accept, and her father—who'd been charmed too—had readily agreed to the match.

Yet a week before the wedding, it had all collapsed.

Pamela had fallen in love with Gaylord too, and Maggie had never been able to decide if it had been genuine fondness for Gaylord or whether she'd done it out of jealousy and spite for not having been wed yet herself.

Pamela and Gaylord had announced to Maggie's father that they'd misbehaved and Pamela was ruined. Gaylord insisted his engagement to Maggie be severed because of what had occurred. Pamela had been their father's favorite, and as the oldest daughter, she'd had a much larger dowry than Maggie.

Initially Maggie had tried to tell herself that Gaylord couldn't have been that crass or greedy that he'd have switched his focus to Pamela merely because of the size of her dowry, but with how matters had played out, Maggie was certain it had been about the extra money. It didn't hurt that he had an enormous ego, and Pamela was a weak person who worshipped Gaylord in a way Maggie never would have.

Pamela was also too timid to put her foot down over any of his misdeeds—and there had been plenty.

Their widowed father had been a rich gentleman who'd never sired any sons. Gaylord had flattered and cajoled until the poor man was blinded to any of Gaylord's faults. But hadn't they all been blinded?

With Gaylord promising to look after Pamela, Maggie, and Rebecca, their father had named Gaylord as his heir so that, after he'd died, Gaylord inherited the estate. Yet as they'd subsequently discovered, Gaylord was a profligate gambler who was swiftly pushing them to the edge of ruin, and they were at his mercy.

Had Gaylord gotten his hands on Maggie's dowry? Had he spent it? If Maggie's allowance was gone, how would she remain in London? How would she keep the charity mission open?

If she was forced to close it she'd have to move back to Cliffside, and the notion of living with Gaylord and Pamela was no more palatable than it had been on their wedding day when Maggie had watched her great love marry her duplicitous, conniving sister.

"You haven't answered me," Maggie said to Pamela.

"What was the question again?"

"My allowance wasn't deposited in the bank this month. What

happened to it?"

"How would I know? You'll have to ask Gaylord."

"Believe me, I will," Maggie fumed, but Pamela had already sauntered away.

As she departed, Rebecca sidled up. She and her two sisters were the same height, and they'd previously been the same size, but over the years Pamela had gained a substantial bit of weight while Rebecca was still slender and shapely. They all had their father's blue eyes, but Maggie had auburn hair while Pamela's and Rebecca's was a chestnut brown that they'd inherited from their mother, who'd passed away when they were girls.

"What did Pamela tell you about the blue salon?" Rebecca inquired.

"She claims she's redecorating."

Rebecca snickered. "It's Gaylord's gambling debts. He's quietly selling our belongings."

Maggie was aghast. Her visits to Cliffside were always contentious, so she'd arrived late to the party, the festivities in progress. She'd been too busy to notice many changes.

"He's selling our furniture?" She was stunned and irate.

"Yes. Wait until you have more time to explore. Most of the upstairs rooms are empty."

"Oh, my Lord! Why didn't you write me?"

"What could you have done?"

That was a question for the ages, wasn't it? What could any of them have done?

Gaylord had been a perfectly acceptable young man from a good family, so when he'd ingratiated himself, there'd been no reason to beware. He'd seduced them into thinking they couldn't live without him, and he'd wound up taking everything they had.

Had any three women ever been so naïve? Why had they trusted him? Why hadn't they seen him for the snake he was?

"If Gaylord and Pamela are desperate enough to sell the furniture," Maggie said, "why are they hosting this lavish party?"

"Honestly, Maggie. It's my birthday. What were we supposed to do? Ignore it?"

Rebecca gaped at Maggie, appearing truly perplexed by Maggie's query. It would never have occurred to Rebecca that she couldn't afford a party.

Maggie could have launched into a lecture about finances and budgeting, but what was the point?

They'd grown up prosperous, pampered, and spoiled, and reality hadn't crashed down for Rebecca. Maggie was the only one who'd left Cliffside, the only one who'd ever had to pay a bill or water down the soup so it lasted a few more days. Rebecca and Pamela still deemed themselves to be wealthy, and they hadn't the vaguest idea what it meant to be poor.

What would become of them? If Gaylord beggared them completely, where would they go?

Rebecca leaned in and whispered, "Guess what else?"

Maggie was almost too terrified to know. "What?"

"The man who holds Gaylord's markers? He's coming here tomorrow."

Maggie gasped. "They'll welcome him into our home?"

"Yes, *and* Gaylord wants me to charm the stupid oaf."

"To what end?"

"Gaylord thinks he'll be smitten and decide to marry me." Rebecca laughed and batted her lashes. "Isn't that the most ridiculous news you've ever heard?"

"He hopes you'll marry this…this gambler?"

"Yes. Apparently he assumes if I'm the man's bride, the debt might be forgiven."

"Gaylord would betroth you to square his gambling debts?"

"Can you believe it?" Rebecca laughed again. "As if I'd lift a finger to help him."

Maggie gazed across the room to where Gaylord was regaling a group of neighbors with one of his humorous stories. It would be a ribald jest that would have them chuckling and murmuring about what a jolly chap he was.

He liked others to view him as smart, shrewd, and successful, but he was simply cruel and amoral.

When Maggie had first met him, she'd often stood on the edge of similar groups, yearning for him to notice her. She'd been seventeen, and he'd been a much older twenty-four. He'd seemed mature and sophisticated, and she'd been imprudently and rashly smitten.

With his blond hair and blue eyes, he was still handsome, but in a dodgy, deceitful fashion. At five-foot ten, he'd once been virile and fit, but as with Pamela, he'd thrived on the rich diet at Cliffside and now had a definite paunch.

She'd like to march over, pinch that paunch, and order him to stop gorging on the last of their food.

In an adjoining salon, a neighbor's daughters banged out some chords on the harpsichord and violin, an indication that the dancing was about to commence.

Rebecca beamed with pleasure. "Let's go in, Maggie. We have to snatch up the best partners before they're all taken."

"You start without me."

"Don't be silly. You can't have danced in ages."

"I'm tired. I'll join in later."

"Promise?"

"Yes."

Rebecca flitted off, and Maggie was relieved that her sister hadn't pressed. Rebecca was a frivolous girl who could dance all night and not worry for a second about hosting a party they couldn't afford.

But they weren't aristocrats and couldn't ignore a creditor's demand. As the bills came due, who would pay? Gaylord obviously, but after he'd sold all the furniture, what then?

Suddenly she felt as if she was choking, but then she always felt that way at Cliffside. There were too many painful memories in the place.

After Gaylord had jilted her, after he'd set Maggie aside to marry Pamela instead, Maggie had had to sit through their wedding, to mourn and fret while they flitted off on their honeymoon, to welcome them back as newlyweds, to watch them coo and snuggle as husband and wife.

She'd never previously understood how a person could be driven to homicide, but occasionally during those awful months, she'd suspected if she'd owned a pistol she might have murdered them both. She'd been that humiliated.

Her father and others had constantly told her to get over her woe, to be happy for her sister—for the good of the family.

She'd been friends with Vicar Sterns and his wife, and they were the only ones who'd comprehended Maggie's anguish. When the vicar had inherited some money, the Sterns had decided to live out their dream of moving to London and starting their rescue mission. They'd asked Maggie to go along, and with a bit of coaxing her father had agreed. Their kindness had allowed her to escape Cliffside, and she would never forget the blessing they had bestowed by inviting her.

She slipped out of the parlor and stepped onto the verandah, gulping in the cool night air as she walked down the stairs into the garden. The groomed paths were lit with hanging lanterns, the moon up and brightly shining, so she could easily see the route. She headed for the lake to relax in the gazebo and stare out at the water.

With each stride, the sounds of the party faded away until she couldn't hear the merriment. She arrived at the lake and was relishing the quiet, but as she climbed into the gazebo, she frowned. A man was already seated on her favorite bench, and he glanced at her over his shoulder.

"Hello," he said.

"I beg your pardon," Maggie mumbled. "I didn't mean to interrupt."

"You haven't." He gestured to the empty spot next to him. "There's plenty of space if you'd like to join me."

She hesitated, thinking it probably wasn't appropriate to tarry with a strange man in the dark, but she shrugged off her reservations. Who would notice or care? Besides, he had to have been invited by Pamela, so she'd meet a new neighbor.

"I will join you," she said. "Thank you."

As she approached, he rose politely to greet her. The moonlight illuminated his features, and he recognized her the same moment she recognized him.

"You!" they charged in unison.

"What are you doing here?" Maggie inquired of Michael Scott.

"I could ask you the same."

"I live here. What's your excuse?"

"You live here? I could have sworn you lived at that wretched charity mission down the street from my club."

"Usually but Cliffside is my home. It's where I grew up. I'm visiting."

"So Pamela Farrow is…what? Your sister?"

"Yes."

"And Gaylord?"

"My brother-in-law."

"Ah…"

His stunning blue eyes took a slow meander down her person. His perusal was so thorough and so seductive that she squirmed and could barely keep from crossing her arms over her chest to block the heightened assessment.

"You still haven't explained why you're here," she said.

"I'm a guest."

"Of Gaylord or Pamela?"

"Both, I suppose."

"You suppose?" She snorted with disgust. "Don't tell me you're friends with them. I'll never believe you."

"Not friends, no."

"Then why would they include you? You can't have come for any innocent purpose. Are you about to rob us? Should I run inside and hide the silver?"

He smirked. "You still have silver?"

"What do you mean?"

"I heard Gaylord is in financial trouble. Hasn't he sold it by now?"

"You heard wrong," she staunchly lied. "Our finances are perfectly fine."

"Are they?"

He stared at her, looking smug and certain—as if he knew secrets he would never reveal—and she yearned to slap that haughty leer off his handsome face.

"I don't like the company in this gazebo," she complained. "I'm returning to the party."

She would have spun and stomped off, but he stopped her by saying, "What color is your dress?"

"My dress?"

"Yes. It's difficult to tell in the moonlight."

"Not that I feel it's any of your business, but it's blue."

"Just like your eyes," he murmured.

She scowled, not sure how to reply.

The fabric was the exact color of her eyes, and she'd specifically chosen it because it highlighted their merry effect. She'd once owned a flattering wardrobe, and of course Rebecca had dozens of gowns and always offered her cast-offs to Maggie. There were few occasions in London to wear pretty clothes though, so Maggie had given most of them away.

It was one of the joys of visiting Cliffside—the chance to prance about in Rebecca's beautiful garments, to pretend circumstances hadn't ruined Maggie's life. But she wasn't about to admit any of that to him.

"It's just…blue," she muttered. "The shade has naught to do with my eyes or anything else."

She should have left as she'd intended, but she was frozen in place. He was gazing at her, the silver of the moonlight painting him in stark tones of white and black.

He was attired in very fine clothes again, but not casual ones this time. The items were suitable for a country party, elegant but understated, his wealth and style clearly displayed but not flaunted.

Though they'd met previously, her view of him being an ogre hadn't changed. He was a brigand who'd grown up an orphan on the streets of London. Where would he have learned how to dress, how to comport himself?

He could have been standing in a room of the most pompous, arrogant aristocrats and he'd have fit right in.

"What are you looking at?" she grumbled, unnerved by his attention.

"You."

"Why?"

"You're very fetching tonight."

"Well...thank you, I guess."

"You should wear pretty gowns more often."

"They don't mix with my life and work."

"Why *are* you working? When your family owns this large estate, why are you in London toiling away?"

She'd never confess what had happened with Gaylord and Pamela. She never talked about it to anyone. There was no point in dredging it all up, and she was certain if he discovered the truth, he'd use it to her detriment.

She stepped to move away, but he stopped her simply by placing his hand on her wrist. His skin felt so hot that he might have scalded her with boiling water. She leapt back, and he chuckled.

"Tell me," he quietly said.

"Tell you what?"

"What drove you to London? Tell me why you're there alone instead of here where any decent British girl would be."

Even though she'd jumped away, he was much too close. She could smell the soap with which he'd bathed, could smell a hint of horses and tobacco in the fabric of his coat. There was another smell too, one that was masculine and delectable, and it lured her in, making her want to rub herself against him like a contented cat.

There was a strange current of energy flowing from him to her. It was electric and stimulating, and it enlivened her as nothing ever had.

He towered over her, and while she should probably have been afraid of him—they were sequestered in the gazebo and far from any other guests—she wasn't worried. As had occurred in his office in London, she sensed no menace. Clearly he was the type of male who liked to bark and strut about, but he wouldn't lash out unless provoked, and she had no intention of provoking him.

Yet as he took a step toward her, she took a step back. He took another, and she did too. Finally she was up against a post and he was in front of her, not blocking her exit precisely, but not letting her go either.

"I always get my way," he said, "so if you don't confide in me, I'll badger you until you relent."

"Why would you automatically assume I was driven away from Cliffside?"

"Why else would you have left?"

"You don't know everything, Mr. Scott. Sometimes there's no explanation. Sometimes a fact just *is*."

"I can keep a secret, and I'm a good listener."

"I don't have any secrets, and I doubt that *listening* is what you do well at all."

He clutched a teasing fist over his heart. "You wound me, Miss Wells."

"You need to be brought down a peg or two."

"I'll just poke around until the servants spill the whole, sorry tale. Wouldn't you rather give me your version before I hear it from them?"

"The servants would never gossip about me," she absurdly stated.

"If that's what you suppose, then you're sillier than I imagined you to be."

"You imagined me to be silly? I can't fathom why you'd have been contemplating me at all."

"Apparently you made an impression when you visited me in London."

He shifted and leaned in so he was touching her all the way down. His behavior was rude and brash, and she should have shoved him away, but to her eternal disgust she didn't.

She been kissed a few times—by Gaylord years earlier—but the embraces had been quick pecks of lips to lips, with no hands or bodily parts involved. So she'd never been intimately connected to a man.

Mr. Scott was large and virile and all male, and his proximity had her pulse racing. She was experiencing so many wild and unusual sensations that she felt dizzy.

Was this why women swooned? Was this why they became overheated and lost all reason? Surely she was made of sterner stuff.

After Gaylord had betrayed her so hideously, she'd sworn off men. She would never trust a man again, would never be enticed, would never be sweet-talked or seduced, would never...*care*.

Gaylord had shown her that she had a very tender heart, and she would never let it be broken again. So why was she dawdling in the dark and allowing Mr. Scott to snuggle her to a gazebo post? Why was she enjoying it so much? Why was she being overwhelmed by him?

She had no idea.

"I'll be here for a week," he said.

She sighed with exasperation. Were all the guests staying for a week? How could Pamela afford it?

"Why would you stay so long?" she asked. "Don't you have crimes to commit in London?"

"Not at the moment, but I'm certain there will be plenty waiting for me once I get back."

"I'm certain there will be too."

He reached out, and her initial reaction was to flinch away but she didn't. She wasn't about to exhibit any weakness.

A lock of her hair had fallen from its comb, and he twirled it around his finger and used it as leverage to pull her closer. His face was inches from hers, and he was staring at her so intently that she wondered if he might kiss her.

She didn't know why the peculiar notion would have entered her mind, but oddly she seemed able to read his thoughts. He was really and truly considering whether to kiss her.

What if he tried? What if he succeeded?

She suspected he'd probably be very adept at kissing and as she recollected the trollop in his office, she figured he'd kissed dozens—nay, hundreds!—of women.

"I'd convinced myself that I didn't like you," he said. "You're bossy and rude, and you assume you're smarter than everyone else. I hate that in a female."

"If you keep flattering me like that, I'll get a big head."

"But"—he raised a brow, looking wicked and handsome and very, very dangerous to her equilibrium—"I might have been wrong."

"About what?" Her voice was breathless and ragged and sounded nothing like her own.

"About you. I think we're going to be very good friends."

"I *don't* think so."

"Yes, but I'm always right, and *I* always get my way. Remember?"

With that parting quip, he stepped away and left. She watched him depart, not glancing away until he disappeared around a corner.

She wanted to call to him, to hurl a pithy remark, to have the last word, but she couldn't devise a comment that would have been sufficiently clever or biting.

She staggered over to the bench where he'd been sitting, and she plopped down. For several minutes she tried to relax, but his essence lingered like a tangible object, and there was no respite to be had.

Ultimately she rose and went back to the house, but she decided she wouldn't return to the party.

If she did, she was positive she'd run into him. He had an ability to fluster her, to leave her bewildered and feeling as if she was young and foolish and ridiculous, and she'd never let a man have that sort of power over her.

She sneaked in a side door and climbed the servants' stairs to her room.

CHAPTER THREE

"What do you think?"

"Bugger them all."

"My feeling exactly."

Michael Scott grinned at his friend and partner, Ramsey Scott.

They shared the same last name, but they weren't related. The orphanage where they'd lived off and on as boys had been owned by a man whose surname was Scott, and he'd given every child his name. It had been an establishment filled with little Scotts.

People occasionally asked if Michael and Ramsey were brothers, but Michael had never understood why. They looked nothing alike and had nothing in common—other than their ability to run scams and make lots of money. And Michael thought he might have had a brother once, but it hadn't been Ramsey.

They were out on the verandah at Cliffside, their hips balanced on the balustrade as they stared into the parlor. Music wafted out, and dancers promenaded by.

Gaylord Farrow was over in a corner, his wife Pamela whispering in his ear, their heads pressed close. Whatever the comment, Gaylord responded quietly but viciously, and Pamela slithered away.

Clearly matters were tense in the Farrow-Wells household, husband and wife so at odds that they would bicker in front of the guests.

Michael figured he should have been suffering a spurt of conscience over what would become of the unhappy couple after he was through with them, but he didn't remember ever having a conscience. If he'd once possessed one, he'd lost it somewhere along the way.

"No mercy?" Ramsey inquired.

Michael scoffed. "Gaylord Farrow is an ass. He doesn't deserve any."

"He wants to introduce you to his sister-in-law, Rebecca, so you can take her riding in the morning."

"She's the slender brunette? The birthday girl?"

"Yes."

"I don't fraternize with children."

That wasn't precisely true. His likely fiancée, Lady Felicia Gilroy, was eighteen.

"Rebecca just turned twenty-two," Ramsey said.

"She acts as if she's ten."

"She doesn't look ten. She appears all grown up to me."

"Leave her alone," Michael cautioned. "I won't have you causing trouble before we leave."

"You mean besides foreclosing on their home, their property, and everything they own?"

"Yes, besides that."

They chuckled then were silent, sipping their whiskey. It was a companionable interval, and Michael recalled—as he always did—that the best times were when he and Ramsey were together, just the two of them with no business to distract them.

Michael's first genuine memories were of Ramsey, but before the orphanage—long before—there had been a chaotic night, a huge fire, crowds running and screaming. Michael had stood in the street with people shouting and asking him his name, but he'd been too terrified to reply.

Then…quite a bit later, he'd been older and with Ramsey at the orphanage.

He never felt he was supposed to have ended up there, because sporadically other memories surfaced. Siblings maybe? A father? He recollected a large, jovial man who used to grab him and toss him in the air. Who could it have been but a father?

How are my boys? You got so big while I was away! You're all grown up!

The ancient comments flitted by in his head, and he shoved them away.

He often heard whispers and saw visions that made no sense. Sometimes it seemed as if he was staring through another man's eyes and reading his mind. Sometimes they were together in the same dreams. Sometimes he jolted awake from a deep sleep, certain that an arm or a leg was missing, that part of him had been stealthily cut away while he'd slumbered.

Sometimes he wondered if there was madness in his blood.

He glanced over his shoulder again, hoping to observe Miss Wells walking back from the gazebo. She was probably safe enough. After all, they were at a country estate in the middle of nowhere, and Cliffside was her home. What could happen?

Still though, he shouldn't have walked off without her. Then again, with such a prickly personality, what harm could befall her? A miscreant might approach with bad intentions, be impaled by her sharp tongue, and he'd move on to find an easier, quieter victim.

"What the hell are you looking at?" Ramsey asked.

"Remember that harpy who stopped by the club last week?"

"Miss Magdalena Wells from the Vicar Sterns Rescue Mission?"

"Yes. She's Farrow's sister-in-law."

Ramsey scowled. "What are the odds of that?"

"I bumped into her out in the garden, and I left her out there by herself. I'm watching for her to return."

"How gallant of you. Was she bitching and complaining?"

"Worse than ever."

"Figures."

"She's prettier in a party gown."

"Wouldn't any girl be?"

They sipped their drinks again, studied the dancers again.

After a lengthy interval, Ramsey said, "If you weren't considering that deal with Lord Stone over Lady Felicia, Gaylord wouldn't be throwing Rebecca at you."

"What do you mean?"

"Gossip has spread that there's a heart in that empty chest of yours."

Michael snorted with disgust. "I have no heart."

"You and I know that, but Lord Stone has been telling people he's coerced you into an agreement."

"Let him. Why would I care?"

Lord Stone was Felicia's father. His real estate was entailed by his title, so he couldn't gamble away his houses or land, but he could gamble away everything else. And he had. To Michael. Lord Stone's holdings had included a sugar cane plantation in Jamaica, ships that sailed to and from America, a gold mine in Africa, and a coal mine in Cornwall.

Michael could return some of it in exchange for Felicia's hand in marriage, but he couldn't decide what he thought about the proposal. It would be amusing to marry into the aristocracy. For some reason, he felt he belonged in that exalted company, and it would serve Lord Stone right for being such a profligate idiot.

Yet Michael had never planned to wed, even though—deep down—he secretly yearned for a home and family. It was an ache that was very much like the sensation of his having lost a limb. It seemed he might once have had a stable, happy life, but it had slipped through his fingers when he wasn't looking.

He enjoyed ruining rich assholes, taking what they had, making them pay. He never bothered with men who were friendly or courteous, but if a man was arrogant and unbearable, he ought to watch his back around Michael.

Lady Felicia hadn't been apprised of her father's fiscal troubles, but if Michael accepted Lord Stone's offer her father would order her to wed Michael, and she was an obedient daughter. She'd probably be a good sport about it, and if she wasn't, Lord Stone was the sort who'd beat a concession out of her, so Michael hoped she wasn't too obstinate.

He'd been introduced to her, and she'd been cordial and polite, but there was no telling how she'd act if she was informed that Michael was to be her husband. She'd likely spend every night weeping into her pillow, having assumed her father would arrange a grand match for her, that she'd have had a highborn oaf for a husband. But her father was an irresponsible wretch, so she might get Michael instead.

The barbarian was at the gate!

He smirked, relishing a vision of the family dinners he'd attend. His presence at Lord and Lady Stone's table would send Lady Stone to an early grave, and the notion made Michael even more inclined to follow through.

"Gaylord is such a prick," Ramsey said.

"Never met a bigger one," Michael concurred.

"I wouldn't be surprised if he offered you Rebecca's chastity in case it might convince you to cancel a couple of his markers."

"She seems awfully flirtatious to me. Why would you think she still has any chastity for him to offer?"

Ramsey chuckled caustically. "Ooh, a low blow."

Gaylord Farrow had already lost everything to Michael. It had been a slow process, his debts mounting for the prior year as he'd dug himself into a hole, and he could never have dug himself out. With an opponent as loathsome as Farrow, Michael wouldn't have allowed Farrow to best him. He won fair and square, or he cheated to win.

The obnoxious Mr. Farrow hadn't stood a chance, and all that remained was to negotiate the transfer of occupancy. Michael was happy to give them a month to vacate, and the ladies could keep the clothes on their backs—even though he owned their clothes too.

Rebecca Wells took that moment to prance by the window in the line of dancers. Ramsey came to full alert, like a hunting dog scenting the fox.

"I'm going in to dance," he said.

"You hate to dance," Michael told him.

"I've changed my mind."

"Don't involve yourself in a mess with her where I'll end up having to drag you out of it."

"She winked at me a bit ago over by the buffet table."

"It was a trick of the light."

"No, it wasn't," Ramsey insisted. "Something tells me she's no better than she has to be."

He strutted off, and Michael was alone in the quiet. He gazed out at the garden, and someone was approaching on one of the paths. Shortly he could see it was Miss Wells, but she didn't notice him lurking on the verandah.

She didn't return to the party, but skirted the house and disappeared into the shadows. A door opened and closed, and he peered up at the mansion. Before too long, a candle flared in an upstairs bedchamber.

He stared at it, stared at the dancers in the parlor, stared at her window again, and he shrugged.

What the hell? Why not pay her a visit?

She still hadn't confided why she was in London, why she worked at the mission, and he was dying to know the whole story. He suspected it would have very much to do with Gaylord Farrow, and if so, the details would add to the reasons Michael detested the man.

He downed his whiskey, then pushed away from the balustrade and walked down the verandah until he located the door she'd used. He climbed the stairs and wandered down the hall, peeking into rooms until he found the correct one.

He sneaked in and dawdled for a minute, assessing the décor and trying to decipher what it revealed about Miss Wells.

It was a small suite, with a sitting room and a bedchamber beyond. No doubt there would be a dressing room beyond that. A candle burned in the bedchamber, so there wasn't much light, but even so, he noted that there weren't any personal items, no family portraits on the fireplace mantle, no bric-a-brac on the tables.

The sitting room had a French window that led out onto a narrow balcony. Through the gauzy curtains, he could see Miss Wells was standing outside and gazing up at the sky. To his delight, she'd taken down her hair. It was an unusual and vibrant shade of auburn, and the lengthy tresses fell to her bottom in a curly wave.

Was she wishing on a star? If so, what would she request? He was extremely curious about the answer to that question, which was definitely interesting.

He never bothered much with women. They served only one purpose, that being sexual relations, and he gladly paid for the services that were rendered. He was surrounded by trollops, so when he was in the mood he never lacked for lewd companions.

But other than a quick tumble, he rarely thought about women at all. His world was a world of men, of violence and betrayal and strife. He was besieged by adversaries, enemies, and competitors who would love to see him brought low, or even murdered if they believed they could get away with it.

Of course if he was ever killed, Ramsey would learn who had harmed Michael, and Ramsey's revenge would be swift and brutal. He had fewer scruples than Michael, and while Michael would occasionally relent and grant mercy, with Ramsey there was only retaliation and vengeance.

So it was odd to find himself mulling Miss Wells, and he was confused as to why she'd captured his notice. He'd always hated the country, with its quiet lanes, fancy houses, and manicured gardens. Most likely he was merely bored to tears and hoping she'd enliven what was otherwise a very dull evening.

Stealthily he shut the door and spun the key in the lock. Lest she not welcome a visitor, he removed it and stuck it in his pocket. Then he tiptoed over to the balcony and slipped through the curtains.

"Hello, Miss Wells," he said from directly behind her.

She didn't shriek with alarm, but she leapt with such fright that he had to grab her arm so she didn't topple over the rail.

"What are you doing in here?" she demanded when she could speak again.

"I have no idea."

"You can't stay." She pointed into the sitting room. "Get out."

"No."

She shoved by him and stomped into the suite, hurrying to the door and turning the knob.

"You stole my key?" she fumed as he sauntered in after her.

"Yes."

"Give it back to me."

"No."

"Yes. No. Yes. No. Is that all you can say?"

"No."

"If you don't give it back to me right now, I'll scream. I will. I mean it."

"Do you suppose anyone would hear you, and even if they did, would you want them to rush to your aid? If you were found locked in with me, your reputation would be shredded."

She was so angry he could practically see steam coming out of her ears. Yet despite the danger, she pounded her fist on the door. She paused, listened for footsteps, and pounded again.

She repeated the process numerous times, but everyone—servants included—was down at the party. Ultimately she whipped around, her eyes flashing daggers.

"What is your plan?" she inquired.

"I don't have one."

"Am I to be ravished? Is that what you intend?"

"You should be so lucky."

"Give me my key," she said again. "Let me go."

There was a decanter of wine on a table in the corner. He ignored her and went over to it and pulled out the cork.

"Let's sit by the fire and have a glass of wine," he suggested.

She gaped at him as if he had two heads, then muttered a comment under her breath that sounded very much like an epithet.

"Foul language, Miss Wells?" he facetiously said. "By a person of your stellar profession of noble do-gooder? I'm shocked, I tell you. Shocked!"

"You are a lunatic."

"Yes, I always have been. Ask anyone."

"I don't need my opinion confirmed by others. The evidence is too blatant."

They stood, her glaring, him grinning. Hadn't he told her he always got his way? She was very stubborn, so apparently it would take her a while to accept reality.

"Fine," she finally mumbled. "Be a horse's ass. See if I care."

She swept by him and returned to the balcony, and he was irked by her insolence.

No one was ever allowed to disrespect him. No one would dare. He simply took up too much space in any room he occupied, and his wishes and commands were paramount.

He couldn't guess where he'd come by such imperious arrogance, but he figured he'd inherited it from the father he didn't remember. How else was he to explain his obstinacy and domineering traits?

He followed her onto the balcony. She was staring at the stars again, and he stepped in very close and eased her into the balustrade so she was trapped in the circle of his arms.

He nuzzled his nose into her hair, and he recognized he was being an incredible boor—he actually had a few manners and knew how to display them.

"Stop that," she said.

"No. I like the way you smell."

She elbowed him in the ribs. "Go away."

"I don't want to."

"Well, *I* want you to."

"So? I never listen to women."

"Couldn't you start? Just for me?"

He chuckled, and she glanced at him over her shoulder, and it dawned on him that she was outrageously pretty. When she'd stormed into his office in London, she'd been buttoned up in her drab gray dress, so he hadn't really noticed much about her other than her sharp tongue.

Out in the gazebo he'd complimented her gown, but it had been dark, and he hadn't yet realized her hair was red.

He hadn't assumed he liked red hair on a woman. If he had a choice, he preferred blond trollops, buying into the generally held belief that a red-haired woman had a temper, and Miss Wells's caustic attitude seemed to prove the rule.

Her big blue eyes were wide, twinkling in the moonlight, and for the moment providing every indication that she was extremely distressed.

Gad, was it tears he was witnessing?

"Are you crying?" he asked almost in accusation.

"No."

But she swiped a furtive hand across her cheek, and he scowled and studied her more closely.

"You are! You're crying."

"So what if I am? It's my bedchamber, and I was all alone and minding my own business until you barged in. I can cry if I want to."

"What's wrong?"

"Nothing."

"You're up here bawling and—"

"I'm not bawling."

"Stop it."

"Stop what? Crying?"

"Yes. I can't abide feminine histrionics."

"You poor thing! You don't have to stay and suffer them."

She wiggled around so she was facing him, and suddenly the front of his body was pressed to the front of hers, and he was delighted to report that—for all her slender stature—she was very shapely. He could feel her breasts, her flat tummy, her mons crushed to his phallus.

Not surprisingly, his cock sprang to attention. Evidently he was attracted to her, but then he was attracted to any female who walked by. He wouldn't read anything into it, wouldn't give it more import than it deserved.

Still though, he was flummoxed by the flood of gladness that swept through him. He was so happy, so content. There was a current of energy flowing from him to her that was electrifying. It made him feel grand and omnipotent—well, he always felt omnipotent—but the impression had never been caused by a woman.

"What's wrong?" he posed more gently.

"I'm sad, you oaf."

"Why?"

"Because life is hard, and I get tired sometimes."

He gazed at her, dizzy with conflicted emotions. The strangest urges were washing over him. He wanted to cherish and shelter and protect as he'd never wanted before.

The feelings were so powerful and so riveting that he might have been bewitched. If he'd been a superstitious fellow, he'd have rushed out, found a wise woman, and bought a charm to ward off evil spirits.

But he wasn't superstitious, and he had no idea what to make of the sensations she produced. It was eerie, it was extraordinary, and he caught himself thinking he'd like to wallow in her company for hours merely so he could keep being barraged by the agitation she stirred.

"Why are you in London?" he asked. "Tell me the truth."

"I went years ago, when I was seventeen."

"Why?" he said again.

"Vicar Sterns was the minister in the village. He and his wife invited me to accompany them when they started the mission."

"Your parents permitted you to join them?"

"My father did. My mother has been dead since I was a girl."

"Your father, he didn't mind? He didn't care?"

"I begged to go."

"I can't imagine you had a driving need to live in poverty and serve the poor. What happened?"

The night seemed to encourage confessions, and he thought she'd confide in him, but she shook her head.

"It doesn't matter. Not after all this time."

"It matters to me."

"I can't fathom why it would."

"I'm not sure either, but for some bizarre reason I'm dying to know more about you."

"If you die, it will be from boredom after listening to my life's story."

"I doubt it."

They stared, her blue eyes probing, delving, as she struggled to figure him out. Usually he shielded himself from such intense assessment, but for once he let her look, let her see.

For all his wealth and pomp and power, he was very lonely, an orphan with no kin, no past, and only violent, loyal Ramsey as his friend.

Apparently she viewed something in him that made a difference, for she said, "I was engaged."

"What became of your fiancé?"

"He married my sister."

Michael bit down a gasp. "Gaylord Farrow was your fiancé? He married your sister after you'd been betrothed?"

"Yes, so I had a chance to leave with Vicar Sterns and I took it. It's humiliating now to admit that Gaylord broke my heart, but in my own defense, I was just seventeen. I didn't know any better."

"I'm acquainted with Mr. Farrow," he cautiously stated. "We've had many business dealings."

"Then you're aware that he's…well…"

She cut off, being reluctant to air the Farrow dirty laundry, and he said, "He's an odd duck."

"Very odd." Bitterly, she added, "A reckless, odd duck."

Michael knew what she meant, but he asked, "In what way?"

"He has a terrible gambling habit. He can't control it."

"I've heard that about him."

"We're in a jam because of his wagering."

Michael nodded, not providing the slightest hint that he was cognizant of the facts.

Clearly her sister and brother-in-law hadn't shared the details about Farrow's downfall, and Michael didn't believe that *he* should have to enlighten her. She'd find out soon enough, and he was certain she'd blame him, would accuse him of taking advantage, of filching what wasn't his.

He was always blamed. In all of the men who'd ruined themselves with Michael, he'd never met a single family member who blamed a father or a brother. They were all positive that if Michael hadn't come along, there would have been no horrid ending.

"What sort of jam are you in?" he inquired.

She paused, then forced a smile. "Oh, listen to me babbling on. It's nothing, really. We've hit rough patches before, and we've managed. We'll get through this one too."

Her remark underscored how little she'd been told about the pending crisis. Luckily she had a place to live at the charity mission in London. He wondered where Gaylord, Pamela, and Rebecca would go. Somehow he couldn't picture them moving in with Miss Wells and residing in Michael's seedy neighborhood.

He thought he had no conscience, but a sliver of one flickered to life, and he felt bad about what would transpire. Not because of what would happen to her kin, but for how it would impact *her*. She had a kind heart, as was obvious by her choice of employment, by her continued contact with the sister who'd stolen her fiancé.

She would fret. She would grieve. She would hold Michael responsible, and though it was completely out of character for him, he hated to suppose she'd think poorly of him.

Before he could stop himself, before he could reconsider, he dipped down and kissed her. He hadn't meant to, hadn't planned to. At least he didn't assume he'd planned to. She just looked so wretched. What was a fellow to do?

His lips touched hers, very lightly, very sweetly, and for a brief second she allowed the embrace, then she eased away.

"I don't want this from you," she protested, but without much of a fuss.

"Hush," he murmured.

"If I behaved in a way that made you believe I—"

"Hush," he said again.

She gazed up at him, appearing forlorn and weary and so very, very lovely. Those masculine instincts flared again, to shelter, to protect, and he couldn't help himself.

He slipped an arm around her waist and pulled her more tightly to him so he could kiss her in earnest. He kissed her as if she was the last woman on Earth, as if he was about to draw his last breath and would never kiss anyone again.

He didn't know how long they continued. He didn't run his hands over her person, didn't clutch or grope or maul her. He simply tasted her lush mouth, letting the connection of their bodies provide a soothing balm he hadn't realized he'd been missing.

When he finally decided to halt, a protracted amount of time had elapsed. She didn't scold him or push away from him, which he took as a very good sign. Her knees were weak, and he suffered from the strongest sense that if he released her, she'd slide to the floor.

The moment was fraught with unspoken emotion. There were a thousand comments perched on the tip of his tongue. For inexplicable reasons, he wanted to unburden himself, wanted to tell her about his haunting dreams and strange visions, but he never talked about the past except with Ramsey and that was only on the rarest occasions.

Most shockingly, he wanted to ask for things he should never receive from her and she would never bestow. He yearned to have her, to keep her for his own, and the poignant ideas were so peculiar that he felt bewitched again.

In his rough and tumble world, he never made commitments. He was a liar and fraud, and he never gave his word or made promises because he never kept them.

She broke whatever spell had been festering. Flashing a lazy smile, she said, "That wasn't so bad."

He snorted with amusement. "High praise indeed."

"You're different than I assumed you to be."

No, I'm not! "What did you assume?"

"I pictured you as an ogre who lurked under bridges and ate passing travelers."

"I can be an ogre—when I'm riled."

"But that's not who you are deep down."

"Are you sure about that?"

"You like to bluster and preen. You like people to think you're tough and cruel."

"I *am* tough and cruel."

"You might be sometimes, but it's not who you really are."

She voiced it with such conviction, as if she knew facts about him she couldn't have known, as if they'd been friends for a dozen years and she'd uncovered all his secrets.

She was idiotically wrong, of course. He had no gallant tendencies and every awful story she'd heard was true. Yet he liked to imagine he was the man she believed him to be. It would be intriguing to pretend.

"You should go," she said.

"I suppose I should."

She linked their fingers and led him out. It was a dear experience for him, as if she was his adolescent sweetheart and they'd sneaked away from her chaperone. He meekly followed along as if he were a pet dog.

She stopped by the door.

"Give me my key," she told him.

He thought about refusing, about demanding to keep it so he could visit again, but he still couldn't figure out why she provoked him in such odd ways, and he wasn't about to foster a relationship. There was no point to it, and in the coming days and weeks she'd have plenty of reasons to hate him.

He handed it over, and she stuck it in the lock and turned it. She opened the door a crack and peeked out to ensure no one was walking by.

"Don't you dare tell anyone you were in here with me," she said.

"I might."

She studied him, then scoffed. "You liar. You never would."

He studied her too, then grinned. "No, I never would."

"Goodnight, Mr. Scott."

"Goodnight, Miss Wells."

He swooped in and stole a quick kiss, then strolled out, bold as brass.

CHAPTER FOUR

In Rebecca's opinion, men were thick creatures. She'd flirted with enough of them to know.

During her final year of school, when she was sixteen, she and her fellow students had constantly plotted over the precise types of husbands and marriages they intended to have.

Most of her classmates had travelled home to enjoy the courtship rituals that would turn them into brides. Most of them had succeeded. She was the only one lingering in the ranks of the unwed, and if something didn't happen soon she would move into the ranks of spinsterhood.

After a lengthy round of chaos—her father dying, Gaylord inheriting—Rebecca's dowry was gone, and every suitor in the kingdom had heard about it.

In the beginning, she hadn't understood why she'd received no proposals. She'd sent out plenty of hints that she was available, but her suggestive manner hadn't elicited the slightest interest.

A school friend had enlightened Rebecca, mentioning how sad it was that Gaylord had frittered away her dowry. Up until that moment,

Rebecca hadn't realized there was a problem.

Still though, she was determined to wrangle herself a husband, and if she couldn't, then she wasn't too proud to wrangle another sort of arrangement entirely. She would do anything—literally *anything*—to escape Gaylord and Cliffside.

They were all on a downhill slide, and when Pamela and Gaylord crashed at the bottom, Rebecca refused to crash with them.

She was over by the French windows that led out onto the verandah. The latest set of dancing had just ended, so the room was crowded, and no one was paying any attention to her.

Ramsey Scott glanced at her, and she winked and waited for a reaction. Once she was certain he'd gotten her message, she snuck outside and hastened down into the garden, stopping under a lantern so he'd have to be blind to not see her.

When he appeared on the verandah she could barely keep from waving, but she didn't. He started toward her, and she took off too, rounding a hedge so she couldn't be observed from the house. Not that anyone would care.

The neighbors ignored her. She was the unwed sister, the forgotten sister whose future had been destroyed by Gaylord. Pamela might complain about misbehavior though. Pamela wallowed in a fantasy where she pretended their life was still the same, that they were still rich and respected and Rebecca had a reputation worth protecting.

Ramsey Scott was the first bachelor Rebecca had met in ages, and she was incredibly intrigued. He was big and tall and handsome. Dressed in black, he exuded danger and menace, and when he sauntered through a parlor people stepped out of his way, scowling as he went by.

She'd never encountered a man who had that kind of effect, and she wanted to know all about him. Why wasn't he married? From his clothes and demeanor, she figured he was wealthy. Gaylord had many posh London friends. Was Ramsey Scott one of them?

If so, might he be in the market for a very pretty, very accommodating wife? If he wasn't in the market, there was no law to prevent her from working to change his mind.

She listened as his boots crunched across the gravel, and very quickly, there he was. He towered over her, looking grim and mysterious and lethal, and her tummy tickled.

"You've been chasing me all night, Miss Wells," he said, "and it seems you've caught me. Now that you have, what will you do with me?"

"I have several good ideas," she saucily retorted.

"I'll just bet you have."

"Let's walk out by the lake."

"I hate walking."

"What do you like?"

He peeked over his shoulder to ensure no guests were behind him on the path. Then he turned to her again.

"Come here and I'll show you."

When she'd lured him out with that wink, she'd assumed they'd chat and flirt and she might eventually let him steal a kiss or two. That's how her other breathless swains had acted—before they learned she was broke.

But there was an air of authority and maturity about him that told her she might have bitten off more than she could chew.

He wasn't the type to stroll along holding hands in the moonlight. He wasn't the type to woo and admire. No, he blustered in, took what he craved, and the woman had very little to say about what transpired.

It was probably a mistake to have lured him outside, and she ought to have pushed by him and hurried back to the house, but she couldn't remember the last time a man had glanced in her direction.

What if she misbehaved with him? It's not as if illicit conduct would matter. She spent her days wandering through the increasingly empty mansion, feeling invisible. Didn't she deserve to have an adventure?

She leaned in, ignoring her racing pulse and pretending she was in the habit of seducing strange men. In response, he slid an arm around her waist and pulled her nearer so they were crushed together from chests to toes.

"What is it you want from me?" he asked.

"I haven't decided."

"Well I think I know, and I'm positive if I gave it to you, you'd die of shock."

"I'm not a child," she huffed.

"But are you a tender maiden? Are you a fresh English rose whose petals are just waiting to be plucked?"

She scowled. "You make virtuous character sound like a bad thing."

"I detest innocent girls. Are you one? Tell me right up front, so I can determine whether you're worth the bother."

"You have a very high opinion of yourself."

"It's all deserved, and you haven't answered my question."

"What question was that?"

"You're no spring chicken. Are you still a maid? Has some bloke taught you how to be a woman, or are you floundering around?"

She'd never heard such scandalous remarks verbalized, and she was greatly flummoxed by them.

"You're from London, aren't you?" she said.

"Yes."

"Is that how a gentleman talks to a lady in the city?"

"I'm not a gentleman, and I'm trying to find out if you're a lady."

"I'm a lady."

"But are you a maiden? Confess your condition, and put me out of my misery."

He laid a finger on her chin and he traced it down her neck, her chest, stopping at the bodice of her gown just at the spot where her corset created a bit of cleavage. For a wild, insane moment, she thought he would slip his hand under the fabric to touch her breast, and she stood perfectly still, aware that she should shove him away, but if she did he'd never follow her into a dark garden again.

"I might be a maiden, and I might not," she blustered.

He scoffed with derision and stepped away. "You've told me all there is to know about you."

"I couldn't possibly have."

"You're pure as the driven snow."

"So what? Maybe I'd like you to be the one to…to…"

Salacious discussion was beyond her, and she couldn't finish her sentence. He finished it for her.

"To what? To plow your field? To hoe your row? To plant a few seeds?"

"Ah…"

"Look, you're very pretty, and you obviously need to have a man between your thighs."

She frowned. "I have no idea what that means."

"Which is why I don't have the energy to fuss with you."

"Fuss with me! As if I'd let you."

"Trust me, sweetheart, if I snapped my fingers, you'd come running. You should have been tumbled years ago. With how you sashay those hips of yours, I'm surprised no man's ever pressed the issue."

"You're talking in riddles."

"Yes, I am, and if you'd ever had a single valuable experience in your life, you'd know what I'm saying. I wouldn't have to explain it to you, and you wouldn't have to guess."

"Then don't make me guess. Just say it flat out."

He leaned in and murmured, "Virgins bore me. I like trollops who've learned their way around a bedchamber, so I can't imagine how you could entice me at all. Can you?"

There was a challenge in his gaze, almost as if he was daring her to proceed to the secretive physical conduct engaged in by husbands and wives. Unwed people occasionally engaged in it too, but she had only vague notions of what those acts entailed. Still, she recognized he was taunting her, suggesting she ruin herself.

What a vain oaf! They'd danced twice in the parlor and had shared a few words at the buffet table. This was the sole time she'd been alone with him.

Was this sort of prurient conversation normal among adults in town? If this was what passed for flirtation in London, then it was a good thing she'd remained at Cliffside. Men in the city would have eaten her alive, yet she hated to have him view her as an annoying child.

So she boasted, "I could do what you want. You could show me, and I'd do it."

"That's precisely the problem, little lady. Some fellows like to teach and train a girl. I like a girl who already knows."

"Oh."

"Besides, if I laid a hand on you, Michael would have my head."

"Michael?"

"My friend, Mr. Scott."

"I thought you two were brothers."

"No, we're friends, and I work for him."

"Why do you have the same last name?"

"It's a long story."

She digested the odd comment, then asked, "Why would Michael Scott order you to stay away from me? What are you? His slave? Must you do what he says?"

"I'm not his slave, but yes, I do what he says."

"Why would you?"

"Because...he's Michael *Scott*."

"And...?"

"Who wouldn't do what he says?"

"Me! I wouldn't. I demand that we have an affair, and I don't care what Michael Scott thinks about it."

It was the most peculiar remark she'd ever uttered. She was demanding an affair? Would she despoil herself with this dangerous stranger from London?

No doubt about it. Gaylord and Pamela had driven her insane.

"You demand it?" He chuckled over her ridiculous naïveté.

"Yes, I insist!"

"Well, my dear, there's a lesson I've learned in this hard life that you never have."

"What's that?"

"We can't always get what we want, and I would never defy Michael on any topic—especially not over a female."

He put a palm on her bottom and shoved her toward the verandah.

"Now get your shapely ass inside," he said, "before you buy yourself a load of trouble."

She glared at him, a thousand caustic retorts begging to spew out. She yearned to call him rude names, but couldn't devise one that was sufficiently cutting.

To her eternal disgust, she marched off and proceeded to the verandah as he'd commanded, and while she was anxious to glance back, to find out if he was watching her, she wouldn't give him the satisfaction.

"What did Rebecca say?"

"She laughed in my face."

Gaylord glowered at Pamela in that way he had, as if every calamity was her fault.

"If you can't convince her," Gaylord threatened, "I'll have to speak with her myself."

"There's no need for you to speak with her. She's my sister. I can make her see reason."

"How will you, Pamela?"

"I'll explain the stakes again."

"You'd better."

Gaylord shook a fist as if he might strike her, and she stood her ground. He'd never hit her, but he often blustered as if he might, and he exhausted her with his preening and temper. Before their wedding, she'd assumed their relationship would be all roses and poetry. It had never occurred to her that it might be awful.

They were in Pamela's bedroom suite, the morning sun shining in the window and highlighting Gaylord's thinning blond hair, the frown lines bracketing his mouth, the paunch of his belly. He'd once been handsome and dashing, suave and smooth, but anymore he simply looked like the lazy ne'er-do-well he truly was.

When Pamela had first met him, she'd figured he'd be the ideal spouse, but she'd had limited experiences with males or romance, and she blamed her father for not being wiser.

A father was supposed to pick a good spouse for a daughter. Why hadn't he warned her to be careful? Why hadn't he seen the danger signs that Pamela had been too besotted to see?

If only Magdalena hadn't wanted him so desperately! If Maggie hadn't been so intent on having him, Pamela wouldn't have bothered, but she'd been incensed by Gaylord's interest in Maggie.

With Pamela being prettier and in possession of a much bigger dowry, it wasn't fair that Maggie had snagged him before Pamela had had a chance. So Pamela had stolen him from Maggie, and in the intervening years she hadn't suffered an ounce of remorse over seizing what should have been hers all along.

She'd suffered other regrets though. Regrets that she hadn't acted more shrewdly and not shackled herself to Gaylord. Regrets that she hadn't noticed what was really there. Regrets that she hadn't realized what he was like until it was much too late.

But she'd never admit her mistake, would never confess how horrid it was or how ridiculous she deemed him to be, for she would never give Maggie the pleasure of gloating.

She hated that Maggie hadn't fought for Gaylord, that she'd let Pamela have him so easily. If Maggie had exhibited the tiniest fuss, their father might not have handed Gaylord over to Pamela. It was a great sin to lay at Maggie's feet. If Maggie had demanded her betrothal be honored, Pamela would never have been wed to him.

So…in a convoluted way Pamela's dreadful marriage was Maggie's fault, and Pamela would never forgive her sister for putting her in such a hideous predicament.

"Rebecca won't help us," Pamela said, "because she doesn't like Michael Scott."

"What has that to do with it?" Gaylord asked.

"If she doesn't *like* him, we'll never persuade her to participate."

"I'll persuade her by taking a switch to her backside."

Pamela rolled her eyes. Gaylord never thought he was in the wrong, and even though he'd wrecked their lives, he never felt *he* should have to fix anything. He expected Pamela and Rebecca to fix it.

The bloodthirsty Michael Scott was in residence, ensconced in their nicest guest bedchamber, and Pamela had spoken with him several times. He was determined and resolute in a manner Gaylord could never dream of being, the exact sort who would enjoy humiliating Gaylord. Mr. Scott exuded rude pride.

Gaylord had plenty of rude pride himself, so he should have recognized the same trait in another man. But Gaylord viewed himself as perfect, and he imagined everyone else viewed him as perfect too.

He assumed they could throw Rebecca at Michael Scott, that the notorious brigand might be smitten and beg to marry her. If Rebecca became his bride, Gaylord insisted Mr. Scott would be driven to mercy and cancel Gaylord's debt.

On the odd chance that it would work, Gaylord was happy to sacrifice Rebecca to Mr. Scott, and Pamela wasn't necessarily opposed to the idea. Pamela had no intention of losing her home, and if Rebecca could simply prostitute herself for a few months and save them all, why shouldn't she?

Yet Pamela hadn't completely acceded to Gaylord's scheme, because she kept envisioning how angry Magdalena would be. Maggie was too prim and proper, too morally upright. She'd escaped Gaylord and Cliffside—another sin to lay at her feet!—by moving to London, so she was safe no matter what happened to Pamela.

With Pamela in such jeopardy, it didn't seem she should have to suffer recrimination if she took drastic measures. Still, she hesitated, but maybe it was pointless to debate. If Rebecca refused to agree…

"If Rebecca won't assist us," Gaylord nagged, "are you aware of what will occur?"

"I'm not a dunce, Gaylord. I'm clear on what the consequences will be."

"Are you really? Michael Scott is a pitiless tyrant."

Then perhaps you shouldn't have gambled with him! "Yes, yes, you've been very blunt in your descriptions."

"We haven't planned our departure. Can you picture yourself packing a bag and walking down the road? To where, Pamela? Let me ask you that!"

They had nowhere to go. She had no kin except Maggie and Rebecca, and Gaylord had an elderly aunt who'd once doted on him, but who had cut ties after he'd embezzled from her.

"I don't know where we'll go," she fumed. "I've admitted it, so why must you continue to harangue?"

"Michael Scott won't allow us an extra minute to make arrangements."

"Whose fault is that?"

Gaylord's expression grew thunderous. "What do you mean?"

"If you'd have given me a bit of warning, I could have squirreled away more of our possessions. But no, you had to keep me in the dark until the last second."

She'd known that his debt was very large. However, the true extent of the dilemma hadn't been revealed until the prior week when he'd brashly announced that the entire estate was lost, and Michael Scott was coming to claim it. The whole affair was so bizarre that it didn't seem real.

Even the fact that Michael Scott was on the premises, that he'd brought clerks to inventory the contents, didn't quite register. If she'd been shaken awake and told she was having a bad dream, she wouldn't have been surprised.

"You're blaming me for the short notice?" Gaylord snapped. "How dare you! If you want to blame anyone, blame Michael Scott and his wretched club. Blame Fate. Blame your precious Rebecca for refusing to do her duty to this family! But don't you dare blame me!"

He spun and stormed out, which was a minor relief.

She loathed quarreling and usually wouldn't. The servants gossiped too much, and she wouldn't provide fodder to fuel their fury. None of them had been paid in months, and when Pamela passed them in the hall, she noted their contemptuous glances.

She'd like to take a whip to them. She'd like to fire them all. It was maddening that they would complain over a trifle. She still fed them, didn't she? She still gave them a bed to sleep in and a roof to keep them out of the rain. Their ingratitude was galling.

A knock sounded on the door, and a maid poked her nose in.

"What?" Pamela barked.

"Your sister is leaving, Mrs. Farrow."

"Magdalena is leaving?"

"Yes, the butler thought you should know."

"Where is she going?"

"The butler says to London."

"Already?"

Maggie was supposed to have stayed for a week. The night before, she'd arrived late, after the party had begun, had hardly socialized, and now the very next morning she was waltzing back to the city? What was wrong with her?

Pamela would be the first to concede that her relationship with Maggie remained a tad contentious, but honestly, it had been seven years since Pamela's wedding. Maggie needed to get over it and move on. Pamela certainly had.

The maid was hovering, and Pamela grumbled, "I'll be right down. You're excused."

She couldn't fathom why she should have to say goodbye. After all, Maggie was departing without a word to Pamela. If Maggie wanted to pout and act like a baby, why was that Pamela's problem?

Yet she stood and started out, and as she did, she went by a window that looked out on the rear garden. Maggie was there, wearing her shawl and bonnet, carrying her portmanteau and headed for the stable.

To Pamela's astonishment, Michael Scott was there too, and as Pamela watched them she was amazed to discover that they were friendly. *Very* friendly.

Pamela hadn't known that Maggie and Mr. Scott were acquainted, and Maggie had only been in the house for twelve hours or so. When would they have had the chance to become so cordial?

As Pamela spied on them, Mr. Scott stepped in very close, his body nearly pressed to Maggie's in a suggestive way, and Maggie didn't show any sign that she was bothered by his boldness.

He murmured a comment that made Maggie laugh, and he grinned a heart-stopping grin that would have left Pamela weak in the knees if she was prone to that sort of reaction. Which she wasn't.

Mr. Scott appeared very smitten, and though it was ridiculous to think so, Pamela wondered if he might kiss Maggie. Right there in the garden, where anyone could see! It was a shocking turn of events.

He said something else and Maggie laughed again, then he took her bag from her and they walked off, with Mr. Scott accompanying her out to the barn. Shortly they vanished from view, and Pamela tarried in her spot, considering what she'd witnessed. Clearly affection had blossomed. Who would have thought?

After Maggie's failed attempt to snag Gaylord she'd sworn off romance, and Pamela had always assumed her sister would live out her days a bitter spinster. Had she changed her mind?

Whatever was happening, the sudden reversal of attitude would work to Pamela's advantage.

She hurried into her bedchamber, raced through the inner rooms and came out the other side in Gaylord's suite. He was still there, fuming over their quarrel and generally feeling sorry for himself.

"I have an idea," Pamela said.

"What is it? And don't propose a stupid plan. I haven't the patience for your nonsense this morning."

"It's not nonsense."

"What then?"

"We don't need to push Rebecca about Michael Scott."

"Why—in your infinite wisdom—have you decided we shouldn't?"

"Because I have a better solution, and it will be much more to Mr. Scott's liking."

"Really?" Gaylord sneered.

"Yes. Let me tell you what I saw, then you can tell me how we should proceed."

CHAPTER FIVE

"Miss Wells, we meet again."

Maggie glared at Michael Scott. "Every time I turn around, there you are. Are you following me?"

"Absolutely."

"Don't you have anything better to do?"

"Not really."

They were in the garden, with Maggie on her way to the stable when she'd stumbled upon Mr. Scott. He'd been out riding and had been trotting up the lane as she'd left the house.

To her consternation, he cut a dashing figure on a horse, looking manly and intriguing, like someone she might like to kiss in the moonlight. The fact that she'd drooled over him as he'd approached only underscored the wisdom of her decision to depart immediately.

She was to have stayed at Cliffside an entire week, but she'd arisen to the realization that she couldn't bear to remain.

A list of dreary tasks had needed accomplishing. She'd have had to explore the upstairs rooms to find out what had been sold. She'd have had to sit down with Pamela to ask biting questions and force answers from her sister. She'd have had to corner Gaylord and press him for information about his gambling debts, about her missing allowance.

The conversations would have been highly unpleasant, and just from considering how horrid they would be, she'd been too nauseous to eat any breakfast.

Coupled with her worries about their financial situation, a housemaid had stopped Maggie to confide that Rebecca had been out in the garden the previous night with Ramsey Scott. No one could say how long the tryst had lasted, but several servants had observed her sneaking back in, and the news was aggravating.

Rebecca had loose tendencies and had nearly gotten herself into trouble with a few different fellows. She wasn't a girl who should be single and desperately needed a husband, but she had no dowry. In the meantime, she aggressively flirted with various men, and it was terrifying to think of her trifling with such a disreputable character as Ramsey Scott.

On top of all that, she was consumed by an odd excitement over Michael Scott being on the premises. She had no idea why he'd visited her room the prior evening, why he'd kissed her on her balcony. She was even more confused over why she'd participated.

Their embrace had continued for a lengthy period, and while she'd tried to convince herself it had been inconsequential, it hadn't been. She felt all jumbled on the inside, hot and cold and prickly all over as if her skin didn't fit over her bones just right.

She didn't want to fight with her family, didn't want to see Michael Scott ever again, so she'd packed her bag and headed off. She planned to take the carriage into the village, then purchase a ticket on the mail coach to London. She'd been so intent on fleeing that she was creeping away like a thief in the night.

Yet she'd run into Mr. Scott anyway. Why was Fate so fickle? If she'd left five minutes earlier, she'd have escaped without having to gaze into those magnificent blue eyes of his.

"Tell me something." His voice was low, seductive, and much too tempting.

"If I can."

"Why is this place called Cliffside? I've been riding all morning, but I haven't seen a cliff anywhere."

She didn't know what sort of query she'd been expecting, but the question made her laugh. "There used to be a cliff."

"Where?"

"Out by the lake. Decades ago, a huge flood washed it away, so the river was dammed and the lake formed."

"It's lucky I bumped into you then. I hate mysteries, and if you hadn't enlightened me, I'd likely have spent the rest of my life searching for it."

She laughed again. "Stop being charming."

"You think I'm charming?"

"Yes, and I also think you're flirting with me."

He grinned. "I might be."

"Please don't. I don't like it."

"What's wrong with you? Every female likes a man to flirt. That's the strangest thing I've ever heard a woman say."

"I'm sure that's not true. I'm sure your trollops have said things that are much stranger."

His grin widened. "You could be right about that."

"What's it like, dabbling with trollops?"

She'd hoped to disconcert him with the indiscreet inquiry, but he wasn't bothered a bit.

"It's grand."

"Grand?" she scoffed.

"Yes. They don't have reputations to protect, so I never have to worry about breaking any fussy rules of decorum."

"Only a libertine such as yourself would deem that a benefit."

He stepped nearer, coming so close that the toes of his boots slid under the hem of her skirt. His brazen personality riveted her, freezing her in her tracks so she couldn't move away.

"Tell me something else," he said.

"What?"

"Are you in the habit of welcoming a man into your bedchamber and letting him kiss you senseless?"

Her cheeks flamed bright red. "You are a cad to mention it."

"Should I take that as a *no*?"

"You should take it as a *no*. After my experience with a certain sector of the male population, I've sworn off all of you."

"Not *all* of us," he countered. "You seem to like me just fine."

"Don't be so pompously annoying."

"Too late." He studied her portmanteau. "Are you leaving?"

"Yes."

"For London?"

"Yes."

"But…you just arrived."

"And now I'm going."

"How are you getting to town? You'd better not be traveling alone."

"I'm not," she lied, for she didn't choose to debate the issue with him.

"If you're no longer at Cliffside, who will entertain me?"

"The neighbor ladies will line up in my place."

As she voiced what was to have been a teasing remark, the oddest spurt of emotion swept through her. She frowned, curious to determine what it was, and when she recognized it as jealousy she was aghast.

"Why are you scowling?" he asked.

"I'm trying to figure out why you're pestering me—and why I allow it."

"You're crazy about me. Most women are."

"*I* am crazy about you?"

"Yes, you can't help yourself. It's a fairly common problem that females encounter when they meet me."

"Your vanity knows no bounds."

"No, it doesn't."

"Goodbye, Mr. Scott."

She attempted to push around him, to continue on, but he wouldn't permit her to go.

"Let me carry your bag."

"I can manage."

"I *said*, let me carry it."

He slipped it from her hand and into his own. "Didn't I tell you that I always get my way?"

"You certainly did."

"Where to, Miss Wells?"

"The stables. My carriage is ready."

It was only taking her into the village, but she was happy to have him assume it would convey her to London. She wasn't about to confess that she'd ride on the mail coach, that she'd purchase her own ticket.

She never accepted any aid from Gaylord and Pamela, and she prided herself on her fiscal autonomy. But she had a sneaking suspicion that Mr. Scott—for all his criminal habits—wouldn't approve of her using public transportation. Buried under his base traits, she was noticing some gallant tendencies.

"I'll walk you to it," he told her.

"I suppose it's pointless to inform you that I don't need your assistance."

"Yes, it's pointless. Stop being so independent. You're a woman. It won't kill you to lean on a man once in a while."

"It might."

They headed off, side by side, Mr. Scott near enough that their arms and legs occasionally brushed together.

The carriage was parked and waiting for her, a footman up in the box. Mr. Scott tossed in her bag, then he helped her climb in and he shut the door after her. She peered out the window, disturbed to find herself regretting her hasty decision to flee.

"I'll miss you after you're gone," he said.

"You will not."

"I will. I'll be so dejected, I'll be like a wilting flower, deprived of sunshine."

"You will not," she repeated.

He shrugged. "Well, I might not waste away, but I'll probably be bored to tears. Who will I kiss in the moonlight if the mood strikes me?"

"Who indeed, Mr. Scott?"

He stunned her by reaching out and squeezing her fingers in goodbye, and for some strange reason, it was a poignant farewell. She felt as if she'd always known him, as if they were lovers parting forever and she would be bereft without him.

The sentiment was out of character for the person she deemed herself to be, but then it had been a long time since a handsome man had paid her the slightest attention. She hadn't thought she minded her lonely existence, but apparently she was as desperate as every other spinster in the world.

"You live down the street from me in London," he said. "I might visit you someday."

She suffered the most annoying spurt of delight, but she quickly tamped it down. "Please don't."

"Why shouldn't I? I ride by that stupid mission constantly."

"There's nothing to see, so you needn't stop."

"I like you better now, and don't forget that I'm obscenely rich. Maybe I'll hand over that donation after all."

"You're toying with me, hoping to entice me with the promise of money."

"I might be, or I might be lying. With me, who can predict what I'll do? I like to keep people guessing. I could be persuaded into tossing you a few pounds—but you'd have to be very, very nice to me in order to get it."

"I doubt I could be *that* nice."

"You just never know."

She leaned out, not wanting the footman to overhear. Mr. Scott leaned in too, and they whispered, their heads pressed close.

"Last night was a mistake," she insisted.

"A mistake! I've never kissed a woman who thought so afterward."

"*And* I don't like you, remember?"

"Yes, but I'm gradually changing your mind."

"You can't possibly."

"We'll see about that, Miss Wells. We'll definitely see."

Looking cocky and magnificent, he drew away and motioned to the driver. The man clicked the reins, and the horse trotted off so swiftly that she was forced back against the seat.

She was grinning, happy as she hadn't been in ages, and dying to move into the window again, to wave and call out her goodbyes. But common sense prevailed, and she remained right where she was.

"Felicia, would you come in here please?"

Lady Felicia Gilroy stared into her father's library. She'd been walking by in the hall when he'd asked her to enter, and the request was an enormous surprise.

In all her eighteen years of living, she couldn't previously recollect being invited in. Her father, the great and glorious Lord Stone, was an enigmatic figure, rarely home, rarely spoken to. He was little more than a stranger to her, and she viewed him as a sort of distant relative who showed up on occasion for important events.

When he was in residence, he scarcely noticed his children, but then he'd had three daughters—Felicia being the third and youngest—and no sons, and everyone knew daughters were an expensive waste of effort.

He'd already had to provide two dowries for her older sisters, so Felicia often felt like an unwanted burden, like a guest who had overstayed her welcome.

Her mother had frequently counseled that Felicia's father had lost the energy to arrange a grand match, and there was no money to pay for one. She'd have to take what she could get.

While she was trying to be brave and accommodating, the situation was galling. Her father was an earl, and she was an earl's daughter. Her sisters had been given rich spouses from esteemed families, and she'd grown up imagining the dashing swain Lord Stone would ultimately catch for her. Yet now that the time was at hand, she was being advised to lower her expectations. It was so unfair!

Still though, she was amazed by his summons and suffered a trill of excitement. If he'd deigned to talk to her, he must have a significant topic to discuss. Marriage, perhaps?

"Sit, sit," he grumpily said. He was seated behind his desk, and he gestured to the chair across.

She eased down, struggling to look calm and composed. "What did you need, Father?"

"I have some…news to share."

"What is it?"

She could smell alcohol on his breath and clothes. The sour odor wafted toward her, and she could barely keep from gagging and covering her nose. His skin was pale and blotchy, and there were bags under his eyes. He appeared to have aged considerably too. Was he ill? Was he dying? Was that what he was about to impart?

"I've accepted an offer of marriage for you." He might have been sucking on sour pickles.

"How nice. Who is it? Is it anyone I know?"

The prior afternoon, she'd met Lord Barrington's son in the park, and she'd always had the worst crush on him. Had he finally realized how much she liked him? Had he spoken to her father? After all her mother's negative counsel, could Felicia be that lucky?

"Yes, you know him," her father said. "It's Michael Scott. I introduced you to him a few weeks ago at Lord Gladstone's ball."

"Michael…Scott."

"Yes."

She formed a picture of him in her mind. He was tall, dark, and handsome, but a bit rough around the edges. He'd constantly searched the crowd as if expecting an attack. If she'd been informed that he'd been armed, she wouldn't have been surprised.

That man, that stranger, was to be her husband?

"I remember him," she tentatively stated, "but I don't believe his title, status, or family was ever made clear."

"Well...ah...he doesn't have a family."

"He was raised by wolves? He's an orphan? What?"

Lord Stone chuckled as if she'd told a humorous joke. "I'm guessing he's an orphan. I'm not sure as to his history—no one is—and he doesn't have a title."

"No title?"

"No."

"How does he earn his living? He's in trade?"

"You could say that. He's...he's..."

Lord Stone's voice trailed off, and apparently he couldn't describe Mr. Scott's true situation. Felicia was panicked and offended and furious.

"He's what?" she pressed.

Her father sagged in his chair as if he might slide to the floor in an exhausted heap. Ultimately he groused, "Look, I'll be blunt, all right?"

"Yes, please be blunt."

"He's a gambler."

"A gambler!"

"Among other things."

"What other *things?*"

"It doesn't matter."

"It certainly does to me."

"I owe him a bit of money."

"How much money?"

"A *lot* of money."

Felicia glared, wanting to scold and chastise, but she had no idea how. She'd never had a contentious discussion with him. She'd hardly ever had a plain, ordinary discussion with him. What was she supposed to say?

"So…you owe him some money," she carefully said. "What has that to do with me?"

"He'll cancel some of my debt if I let him marry you."

"You're using me to pay off a debt?"

"A rather large debt. I didn't give you away cheaply."

"What was I worth?" She was very snide; she couldn't help it.

"Quite an enormous amount, actually."

"Be more specific."

"I only have to part with my plantation in Jamaica and a few ships."

"As opposed to what?"

"As opposed to everything we own in the world."

"You gambled away everything?"

"Yes." He was unable to hold her irate gaze, so evidently he was capable of some shame.

"What if I don't wish to wed him?"

"That is not an option, Felicia."

"Why isn't it?" she fumed.

"Because if you refuse, we'll be allowed to keep Stone Manor, but that's all. We'll be walking around in empty rooms."

"He'd take our furniture?"

"Yes, and every stitch of clothing in your closets, all the animals and equipment on our farms, all our stocks and bonds and investments. He'll take everything that isn't entailed by the title."

Felicia was aghast. What type of father would ruin his family like this? And over a silly game of cards! She'd always viewed him as being very stoic and responsible, so it was a shock to learn that he was simply a negligent spendthrift.

"All the years I was growing up," she said, "you were never home. I assumed you were busy with important issues. Imagine how stunned I am to discover that you've been wallowing with sordid companions in gambling halls."

"Don't use that tone with me," he snapped. "I have enough problems without listening to you nag."

She rose to her feet. "I want to talk to Mother about Mr. Scott. I want to hear her opinion about this."

"I've already spoken to her. We've agreed this is for the best."

"The best for whom?"

"For you *and* for us. You're an obedient daughter, and I expect you to be in this situation too."

"If I'd known all this compliance and submission would lead me to such a horrid spot, I might have misbehaved occasionally."

He ignored the jibe and waved her away. "Go meet with your Mother. You can pick dates and plan your schedule."

"The wedding is to happen right away?"

"Not *right* away, but soon."

Felicia gaped at him and he glowered back, studying her in a way he rarely had.

"You're upset," he muttered.

"Who wouldn't be?"

"I need your consent, Felicia—for the good of the family, for your mother and me. I *need* your help."

It was a plaintive appeal, and to her disgust, she was deeply moved by it. Her father had never previously asked a favor of her. How could she decline to assist?

"Yes, I suppose I can do it," she mumbled, having no idea why she'd think so.

"And he's not a bad fellow." Lord Stone flashed a ghoulish smile. "He's a self-made man, a real bootstraps sort of chap, seized his destiny and all that. I'm sure, after you get to know him, you'll be impressed."

"Impressed? Seriously?"

"This is for the best, Felicia," he said again. "For the family."

"Then I'm certain it'll be fine, won't it?"

She swept out, so furious she was blinded by rage, and she bumped into someone in the hall, having to blink three times before she saw it was her father's driver and guard, Mr. Blaylock. He'd once worked as a pugilist and was forbidding and scary, always lurking in the shadows, eager to carry out whatever task Lord Stone required.

It dawned on her that she'd like to have her father murdered. But no, not her father. Michael Scott. She was in such a violent temper that she wildly wondered if Mr. Blaylock could be bribed to commit such a heinous act. She suspected he might.

"Lady Felicia"—he reached out to steady her—"are you all right?"

"Yes, I just received some distressing news."

He oozed commiseration, which was much more than her accursed parents would ever bestow.

"Is there anything I can do?" he inquired.

How about kill my father—and my fiancé! "No, there's nothing."

He leaned in and whispered, "Is it your engagement? Has he finally told you?"

Gad, was she the last to learn of it? Had the whole city been apprised? Were people tittering behind her back?

"Yes, he told me. It's a bit of a shock," she incautiously mentioned.

"I dare say." His gaze turned sly. "I know Michael Scott very well, and I'm very discreet. If you'd ever like to discuss him…?"

He let the question dangle, and she didn't reply. He was a servant, and he had no business talking to her about Mr. Scott or any other topic, but she was intrigued that he knew Mr. Scott *well*. Yes, she thought, they would definitely have to have a private conversation—when she could escape all the prying ears in the house.

"If you'll excuse me?" she murmured. "My mother is waiting."

"Oh, my apologies. I didn't mean to delay you."

He stepped away, and she kept on, relieved that her father's choice hadn't been worse.

Lord Stone might have selected someone decrepit and elderly, might have wagered with someone blind or deformed. But no matter how hard she tried, she couldn't find a silver lining. In the coming weeks and months, how would she ever bear up?

What would she tell her friends?

"What can you reveal about any of it?"

"Not much, I'm afraid."

At Mr. Thumberton's response, Evangeline Etherton Drake sighed. Thumberton was a renowned London solicitor who served the wealthiest clients. She and her brother, Bryce Blair, were in his office, requesting details about their past.

She'd been hoping she'd get lucky, that the answers she sought would be easy to attain, but there would be no simple resolution.

She had a convoluted identity, having recently learned that her maiden name had never been Etherton. Nor was her first name Evangeline. It had been pinned on her as a toddler, but she had no idea why.

She'd grown up believing she was an orphan, so she'd been astonished to accidently stumble on her older brother, Bryce. He'd explained that she'd been born Anne Blair and named after their mother. She'd been called Annie, and as a baby her three brothers—Bryce and the twins

Michael and Matthew—had called her Sissy. She'd been the only daughter—the only sister—in a family with three sons.

Although she had vague dreams about the time when she was Annie Blair and Sissy to her brothers, she didn't remember that period. In her earliest genuine memories, she'd been living at Miss Peabody's School for Girls, and her name had been Evangeline Etherton.

It was bizarre to suddenly discover she was a different person from whom she'd always presumed herself to be. She hadn't yet returned to using the name Anne Blair—and wasn't sure she ever would. Evangeline was the sole name she recollected, and she was Evangeline Drake now, having married her husband, Aaron Drake, Lord Run.

Aaron was a viscount, heir to Lord Sidwell and would someday be an earl, so she was Anne, Annie, Sissy, Evangeline Blair Etherton Drake, Lady Run. Out of that long and elaborate list, how could any sane woman pick the correct moniker?

She'd been a charity case at school, her tuition paid by an anonymous benefactor, so it had definitely been a shock to meet Bryce and hear that her history was a lie.

They'd once had a loving, happy existence, their home filled with laughter, music, singing, and joy. Their mother had been extremely talented, likely an actress or singer, and their father a dashing sort, maybe a sailor or soldier who wasn't often present in London.

But a misfortune had ripped them apart. Why had that idyllic life ended? What had ended it?

Their mother seemed to have been convicted of a crime, perhaps transported to the penal colonies. Bryce had a traumatic memory of them being at the docks and saying goodbye to her, but he'd been too young to fully understand what was occurring. Only with adult hindsight had he pieced together what must have transpired.

Their father had perished, then their mother's troubles had started. And as to the twins? There was no trace. What had become of them?

Mr. Thumberton had occasionally checked on her and Bryce over the years, so they'd come to speak with him. If he didn't know the truth, who would? Yet so far, the visit had been pointless.

"Have you any information about our parents?" she asked.

"No."

"How about the boarding schools where we grew up? How were they selected for us? How was the headmaster convinced to accept Bryce when he was so little? What about me and Miss Peabody? I was even younger than Bryce when I was enrolled there, and she always hated me. Why did she keep me as a student if she disliked me so much?"

"I'm sorry," Mr. Thumberton said. "I simply don't know. I wish I had better news for you."

It had been Thumberton's reply to nearly every question.

"Bryce and I made it to our respective schools, but why is there no record of the twins? What happened to them?"

"I don't know. No one knew. It was a great mystery that always vexed Etherton."

"Is there any tidbit you can share?" Bryce inquired. "If we had the smallest hint of a clue, we could begin our search." He paused for a moment, studied Thumberton, then asked, "Were you paid to remain silent? Is that why you're so reticent?"

Bryce had hit on something. Thumberton stared at Bryce, at Evangeline, at Bryce again. For the longest while, he pondered. Finally he stood and went over to a locked cabinet. He opened it, drew out a file, and came back to his desk.

"I checked on you for Mr. Etherton," he said. "He retained me for that sole purpose."

"Now we're getting somewhere," Bryce muttered.

"I wasn't told much about either of you. Mr. Etherton needed me to establish your welfare, that you were being taught and fed and housed adequately in accordance with the money he was tendering for your care."

"Why didn't he check himself?" Bryce asked.

"He was incapacitated in an accident, so travel was difficult for him."

Evangeline popped in with, "What about Miss Peabody? She hired me as a teacher after I was finished with my education. Why?"

"I believe she was paid to do that."

"By Mr. Etherton?"

"Yes."

"That must have made me a bargain as an employee—if he provided my salary."

He nodded. "I'm sure it was a factor in your retention."

"I don't understand any of this," Evangeline said.

"Neither do I," Bryce agreed, and he turned to Thumberton. "You never met Etherton face to face?"

"Just the initial time when he retained me. After that, we corresponded through the mail."

"To what address?" Bryce asked. "Is he here in London? Could we visit him?"

"I'm afraid that won't be possible," Thumberton said. "He passed away many years ago."

And likely took his secrets to the grave!

Evangeline wanted to weep with frustration.

"But," Mr. Thumberton added, "his niece has managed his affairs since he died. She's in possession of his personal papers."

"Where is she? Is she in town?"

"No. She resided in a village near Southampton—if she's still alive and there. I haven't heard from her in awhile."

"We could locate her?"

"Yes, certainly," Thumberton said, "but if I may offer a word of advice?"

"Of course," Evangeline and Bryce replied in unison.

"I've been helping people with their legal problems for many decades, and I've learned that some secrets are best left buried. You should think long and hard about whether to reveal the truth. Someone went to an enormous amount of trouble to hide it from you."

Evangeline and Bryce smiled at each other, and Bryce told him, "We'll be happy with whatever we discover."

"And I'm desperate to find the twins," Evangeline added.

"Well then, I wish you Godspeed in your investigation," Thumberton said, "and let me know if I can be of assistance in the future."

"We will."

She and Bryce made their goodbyes and Thumberton's clerk escorted them out. They hovered on the sidewalk, their driver waiting in the carriage down the street.

"Are you free next week?" Bryce asked her.

"Why? Are we going to Southampton?"

"Absolutely," Bryce said.

"What if I ran an advertisement in the newspapers?"

"To say what?"

"To say we're looking for the twins. Maybe they're living down the block. Maybe they're together and safe and sound. They'll see the notice and appear on my doorstep tomorrow morning."

"I doubt it will be that easy," Bryce gently stated. "Please don't get your hopes up too high. I'd hate to have them dashed."

"Don't worry about me. I'll be fine—no matter what."

"I know you will."

"It's worth a try, don't you think? My contacting the newspapers?"

"I suppose."

"Should I mention a reward?"

Bryce scowled, then laughed. "Gad, no. We'd have every confidence artist in the kingdom show up with a sob story and claiming to be our lost brother."

Evangeline laughed too. "I hadn't thought of that."

"But purchase your advertisement, and pack a bag. I can't wait to meet the elusive Miss Etherton and ask her about her uncle. I intend to make her spill all."

CHAPTER SIX

"I was reading the newspaper."

"You were? I hope you didn't hurt yourself."

"Very funny," Ramsey muttered.

Michael glanced over at his friend and laughed. They'd been back in London for several days and were riding down the street toward his gambling club. As usual, a crowd had gathered behind them, mostly children, all of them eager for Michael to throw some coins or enlist one of them to perform a chore.

He and Ramsey had had quite a bit of schooling at the orphanage where they'd been raised, but it was a regular joke between them that Michael was a scholar and Ramsey wasn't. Ramsey could read people and situations better than any man alive. But printed words? No. He'd been too restless to learn his lessons and always said that he liked to speak with his fists.

"What was the article about?" he asked Ramsey. "If it attracted your notice, it must have been shocking."

"It wasn't an article. It was an advertisement."

"About what?"

"Someone is searching for Michael Blair—approximately thirty years of age, dark hair, blue eyes."

"Michael…Blair?" Michael carefully inquired. "What has that to do with me?"

"What has it to do with you? Don't be an idiot."

"It's a common enough name. There are likely thousands of Michael Blairs in the kingdom."

"They're hunting for one in particular."

"Who would look?"

Though he went by the name Michael Scott, he had a faded birth certificate and some other papers that proved his real name was Michael Blair. His parents had been Anne and Julian Blair, which meant nothing to him. The documents were in a crumpled brown envelope in his safe. He remembered someone stuffing them in his shirt on the tumultuous night of the fire when he'd been very tiny.

An adult had bent down and told him they were important, to never part with them, and he never had.

"Maybe," Ramsey mused, "you have a rich grandfather who's suddenly dying to find you."

"If I have a doting relative, how was I lost in the first place? Wealthy people's children don't get lost."

"You're such an obnoxious ass. Perhaps they thought they wanted to be rid of you, but they forgot how insufferable you can be and they changed their minds."

For all of Ramsey's violent ways, he was actually a very romantic fellow. He believed in happy endings, and while he had no information about his own family, he'd always claimed Michael's father must have been a prince or a duke. How else could Michael's imperious tendencies be explained?

When they were small, Ramsey would weave stories about how Michael's aristocratic father would locate him someday, how he'd arrive in a gilded coach drawn by six white horses. In case it had ever happened, Ramsey had made Michael promise he'd take Ramsey along and not leave him behind.

"The advertisement didn't mention a reward," Ramsey said, "but I was wondering if I shouldn't turn you in myself. You might be worth a pretty penny."

"I doubt it. Who would pay to bring me back?"

"I agree. Who would?" Ramsey shrugged. "It probably wasn't you."

"I'm sure it wasn't."

"The person was looking for a Matthew Blair too. Twins, it said. Michael and Matthew Blair. You didn't have a twin brother, did you? Not one you ever talked about anyway."

For the briefest second, the Earth seemed to stand still. Michael's horse paused in mid-step, birds halted in flight, voices hushed, passersby froze in their spots.

He might have been staring into a mirror at a little boy who looked just like Michael. They were nose to nose, smiling, whispering in a secret language no one understood but them. The most terrifying wave of anguish swept over him. He couldn't breathe, couldn't keep his balance. Frantically he grabbed for his arm, feeling as if it had been hacked off and was no longer attached to his body.

"Hey!" Ramsey snapped his fingers in Michael's face. "Where were you?"

"I was…daydreaming."

"Seeing what this time?"

"Nothing but myself in a mirror."

Michael physically shook himself, the peculiar vision providing the distinct impression that he was missing a precious treasure in his life. Since he had no idea what it was, he had no idea how to get it back.

Ramsey was used to Michael's abnormal hallucinations. He was used to them, but didn't like them. As children, he'd often had to awaken Michael when he was in the throes of a nightmare.

"You know I hate it when you wander off in your mind," Ramsey complained. "I'm always afraid you won't return."

"Don't worry. If I ever vanish completely, I'll find a way to haunt you."

"Just my luck."

Michael glanced around, not surprised to discover they were directly in front of the Vicar Sterns Rescue Mission.

After Miss Wells had fled Cliffside, Michael hadn't stopped thinking about her. The lengthy kiss they'd shared on her balcony had rattled him, and she'd wedged herself into his head like an irksome gnat. For some bizarre reason, he felt as if they were connected, as if she was his now, which made no sense at all.

He didn't even *like* her, and considering her line of work—and his—they had naught in common. What would be the point of fraternization? If he spent any extended time with her, she'd drive him batty.

But he reined in his horse.

"What are you doing?" Ramsey asked.

"I thought I'd visit Miss Wells."

"Are you mad?"

"Very likely."

"Our shipment is at the docks."

"I know."

"You wanted to check it."

"I *know*, Ramsey."

Ramsey studied the ramshackle building, the crooked sign. The whole place was a stiff wind away from collapse. He chuckled. "She might be worth it."

"Worth what?"

"Worth...*whatever* you're contemplating. Did I tell you her sister lured me out into the garden at Cliffside."

Michael scowled. "No, you didn't tell me."

"She begged me to tumble her in the grass, but I refused."

"You better have. I can't have you involved with her."

"That's what I said, but she insisted I shouldn't listen to you."

"I hope you told her to stuff it."

"Rebecca Wells is as loose as I imagined." Ramsey gestured to the mission. "Perhaps her sister is too."

"I'm not here to seduce her."

"Why are you here then? Are you claiming we just happened to ride by?"

"I promised her a donation."

"Sure you did, Michael. Sure you did." Ramsey urged his horse into a trot. "I'll check the shipment for you," he called over his shoulder, "and meet you at the club."

"All right."

"Once I'm back, I'll expect you to describe the color of her drawers."

"I'm giving her a donation!" Michael said again.

"Donate a bit for me, would you?"

Ramsey rounded the corner and disappeared.

Michael dismounted, and a dozen boys rushed up, begging to watch his horse while he was inside. He knew most of them by name, and he motioned to three of the shyest ones, trying to spread around the coins he'd toss to them later when he departed.

The door was open, with her not bothering to lock it, but then she probably didn't need much security. What was there to steal?

He entered the main room. It was empty and Miss Wells nowhere in sight. There were several long tables set in rows, and through a doorway beyond he could see a kitchen, but it was quiet, the lull in the afternoon when nothing much occurred.

Previously, he'd heard rumors about her operation, and he'd asked about her and found out more.

She served two meals a day, breakfast and supper, to anyone who was hungry. In the mornings, after breakfast, she ran a school that any child could attend. On Sundays, a pastor stopped by to conduct a prayer service, but other than that short ministry there wasn't much religious fervor attached to her activities.

If she had no spiritual leanings to spur her on, what kept her motivated and inspired? Especially after the Vicar and Mrs. Sterns had passed away, it couldn't have been easy to continue, and she was a woman on her own with no male to offer guidance. How did she manage?

When he caught himself obsessing over her, he rolled his eyes and shook away his fixation. There was no reason to be fascinated by her, but apparently he was.

She lived in an apartment upstairs and had a few helpers, volunteers who'd been *rescued* by Vicar Sterns. None of them were present to welcome him or shoo him away.

He strutted in as if he owned the place, but he was curious about the proprietor. Miss Wells didn't appear to have two pennies to rub together, so he doubted the building belonged to her. Maybe he would approach the owner and buy it. The notion of being her landlord, of having some authority and control over her, was vastly amusing.

There was a rickety staircase in the back that led up to the second floor, and he went over and climbed. He walked down a narrow hall, peeking into clean, sparse rooms that were like cells for a group of monks. Only the door at the end was closed.

He spun the knob and looked into a parlor, noting immediately that it was her private quarters. Dilapidated furniture was neatly arranged, and an effort had been made to create a comfortable and homey abode. There were rugs scattered, doilies on the tables, curtains on the windows.

But it was a far step down from the opulence of Cliffside, and he wondered how her pride had stood the descent to the lower rungs of society. Gaylord Farrow had jilted her and broken her heart, so Michael comprehended why she'd fled her home, but on viewing the dire condition of her situation, he certainly questioned whether her father had ever visited.

What man would have let his daughter stay in such a dreary establishment?

A bedchamber was located behind the parlor, and he could hear her in there humming to herself, and it sounded as if she was washing. Water splashed in a bowl.

On realizing he was about to be with her again, he suffered such a thrill that he was alarmed by it. What was wrong with him?

He turned the key in the lock, and as he stuck it in his pocket, he grinned. Would this become their typical mode of interacting? He'd bluster in without warning, she'd scold and order him out, but he wouldn't leave until he felt like it.

He sauntered over and leaned against the door jam, and her back was to him, so he had a moment to watch her before she figured out he'd arrived.

Her glorious auburn hair was down, and it hung to her waist in a curly wave. It was such a stunning shade, red but with strands of gold and mahogany woven through as well. He'd never seen hair like it, and he thought of her sisters, with their plain brunette hair. In comparison, she looked like a goddess.

Gaylord Farrow could have had her, but he'd chosen tepid Pamela instead, which only underscored Michael's opinion that Farrow was an idiot.

To his eternal delight, Miss Wells was stripped down to chemise and petticoat, her feet and arms bare, her corset tossed on a nearby chair. The garments were functional, faded from many launderings, but nevertheless she was sexy as hell.

She was standing by her dresser, dipping a cloth in a bowl of water and smoothing it over her face and shoulders.

"Nan, is that you?" she asked. "Could you help me pin up my hair? It's rioting today, and I can't manage it on my own."

She glanced over, expecting someone named Nan, and when she saw him she gasped with astonishment. Thankfully she didn't scream bloody murder, but she scrutinized him as if trying to determine if he was an apparition or if he was actually in her bedchamber.

Unfortunately for her, he was all too real.

"Mr. Scott!" she snapped. "What are you doing here?"

"I have no idea."

"I could have sworn at Cliffside I told you not to visit."

"Did you? I must have forgotten."

"You can't just barge in."

"I already have. You should lock your door."

He pulled out her key and held it up.

"I'm trapped with you again?"

"Yes, until I decide to let you out."

There was a knitted throw on the bed, and she reached for it and wrapped it around her torso as if it was a large towel. While it concealed her a bit, it *was* knitted, so it didn't provide anywhere near the coverage she was hoping.

"As you can see," she fumed, "I'm in no condition to receive you."

"I don't care."

"Well, I do. Please go."

"Sorry, but I can't oblige you."

"Yes, you can."

"You keep ignoring one very important fact about me."

"What is that?"

"I never listen to women, remember?"

"I dare say you never listen to anyone, but this isn't funny. I'm not dressed and you can't be in here."

He walked toward her, and with each step he was inundated by a strange sense of destiny. If he'd tried to turn and leave, he couldn't have. Fate seemed to be holding him in place, as if he'd finally arrived right where he belonged.

As to Miss Wells, it was clear from her exasperated expression that she wasn't sensing the dubious hand of Fate. No, she was gaping at him as if a lunatic had entered and was about to commit unspeakable acts.

She wasn't too far off. He'd always deemed himself to be quite insane. When he considered the chances he'd taken in his life, the risks he'd assumed, it was obvious that only a deranged person would have behaved so recklessly.

And as to unspeakable acts…

He'd definitely like to commit several. What was his plan? What did he intend? How badly did he want her?

He approached until his body touched hers, the rough edges of the knitted throw scratching against his clothes.

That invigorating energy flared, the one he always perceived when he was close to her. He felt half-crazed with desire, but she was a spinster, and he hated innocent women. He liked women who knew what they were about in the bedchamber, who knew what he preferred so he didn't have to waste any effort getting it from them.

If he pressed her into a tryst, he'd have to do all the work and would be annoyed when he was finished. So…why was he titillated? His aroused state was ridiculous, but she stirred him as no female ever had, and there was no possible solution but to forge ahead.

He drew her into his arms and dipped down to nibble at her nape.

"You smell good," he murmured.

"Mr. Scott!"

Her bed was next to them, and he lifted her and tumbled them onto the mattress. She didn't cry out with alarm, didn't try to squirm away. If anything, she appeared even more exasperated.

"Are you about to ravish me?" she asked.

"No, I never would."

"Then explain yourself, for I must tell you that you're making me very afraid."

"You're not afraid of me," he scoffed.

"No, but I'm afraid of what you might do."

So am I!

"If I see something I crave, I take it," he said. "I'm not the type to sit around in fussy parlors, drinking tea, and fretting over what I'd *like* to have."

"I realize that about you, but *I* am not the kind of woman to dawdle on a mattress with any man, let alone a man I barely know."

"I think you know me quite well."

"Why? Because I've figured out that you're an unrepentant rogue and criminal?"

"Yes."

He grinned, and she rolled her eyes in frustration.

"Let me up."

"No."

"Please."

"No."

"If we're at the point where you're uttering one-word replies, it's futile to argue with you."

"It's always futile, so you're finally learning that I always get my way. There are few people who have the stamina to battle my stubbornness, and you certainly don't. Give over and give me what I want."

"What is it you *want*? I've fascinated you, but I have no idea why."

"Don't you?"

"No."

She gazed up at him, looking perplexed and confused and very, very pretty.

Was she aware of her beauty? Had any man ever told her? Gaylord Farrow should have flattered her to the moon and back, but no doubt, he'd never voiced a single glowing comment.

Michael wasn't the sort prone to romantic declarations, but suddenly he was desperate to shower her with praise. Yet she didn't like to flirt and didn't like compliments. With her having such odd female proclivities, how could he make her feel special?

He wouldn't waste time talking. He was a man of action, not words, and he was clearer when he used his body and hands to clarify his position. He kissed her, and there was such sweet relief in the embrace that he was glad he was lying down. If he'd been standing, his knees might have buckled. He was that besotted.

"Mr. Scott," she scolded as he drew away.

"Call me Michael."

"No."

"Miss Wells, let's review what you know about me."

"You always get your way."

"Yes, so you might as well call me Michael. I won't stop pestering you until you agree."

"We're barely acquainted, and you're pressuring me horridly."

"How am I pressuring you? We're just chatting."

"On my bed, when I'm not wearing any clothes."

"Tell me to leave and I will."

"Leave."

"No."

She laughed a full, but miserable laugh.

"What am I to do with you?" she inquired.

"Call me Michael, and we'll proceed from there."

"Fine, Michael, let it be as you wish. There will be no formality between us. From here on out, we'll carry on as if we've known each other for decades. You've insisted, and I can't seem to go against you."

"Good. Now then, your name is Magdalena, but your sisters call you Maggie. Which shall it be for me?"

"You're not using my given name."

"I'm not? Let's review. I always get my—"

"All right, all right," she huffed. "You may call me Maggie—when we're alone. If I have the misfortune to encounter you out in public, I am Miss Wells to you."

He considered, then grinned again. "Perhaps."

"If you're not careful, I'll have to demand you marry me."

He scowled. "What?"

"When two people misbehave as we are, matrimony is the penalty they pay."

"We're not misbehaving—not in my world anyway."

"Well, in *my* world you're one step away from being dragged to the altar."

"I'm not exactly the marrying kind," he lied. In fact, he'd just heard from Lord Stone that Stone had decided to save himself by sacrificing his daughter, Felicia.

"Every bachelor claims he'll never wed," she said.

"But *I* mean it."

"I'm sure you do, but if you commit a carnal lapse with me, you'll quickly find yourself fettered. You'd hate for that to happen, wouldn't you?"

"Who could make me wed you? Your silly, trembling sister? Your idiotic brother-in-law? Somehow I can't picture you asking him to help you."

"*I* could make you," she said. "I would rail at you until you relented."

"We've already established that I never listen to women."

"If the threat of marriage can't deter you from mischief, what will?"

"Nothing."

"Haven't you a trollop who could entertain you this afternoon?"

"Dozens of them."

"Yet you're forcing me to be the one."

"Yes. Aren't you lucky?"

She flashed a stern frown. "I don't want this from you."

"You just think you don't. You're still a maiden, so you don't know what you need."

"I'm pretty sure I don't need you bothering me."

"What if you're wrong? What if I turn out to be precisely what you require?"

"Only a man as vain as yourself would suppose you could be the answer to a woman's prayers."

"Let me show you something."

"I'd rather you didn't."

"You'll like it. I promise."

In his opinion she spent entirely too much time talking, so he kissed her again, more passionately, and for all her protesting she didn't attempt to stop him. Apparently she'd enjoyed their previous romantic foray as much as he had.

He kept on for what seemed like forever, and gradually she relaxed and joined in, her arms slipping around his neck to pull him close. The knitted throw had come loose, so there was little separating them. The fabric on her chemise was so thin and faded, she might not have been wearing any clothes at all.

He placed a hand on her breast, and he kneaded it, caressing the soft mound, feeling the taut nipple pressed to his palm.

Without a doubt he'd pushed her much farther than she'd intended, but he couldn't desist. He was so happy when he was with her and didn't want the sense of contentment to ever abate.

He slid his fingers under her chemise, but she clasped his wrist and yanked him away. Their lips parted, their riveting kiss ending, and he couldn't believe how he regretted its concluding.

"You are so wicked," she said, but she was smiling.

"I try to be."

"And very dangerous to my equilibrium. You make me eager to misbehave."

"Didn't I tell you I'd turn out to be just what you need the most? Besides, you're too old to be a maid. You should lie down with me more often. There are all kinds of pleasurable activities I could teach you."

"No, thank you. I think I'll hold on to my chastity—if that's all right with you."

"It's not all right."

"Well, it's all right with me, and that's what matters."

He could have mentioned that his wishes were always paramount, that the world rotated in his direction, but he didn't, for he wouldn't wreck the moment with bickering.

Their banter dwindled and they were nose to nose, gaping like half-wits, with him still stretched out on top of her. He knew he had to depart, but couldn't leave.

She glanced over to the window and saw the shadows lengthening, the afternoon waning.

"I have to get downstairs," she said, "to check on the preparations for supper."

"In a minute."

"Rumors will spread that I'm growing lazy."

"I'll beat any man who says so."

"You will not," she scoffed.

"I might—if you asked me to."

"I'm quite capable of taking care of myself."

"You don't even lock your door."

"I never had to until you stumbled into my life."

He raised a brow. "If I recall correctly, *you* stumbled into mine. I was minding my own business when you blustered into my office."

"I guess you could describe it that way."

"I could and I have. If you're upset over my heightened interest you have only yourself to blame for it."

"I suppose." She sighed. "Will you be popping in all the time now?"

"Maybe."

"I can't figure out what's happening with us."

"Must you figure it out?"

"In light of my history I've sworn off men, and even if I hadn't, you're the very last sort I'd welcome as a suitor."

"I'm not a suitor."

"Precisely, and I'm not loose, so I have no idea why I'm lying here without my clothes."

He grinned his most cocky grin. "It was pleasant though, wasn't it?"

"Very pleasant," she agreed.

"I'm growing on you."

"Perish the thought, Mr. Scott."

"It's Michael, remember?"

"So it is, Michael. So it is."

He slid away and stood. She remained on the bed, looking lovely and rumpled and adorable, and the strangest emotions rocked him. He felt sad and grand, wonderful, but wretched too. He ached to say things to her he'd never said to anyone, about his difficult childhood, about how successful he'd become.

He'd like to tell her about the vision he'd had out on the street when he was riding up with Ramsey. Why did he always observe another boy? A boy who was so much like him? A boy who might be his other half?

He wanted to tell her about his real name being Michael Blair, that someone was searching for a man with that name. The need to belong, to know his past, to stare across the supper table and have a familiar face staring back, was so strong that he often felt ill just from contemplating it.

But he never talked about any of those topics, and it was a mark of the peculiar hold she exerted over him that he would yearn to unburden himself.

She'd insisted he wasn't the sort of fellow she'd ever welcome into her life, and she was absolutely right that she shouldn't. Still though, as he imagined never seeing her again, the notion was preposterous.

Yet what point would be served by socializing? What was he hoping to accomplish by bothering her?

"Goodbye," he murmured.

"That sounded awfully final. Does that mean you've come to your senses and won't stop by again?"

"I haven't decided."

He swooped in and stole a last kiss, then he strolled out. He left the key on her dresser so she could find it easily when she remembered to lock her door.

CHAPTER SEVEN

"I have a proposition for you."

"It's a little late for propositions."

Gaylord Farrow stared at Michael Scott, feeling nervous in a manner he rarely was. Mr. Scott had a reputation as a bully and a fiend. He was the sort who took advantage, who preyed on the weak, so Gaylord couldn't exhibit an ounce of anxiety.

They were in Scott's London club where Gaylord had reveled and amused himself to the point of total ruin. Currently it was the most fashionable spot in the city to wager, and a person needed Mr. Scott's invitation before he could join in.

Gaylord had once been a valued customer, but as soon as he got into a bit of difficulty, he'd been refused admittance. Michael Scott was fickle that way. He'd kick a man when he was down, and Gaylord blamed Scott for all his fiscal troubles.

Michael Scott could have reined in Gaylord's excesses, but he hadn't. He'd allowed Gaylord to keep on until he'd tumbled over the cliff of financial catastrophe.

The most galling fact was that Gaylord could no longer socialize at Scotts. Every gentleman of consequence gambled there, but Gaylord was excluded, and everyone would eventually learn of how he'd been shamed.

"Hear me out," Gaylord pleaded. "I think you'll be intrigued."

"What is it?"

They were in Scott's office, with Scott seated behind his desk and Gaylord in the chair across. The violent rogue, Ramsey Scott, stood off to the side.

"You were at Cliffside," Gaylord said.

"I was," Michael Scott agreed.

"You met my sister-in-law, Rebecca. She's quite stunning."

Scott shrugged. "I suppose."

"She'd like to marry."

"Would she?"

Ramsey Scott piped in with, "She's too busy flirting. I spoke with her, and matrimony wasn't what she was considering at all."

Michael Scott didn't look at Ramsey, but waved a hand, silencing him.

"She's not a flirt," Gaylord insisted. "She's an upstanding young lady of good reputation."

"Fine," Michael Scott muttered, "she's upstanding and good. What has that to do with me?"

"As I said, she's eager to wed, but with her father's passing, we haven't had an opportunity to select a husband for her."

"Her father died five years ago," Michael Scott scoffed. "It must have been a lengthy mourning period."

Gaylord ignored the snide remark. "Anyway, Pamela and I discussed the matter, and what with your interest in Cliffside—"

"My interest? I don't have an *interest*. I own the bloody place. We're just dickering over the date you have to be out, which I believe is July first."

"So it is." Gaylord nodded, all smiles, all accommodation.

Gaylord would try any ruse in order to keep Cliffside. He would lie, cheat, steal, and perhaps even murder Michael Scott if that's what it took to retain the property.

He'd spent ages hunting for just the right situation, and the Wells family had suited his purposes perfectly. He'd been born to an acceptable family of his own, but his father had been a wastrel, so Gaylord had always understood that he had to find a rich bride. Prosperous, thriving Cliffside had been exactly what he'd sought.

Initially he'd wooed Magdalena, but she'd proved too smart and stubborn, so he'd seduced Pamela instead, then had ingratiated himself to her father. The old man perished soon after Gaylord's wedding, so Gaylord had had the entire estate all to himself, but it had never been enough to support his dissolute habits.

He loved the excitement of town where he cavorted and gamboled as was expected of a gentleman. He dressed well and dined well and drove around in the sleekest, fastest carriages. He would not lose any of it!

"You're such a successful fellow," he said to Michael Scott, "and Rebecca was fascinated by you."

"Was she?" Michael Scott appeared bored and one second away from tossing Gaylord out on his ear.

"Oh yes, after you left, all she could talk about was you."

"I'll bet."

"With her being so smitten, Pamela and I thought it only fitting that I approach you."

"About what?"

"We were wondering if you'd entertain a betrothal."

Michael Scott looked astonished. "Between Rebecca and myself?"

"Yes. You have to admit she's fetching, and she's accomplished at all the feminine arts. She could bring flair and style into your life."

"I don't need any flair, and I don't need a wife."

"Come now," Gaylord cajoled, "every man needs a wife. You're reported to be thirty already. Surely it's time for you to settle down."

"And if I marry Rebecca, you'd get…what? Are you hoping I'll relent about Cliffside and sign it back to you?"

"If we were *brothers*, it would certainly smooth over our contentious issues."

"We have no issues," Scott said, "except that you've wagered away every pound, scrap, and furrow of ground you ever possessed, and you wagered them away to me." He studied Gaylord, his dislike palpable and infuriating. "Besides, I'm not in the market for a bride. I just became engaged."

"I hadn't heard." Gaylord was incredibly deflated by the news. "Anyone I know?"

"My fiancée will be making the announcements."

Gaylord squirmed in his seat, struggling to come to grips with this latest development. There had always been rumors that Scott accepted all sorts of boons to allay debts that were owed. Obviously Gaylord had been beaten to the punch, and he gnashed his teeth. Who had barged in and stolen Gaylord's thunder? Who had offered a girl before Gaylord could offer one himself?

"Perhaps we could work out a different arrangement," Gaylord slyly stated.

"Meaning what?"

"Rebecca is so pretty, and she's still a maiden. She's just ripe for the plucking."

Ramsey Scott shifted in the corner, but Michael Scott raised a hand again, preventing any comment.

"You'd like me to *pluck* her for you?" Michael Scott inquired.

"A man might take a bride," Gaylord said, "but it doesn't dampen his interest in other…things."

"You're offering me Rebecca's virginity?"

"Yes."

"In exchange for what?"

"For six more months of residence at Cliffside."

Six months was an eternity where Gaylord could figure out a better conclusion. He could try his luck at other clubs. Maybe his losing streak would end, and he'd win so much money he'd be able to buy back Cliffside and send Michael Scott packing.

"Let me get this straight," Michael Scott said. "I'd get one unpleasant night with your virginal, annoying sister-in-law, and you'd get six months longer at Cliffside?"

"Yes."

"No. I hate fussing with virgins, and I won't have you loitering on my property. I've been more than fair in permitting you to vacate on July first."

"All right, all right," Gaylord hastily concurred. "You can have her as your mistress for six months. That's an even trade, isn't it? Six months for six months?"

"During that period, I could do whatever I wished to her?"

"Yes," Gaylord said.

"And after the six months are over, then what?"

"Then…what?" Gaylord gaped as if he didn't understand the question.

"What would become of her? She'd be ruined."

What happens to her is not my problem!

Gaylord was sick of supporting the idiotic girl. Years earlier, he'd blazed through her dowry, and she never stopped nagging about it. Despite her disagreeable nature, he'd allowed her to stay at Cliffside, and he'd been much too patient. She needed to lower her standards, find the best possible husband available without a dowry, and get out of Gaylord's house.

"If you're not keen on Rebecca—" Gaylord started.

"I'm not."

"Let me make another suggestion."

"You might have reached the limit of what I'll listen to."

"Hear me out," Gaylord pleaded again, sounding ever more desperate. "My wife mentioned that you seemed smitten by her other sister, Magdalena."

"I have no idea why she'd think so," Mr. Scott claimed. "I barely know Magdalena Wells."

"I guess the two of you socialized when you visited Cliffside."

"The mansion was packed to the rafters with guests, so I socialized with many people. What of it?"

"You won't consider a liaison with Rebecca, so I'm happy to extend the offer to Maggie."

Pamela had urged him to propose Magdalena from the outset, but Maggie wasn't as much of a pest as Rebecca. She never bothered Gaylord, and she supported herself, although it would be more difficult now that he'd gotten his hands on her dowry trust. She was as broke as everyone else in the family.

Why shouldn't she chip in to help? Why shouldn't she suffer as the rest of them were suffering?

"We're dickering over her chastity?" Michael Scott said.

"No, the six months for the six months."

Mr. Scott snorted with amusement. "Magdalena might have something to say about that. I can't imagine her consenting."

"It's not up to her."

"It's not? You assume you can command her?"

"I won't have to. She's absurdly devoted to her sisters. When she learns what's at stake, she'll be eager to assist them."

"Even if it includes spreading her legs for me for six months?"

"Even that."

Michael Scott glanced over at Ramsey Scott, seeking the other man's opinion, but Ramsey glared and gave no indication of what he thought his partner should choose.

"If I might comment on Magdalena?" Gaylord asked.

"No, you may not."

Gaylord continued anyway. "She's the prettiest of the Wells sisters, and she's the smartest too. She can carry on a conversation. You'd never be bored with her."

Michael Scott scoffed. "Just what I'm looking for in a bedmate. Conversation!"

Still though, it was clear Scott was intrigued, his cunning mind sifting through the benefits and detriments. The excruciating seconds ticked by. Scott drummed his fingers on the desk and finally said, "I'll do it for a month. If she pleases me, *and* if she's not annoying as hell, I'll keep her for the whole six months."

Gaylord was so relieved, he nearly slid to the floor in an exhausted heap. An entire month! And it might grow to half a year! Any dastardly *accident* could happen to Michael Scott during such a lengthy period.

"She'll please you! I swear it."

"We'll see, I suppose. Will you tell her or will I?"

"My wife and I will tell her. She may take a bit of convincing."

"It's Wednesday afternoon. I'll expect to begin on Saturday."

"Saturday will be fine."

"If she refuses, you'll leave Cliffside at once with no delay."

"Wait a minute!" Gaylord huffed. "I can't be responsible for—"

"Those are my terms, Farrow. She agrees and we begin on Saturday, or you vacate sooner than planned."

Gaylord wanted to hurl invectives, wanted to curse and ask where such a lowborn person as Michael Scott mustered the gall to dictate terms to Gaylord. But he'd gained what he'd come to achieve.

He stood and held out his hand as if they might shake and pretend they were cordial, but Scott simply glowered at the extended hand, and Gaylord dropped it to his side.

"I'll just be going," he mumbled.

Mr. Scott waved to Ramsey. "Follow him out. I won't have him lingering."

Ramsey Scott pushed away from the wall, and the tall, violent oaf blustered over as if he might drag Gaylord out. Gaylord hurried off before Ramsey Scott could touch him.

As he started down the hall, Michael Scott called, "Saturday morning, Farrow. She'll be mine by eleven o'clock on the dot. I won't give her a second more."

Gaylord shuddered with dread, worried about Magdalena's reaction, but a wisp of excitement slithered by too. Maggie was shrewd and practical. She'd recognize the importance of her task, would grasp how her sisters needed her in their most dire hour.

She would finally have the chance to prove her loyalty. She'd save them all—or Gaylord would extract a retribution he was certain she'd never wish to pay.

"Let me kill him."

Michael pondered the request, then said, "No."

"Please?" Ramsey begged. "I'll make it slow and painful, and I'll enjoy it so much."

"No. If Farrow died, we'd be the first ones under suspicion."

"So? They'd never be able to pin anything on me."

"He's not worth the risk."

"What risk? I can ride up behind him on the road, knock him senseless, and drown him in a creek. He's a renowned drunkard. People will figure he fell in and was too inebriated to climb out."

Michael chuckled, but shook his head. "I want Cliffside."

"He's already signed it over to you."

"I'm regretting that I gave him time to vacate. It's put me in a position of having to constantly deal with him."

"Why scheme with him over Miss Wells then?"

"He'll never persuade her." At least Michael didn't think Farrow would. With a woman, who could predict how she'd behave? "She loathes him, so he'll never convince her. By Saturday, we'll be through with Farrow. I won't have to wait to evict."

"What about the other sister? What about Rebecca?"

"What about her?"

"Will you abandon her to Farrow?"

"You talk as if I'm her savior."

For some reason, Ramsey had become fixated on Rebecca Wells, and Michael didn't understand it. Ramsey could have his pick of any loose doxy in the city. Why bother with Rebecca?

She was pretty, but flighty and foolish. At twenty-two, she was past the marrying age, past the interval when a man could have trained her to her marital duties with any confidence that she'd conduct herself appropriately.

"You can't assume she's safe with Farrow," Ramsey complained.

"I don't assume it."

"I'm getting her out of there," Ramsey ridiculously boasted.

"To do what with her?"

"I don't have any idea, but whatever I choose, it will be better than what she's facing with that prick."

"Leave her alone," Michael scolded. "After the deal collapses on Saturday, after *we* move in and they move out, I don't want any further contact with them."

"Maybe I won't listen to you for once."

Ramsey's announcement was so out of character that Michael was taken aback by it, and he scowled. "Don't argue with me. Just stay out of trouble."

"How can it matter if I have a fling with Rebecca? You don't care about Cliffside. You plan to sell it after they're gone."

"I might keep it."

"You, keep Cliffside? Why would you?"

"Now that I'm engaged, I need somewhere fancy to stash my wife."

He and Lord Stone had just agreed to terms. Michael would gain a sugar cane plantation and three ships—and an unwanted daughter—and Lord Stone would retain everything else.

Michael thought he should feel some emotion, happiness, pride, contentment. But he had no feelings about Felicia one way or the other. He supposed he'd have to make a trip over to her house to be properly introduced, to propose in person, but the entire notion was exhausting.

Ramsey looked dubious. "You'll live at Cliffside—in wedded bliss with Lady Felicia?"

"If she likes the place. If not, I'll buy her another."

Michael had a home in the country—ludicrously named Orphan's Nest—but he rarely visited it. He didn't like the deserted country lanes or the quiet country evenings that went on forever. He was too used to action and adventure.

Nevertheless, it was a fine residence, comfortable and stylishly furnished. There was nothing grand about it though, and Felicia would expect lavish surroundings. Plus, if Michael intended to wedge himself into her social circle—which was the whole point of the marriage—he had to own the right kind of property.

"What if you're wrong about Miss Wells?" Ramsey asked.

"What do you mean?"

"What if she's so worried about her sisters that she consents?"

Michael suffered a rush of excitement thinking how thrilling it would be to have Maggie all to himself for a month. Or perhaps even six months!

Yet as quickly as he recognized his heightened interest, he shoved it away. Apparently he was as besotted as Ramsey, and while Ramsey might pine and mope for Rebecca Wells, Michael never grew attached to anyone. It wasn't in his nature.

Bonds were always severed, so his past had been a depressing story of separation and disaster. People moved away. People died. Ramsey was the only one who'd stayed. Over all the years of Michael's life, it had been Ramsey and no one else.

"Magdalena Wells won't give Farrow the time of day," Michael said, "and she would never lower herself to consort with me. Not if the fate of the world depended on it."

"The fate of *her* world does depend on it."

"So what? She's been very clear in her opinion of me, and Farrow will never persuade her to participate."

"We'll see," Ramsey mused.

"Yes, *we* will."

"Don't say a word."

"Who's there?"

Ramsey slipped a hip onto the mattress of Rebecca's bed and clasped a palm over her mouth so she wouldn't cry out.

It was dark, just a hint of moonlight shining in her bedroom window, and he didn't want to scare her where she'd scream and servants might come running. Not that anybody would. He'd snooped through the empty halls and hadn't encountered a single soul.

Still, he had to be careful and couldn't be caught—for he wouldn't cross Michael. In the horrid years they were boys, Michael had saved him on a thousand occasions. Michael had patiently trained Ramsey so he'd become the shrewd, tough criminal he was.

Most of all, Michael had taken Ramsey with him on their journey to wealth and power. Michael wasn't the sort to leave a man behind. He was the most fiercely loyal person Ramsey had ever met, and Ramsey was fiercely loyal in return.

Except now, with Rebecca in the picture, he was considering a bit of betrayal. Michael had warned him away from Rebecca, but if Michael never learned of Ramsey's folly, where was the harm?

"It's me, Ramsey Scott," he whispered. She nodded against his palm, letting him know she understood. "I'm moving my hand away. Don't make a sound."

He eased away as she said, "I won't."

"Good."

She sat up, the blankets clutched to her chest, her brunette hair flowing around her shoulders. "Why are you here?"

"I came to see you."

"Seriously? Don't you live in London?"

"Most of the time."

"And you rode all this way?"

"Yes."

"I thought you weren't interested in me. That night in the garden, you were very clear."

"Can't a fellow change his mind?"

"A fellow *can*, but it seems awfully peculiar." She batted her lashes. "I'm still the naïve maiden you can't abide."

"Maybe I've decided to try new things."

She stuck her pert nose up in the air. "You won't be trying any new things with me."

"Are you sure about that?"

"Very sure."

"I'm surprised to hear it. I took you for the type of girl who was innocent but curious."

"Curious about what? About you?"

Her big blue eyes wandered down his torso, and there was a lot of him to see.

"I want to show you something," he told her.

"What is it?"

"I want to *show* you, not tell you."

"I'm not certain I like you, and from that gleam in your gaze, it's obvious you're contemplating mischief."

"I am. I admit it."

"I can't involve myself with you now. Gaylord went to London to engage me to Michael Scott. I'm to be married."

"To Michael?"

"Yes."

"You haven't spoken to your brother-in-law?"

"No, he's not back yet."

"You're not marrying Michael."

"He said *no*?"

"He said *no*."

"Oh."

Her shoulders slumped with defeat, and he suffered the worst wave of pity for her. Farrow had bartered over her like a fattened sow, hoping Michael would feast, but Michael would never have considered it, and Farrow was mad to have proceeded.

She foolishly assumed Farrow had sought a betrothal to Michael! She believed her brother-in-law had traveled to town with good intentions!

Ramsey bit down the scathing rebukes he yearned to hurl about Farrow. He would never inform her that her brother-in-law had started out talking marriage, but had ended up proposing another arrangement entirely.

Ramsey made his living off of disreputable gentlemen. They regularly ruined themselves, and as they raced to undo their recklessness, the despicable swine tendered bribes and other inducements too hideous to mention in polite company.

Nothing astonished him any longer, but even in his jaded view he'd been disgusted by Farrow. The poor girl wasn't safe with her brother-in-law. If Farrow would offer her as mistress to a fiend like Michael, what dastardly fate might Farrow engineer for her next?

"Were you eager for a betrothal to Michael?" Ramsey asked. "Were you counting on it?"

If she'd set her heart on Michael, Ramsey would be crushed. Michael was handsome and dashing and civilized as Ramsey could never be. Ramsey was handsome enough, but he was too rough around the edges for any genuine lady to pick him over Michael.

"I wasn't counting on it precisely," she claimed. "I'm simply desperate to escape Cliffside. Gaylord is in financial trouble with his gambling, and I'm anxious to flee before the walls crash down on us."

"That's very wise," Ramsey agreed, but didn't provide any pertinent facts. Evidently she wasn't aware that the estate was already forfeit, and Ramsey wasn't about to apprise her. Farrow could explain his own sins.

"Marriage to Mr. Scott would remove me from Cliffside," she said, "but I wasn't obsessing over it. Gaylord could have given me to him or anyone, and I'd have been relieved. At this late date, I'm not choosey."

Ramsey snorted with amusement. She was keen to be rescued, and while Michael was nobody's savior, could Ramsey jump into the role of champion? Was it possible?

He wasn't sure. There was the major problem of where to take her. He was a confirmed bachelor who had no plans to wed, so if he convinced her to steal away, what was his purpose? Somehow he couldn't see her staying in his rooms over Michael's club, and Michael would never allow it, so what did he intend?

"Why have you visited me?" she asked. "Are you here to climb under the blankets? Am I about to be ravished?"

"I might climb under the blankets, but I don't know about the ravishing part. I haven't decided what I want from you."

"You won't get very far unless you have marriage in mind."

"I don't have marriage in mind."

"I didn't suppose you would."

"I like to be clear about that right up front." Actually, in light of the trollops who usually serviced him, no woman of his acquaintance would have assumed matrimony was on the table.

"We're just chatting?" she inquired.

"Maybe."

He reached for the blanket she had clutched to her bosom, and with only a minor tug of war, he pulled it away and pushed it down her legs.

She was clad in a frilly nightgown, pristine white with flowers stitched on the bodice. It was sewn from too much fabric, so it billowed around her, hiding any pertinent areas.

"Do you always sleep in a nightgown?" he asked.

"Doesn't everyone?"

"Not me."

"That sounds perfectly scandalous."

"From now on, you're to sleep in the nude."

"Why?"

"So next time I stop by, you won't be wearing anything."

"You might stop by again?"

"I might."

"Who said you'd be welcome?" she snottily taunted.

"You'll be glad when I arrive. I'd bet a hundred pounds on it."

"I might not be glad. I might be furious."

He chuckled. "Sleep without a nightgown—starting tomorrow."

"I'll be naked!"

"I certainly hope so."

He was feeling less and less sure, not convinced that he should proceed. No matter what he did, there was the specter of Michael lurking in the background, advising him to tamp down his most riotous behaviors.

He'd had no business sneaking into her bedchamber, no business riding from London merely to speak with her. He'd been prepared to deflower her, but had no plan after that.

"I have to head out," he said.

She scowled as if he was a lunatic. "You just got here."

"I probably shouldn't have come."

"You're making no sense at all."

"Let me see your breasts," he suddenly requested. "Give me a treat for my troubles."

"Absolutely not."

"I heard a few rumors about you."

"What were they?"

"You're a slattern at heart."

"Just because I flirt occasionally doesn't mean I have low morals."

"I like girls with low morals. They're my favorite kind. I just don't like innocent girls, but a girl with slatternly tendencies has a way of shedding her innocence very quickly."

The front of her nightgown was tied with a prim bow. He grabbed the dangling string and tugged to undo the knot.

"Stop that." She clasped his wrist, which was pointless. He couldn't be deterred.

"No. I want to see if you have any feminine parts that are worth looking at. I can't tell what's under all that virginal white fabric."

"I have plenty to *look* at."

"Show me."

She didn't move, and he shoved the garment down and off her shoulders. Two very pert breasts popped out. She yelped with alarm and tried to cover herself, but he pinned her arms at her sides and took a thorough assessment. He stroked a palm over them, the nipples jumping to attention as he pinched them with finger and thumb.

"Very nice," he murmured.

"I'm delighted that you approve."

"Oh, I definitely approve."

He leaned down and sucked a nipple into his mouth, and he held her close, her slender torso pressed to his chest. It seemed as if she fit against him exactly right, as if she'd been created specifically for him.

He eased her onto her back, and he came over her, nibbling a trail up her neck, her chin, to capture her lips in a torrid kiss. She leapt in immediately, providing ample evidence that she wasn't a novice. Her apparent amorous skill made him wonder just how chaste she actually was.

If they forged ahead, perhaps there'd be no deflowering. Perhaps there'd already been one.

He kissed her until he couldn't stand it anymore, until he was on the edge of serious transgressions. There were always consequences, and since he was in the habit of acting rashly, Michael frequently had to clean up Ramsey's messes. With Michael having warned him away, Ramsey might be biting off more with Rebecca than he could chew.

During every mile of the lengthy trip to Cliffside, he'd told himself that it would be fine to initiate illicit conduct, but what if it wasn't? He had to ponder the ramifications, had to be confident of his path.

He drew away, and she grinned at him, appearing happy but sly too, as if *she* had seduced him instead of the other way around.

"What is it?" he asked.

"You're not so bad."

"Neither are you."

"Tell me why you're really here."

"I just..." He paused, considering how much he should reveal. Finally he said, "You're not safe with your brother-in-law."

"I've always felt imperiled by him—ever since the day he jilted

Magdalena."

"He's gambled away Cliffside. Were you aware of that?"

She frowned. "He's lost the whole property?"

"Yes."

"We realized he was having difficulties, but I had no idea it had gone so far."

"Michael Scott owns Cliffside."

At the news, she was horrified. "It's not ours?"

"No, and when a man like Gaylord Farrow is under a lot of pressure, he might do any awful thing."

She stared at him, waiting for him to say more, but he'd cut off his tongue before he'd inform her of Farrow's pathetic attempt to sell her to Michael.

Ultimately she inquired, "Would you take me away with you?"

"I might."

"Would you take me right now?"

"I have to make some arrangements first."

"What kind of arrangements?"

"If I snatched you away, I don't have a place to put you."

"I wouldn't be any trouble. You won't even know I'm there."

He scoffed. "Little lady, I'm guessing *trouble* is your middle name."

"I swear I won't be a nuisance. And you wouldn't have to wed me. Just take me with you."

There was nothing more riveting she could have said. She was willing, without the bother or demand of marriage. What more could a dissolute fellow such as himself hope to find?

"Even on those terms," he replied, "I still have to prepare for your arrival."

She sighed. "Fine, but promise you'll come back."

"I'll come back. Pack a bag and stow it under your bed—just a small satchel we can tie on a horse."

"I'll need clothes to wear, so I'll have to have more than a single bag."

"I'll buy you clothes. I'll buy you a whole damned wardrobe, fit for a queen."

He swooped in and enjoyed another lush kiss, then he slid off the mattress and stood.

"Be ready to leave at a moment's notice," he said.

"How long will you be, a day, a month, a year? What?"

"Give me a few weeks."

"Weeks! Any tragedy could happen in a few weeks."

"Yes, but you'll be away from Cliffside before anything too terrible can occur."

"That doesn't make me feel any better."

"Be ready," he repeated, "and remember our agreement. I'll help you, but there will be no strings attached, and you'll cause me no trouble."

"I'll remember."

"Keep peeking over your shoulder," he said. "You never know when I'll be standing there."

He spun away and went over to the French window that led out onto a balcony. He leapt over the rail, caught a tree branch, and slithered to the ground, vanishing so fast and so quietly that he might never have been there at all.

CHAPTER EIGHT

"Where is your home, Mr. Scott?"

Michael stared at Felicia, figuring he shouldn't say, *I mostly stay in the rooms over my gambling club.*

"I recently came into possession of an excellent estate in Surrey."

"What's it called?"

"Cliffside."

"But...it's not really your home."

"No, but I've never had a home."

"Everyone has a *home,* even if it's a hovel in the forest."

"I never did."

"Why is that?"

Michael gaped at his fiancée, but didn't answer. He'd already slipped up in his replies. He should have simply claimed he'd grown up at Cliffside.

With her father being an earl, she was from a world where status meant everything, so he wasn't about to tell her he was an orphan and criminal celebrated for his tough demeanor and stubborn determination.

He'd stupidly assumed he could betroth himself to her with very little consequence. Her father had agreed to Michael's terms, and Michael had given scant thought to the situation beyond that. He hadn't considered *her* feelings about what had happened, hadn't considered that she might be unhappy, even angry.

She would marry Michael because her father had ordered her to, but no one—not even her exalted father—could force her to be glad.

"Shall we keep walking?" he asked. "We could follow the path down to the river. It might be cooler down there."

"I'd like to stand here and chat—if that's all right with you."

"Yes, that's fine."

They were at her father's London property. It was located just outside the city, with Lord and Lady Stone having hosted an afternoon engagement party for their daughter. There were white tents set up in the garden, tables overflowing with food and champagne. Waiters hovered, eager to grant every person's immediate wish, but he and Felicia were away from the festivities, with her dragging him off for a private talk.

The guests were a conglomeration of London's elite citizenry. The men were mostly the snooty aristocratic pricks he loathed, and most of them owed him money. They had certainly looked chagrinned to have him welcomed into their hallowed halls where he was entitled to rub elbows on an equal footing. He'd love to go up to all the wives and whisper some of their husbands' secrets.

Having very typical blond hair and blue eyes, Felicia was a fetching girl, short and plump, with rosy cheeks, fleshy arms, and plenty of bosom. She could have passed for a healthy dairy maid—that is if she'd been dressed in common clothes rather than an immaculate gown.

It was a pretty shade of blue, the color highlighted by gaudy sapphire jewelry, and he gleaned satisfaction from knowing the jewels could have been his and that she'd been able to keep them because of the deal he'd struck with her father. Did she understand that fact? How much had her father told her about what had transpired?

No doubt she blamed Michael for the debacle. The family members always blamed him.

"Why did you pick me?" she inquired.

"What do you mean?"

"My father has decreed that I shall marry you, and I've agreed, Mr. Scott. We may end up wed for decades, but we haven't spoken a dozen words to one another. So I ask again, why me?"

"Because your father offered."

"*He* offered you my hand? You didn't seek the betrothal yourself?"

"No, it was his idea."

She scowled. "I don't know if that makes me feel better or worse. I was hoping you'd humor me and pretend you'd been dying to have me, that you'd begged him to give me to you."

"I've never begged in my life, and I've never been *dying* to have anything."

That wasn't precisely true. When he was younger, he'd often been hungry and cold, and of course he'd been desperately poor. He'd frequently worried he might die—literally—if he didn't find food to eat. But those days didn't count anymore.

She studied him. "Yes, I can see you're not the sort of man to have ever begged."

"I usually take what I want."

"Did you *want* me?"

Michael shrugged. "You'll do."

She laughed miserably. "If I was a wilting violet kind of girl, that reply might send me into a weeping swoon."

"I'm glad to hear you're not weepy. I hate hysterical women."

"Well then, I'll be sure to never suffer an upset in your tender presence."

Michael chuckled. "Thank you."

"You're welcome." She scrutinized him more closely, assessing his expensive clothes, the diamond ring on his finger. "Are you wealthy?"

"Very."

"I won't live in rags and have to milk the cows before supper?"

"No."

"Praise be!" she sarcastically said. "I'm sorry to pepper you with questions, but my father won't answer any, and I believe I'm entitled to know a bit about you."

"You can ask me whatever you like." He couldn't guarantee his responses would be truthful, but she could certainly ask.

"What type of life have you envisioned for us?"

Michael frowned. "What type of life?"

"We're barely acquainted. How will we get on?"

"As most couples do, I suppose."

"Are you being deliberately obtuse or are you not much of a one for conversation?"

"I don't mind a hearty conversation, but this is more awkward than I'd imagined it would be."

"You're right about that."

"I don't mean to offend you," he said, "but I haven't spent much time contemplating what this would be like."

"This being…?"

"Our engagement. You."

She batted her lashes. "There you go again, making me feel special."

Michael smiled. She was being a good sport, and he was being an ass, but he simply couldn't exhibit better behavior.

All his life, he'd detested the aristocracy, seeming to have an almost inbred abhorrence for them. He'd assumed it would be amusing to force his way into their inner circle, to breach the gates and steal one of their precious daughters. Yet now that he was on the inside, now that the future was barreling down on him like a runaway carriage, he was sensing a huge mistake in progress.

He didn't care about the Jamaican plantation or the ships he'd receive. He'd enjoyed Lord Stone's squirming, had enjoyed having the lofty man under his thumb. But evidently Michael was aggravated by his betrothal, and it was an awful time to figure it out. He wasn't actually opposed to marrying and wasn't overly opposed to marrying *her*. So what was wrong?

A memory of Maggie Wells flashed into his head, and the problem with Felicia became very clear.

When he was around Maggie, there was a physical connection between them that was so strong, the air sizzled with energy. With Felicia, he didn't feel a thing. Not lust. Not passion. Not piqued interest. Not even mild curiosity.

He was simply wondering how tedious the approaching years would be. Since he hated her father, hated all her acquaintances, and thrived on ruining people like Lord Stone, how would they ever get along?

His secret wish—too unmanly to mention aloud—was that he yearned for a home and family, but he craved a *genuine* family, a wife who loved him, who would be his partner through thick and thin.

Felicia would provide polite company and courteous exchanges, and the underlying impression would always be that she couldn't abide him, that he'd won her under false pretenses. Could he carry on like that? Would it be worth it?

"What is Cliffside like?" she inquired.

"Very grand, but if it doesn't please you, I'll buy you another property."

"Whatever I want?"

"Yes."

"You really are rich."

"Yes, I really am."

"Good. From how my father talks about you, I thought maybe you gambled to earn your living."

"I gamble occasionally, but I make money other ways too."

"What ways?"

I smuggle, embezzle, steal, threaten, blackmail, and rob.

"I'm a businessman."

"A successful businessman?"

"Enormously successful, and I oughtn't to brag, but in light of your father's penury, you're lucky you latched on to me."

"Why, I'm the luckiest girl in the world these days."

"I wish I could say I'm the man of your dreams."

"You're not." She gasped. "Mr. Scott, I most humbly apologize. Forgive me. I'm not myself this afternoon, and I'm ashamed to have voiced such a rude remark."

"It's all right. I realize you expected to land a fellow who was much more refined."

"Yes, I was raised around the sons of the peerage, and I assumed I would wed one of them."

"Let me be indiscreet and confide that I likely know every swain you've ever considered as a spouse. You're not missing much by having to abandon them."

"Are you claiming I'm taking a step up with you?"

"I would never claim it's a step *up,* but I can swear to you that I won't ever gamble away your jewels or your children."

"I'm so relieved to hear it."

"I work hard and make good decisions, so you won't ever have to worry that I might foolishly destroy your life without you learning of my folly until it's too late."

"That's a plus."

He'd womanize extensively though, but he didn't suppose it was a sin he should confess. It was information he'd keep between himself and his favorite doxies.

"And I'll be kind and respectful," he added. "I'll never beat you."

"You'll never *beat* me? I never for a single instant deemed that a trait over which I should fret when I was selecting a husband."

"You should have."

"Why?"

"You'd be surprised by the trouble a female can find for herself through matrimony."

"You won't beat me!"

She put her hands over her eyes, and for a moment he thought she was crying. Quickly, he discovered she was chortling, but with dismay.

"I'm sorry, Mr. Scott," she said, "but I have to return to the party now."

"Fine."

He moved to take her arm to escort her, but she pulled away.

"I can get there on my own. You won't be horridly offended, will you?"

"Nothing horridly offends me," he told her, but it was a lie.

Most things horridly provoked him. He had large appetites and was never tepidly emotional about any topic. He was extremely happy or extremely angry or extremely vexed. Where his mental state was concerned, there were no calm sentiments.

"Would you stop by again someday," she asked, "so we can talk further?"

"Of course."

"Could we visit Cliffside? I'd like to see where we'll be living."

"Certainly. The prior tenants are still there, but they'll be leaving soon."

"And if I don't like it…?"

"I'll buy you something else. I promised, and I meant it."

She gaped at him as if he was a heathen—which he was—but he wouldn't judge her too harshly. She was only eighteen, and her father had dumped his problems on her plump shoulders. She was right to be afraid. She was right to worry.

She spun and left, and he trailed after her, watching to ensure she reached her guests with no difficulty. Briefly, he tensed as a man stepped out of the hedges to speak with her, but she appeared to know him. They exchanged a few whispered words, then she kept on, and the man vanished into the shrubbery.

From Michael's fleeting glimpse, the man looked like an old enemy, Blaylock, who worked as a guard for various rich nobs when they were out carousing.

One night on Michael's street, Blaylock had caught one of Michael's young pickpockets in the act, and Blaylock had beaten the boy nearly to death in punishment. Michael had returned the favor, giving Blaylock a thrashing he'd never forget and warning him that Michael would kill him if they ever crossed paths again.

Would Blaylock dare show his face at Michael's betrothal party?

He considered chasing after the furtive fellow, but if it was Blaylock, and Michael cornered him, there would be a huge scene, and he was loath to pick a fight in front of Lady Stone and her snooty friends. Yet if Blaylock was lurking, it couldn't be with decent intentions. Was he scheming with Felicia? Could she be aware of Blaylock's enmity toward Michael? Was she aware that Michael reciprocated that dislike? Should he tell her to be careful?

He couldn't decide what was best. If it hadn't been Blaylock, he'd sound like a paranoid idiot. Perhaps it had been a beau, and if Michael questioned her about the encounter, his relationship with her would grow even more strained.

He wandered over to the party tent, desperate to have more whiskey. He was feeling low and wishing he hadn't set the current madness in motion. Ramsey was the one to engage in reckless, pointless behavior. Not Michael. But Michael was very vain, and with Lord Stone giving him a daughter, Michael couldn't imagine giving her back.

He stood alone in the shade, listening to the people around him and being generally ignored.

A group of women was blathering on, and one of them said, "Lady Run, that is the most romantic story."

"I wouldn't call it romantic, but it's intriguing, isn't it?"

Michael peeked at the woman who'd been addressed as Lady Run. She was beautifully exotic, with gorgeous blond hair and big blue eyes, and he thought she might be the most striking female he'd ever seen. The other aristocratic ladies paled in comparison.

"A lost family," someone gushed, "and lost brothers."

Another said, "If I'd lost my siblings at such a tender age, I wouldn't search for them. I'd be afraid of who I'd find. They might have become brigands or criminals."

Everyone laughed, and Lady Run said, "I'm not concerned about the sort of men I'll find. My brother, Bryce, is wonderful, and I'm positive they'll be much the same."

"Have you had any response to your advertisements in the newspapers?"

"No," Lady Run said. "We've received a few replies, but none that were serious enough to be investigated."

Michael froze in his tracks. Was Lady Run the person who'd purchased the advertisement about Michael Blair? Could it be?

She glanced up and noticed Michael where he skulked in the shadows. Her vibrant blue eyes drilled into him, and under her shrewd assessment he suffered the strangest reaction. His ears were ringing, his heart racing, his head pounding. He was dizzy, as if he might fall to the ground, and it occurred to him that he should get out of the sun and cut back on the liquor.

She smiled, and his disorientation increased. He had an abrupt memory of his mother—who'd been blond and spectacularly beautiful just like Lady Run.

When Michael had been little, he'd dreamed of his mother occasionally, but the visions had gradually faded. Ultimately he believed he didn't remember what she'd looked like. But…she'd looked exactly like Lady Run.

Yes, he recollected now.

Lady Run abandoned her companions and came over to him. With a complete disregard for fussy protocol, she asked, "Aren't you the blushing groom?"

Her vibrant character washed over him, yanking him out of the peculiar cloud in which he'd been temporarily enveloped.

"I'm the groom," he said, "but I don't usually blush."

"We haven't been introduced."

"I apologize for the slight."

"You don't mind if I introduce myself then, do you? I have to leave shortly, and I would hate not to have met you. You won't faint from shock?"

Michael chuckled. "I'll try not to."

"I'm Evangeline Drake. My husband is Aaron Drake, Lord Run. Are you acquainted?"

"No, but I know his brother quite well."

Aaron Drake was one of the few men in the kingdom who didn't gamble. His brother Lucas though, was a different case entirely and in debt up to his eyeballs. Michael hadn't seen Lucas Drake recently and rumor had it that he'd married. Maybe his wife had calmed his more horrid tendencies.

"You own a gambling club, don't you?" She talked as if it was perfectly normal for them to discuss his disreputable business.

"Ah…yes," he admitted, not sure if he should.

"I'm not surprised that you're acquainted with Lucas. He's a renowned scalawag."

"He definitely is," Michael agreed.

"I hope you won't deem me indiscreet, but I'm told you and Lady Felicia will be living at Cliffside in Surrey."

"Yes."

"I'm confused by this situation. I went to school with a girl named Magdalena Wells, and her family owned Cliffside."

"It's the same family," he cautiously stated. "They've had a bit of trouble over the years."

"How dreadful. Have you any news of Magdalena? We were great friends, and after we finished school, we corresponded for awhile. Then her letters stopped. Last I heard from her, she was engaged to be married."

"She didn't marry."

"Oh, that's too bad."

"Actually, she's here in London. She operates a charity rescue mission near my club."

"Magdalena does that? I can't picture it. How did it come about?"

"I don't know." He wasn't inclined to share Magdalena's secrets. If she chose to confide in Lady Run, it was her story to tell.

"I would love to see Magdalena. Would you take me to visit her someday, Mr. Scott?"

"Well…ah…certainly. It's not a very nice part of the city."

"I'm sure I can bear up. If I give you my card, you could pick me up and escort me. I'd be safe with you, wouldn't I?"

"If you weren't, your husband and his brother would murder me."

Her smile widened. "I imagine they would."

He wanted to decline, but there was a seductive air about her that drew Michael in, that made him eager to linger in her presence and beg for favors. No doubt her home was located on the finest block in Mayfair, and he'd be embarrassed to show her his crowded, squalid street.

But apparently he couldn't refuse her, and Aaron Drake had Michael's sympathies. How could a man ever say *no* to such a woman?

He stared into her blue eyes and his pulse rate soared again. The ringing in his ears was back.

"Have we met before?" she suddenly asked.

"No."

"Are you positive? You look so familiar to me."

"You're quite amazing, Lady Run. I'd definitely remember."

"You're a flirt, Mr. Scott." She grinned. "I've heard many things about you, but not that you're a flirt. Or that you're so charming."

"I'm charming?" He was grinning now too. "I'll have to tell my fiancée you think so. She hasn't yet realized how wonderful I am."

Aaron Drake took that moment to walk up to his wife.

"We have to go," he told her.

Lady Run beamed at her husband in a manner that—had they been in a darkened room—would have lit up the whole space.

"Aaron," she said, "have you been introduced to the groom?"

"No, but Mr. Scott and I have many mutual acquaintances."

He and Aaron Drake made all the appropriate remarks, then Lady Run said to her husband, "Does Mr. Scott seem familiar to you? He insists we haven't met, but I'm certain we have. I'm trying to place him."

"He looks just like your brother Bryce," Lord Run replied, "if Bryce had black hair instead of blond."

Lady Run studied Michael and mused, "My goodness, yes. Mr. Scott, do you know my brother, Bryce Blair?"

"Yes, I know Mr. Blair." Blair was a regular customer, but he never had enough money to land himself in too much trouble.

"The two of you could be twins," she claimed.

On her voicing the word *twins,* he was so overcome he worried he might faint—in the middle of the garden, with every snobbish prick in London watching.

"Is Blair your maiden name?" he managed to force out.

"Sort of. I grew up thinking I was Evangeline Etherton, but I've since learned my name was Annie Blair when I was little. My siblings and I were split apart for some reason. Bryce and I found each other again not too long ago."

She might have prattled on, but she must have noted his disorientation, because she stopped and laid a hand on his wrist.

"Are you all right?" she asked. "You're a bit green around the gills."

"I've had too much sun today," he muttered.

Lord Run added, "And you're newly engaged. That would leave any man weak in the knees."

"Absolutely," Michael mumbled.

He said goodbye and staggered away. At least he *hoped* he'd said goodbye. In such exalted company, he hated to behave like an idiot.

Somehow he left the garden and the party without informing anyone he was departing. When he was able to focus and muster another coherent thought, he was in the city, at his club, in his office. But he had no idea how he'd gotten there.

"Pamela, this is a surprise."

"Hello, Magdalena."

Maggie gaped as if Pamela was an apparition. In the seven years Maggie had been in London, none of her family had ever visited. What could have brought Pamela to the city? It couldn't be happy news.

"Is there a problem at home?" Maggie inquired.

"No."

They were in the main room at the mission. There were several long tables, with benches for the seats. The space was plain and functional and clean, yet Pamela scowled as if she'd descended to the pits of Hell.

Her discomfort was understandable. Maggie's reaction had been much the same when Vicar Sterns had initially shown her the neighborhood. Back then, Maggie had been the cosseted daughter of a rich gentleman. Her prior life experience had consisted solely of her attending Miss Peabody's School for Girls, a posh academy with high tuition.

Maggie had never seen how most people lived, how desperately poor most people were. Her first months at the mission had been shocking and disturbing.

Now though, nothing shocked Maggie. She was used to getting by and making do. But Pamela was dressed in an expensive gown, her hair intricately styled, and appearing so grand she might have attired herself for a royal ball rather than a decrepit charity mission in the slums. What was she thinking with such an ostentatious display? In light of the miscreants out on the street, she was lucky she hadn't been robbed when she stepped out of her carriage.

"Is there somewhere we could talk privately?" Pamela asked.

"We can talk here." Maggie gestured to a table in the corner. "We won't be interrupted."

It was mid-afternoon, with Maggie's cook not having arrived to start supper. The building was quiet as a tomb.

Pamela hesitated, but Maggie walked over and sat on a bench. She stared at Pamela, daring her to sit too, and Pamela sidled over and pulled out the bench across. She hovered, then opened her reticule, retrieved a kerchief, and wiped off the seat. Finally she eased down, but she was ready to bolt, as if the slightest noise would send her scurrying for the door.

"What's wrong?" Maggie said. "And don't tell me everything is fine. If you've come all this way, it must be a horrid calamity."

"Why must you always assume the worst?"

"Because when I'm around you the *worst* is usually what happens."

Pamela sighed. "You are the most infuriating person. I don't know why I maintain a relationship with you."

"Neither do I."

Maggie stared again, waiting for Pamela to explain the reason for her trip to town. There had to be a catastrophe, no doubt caused by Gaylord, but Pamela wouldn't spit it out. She'd stolen Gaylord from Maggie, and she was determined not to ever let anyone suspect she'd made a huge mistake.

The silence might have gone on forever, but Maggie grew impatient and prodded, "Well…?"

"I need to discuss a certain…situation with you."

"What is it?" Still, Pamela dithered, and Maggie snapped, "Is it Gaylord? What's he done now?"

At Maggie's sharp tone, Pamela glanced away, giving every indication that the news was very bad indeed.

"We've lost Cliffside," Pamela murmured.

"You've *lost* it? How could you have? When I visited last week, it seemed to be in the same old spot. Should I come to the country and locate it for you?"

"Don't jest, Magdalena. Not about this."

"All right. I won't jest. What are you telling me?"

"Gaylord has gambled it all away."

"Gaylord has."

"Yes."

Maggie had known Gaylord's gambling debts were increasing. How could she not have known? Much of the upstairs furniture was gone!

"The whole estate has been wagered away?" Maggie asked.

"Yes."

"The house? The barns? The equipment? The animals? What does *all* include?"

"It includes…everything we ever owned. He didn't mean to," Pamela hastily said. "It's just that he's in over his head, and he—"

"Don't defend him to me!"

"He tried to win it back, but he's had such awful luck."

"The poor boy," Maggie sarcastically retorted.

Ever since the day she'd first laid eyes on Gaylord, she'd been regretting the disaster she'd initiated by bringing him into their midst. Would the carnage never end?

"Let me get this straight," Maggie fumed. "He convinced Father to name him the heir, he inherited what should have been ours—"

"We're females, Magdalena. Father wouldn't have permitted any of us to inherit. I was married. It was perfectly appropriate to leave my husband in charge."

Maggie had never shared that view, but she wasn't about to rehash that old fight. "Gaylord was fortunate enough to become the sole owner of Cliffside, and he's frittered it away with his negligent habits."

"I guess you could put it that way."

"Is the damage final? Is there a new owner or what?"

"Yes, there's a new owner."

"Who is it?"

"Michael Scott. You met him at Rebecca's birthday party."

Maggie almost fell off the bench. Michael owned her home? Michael had gambled with Gaylord until he'd won all that had belonged to Maggie's family?

At Cliffside, she'd assumed he was one of Gaylord's dissolute friends. She hadn't realized he was there to take possession of his property. He'd never said a word! He'd never so much as hinted!

An ember of fury ignited in her chest, and it grew and grew until she worried she might simply burst into flames.

"How long have you known about this?" she seethed.

"It's been brewing for awhile."

"When Mr. Scott was at Cliffside, was the transfer of ownership already complete?"

"Yes. He was there to conduct an inventory."

"What now? Are you about to ask if you and Gaylord can move in with me? If you are, I must inform you that the neighborhood isn't up to your high standards."

Maggie's snide tone rankled Pamela and yanked her out of her embarrassed stupor. "I don't need lodging."

"Then why are you here?"

"Gaylord has reached an accommodation with Mr. Scott, and I have to tell you about it."

"Gaylord and Mr. Scott can jump off a cliff."

Pamela glared as if Maggie was five years old and deserved a swat on the bottom. "I told Gaylord it was pointless to speak with you."

"For once you were correct, and while we're on the subject of financial catastrophes, I never had a chance to ask your husband what happened to my allowance."

Pamela slapped a palm on the table, the irate smack echoing off the ceiling. "It's gone, Magdalena. Everything is gone! How many more times must I say it?"

"No more times," Maggie quietly mumbled.

They frowned, their tempers flaring, their misery acute, and ultimately Pamela said, "Mr. Scott has given us some latitude as to when we vacate, but with conditions attached."

"What conditions?"

"It appears he's very taken with you."

"Why would you presume so? He and I are barely acquainted."

"You can help us with him."

"Help you *how*?"

"He's agreed to let you…that is…ah…"

Pamela's voice drifted off. Whatever dubious *help* she envisioned Maggie supplying, it was obviously beyond her ability to explain.

"What has he agreed to let me do?" Maggie pressed.

"If you'll be his…mistress—"

"His mistress!"

Maggie shouted the word and leapt to her feet.

Pamela ignored Maggie's outburst and calmly continued. "Yes, his mistress. For six months."

"Six months? Are you mad?"

"It's the only way, Maggie."

"The only way to what?"

"To buy ourselves some extra time."

"Buy yourselves *time* for what?"

"We haven't made any arrangements, Magdalena."

"Whose fault is that?"

"I thought Gaylord would turn matters around. He's always so confident, and he insisted he could fix what was wrong."

"You believed him?"

"He's my husband. Why wouldn't I have?"

"Oh, Pamela…" Maggie sighed with disgust and sat back down.

It was the closest Pamela had ever come to criticizing Gaylord, and Maggie took it as a sign of just how dire the circumstances.

"I can't do what you're asking," she said.

"You could mend things for us with Mr. Scott."

"How could I? You'd merely have some extra time to leave. At the end of six months, I'd be ruined and disgraced, and you'd still have to depart."

"Gaylord thinks if you could distract Mr. Scott for us we could figure out a different conclusion."

"Gaylord thinks that, does he?"

"Yes, and Gaylord's so clever, Magdalena." Maggie scoffed, and Pamela stated, "He is clever! He had a run of bad luck, and Mr. Scott has been an absolute beast. We can delay the eviction. Gaylord is sure of it."

Maggie thought of greedy, corrupt, foolish Gaylord. Then she thought of the notoriously wealthy criminal and brigand, Michael Scott. Had he tricked Gaylord to win Cliffside? Had he cheated? Or had he won fair and square? However the disaster had unfolded, Gaylord would never succeed in any scheme against Michael Scott.

"Gaylord is an idiot, and you're both insane."

"You won't help us?"

"No."

"If you won't, we have to leave on Saturday!"

"This Saturday?"

"Yes. Is that what we've come to, Magdalena? Forget about Gaylord for a moment. Have you grown so hard-hearted and vindictive that you'd allow me and Rebecca to be tossed out on the road?"

"Don't make this my fault."

"If you won't aid us in our darkest hour, who should we blame?"

It was the cruelest comment Pamela could have uttered, and Maggie studied her sister's malicious expression and wondered why she still possessed any affection for her. Pamela was a dimwitted ninny, and Gaylord manipulated and controlled her. When dealing with Pamela, Maggie often felt as if she was dealing with a child. And Rebecca was no better.

Could Maggie stand idly by and let Michael Scott harm her sisters? Cliffside was Maggie's *home*, the Wells family seat for two centuries, and she had the ability to save it. She need only agree to Mr. Scott's absurd demand, and how awful could it be? She was attracted to him and didn't suppose a physical liaison would be horrid.

Yet as swiftly as the notion arose, she shoved it away. She wouldn't be bullied by Gaylord *or* Michael Scott. She wouldn't let Pamela make her feel guilty. She and her sisters hadn't participated in the wagering between the two men, but wasn't it typical that all of the consequences would fall on them?

Maggie stood and glowered at her sister, her condemnation shining through.

"Go home, Pamela."

Pamela stood too. "What shall I tell Gaylord?"

"Tell him I'll visit Mr. Scott's gambling club to give him a piece of my mind."

"Then what?"

"I'm certain it will have no effect whatsoever, so you should pack your bags."

"I'm begging you, Magdalena." Tears flooded into Pamela's eyes, and she looked sincerely woeful. "Why can't you just do this one little thing?"

"Because I don't want to and—despite what scheme Gaylord and Mr. Scott have concocted—I don't trust either of them."

"You could save me and Rebecca, but you won't."

"I can't save you, Pamela, but I will speak to Mr. Scott. That's all I can do."

"Fine. Be that way." Pamela was so angry she was shaking. "Have your final revenge for my taking Gaylord from you."

"I don't care about revenge. You can have him with my blessing."

"But when you learn that Rebecca and I are living in a ditch, when you learn that Cliffside is no longer ours, I hope you'll be pleased with what you've wrought."

Pamela spun and stormed out.

Maggie yearned to chase after her, to scold and defend herself, but she didn't. She sank down on the bench and murmured, "Nice to see you too, Pamela. Stop by any time."

CHAPTER NINE

"You have a visitor."

"Are you deaf? I told you I didn't want to be disturbed."

Michael was seated at the desk in his office, and he bellowed his remarks to the closed door. But it was Ramsey who'd knocked, and Ramsey had a habit of not listening to orders he didn't like.

Ramsey flung the door open, and Michael was greatly flummoxed when he stepped over the threshold and dragged Maggie Wells with him.

"I tried to make her go away," Ramsey claimed, "but she refused."

"You're a foot taller," Michael snapped, "and probably a hundred pounds heavier. If you couldn't get rid of her, what good are you to me?"

"She's riled about something," Ramsey explained, "but wouldn't tell me what it is. I figured you should talk to her."

Michael's gaze was locked on Ramsey, and he still hadn't glanced at Maggie. He waved Ramsey out, and his friend huffed away, leaving Michael alone with her in the small room.

He finally shifted his focus to her, and she appeared young and defenseless, and Michael wondered what had spurred Ramsey to escort her upstairs.

"Miss Wells," he said, "this is an irksome surprise. What brings you by again?"

"I have to ask you a question."

"If you must."

"I must."

"Will you sit?" He gestured to a chair in the corner. "Last time you were here, you declined, but from your dour expression, I'm predicting this might be a longer appointment."

"Yes, I'll sit, thank you."

If he'd felt like exhibiting his manners, he'd have leapt up and grabbed the chair for her, but he was in the foulest mood ever and couldn't bestir himself.

He was reeling from his engagement party, disoriented from his conversation with Lady Run. Who the hell was she to Michael? It sounded as if she was the one who'd purchased the advertisements about Michael Blair. Should he have spoken up?

To what end?

If there was a family out there hunting for Michael Blair, why would *he* be the person they were hoping to locate? What if he put himself forward, only to learn he wasn't the one? He'd look like a fool.

But what if he was her kin? What benefit was there in being found? What detriment? If he was related to her and her brother Bryce Blair, how had he been lost? What sort of despicable people let such a tragedy happen to a little boy? Why would he choose to be reunited with them?

His life was fine. Fine! He liked his rough and tumble existence, liked the world of men where he thrived and flourished. He had no desire to be hauled into a weepy morass with some rich, aristocratic lady, and at the moment he hadn't the energy to deal with Magdalena Wells.

"You're mad as a hornet," he said. "What have I done now?"

"You can't guess why I'm here?"

"No. What's wrong? Have I recruited another of your street urchins and trained him as a pickpocket? Are my customers making too much noise at night when they depart in their fancy carriages? Are they disturbing your sleep? What?"

"Tell me about your relationship with my brother-in-law."

"With Gaylord Farrow?"

"Yes."

"What is it you wish to know?"

"Don't pretend to be ignorant of the situation."

"What situation is that?"

"Stop it, Mr. Scott," she fumed.

"We're back to *Mr. Scott*, are we? I could have sworn you were supposed to call me Michael when we're alone."

"Don't change the subject."

"What's the subject? Gaylord Farrow?"

"Yes. Tell me about him this very minute."

Michael sighed. Didn't family members always blame him? Didn't they always assume *he* was the one who led every wretch to ruin? Usually he didn't care what they thought, but her snotty attitude incensed him.

"I take it he finally spoke to you," Michael said.

"My sister did."

"Then Gaylord was too much of a coward to handle it himself. He sent his wife to do his dirty work." Michael snorted with disgust. "Typical of him."

"Pamela claims you own our home. She says you own everything, right down to the silver in the drawers."

He nodded. "I do."

"Give it back."

"To Farrow?"

"Yes. Give it all back."

"No."

"How did you win it from him? Did you cheat? I'm aware of your low reputation in the neighborhood. Did you trick him? What?"

Her accusations lit a fuse to his temper. "I'm sure this will come as a great surprise, but your brother-in-law isn't an angel."

"I realize that fact. Considering my history with him, I don't need any lectures from you about what he's genuinely like. Just tell me what you did."

"What *I* did," he furiously retorted.

"Yes. He's a negligent ass, but he wouldn't jeopardize us this way. He was too proud of his ownership of Cliffside and the status it bestowed. He would never willingly part with it."

"You're correct. He didn't willingly relinquish it. I took it from him, and despite how he wheedles and begs, or how he has you traipse over here and bat your pretty lashes at me, I won't sign it over to him."

"You're as vain as he is," she charged.

"I dare say I'm worse."

"Is that a joke? Am I to laugh? Is this a game to you? Is that how you view it?"

"Yes, it's a high-stakes game. Gaylord played it and he lost."

"Give me my home back!"

"No." He leaned forward, his elbows on the desk. "Listen to me, Magdalena."

"Why should I?"

"Because you're making me angry."

"Good, but I must confess that—whatever state you're in—you can't be half as irate as I am."

"You storm in and start throwing around accusations—"

"That are all fully deserved."

"Are they?" He studied her, his exasperation extreme. "You blame me."

"Absolutely. I blame you *and* Gaylord."

"It's *my* fault that he's an irresponsible wastrel?"

"No. It's your fault that you took advantage of him. I'm positive you caught him at a weak moment, and you goaded him into conduct he wouldn't have contemplated on his own."

"Is that right?" he snidely asked.

"Yes. I'm certain that's exactly how it happened."

"For your information, Miss Wells, your brother-in-law has been involved with me for over a year now."

"Are you telling me you've had an entire year to trick and deceive him? Because if that's your defense, you can stuff it."

"It's not my defense. It's simply the facts as they currently exist. He gambled and constantly lost. So he came more often and tried to reverse his fortunes, but he never could."

"Once he got into financial trouble, why didn't you bar him from the premises?"

"Am I his nanny? Am I to tag after him and order him to behave? How precisely would I have done that?"

"I don't care how you rationalize it. You could have stopped him if you'd wanted to."

"There's the problem for you, Magdalena. I didn't want to stop him. I wanted him to keep on and on, because he's a rich, pompous prick, and when I was crushing him I felt like a god!"

He pounded a fist on the desk for emphasis, and they glared, their animosity frightening in its intensity. They were breathing hard, as if they were pugilists in the ring who'd just gone ten rounds.

Ultimately she complained, "You never mentioned any of it to me."

"Why would I have? It was between him and me and none of your affair."

"When you were at Cliffside, I thought you were a guest."

"I wasn't. I was the new owner, and you were all staying there—hosting your idiotic birthday party—with my permission."

"I trusted you. I...*liked* you."

"So? How is that relevant?"

He was being deliberately cruel, but he'd been inordinately stung by her harsh tone. She was being unusually strident in a way he loathed and wouldn't tolerate.

People weren't allowed to chastise or berate him. He was king of his world, and no person could enter it and challenge his authority. If they tried, there were consequences.

"You're being a bully," she nagged.

"I am. I admit it."

"You're enjoying this."

"Yes."

"You're doing it because you can, because you can get away with it and no one can stop you."

He scowled. "Why am I the villain here? Could we pause for two seconds so you can ponder the answer to that question?"

"You're the villain because you committed treachery. You can deny it all you like, but I'll never believe you."

He was stung again, livid that she'd discount his word, his version of events. She knew Farrow was a snake in the grass, yet she was defending him anyway. Her misplaced loyalty to Farrow enraged Michael as nothing had in ages.

She thought he was an ogre? She thought he was a bully? Fine. She could feel the entire brunt of his vanity.

"Whether you believe me or not, the deal is finished. Cliffside is mine"—his torrid gaze slid down her torso—"and so are you."

"You're mad," she spat, "and I won't abide by the terms of your wager."

"I'm not the one who bartered you away. You're blaming the wrong person."

"I've already told you I blame you both."

"Yes, but if you want to toss around charges of lunacy, I suggest you apply them to your own family. Not to me."

"You can't haggle over me as if I'm an African slave."

He shrugged. "Take it up with your brother-in-law. I hardly see how it's my problem."

"Are you claiming it was all his idea?"

"Yes, that's precisely what I'm claiming."

"*He* came to you. *He* proposed the sordid bargain. You were innocent as a lamb?"

"In this matter? Completely innocent." He shook an angry finger at her. "And before you start riding your high horse, you should know that he initially offered your hand in marriage."

"He wouldn't have dared," she huffed.

Michael ignored her indignant retort. "But I have no interest in marrying, and I particularly have no interest in marrying *you*."

"You were happy enough to ask that I be your mistress."

"I didn't ask!" he snapped. "Get it through your thick head! It was Farrow's plan—every stupid bit of it. He offered marriage, and I declined, so he offered you in a different way."

"I won't be your mistress. Not for an hour. Not for a day. Not for a week. I won't do it!"

"I told him you wouldn't, but he insisted on pursuing it."

Suddenly the fight went out of her. She sagged in her chair and tears flooded her eyes. He steeled himself against her woe. Over the years, he'd had plenty of women sit where she was sitting, plenty of women beg as she was begging.

By the time he reached this despicable point, he was out of patience.

"If you're about to weep," he said, "I should probably apprise you that it won't have any effect on me."

"I can cry if I want to."

"Save it. You can't move me. You can't dissuade me."

"I'm so sick of men!" she seethed.

"As I am all male, I haven't a clue how to reply."

"You all think you run the world."

"We do."

"You presume you can engage in any folly, that you can wreck and destroy without consequence. We women have to hover in the corner and let you commit any reckless deed that tickles your fancy."

"I remind you again, Magdalena. *I* committed no reckless acts. I'm in business, and I made a huge profit off another man's loss. I'm simply collecting what I am owed."

"You don't have to follow through."

"You're correct. I don't have to."

"You *want* to."

"Yes."

"Why? Tell me the truth."

"Because Gaylord Farrow is an arrogant ass, and I loathe him."

"So it's personal."

"Of course it's personal. What do you bloody think it is?"

"Don't curse at me."

"We're in my office, in my business establishment. If you don't like my language, you can leave."

"How can I persuade you to mercy?"

"You can't."

"Is there nothing I can say?"

"No."

To his astonishment, she pushed herself to her feet and rounded the desk. She dropped to her knees and clasped his hand, her beautiful blue eyes beseeching.

"Have mercy on my family, Michael. Please?"

"It's too late for begging, Maggie."

"If you won't give the property back to Gaylord, give it to Pamela. Or give it to me. Please!"

"No." He would have added the word *sorry*, but he wasn't. He tried to pull his hand away, but she simply clasped it tighter.

"Why are you doing this to me?"

"I'm not doing it to you. Your brother-in-law is responsible for the whole mess, and you should consider the possible ramifications."

"What do you mean?"

"He was very determined. If you won't dally with me, who might he seek out instead? At least you've met me, and we have a passing acquaintance. What if he approaches a stranger? Are you prepared for that?"

"He wouldn't," she ridiculously claimed.

He bent down so they were nose to nose. "He already has. Aren't you curious how we arrived at this point? And have you thought at all about your younger sister?"

"Rebecca? What about her?"

"Farrow offered her first, but I wasn't interested, so he offered you in her place."

"He offered to let you have Rebecca as your mistress?"

"Yes, so I ask you again. If you don't relent and play your part as has been arranged, what foul deed might Farrow perpetrate next?"

"Give them more time," she pleaded.

"To what?"

"To make plans. To move out."

"Maggie, they've had six months."

"You've owned Cliffside for six months?"

"Yes. Now get up. I can't abide all this drama."

He stood and drew her to her feet. They glared again, hostility flaring.

"Explain the details of your bargain with Gaylord," she said. "What would I be expected to do?"

"You'll be my mistress for a trial period of thirty days."

"A trial period?"

"Yes, so I can see if you're worth the bother."

"If I'm not?"

"Then your family will leave Cliffside at once."

"And if I *am* what you're hoping? You'll keep me for six months, and in exchange, they'll have six more months to vacate. Is that correct?"

"Yes, but you could never be what I'm hoping for."

He'd pricked her vanity, and she said, "I might surprise you."

"I doubt it. No woman ever has."

"What if I tell you to stuff it and walk out of here?"

"I'll evict your sisters immediately. I'll send a messenger on a fast horse, and I have men on the premises to ensure their departure."

"You'd put their belongings out on the road?"

"They don't have any belongings," he grimly stated, "so they won't have much to carry."

"Why are you being so cruel?"

"I'm simply letting you witness my true nature."

"No, you're not. You can be kind. You can be generous and funny and wonderful. I've seen you act that way."

"That's all it is, an *act*."

"No, it isn't." She stepped in, the hem of her skirt swishing over the toes of his boots. She studied him, her blue eyes probing, digging deep. "You're upset about something. Not about this but something else, and you're taking it out on me."

"I'm not upset. You're being absurd."

"No, you're extremely troubled. What's wrong? What happened?"

"Nothing's wrong," he insisted, "and you're annoying me. Would you go?"

She rested a palm on his cheek, and the gesture was very dear, as if she was his wife, as if she'd touched him gently a thousand times prior.

"You can tell me what it is," she murmured.

"There's naught to tell."

He grabbed her wrist and yanked her away, and he hardened his features, irked to have her observe his distress.

Sensing his paltry attempt at indifference, she smirked and announced, "I'm calling your bluff."

"What are you talking about, woman?"

"You're being a bully and deliberately trying to drive me away."

"Why would I bother? You'll stomp out in a huff before too much more time has passed."

"Why is that, exactly? Might it be because—if I stomp out—you get Cliffside with no delay?"

"It might."

She was taking his measure, assessing his attributes and finding few that were redeeming.

"Fine, Michael Scott," she said. "I agree."

"You agree to what?"

"I shall be your mistress for thirty days, and if I please you, I'll stay for six months."

"You will not."

"I will—for you see, Mr. Scott, I evidently know a fact about you that you don't."

"What is it?"

"You bluster and offend and insult, and while it might terrorize others, *I* am not afraid of you."

"You're not?"

"No. You may fume and rage all you like, but you'd never hurt me."

"If that's what you believe, then you're a fool."

"We begin our affair on Saturday. Isn't that right?"

"I won't proceed with you," he firmly asserted.

"A deal's a deal, Michael."

"It's not what you said five minutes ago."

"Well, I changed my mind, and I demand you honor it."

"*You* demand."

"Yes."

She was grinning, preening, as if she'd just bested him in every manner that counted. Didn't the idiotic female fathom what would transpire?

"You understand your role, don't you? I'll take you to my house in the country and have my way with you—over and over again."

"As I'm a spinster and a maiden, I have no idea what that means, but I'm sure you'll show me."

"You won't like it."

"I'll grit my teeth and endure it."

"That makes me eager to start up with you."

"You wagered over my chastity, and you'll receive it, but no bet—no matter how large—can force me to like you."

"I don't want you to *like* me. My plan doesn't involve *liking* at all."

"Yes, you've been very clear. When do we leave? Saturday morning?"

He grimaced with distaste, deciding she actually knew him quite well. He hadn't sought the stupid bargain with Farrow and had only consented because he'd been confident she'd refuse and he'd be able to evict Farrow at once.

Now though, she was practically throwing herself at him. What was he supposed to do? Catch her? Then what?

"Saturday morning." She smiled sweetly. "I'll be ready at ten. Will you come to fetch me, or would you like me to meet you here?"

A muscle ticked in his cheek. He'd like to shake her. He'd like to bend her over his knee and take a switch to her shapely backside. He'd like to get her alone at his country house and perpetrate every wicked, immoral deed ever devised by man.

"You're playing with fire, Magdalena."

"I don't think so," she countered. "I think—deep down—you're a big, fat pussycat. In a quick week, I'll have you wrapped around my little finger."

"In your dreams."

"In my very vivid, very optimistic dreams, where you end up giving me everything I want."

"And what would that be?"

"I'll let you know—when I feel like telling you."

She spun and sashayed out, and at the last second, she tossed over her shoulder, "Saturday at ten?"

He should have told her to sod off, should have told her she was insane and he wouldn't be bossed by a female. But he opened his mouth and the words that emerged were, "I'll pick you up at the mission."

"Perfect."

"Can you ride, or will you need to be pampered by traveling in a fancy coach?"

"I grew up in the country, Mr. Scott, so yes, I ride. Probably better than you."

With that taunt deftly hurled, she left, and he eased down into his chair, wondering what the bloody hell he'd set in motion.

CHAPTER TEN

"I can't believe this is your life."

"Sometimes neither can I."

Maggie laughed with her old friend, Evangeline Etherton, who was now Evangeline Drake, Lady Run. They'd grown up together at Miss Peabody's School for Girls, and after they'd graduated Maggie had gone home, fallen in love, and become betrothed to Gaylord.

Evangeline had stayed on at the school as a teacher, and Maggie had always assumed that's where she'd remained. It was mind-boggling to learn that she'd wound up married to a viscount. Who could have imagined it? The story had played out like a plot you'd read in a romantic novel.

Evangeline had shown up unexpectedly, and Maggie wanted to be irked but couldn't be. She was in a frantic state, packing her bag and calming her nerves as she watched for Michael Scott to arrive so he could whisk her away to his house in the country.

She'd told Evangeline she was leaving town on a brief trip, but hadn't shared any true information, and to her relief Evangeline hadn't asked.

Maggie was simply planning to push Evangeline out the door before Mr. Scott appeared. There was no suitable explanation Maggie could give as to why she'd be traveling alone with him.

"When Mr. Scott advised me you were here," Evangeline said, "I was stunned."

"I'm so glad you crossed paths with him."

"I was twiddling my thumbs, figuring I'd arrange to have him bring me for a visit someday, but I decided I couldn't wait. You're not upset, are you? That I popped in without warning?"

"Absolutely not."

"I'm still as impetuous as ever," Evangeline said, and they laughed again.

Evangeline was a fantastically accomplished singer and musician who'd loved to flaunt her many talents, and her penchant for aggravating Miss Peabody had been legendary.

"You haven't changed a bit," Maggie said.

"It's a good thing too. My husband is a stick in the mud and in desperate need of enlivening, and I'm doing my best to deliver chaos into his life."

"He's very lucky."

"I wrote you several times after graduation," Evangeline told her.

"I know. I was too embarrassed to reply."

"I should have pestered you until I heard back. I hate that you went through all that heartache without a single ally by your side."

"It was definitely horrid," Maggie admitted, "but it's in the past. I rarely think about it anymore."

"You *rarely* think about it? The cad wed your sister."

"Other than *that* part, I try not to dwell on it. I'd drive myself batty."

"I'm disgustingly rich. Have I mentioned that I am? Well, my husband is, but he's incredibly generous."

"From the jewels you're wearing, I suspected your fortunes had improved."

"I'll start donating to you. I'll make you one of my charities."

"I'm not too proud to say *yes*."

"I should hope so. Please take advantage of me. I'm settling into my position, and it's wonderful to be wealthy—much more fun than being poor."

"Yes, I vividly remember that affluent period when I could simply snap my fingers and have whatever I wanted."

"That's my world now. I feel like a princess in a fairytale."

Evangeline had been an orphan and charity case at school, with an anonymous benefactor paying her tuition, but she'd never had an extra farthing to buy a new dress or ribbon for her hair. Maggie had often shared or—when shopping—had purchased two of everything so she could provide one to her poverty-stricken friend.

How odd to have their roles completely reversed!

"But listen to me chattering on and on," Evangeline said. "It's just that I have so much to tell you, and I'm blabbing while you're finishing your packing."

"I'll be back in a few days. I'll contact you the minute I return, and you can fill me in on the details."

"Guess what the biggest one is?"

"You mean besides your marrying a viscount, becoming a viscountess, and joining the top ranks of society?"

"Yes, besides all that." Evangeline's smile lit up the dim room of the mission, illuminating it in a way it would never be again. She had that kind of dramatic effect.

"Give me a hint of your news," Maggie said, "so I can chaw on it while I'm away."

"I have a family," Evangeline announced.

"What? You're joking."

"No, I'm not an orphan and never was. I have a brother named Bryce and two other brothers I'm trying to find. We were separated when we were very young."

"My goodness, Evangeline."

"And when I was born, my name was Annie Blair."

"Now, I'm doubly anxious to hurry back."

"You'll be astonished. My own head is still spinning."

Maggie walked Evangeline to the front door, and they'd just stepped outside when Mr. Scott trotted up the street. Wouldn't you know it? The blasted man was right on time.

He was with Mr. Ramsey, and Ramsey was leading a mare that had no rider, so evidently the animal was intended for Maggie.

She'd hoped Evangeline's carriage might block her view of Mr. Scott, but anymore Maggie couldn't seem to generate any luck. Evangeline glanced over and said, "Oh, there's Mr. Scott. What a coincidence."

She merrily waved, and when he saw her he blanched with dismay.

Evangeline leaned nearer and murmured, "He's so handsome, don't you think?"

"Yes, he's very handsome." *If you like untrustworthy, dissolute brigands!*

"He looks just like my brother, Bryce."

As Evangeline mentioned the similarity, Maggie stared at Mr. Scott, and it dawned on her that he also looked a lot like Evangeline too—although his hair was dark and hers was blond. They both had the most stunning blue eyes.

"Mr. Scott," Evangeline said as he and Ramsey reined in, "we meet again."

"Hello, Lady Run."

"I realize I begged you to escort me to the mission someday, but once you told me Maggie was in the city, I couldn't wait to speak with her." Evangeline grinned up at him, pert dimples creasing her cheeks. "You don't mind, do you?"

"I don't mind," he mumbled.

He had the strangest expression on his face, and he was ignoring Maggie completely, which was fine by her.

Evangeline didn't notice his peculiar demeanor and—praise be!—didn't inquire as to why he was passing by. But then his business establishment was just down the street, so it wasn't that odd to bump into him.

She hugged Maggie, promised to stop by again very soon, then climbed into her carriage. The driver clicked the reins, and they rumbled away.

With a sad sort of yearning, Maggie watched her go. She'd have given her right arm to climb in with Evangeline, to be spirited away to Mayfair and leave all her troubles behind, but she couldn't avoid the pending trip.

Michael Scott thought he'd tricked Maggie into being his mistress, but he was in for a surprise.

She'd agreed to his scheme, but she had no intention of ruining herself. What she *did* intend was to charm and flirt until she lured his kindness to the fore again. He could be funny and interesting and polite, and she would goad those traits to the surface if it killed her. Once she had him back on a more pleasant footing, she'd be able to cajole him into behaving exactly as she wished him to behave.

There would be no illicit affair. He was mad if he presumed so.

"Why was Lady Run here?" Mr. Scott asked almost in accusation.

"She's a friend of mine. Apparently you were blabbing hither and yon about my missionary work, and she came to see it for herself."

"I never blab," he huffed, "and I most especially didn't blab to her."

"I stand corrected," she sarcastically replied.

"Are you prepared to depart? Or are you a typical female who'll make me dawdle for hours while you primp and preen?"

"You're a bachelor, Mr. Scott. Why would you be so familiar with a woman's traveling routines? Are you in the habit of absconding to the country with virtuous young ladies?"

"Yes, all the time."

He glared so ferociously she couldn't decide if he was telling the truth or not. Her confidence slipped a bit.

"You said we were riding," she reminded him.

"We are."

"So I assume I can only bring one bag."

"Yes."

"It's upstairs. Will you carry it down for me or must I do it myself?"

"I can do it," he grumbled.

"See?" she chided. "Your manners are already improving. If you spend a few days with me, I may actually turn you into a human being."

"I wouldn't count on it," Ramsey muttered.

She peered up at him and asked Mr. Scott, "Are you ever going to introduce me to your companion?"

"No."

"I've been in his presence several times," Maggie said, "but haven't had the pleasure."

"I'm Ramsey Scott."

"Ramsey Scott?" she inquired. "Are you two brothers?"

"He should be so lucky," both men grouched in unison, providing ample evidence of a lengthy acquaintance.

"Is he coming with us?" she asked.

"No," Mr. Scott responded, and Ramsey Scott queried, "Who will run the mission while you're away?"

"I have volunteers who know the procedures."

"But...there's no one in charge?"

"No."

"You live here?"

"Upstairs in an apartment."

"Your bed will be empty while you're away."

"I have no idea why that would concern you." She turned to Michael Scott. "May we go?"

"The sooner the better. I'm eager to claim my prize."

"Your prize?" At first, she didn't understand, but his torrid gaze rudely wandered down her torso. "Oh, you mean *me*. I am the prize."

"Will you be worth it?" he snottily inquired. "Time will tell, I suppose."

"I'll be the best thing you've ever won."

He snorted and swung down from the saddle. A group of boys rushed up, all begging to hold his reins. He nodded to one of them, then stared up at Ramsey.

"You have your instructions," he said.

"I'll take care of it. Don't worry."

"You know where I'll be—if there's trouble."

Ramsey Scott scoffed. "As if they'd dare to cause trouble around me."

"You might stumble on an idiot who's unaware of your repute," Mr. Scott replied.

"He'll be aware of it after he meets me," Ramsey Scott boasted.

He laughed malevolently, and Mr. Scott waved him off and led Maggie inside.

"Where is Mr. Ramsey going?" She needed to make conversation to smooth over the awkwardness of the moment.

"To break a few arms for me."

She tripped, and he lurched forward to steady her.

"You're not serious," she scolded. "You're not having anyone's arm broken."

He shrugged but didn't comment, and again she couldn't discern if he was being truthful.

She heard footsteps behind her and peeked back to find a hoard of street urchins following in Mr. Scott's wake. They hovered in the doorway, tracking Mr. Scott's every move, their expressions worshipful, as if he was a hero or saint.

"You have a gaggle of admirers," she told him.

He glanced at them, and with the slightest gesture they hastily disbursed.

"Sorry," he muttered.

"I'm surprised by how they all seem to know you."

"Why would you be surprised? I've lived on this street a lot longer than you have."

"They're enamored of you."

"That's because I'm one of them and on their side." He peered around the room. "This used to be an orphanage years ago. I stayed here sometimes."

She stopped and pulled him to a stop too. "I knew you grew up on the streets, but on *this* street?"

"Yes, and everyone on it is under my protection, so the children are safe. It's probably why they tag after me. I imagine they're grateful."

He offered the explanation as if it was silly or embarrassing, and she scowled. "How did you become the man you are?"

"How does anyone?"

She thought he might reveal a tad more personal information, but evidently he'd already shared more than he'd intended. His cheeks flushed with what might have been chagrin, and he walked on, giving her the clear indication that he didn't want her to realize he was discomfited.

He knew where her apartment was located, and he went to the stairs and tromped up. She strolled more slowly, evaluating his body, his clothes, his erect bearing.

He was dressed for traveling, but in expensive, perfectly-tailored garments, such as an aristocrat might wear: tan trousers, knee-high black boots, a flowing white shirt, a blue coat. His fingers were covered with gaudy rings, the stones appearing to be sapphires and diamonds and, considering his luxurious attire, she assumed the gems were real.

She'd understood that he gambled, that he owned his notorious club. But there were other stories too, that he owned ships and land and other vital assets. She'd discounted the tales as exaggerations. After all, how could a criminal accumulate so much wealth?

It didn't seem possible, and in light of the general opinion that criminals weren't very bright or educated, how could he have had the intellect to thrive? How would he have had the mathematical skills to tabulate the money that was rolling in?

A sliver of unease slipped down her spine. What was she getting herself into?

He strutted into her apartment, and she entered after him, almost tiptoeing, feeling uncertain in a manner she never was. He marched through the parlor and proceeded directly to the bedchamber where her battered portmanteau was on the bed.

He gaped at it. "Is this it?"

"Yes."

He studied her gray gown, her tidy chignon.

"How many dresses did you pack?" he asked.

"Two—besides the one I'm wearing."

"Are they all gray?"

"Yes."

"I won't have you traipsing around my home, looking dowdy."

"You don't have to be rude. I'm not rich like you."

"I wasn't being rude. I'm just stating the facts."

"Well then, thank you for pointing out the obvious."

"You're welcome, and you don't need to worry. I've bought plenty for you."

"Plenty of what?"

"Clothes."

"You bought me clothes?"

"Yes. They'll be delivered over the next week, so you don't have to take any of this if you don't want to."

"You can't buy me clothes!"

"Why not?"

"It's not…appropriate."

"Maggie, we're about to begin a wild, salacious affair. I think *clothes* are the least of your problems." He nodded to the portmanteau. "Are we bringing this raggedy old stuff or not?"

"Yes, we're bringing it."

"Have it your way, but it's a waste of perfectly good space."

"I'll keep that in mind."

He spun and stomped out, her bag under his arm, and she had to run to catch up.

"I'm ready to start."

"Start what?"

"Our affair."

Michael stared at Maggie, his expression shielding his true sentiment, and she couldn't conceal a gasp of alarm.

"Now?"

"Why not? We've been in my home for over twelve hours. I'm not in the habit of waiting for things."

"But…but…" she stammered.

"But what? We came here so I can relieve you of your virginity. Let's begin."

"No."

"No?"

"I mean, I need a little more time to compose myself."

"I don't want you to be composed. I want you anxious and scared."

"Scared? Why?"

"It will be more enjoyable for me if you're frightened and begging me to stop."

She frowned. "That's disgusting."

He bit down on the smile that was struggling to break out.

They'd spent two very lovely days on the road, plus a night at a coaching inn, in separate rooms of course, and had arrived at his country house—Orphan's Nest—on the third day.

Throughout the journey, she'd been engaging and sweet, and he'd found himself liking her more than was wise. Gradually he'd become troubled over his plans with regard to her.

From the outset, when Farrow had first proposed his illicit bargain, Michael hadn't been interested in deflowering her. But she'd needled and nagged at him when he was in a temper, and he'd forced the issue simply because she'd given him an enormous headache and deserved a comeuppance for aggravating him.

Yet he wasn't an idiot or a fool, and when he caught himself yearning to back out of the deal with Farrow, to return her to her family safe and sound, her virtue intact, he'd realized her ploy.

She was hoping to charm him into better behavior. She was hoping to make him feel sorry for her, but she didn't have to earn his sympathy.

He felt very sorry for her. Sorry that Farrow was her brother-in-law. Sorry that Farrow had put her in such a predicament. Sorry that Farrow had destroyed her life when he'd jilted her.

But Michael wasn't sorry that he'd ruined Farrow. It didn't weigh on his conscience at all, and despite how she cajoled him, he would never change his mind about that one pertinent fact.

During the trip, he'd been the perfect traveling companion, so he'd allowed her to indulge in fantasies as to what he was really like, but it was time to rein in her mischief. He was happy to demonstrate how alone she was, that he could do whatever he wished to her and she couldn't prevent it.

He wouldn't harm her or force her, but honestly! How much manipulation was a man supposed to endure?

It was late, almost midnight. They'd dined together—a slow, lazy supper that had lulled her into a false sense of security—then they'd had a quiet brandy on the verandah and looked out at the stars.

Then she'd gone up to bed. He'd tarried a few minutes so she could undress, then he'd barged in as if he owned the place. Which he did.

"Take off your robe," he ordered.

She gulped with dismay. "My robe?"

"Yes." He gestured to it. "Take it off. Your nightgown too. I want you naked."

"I don't think I'd like that."

"And *I* think I'd like it very much."

He took a step toward her, and she took one back. She took another and he took one too. They were in her bedchamber, and he approached until she bumped up against the bedpost and couldn't keep on. He pressed his body to hers and nearly sighed with contentment, feeling as if it had been years, instead of days, since he'd been so close to her.

He untied the belt on her robe and tugged it off so it pooled on the floor at her feet. Her nightgown was old and faded, the cloth worn thin from too many washings. Her nipples poked at the fabric, the pink color just visible.

"I don't like that gleam in your eye," she said, and she was trembling, which annoyed him very much. He liked to imagine she understood him and knew he wouldn't hurt her. Not physically anyway.

"What gleam is that?" he asked.

"It appears you'd like to gobble me up."

"Your perception is correct, Miss Wells."

He dipped down and nibbled at her nape, liking how she squealed with dread, how she squirmed and tried to escape, but he wasn't about to cease his torment.

"Could we discuss this?" she inquired.

"No."

"The whole trip, you've been so…so…"

"What? Complacent? Polite?"

"I thought maybe you'd…ah…decided not to ravish me."

"I had initially believed I wasn't interested, but I'm tired of listening to you talk. There are things I'd like you to do with that pretty mouth of yours—besides babbling on and on—and I plan to show you what they are."

"I don't have to talk all the time. You seemed to be enjoying our chats, but I can be silent."

"I'd rather have you shrieking and clawing at my back with your fingernails."

"I have no idea what you mean."

"Good. Your claims about being a maiden must be true."

"Of course they're true, you oaf."

"Some women have been known to lie about such an important detail."

"Not me."

He abandoned her nape and nuzzled up to capture her lips in a torrid kiss. She permitted the contact for only a moment, then she wrenched away, looking lost and alone and very afraid.

"What's the matter, Magdalena? Don't tell me you're frightened. This is what we came here for, remember?"

"Yes, but…but…"

"A deal's a deal. Isn't that what you said?"

"Perhaps I was a bit hasty."

"And perhaps I finally agree with you. When your brother-in-law offered you to me, I deemed it a terrible notion, but now I can't wait to have you."

"Well, I've changed *my* mind."

"You can't. It's too late."

He picked her up and pitched her onto the mattress, and before she could scoot away, he stretched out on top of her and pinned her down.

He grinned. "This isn't so bad, is it?"

"It's pretty bad," she petulantly grumbled, and he laughed and laughed.

"You greatly amuse me, Magdalena Wells. I'll give you that much."

"So glad I could be of service."

"Will you stop trying to charm me? It's irritating, and you can't alter my character."

"Why would I waste any energy trying to charm you? I realize how stubborn you are, and there's no way I could manipulate you into better conduct."

"You have the most expressive face, and I'm a gambler who reads faces for a living. You assume you can seduce me into forgiving your family's debt, but without you having to furnish what I was promised."

"I never thought that," she huffed with feigned offense.

He laughed again. "You should never lie to me, because you can't."

He pushed away from her and sat on his haunches so he could draw off his shirt, and he tossed it on the floor.

"What are you doing?" she demanded with outright alarm.

"I'm getting more comfortable."

"Would you put your shirt back on?"

"No."

"Please?"

"I love it when a woman begs, but the answer is still *no*."

He grabbed her hands and slid them around his waist, then he stretched out atop her again.

He didn't intend to deflower her. At least he didn't think so. If he proceeded, he'd have to show Gaylord Farrow some mercy, but she inspired a raging amount of lust, and he'd spent several very chaste days keeping his passions in check.

It wasn't healthy to be so titillated. He was determined to assuage some of his ardor, being absolutely convinced that if he dallied with her his fascination would wane.

No woman ever held his interest for long, and he dabbled with trollops so he wouldn't have to flirt and woo. He placed hard cash on the table and bought what was necessary from them. He was very generous, and they were happy to provide whatever he requested. That was as far as his *interest* ever extended.

Yet Magdalena was stirring another sort of fascination entirely.

"Some words of advice, Magdalena? Don't gamble with a man like me unless you can afford to pay the price after you lose."

"I haven't lost."

He cocked a brow. "Haven't you? You're away from the city and all that's familiar. You're tucked away in my country cottage and lying beneath me—barely dressed—in one of my many beds. I wouldn't exactly claim you've won. Would you?"

"Let me up."

"No."

"Ooh, I hate it when you give me simplistic replies."

"Hush."

"Michael, I can't do this with you. I know in London I said I would but—"

"Hush!"

She gazed up at him, her blue eyes searching his own for a hint of kindness, of compassion, but she wouldn't find it.

She'd built up absurd views of him that weren't accurate or true. She had such ridiculous faith in him being different than he really was, and her misconceptions would only damage her in the end.

He couldn't bear to have her studying him so keenly. Nor would his pride allow him to stomp out without making a pertinent point. The fact that he wasn't sure what that point should be was aggravating. He merely wanted her to comprehend that he was in control of her situation, and he would be in control until he'd had enough of playing games with her.

He kissed her. He didn't see why he shouldn't. He enjoyed it, and she enjoyed it too, once she got past remembering that she was typically British and supposed to be virtuous and opposed to pleasure.

Initially she tensed, being certain she was about to be ravished, but when he simply kissed her, then kissed her some more, she relaxed and joined in. Kissing she understood. Kissing she liked very much. It set them on a firmer footing and pushed them onto roads they'd walked before.

Without her noticing, he untied the bow on her nightgown and opened the front, slipping his palm under the fabric until he found her nipple. He pinched and teased it until she reached for his wrist and pulled him away.

He rolled onto his back and rolled her with him so she straddled his lap. Her glorious auburn hair cascaded over her shoulders and arms, her lips rosy and swollen from their potent embrace.

She looked rumpled and magnificent, like a trained seductress in a harem, like a mermaid perched on the rocks, singing her siren song to unsuspecting sailors. If he wasn't careful, she'd lure him to his doom.

"I like kissing you," she said.

"I like kissing you too."

"But that's it. I can't do more than that."

"Can't you?"

"No."

"I guess we'll see, won't we?"

He rolled them again so she was beneath him, and she scowled, but the expression wasn't nearly as scolding as it had been previously.

"I won't bother asking you to let me up," she said. "You wouldn't listen anyway."

"No, I wouldn't."

"What is it you want from me?"

Everything! Nothing at all!

He had no idea what he sought, but apparently she possessed something he desperately needed, and he had to figure out what it was. Then he could be shed of her.

"You know what I want." He gestured down her body. "I want what I bargained for. I want you."

"I don't want *you* in return."

"You're a virgin and a spinster, so your opinion is irrelevant."

"I've sworn off men," she claimed.

"If that's your defense as to why we shouldn't proceed, I'm duty-bound to declare that it's a little late to protest on those grounds."

She was about to argue the issue—did the woman ever stop talking?—so he kissed her again. There seemed no other way to silence her.

He grew more bold, his hands roaming everywhere, caressing her breasts, her hips and thighs. He dipped down and sucked a nipple into his mouth. It was still concealed by the thin fabric of her nightgown, the material adding extra friction as he tormented her.

"What's happening to me?" she managed as she gasped and moaned.

"I'm pleasuring you."

"It doesn't feel pleasurable."

He chuckled. "Liar."

He'd kept her so busy that she hadn't noted him drawing up the hem of her nightgown. He bared her calves, her thighs, his torso dropping in between.

She was splayed wide, at his mercy, his trousers the only barrier to ravishment, and he was a hairsbreadth away from going farther than he'd ever intended. He was hovering on a dangerous ledge, anxious to take her, to have her in the sole manner that counted, and he couldn't imagine relenting.

Why was he such a proud, vain ass? Why couldn't he have left her alone?

Where she was concerned, he had no control at all. Shouldn't he receive some sort of boon for his trouble?

He went to work on her nipples again, pulled on the fabric to move it away, and he bit and licked, while down below his fingers found the woman's hair at the vee of her legs. He slid one finger into her sheath, then another, and he stroked back and forth, once, twice, and she exploded into a powerful orgasm. He'd aroused her that thoroughly.

He'd suspected that—deep down—she was a very carnal creature. With all that sass and temper bottled up inside, she had to be a bubbling cauldron of unfulfilled lust. How delightful that he'd been the man to discover it.

She cried out—quite loudly—and arched against him as she soared to the heavens, the ecstasy spiraling until he wondered if she'd ever get to the end.

Finally, she reached the peak and floated down. She landed in his arms, safe and sated and astonished, and he grinned, preening, thrilled with what he'd accomplished.

"What was that?" she asked when she could speak again.

"*That* was sexual pleasure."

"Can it occur more than once?"

"Definitely."

"Am I still a…a…" She was such an innocent that she didn't have the salacious vocabulary to complete her sentence.

"Yes, my little maiden, you're chaste as the day is long."

She'd had her ardor assuaged, but he hadn't remedied his own, and as he eased away from her, his titillation was so extreme that he decided to ride into the village and visit the local tavern. They employed a serviceable trollop who knew her way around a mattress. If he didn't allay his stimulation, he might injure himself!

But he wouldn't press the issue with Magdalena. If he did, Gaylord Farrow would be able to continue plaguing him.

He slipped to the floor but dawdled like an imbecile, desperate to lie down and snuggle with her all night, which was ludicrous.

If he climbed under the blankets with a female, it was for one reason and one reason only. He never *slept* with women. When he was in a bedchamber, he was busy with other matters.

"Are we finished?" she asked.

"For now."

"What does that mean?"

"It means that I've proved my point."

"What point is that?"

"I wanted to learn if I could coax you into a physical dalliance, and I'm happy to report that I succeeded."

"You did not," she staunchly declared.

"Magdalena, you're halfway ruined. Give over and admit your defeat. I can do whatever I like to you. But"—he leaned down and stole a quick kiss—"I'm not interested in what you're offering, so stop being charming. You can't protect your brother-in-law from me."

He grabbed his shirt and strutted out.

Behind him, she said, "Mr. Scott, get back here." He kept on and she called more sternly, "Michael! Don't you dare walk out. I want to talk to you."

He glanced over his shoulder, thinking she was stunning, and he struggled to maintain a severe scowl.

"Magdalena, you've talked me to death, and I can't bear to hear another word."

"Michael!"

"I'll see you in the morning. We'll make plans to return to the city."

"Already? Why come all this way if we're simply going to leave?"

"We came because you annoyed me, because you thought you were smarter or tougher or cleverer than me. But you're not, and you can't save Gaylord Farrow—and I can't figure out why you'd wish to save him."

He strolled out, and she hurled a pillow, but he was much too far away and her throw was weak and pathetic, so there was no chance she'd have hit him.

CHAPTER ELEVEN

Maggie gazed out the front window of Michael Scott's country house. She could see him out on the road, galloping on a stallion.

He'd been riding for hours, having departed before she'd staggered down to breakfast, and it had been almost a disappointment to have him gone. After what had happened between them in her bedchamber the prior night, she'd had no idea how they would interact. Apparently, he'd been so unmoved by their foray into passion that he'd jumped up at dawn and trotted off.

She shouldn't have been surprised by his indifference. The very first time she'd ever laid eyes on him, he'd had a trollop on his lap. He was accustomed to salacious misbehavior, but she certainly wasn't. She felt lost and confused about what to do with herself.

Though she hated to admit it, she was extremely curious about him. She'd like to snoop and pry for clues in the various rooms and salons, but she hadn't dared. When they'd arrived the previous day, he'd given her a quick tour, and they'd dined together in the dining room, but she hadn't had the opportunity to uncover any details that would reveal more about him.

How could he have started from such a low spot, but risen so high? How had he overcome his early poverty and achieved such amazing success?

He was an orphan, and as far as she was aware had no information about his parents or lineage. But it was an accepted fact that bloodlines determined a person's status and abilities, which was why kings and queens ruled the world. The common people understood that ancestry set the nobility apart from the masses.

Was he from an exalted family? Was it possible? How else could one explain his extraordinary intellect and talents?

As they'd left London, she'd been unnerved about their destination. What sort of residence would be owned by such a dissolute gambler and criminal? Yet she needn't have worried as to what it would be like.

The place was remarkable. Tastefully decorated. Quietly understated. His wealth was evident in every nook and cranny, but not in a garish or vain way. The rooms were bright and airy, the colors pleasing, the furniture posh and obviously chosen for maximum comfort.

It wasn't an overly large abode—she'd counted just five bedchambers. There were no acres and acres of parkland, no rivers for fishing, or woods for hunting, and he employed only a handful of competent, courteous servants.

In the rear of the house, there was a small library with shelves of books on a wide range of subjects such as trade, finance, and farming, and she wondered if he could read and comprehend the contents. She supposed he could, but who had taught him? How had he become educated?

The parlor where she was sitting boasted a pianoforte and a cabinet full of music. Did he play? Could he read music? He didn't seem the type, but then again, nothing about him had turned out to be what she expected.

To her disgust, she found herself being jealous of him. He had so much and hardly noticed his affluence. She had hardly anything, and with Cliffside frittered away she now had even less. Where would they all be on Rebecca's next birthday?

He left the road and started up the drive, and she couldn't stop staring. He was so handsome and dashing, as if he was a great lord surveying his domain. His cheeks were rosy, his dark hair freed from its ponytail and flowing around his shoulders.

Who could have sired such a magnificent male specimen? If he had kin somewhere, what would they think of his current condition?

As he went by the window on his way to the stables, he saw her gawking, her attention riveted as if she was an adolescent girl in the throes of her first amour. He smirked and arrogantly waved as if her heightened scrutiny was exactly what he deserved. Embarrassed, she scowled and whipped away, and he kept on.

She dawdled, uneasy and exasperated with him—and herself. She had naught to do and felt she should write some letters or play the pianoforte or...something. Since she'd moved to London with Vicar Sterns and his wife, she'd forgotten how to loaf. She was used to being busy, to having her time filled with tasks that needed accomplishing.

Eventually she heard him enter out in the foyer. A footman met him at the door, and they had a quiet chat. She tried to eavesdrop, but was frustrated that she couldn't decipher a single word. Were they talking about her?

For a moment she fretted over what the servants thought. When she'd been introduced as *Miss* Wells, none of them had batted an eye over the impropriety. Of course there was no telling what they whispered about her when they were in the kitchen.

She was dreadfully concerned that they weren't bothered by her presence because Mr. Scott made a habit of bringing unmarried ladies when he visited. If so, how many had there been before her? Under what circumstances had they traveled with him? Had he ruined other men besides Gaylord and been given their virtuous sisters or daughters in exchange for cancelled debts?

There were always wild stories circulating in the city about lost fortunes, but she'd assumed the tales to be preposterous and untrue. Who could have guessed she'd find herself in the middle of just such a sordid saga?

Suddenly he appeared in the doorway, having come down the hall without her being aware. She stood and faced him, not certain what would happen, what they would say. But he was grinning, happy and relaxed as she hadn't seen him previously.

"Good morning, Miss Wells."

There was a flirtatious tone in his voice for which she hadn't been prepared, and her cheeks flushed, as if with excitement.

"Mr. Scott."

"I've been riding. Did the servants apprise you?"

"Yes."

"So you didn't think I'd abandoned you?"

"No. I knew you were out."

"Were you fed and looked after?"

"Yes. Everyone's been very gracious and accommodating."

"And how was breakfast? Was the food to your liking?"

"It was marvelous."

"Are you sure? Because if it wasn't, I can—"

"No, no, it was fine. Everything is fine." It occurred to her that he was worried about her opinion of his home, his cook, his staff, so she added, "This is an enormous treat for me. Don't forget that I live at the mission and eat the food there."

"What is usually served? Bread and beans?"

"With bits of ham in it occasionally, if I have the funds to buy some meat."

"I never gave you a donation, did I?"

"No, and I definitely deserve a carriage full of money."

"Payment for your troubles?"

"Yes."

He strolled in and crossed the floor, stopping directly in front of her. She could smell the out-of-doors—fresh air, sunshine, horses—emanating from his clothes and person. The heady, masculine aromas set fire to her feminine sensibilities, and she could barely keep from leaning in and rubbing herself against him. What was wrong with her?

She didn't like him, loathed his highhanded conduct, and had intended to remain aloof and unaffected—especially since he was completely impervious to their amorous encounter. She'd tossed and turned over it until dawn, then had tiptoed down to breakfast, being terrified as to how they'd get on, but the rat wasn't even on the premises and hadn't been for hours.

Mentally she grasped the reasons she detested him, but evidently her anatomy had a different view of the situation. His intimate caresses had altered her, had left her feeling raw and disoriented.

She wanted to ask him about what had happened to her body, but she wasn't sure how to have that discussion. There were probably adults in the world who could parlay over such an indiscreet topic, but she was not one of them.

"I've decided we're not returning to London this morning," he announced.

"We're not?"

"No. We'll stay on for a few days."

"What made you change your mind?"

"It's silly for us to have come all this way, merely to leave."

"Yes...it is," she cautiously said.

She was eager to hurry back to the city. Wasn't she?

It wasn't London that was calling to her precisely. She was simply anxious about being in the country with him. They were too secluded, and in their isolation it seemed that any behavior was allowed. Up in her bedchamber he'd proved she was no better than she had to be, and she was very afraid that—given further opportunity—she'd shame herself again.

"What if I say I'd like to head back right now?" she asked.

"You can *say* it, but we're staying, so it's pointless to complain."

"You are the most infuriating man."

"Yes, I've constantly been told that I am."

"Were you arrogant and domineering from the start?"

"From the start? You mean as a boy? Yes, I suppose I was. Ramsey claims I was always horrid and impossible."

"How old were you when you met him?"

"Three? Four? I don't recollect."

"He would know then—if he's had to put up with you that long. Have you ever wondered where you come by such imperious traits?"

He scowled. "I had to be arrogant, or I wouldn't have survived. I didn't grow up rich and spoiled—like some people I could name."

She was rattled by his use of the word *survived*. It conjured up too many images that made her feel sorry for him.

"Yes, I'm aware that you were a homeless waif. How were you orphaned? Who were your parents? Have you any idea?"

"Miss Wells, why are you asking?" he slyly said. "Are you curious about me?"

"No."

He laughed and shook a scolding finger in her face. "Remember what I told you about lying to me? You shouldn't. You are awfully bad at it."

"I *might* be a tad curious," she admitted.

"With good reason," he pompously retorted. "I dare say you've encountered few men like me in your life."

"That would be an understatement."

He plopped down on the sofa and clasped her hand, dragging her onto his lap. She made a halfhearted effort to remain standing, but of course he won the battle.

"What is it you wish to learn about my past?" he said. "I'll tell you what I can."

"Where were you born?"

"I don't know."

"Who were your parents?"

"I don't know."

"How did you end up in an orphanage?"

"I don't know."

It took her a moment to realize he was teasing her, and she didn't like him to exhibit a playful demeanor. She'd start liking him again, but then wasn't that why she'd come to the country? Wasn't she determined to lure better behavior to the fore?

She glowered. "Would you be serious?"

He chuckled. "All right. In my very first memory, I was tiny. There was a terrible fire, and I was out in the dark, watching huge flames engulf a building."

The story raised the hairs on the back of her neck. "You were alone?"

"I think someone was with me, but it was very chaotic. I couldn't find the person who was minding me." He shuddered dramatically. "I hate fire to this day."

"Was it your parents' home?"

He thought and thought. "I don't believe so. It might have been a hotel or a coaching inn?"

"What makes you assume so?"

"It just seems to be true." He shrugged. "In my next memory, I was at the orphanage with Ramsey. I was young. Maybe three or four?"

"Was it the building where my rescue mission is?"

"Yes."

"You grew up there?"

"No, I lived there occasionally. Ramsey and I would sneak off and try to manage on our own, but when we were too hungry or too weary, we'd go back. I guess they felt sorry for us, because they always took us in."

"Mostly you lived on the streets?"

"Yes."

"You were just a boy. Wasn't it scary?"

He scoffed at her concern. "It wasn't so bad. I discovered some nasty tricks that helped me get by."

"What sorts of tricks?"

"Thievery. Pickpocketing. The usual crimes."

"You're rich and prosperous now."

"I definitely am, and since you've noticed—and we're both aware that you're a poverty-stricken spinster—will you glom on to me for my money?"

"No. It would require more than a large fortune to make me like you. And don't change the subject."

"What was the subject again?"

"How have you become so wealthy? You began with petty crimes."

"Yes, but I was smart and shrewd—as well as vicious and driven—and I refused to be poor. I gradually elevated myself above everyone else."

"With your gambling?"

"Among other things."

"What *other* things?"

"That, Miss Maggie, is probably more than you need to know about me."

He pushed her to her feet, and he stood too.

"I thought I hated it here in the country," he said.

"Then why did we come?"

"So I could ruin you, remember?"

"It's not happening, so why are we staying?"

"I'm enjoying myself for once. Normally I can't abide the quiet and the deserted country lanes. I'm a city boy through and through, and I've always had to work very hard. I have no idea how to relax."

"I have no idea either," she agreed. "At least not since I was seventeen and moved to town. I can't stand to be idle."

"Well, we're going to be idle and pamper ourselves. Do you paint?" he strangely asked.

"Every girl of my station learns how to paint."

"I have brushes and canvases in a cupboard. We'll sit out in the garden and you can paint me a picture."

"I will—as long as you promise not to laugh at my lack of skill."

"Later, you can play the pianoforte for me."

"I had lessons, but I'm awful at it. How about you?"

She'd expected him to say the same, but he stunned her by claiming, "I'm very good at it."

Her jaw actually dropped in surprise. "You are?"

"Yes."

"Who taught you?"

"No one. I just always knew how." He winked at her. "I can sing too. Wait until you hear me. You'll be amazed."

"Are you pulling my leg?"

"No. Trust me, you'll be floored."

"Could it be a talent inherited from your parents?"

His brows rose—as if he'd never considered the prospect. "It could, I guess."

"My friend, Evangeline, was an orphan too, and she can play and sing so beautifully. She assumed it was an inherited gift."

"I suppose it's possible." As if the topic bored him, he waved it away. "Go upstairs and change."

"Into what? All I have with me are my three gray dresses."

"The servants tell me that some of your new clothes were delivered a bit ago."

"And I told you not to buy me any clothes."

"Why would I listen to such a silly comment?"

She peered up at him, finding him elegant and fascinating and—at that moment—so very, very likeable.

"No, you'd never listen to me."

"Now we're getting somewhere." He nodded and motioned to the stairs. "If there's a straw bonnet in the pile, wear it for me."

"Why?"

"We're going on a picnic, and I want to see you sitting in the grass in a bonnet that matches your gown—with a bow tied under your chin."

She stood gaping at him, and finally he said, "What?"

"A picnic?"

"Yes, and I'll fetch the brushes and canvas so you can paint me that picture I requested."

"If I have to paint for you, you'll have to perform for me once we're back inside."

"I might. We're on holiday, aren't we? We can act however we please."

"Yes, we can, Michael." She paused and dared to inquire, "How many female guests have you brought to Orphan's Nest before me?"

"None. You're the only one ever."

Should she believe him? To her dismay, she desperately yearned to.

They hovered, perched on the edge of something wonderful. He was staring at her with an intense expression, his gaze warm and affectionate. He was looking at her as if they were sweethearts, as if genuine fondness was blossoming.

But that couldn't be. Could it?

"Would you get a move on?" he scolded.

She braced, positive he would kiss her. After what they'd shared in her bedchamber, it certainly seemed like he would—or like he *should*—yet for some reason, he didn't. He put a hand on her bottom and urged her toward the door.

"Go change," he said again, "and come down in a dress that's not gray."

She hesitated, feeling as if she should toss out a pithy retort, but she couldn't think of a remark that was appropriately flirtatious, so she settled for, "I'll pick out the prettiest one—just for you."

"Perfect," he murmured. "Absolutely perfect."

CHAPTER TWELVE

"I'm going to London."

Pamela glared at Rebecca and said, "No, you're not."

Rebecca glared back and said, "I am."

They were in the front parlor at Cliffside, Gaylord lurking in the corner, and Pamela cooed, "Gaylord, darling, what is your opinion?"

"Why would I care what she does?" he replied.

Pamela bit down a furious retort and forced a smile. "You're the head of the family, Gaylord. You can't consider it appropriate for her to traipse off on her own. What would people say?"

"I don't give two figs what people say. She's embarrassed herself with all the young men in the neighborhood. Who would be surprised if she starts in with the young men in the city?"

"Gaylord!" Pamela snapped. Her constant regret was that he never behaved as she wanted him to, that he'd never turned out to be the husband she needed.

"I'm not asking your permission," Rebecca declared. "I'm simply telling you where I'll be."

"You're not asking?" Pamela fumed. "You're telling? I won't have it, Rebecca. I truly won't."

"To quote your husband, I don't give two figs as to your opinion."

"Don't expect me to cough up the money to finance your little jaunt," Gaylord bestirred himself to complain.

"As Pamela has no jewels you haven't sold," Rebecca sniped, "I'm certain you have no money, so it's a moot point."

"What are you planning to do?" Pamela asked.

"Maggie was called away from the rescue mission," Rebecca explained.

"Was she?"

Gaylord and Pamela shared a furtive grin.

"She's having me stay in her apartment and keep an eye on things while she's away."

Rebecca had always been a bad liar, and she glanced away, looking dodgy and dishonest. Pamela couldn't guess what was really occurring.

Gaylord snorted. "You'll stay at Maggie's rescue mission? You've never been to that seedy neighborhood before, so I must caution against it. You could be endangering yourself."

"Maggie's been there for seven years, and no mishap has befallen her."

"She's such a harridan," Gaylord snidely said, "that no miscreant would risk getting close enough to harm her."

"Don't you dare denigrate her to me," Rebecca scolded, "and since *you* are responsible for her being in London, you have an enormous amount of gall to criticize. She's spent her time helping others. What have you done?"

Rebecca hovered, waiting for Gaylord's answer, but of course he couldn't supply one. Rebecca and Pamela knew his sins, and he knew too. Not that he'd ever admit them aloud.

Rebecca smirked. "I'll write once I'm settled."

"I told you that you may not leave, Rebecca," Pamela seethed.

"Yes, and I told *you* that it doesn't matter what you think. If I remain here with you two another second, I'll go mad."

She swept out, and Pamela was so angry she had to grip the arms of her chair to physically prevent herself from running after her sister. She'd like to slap Rebecca silly, would like to insult and humiliate her until she was brought down a peg, but there weren't words in the world sufficient to vent Pamela's frustrations.

She'd coveted Gaylord so desperately that she'd stolen him from Maggie, and she would stand by him through thick and thin. They were just having a rough patch, but Gaylord was very clever. He insisted he would fix their problem, and she believed him. She couldn't *not* believe him. If she suffered the slightest glimmer of doubt, the foundation of her life might collapse.

"The disloyal witch," Pamela muttered as Rebecca's strides faded down the hall.

"Don't fret over her," Gaylord breezily said. "She's always been a pain in my ass. If she wants to journey to the city and wallow in Maggie's squalor, let her."

"She's my sister, Gaylord, and I'm her guardian. With no parent to guide her, I should try to keep her under control."

"To what end? Haven't you done enough? Haven't I? She's lived with us, and I've supported her. Any normal, pragmatic girl would have wed ages ago."

"I suppose," Pamela hesitantly said.

"If she chooses to be a spinster, that's her option, but must we put up with her?"

Gaylord had squandered Rebecca's dowry, so she couldn't wed even if she wished to, but Pamela would never raise the topic for she wouldn't discuss the contentious issue.

"What about Maggie?" Pamela asked him. "I've never heard of her being away from the mission before. Where would she go? How could she afford to travel?"

"It seems, dearest Pamela, that she's off frolicking with Michael Scott."

Pamela gasped. "She agreed to ruin herself for us? When I spoke to her, she was vehemently opposed."

Gaylord came over and clasped Pamela's hands, pulling her to her feet. He twirled her around as if they were celebrating.

"It appears Maggie has changed her mind," he said.

"We have a month until we have to move?"

"Yes, and despite what Michael Scott decides about her, I'll claim he owes us the whole six months. After we've taken the drastic step of surrendering your virginal sister, it's only fair that we be allowed to remain for the entire period."

Pamela didn't deem Mr. Scott the sort to deal in fairness, but she nodded. "Yes, it's only fair. I don't understand why he wouldn't marry her when you offered. That day I saw them together, he was totally smitten."

"Didn't I tell you? He's engaged to someone else."

"But…but…what will happen to Maggie when he's through with her? What if she winds up with child?"

Gaylord scowled. "Why would that be our problem, Pamela?"

"She *is* my sister, Gaylord."

"Just barely. Let's not imbue her with a connection she no longer deserves. If she winds up in trouble, whose fault is that?"

"Ours?"

"No, it's Michael Scott's. He'll have to make arrangements for her and the baby, and I'll force him to pay *us* for any damage he caused to her."

He dropped Pamela's hands and started out.

"Where are you going?" Pamela nervously asked.

"I'm off to town too."

"Should you, Gaylord?"

"What with Maggie's capitulation, I'm feeling lucky, Pamela."

"Oh." Whenever Gaylord voiced the word *lucky* they were in grave jeopardy.

"I've found a new club that's let me join."

"A gambling club?"

"No, a gentleman's club, but the members have been known to throw the dice occasionally. With this reversal of my fortunes, I can't refuse to play."

Yes, you can!

"I'm afraid I must object." Pamela sounded uncharacteristically shrewish.

"Object all you want," he flippantly retorted as he strolled out. "Why would I care?"

She sank down on the sofa, realizing she would be alone in the big mansion until he deigned to return. What catastrophe would he bring with him?

"What am I to make of it?"

"I wouldn't try to guess."

"Is Mr. Scott being deliberately rude? Or is he oblivious to social etiquette?"

Felicia had written to Mr. Scott to inquire about the wedding. He'd finally replied, and she was at her wit's end. She was with her mother in her mother's solar, and just one blasted time she'd like to obtain some commiseration or guidance, but her mother was stoically silent.

Ever since Lord Stone had apprised them of his fiscal calamity, her mother had been in a state of shock. She had no counsel to share.

"He's not highborn," Felicia said, "but he has some manners. Why doesn't he exhibit them?"

"If you're hoping for stellar behavior from the man, you need to reassess what will be possible with him."

"What are you saying? Are you saying I shouldn't obey Father?"

She was on tenterhooks, praying her mother would order Felicia to cry off, praying her mother would develop a spine and advise Felicia to develop one too. Together, they could tell Lord Stone and Michael Scott to stuff it.

To her great frustration, her mother responded, "No husband is ever what his bride is expecting."

"Couldn't he pretend to be interested in marrying me? Here at the beginning, when he went to so much trouble to win me from Father, couldn't he pretend to be glad? Is that too much to ask?"

"Mr. Scott went to no trouble over you." Lady Stone tsked. "It was all your father's mess. Mr. Scott just sat there and watched your father race to ruin."

Felicia still couldn't believe it. She yearned instead to believe there had been some treachery involved on Mr. Scott's part, but apparently Lord Stone had merely wagered until he'd had naught left to barter but Felicia. Why would Mr. Scott have declined to take what was so gleefully and recklessly squandered?

She waved the infuriating note from Mr. Scott in her mother's face and read the curt, offending missive again.

"*Whatever you want is fine with me.* One sentence! One meager, idiotic sentence! It tells me nothing! Will he pay for the wedding? What sort of ceremony does he envision? Should I book the cathedral and invite a thousand guests? Can he afford such an extravagance? Or is he assuming *we* will pay? When he's beggared us, how would we? Or should we hold a simple ceremony at the house? And whose house? Ours? His? Has he friends he'd like to attend?" Felicia threw up her hands. "How should I interpret this?"

Her mother scowled. "You should interpret it in precisely the way it's stated. *Whatever* you wish is fine. He's very rich. If he doesn't like your expenditures, who cares?"

Besides her pointless questions about the wedding, Felicia had also invited him to supper and to the theater. But the messenger who'd delivered the letter had said Mr. Scott was out of town, and no one knew when he'd return. Was Mr. Scott away for an extended visit? Should she proceed without him? Should she wait until he was back and could provide input? What? What?

"Is this how my marriage will go?" she asked.

"What do you mean?"

"He's out of town, without a word to me—even though I'm his betrothed. He can't be bothered to answer my requests to socialize. I'm already an afterthought, and I'm not yet his wife!"

Lady Stone's scowl deepened. "Yes, I'm sure this is exactly how your married life will go. It's the same for every female. If you were anticipating it to be different, you're a fool."

Felicia recalled her parents' dull existence, how Lord Stone was never home, how Lady Stone was always alone. Months would pass, with Lady Stone and her daughters stuck in the country and Lord Stone cavorting in town.

Her mother had suffered silently, had never criticized or complained.

Her reward for all those years of loyalty was to have lost everything due to her spoiled husband's profligate habits.

Was that to be Felicia's experience? Mr. Scott had insisted he was very reliable, but what if he'd been lying? What if he was actually an irresponsible wretch?

"Have you ever heard of Cliffside," she said.

"No."

"He claims he just bought it."

Lady Stone shrugged. "More likely, he won it from someone."

Felicia gasped. "He'll move me into a home he stole?"

"It could be. You shouldn't ever forget how he earns his income." Lady Stone's expression soured even more. "I'm relieved he's not demanding you live over his gambling club."

"I'm the daughter of an earl, Mother. He wouldn't dare."

"Wouldn't he? I've typically found that—no matter the husband's station or status—he can pretty much behave as he wishes toward his wife. If he orders you to live over his club, then that's what you'll have to do. You're lucky he has a place for you—despite how he came by his ownership."

"Oh, how could Father shame me like this?" Felicia wailed.

"He shamed all of us, Felicia."

"But why am *I* paying the price?"

"We're all paying," her mother declared.

"It doesn't seem that way to me."

"Gossip is all over the city that we're ruined," her mother whined. "Imagine how it feels to be me."

"Yes, poor you, having your reputation tarnished. It sounds ever so much more horrid than my plight of having to marry a man of no name, no rank, and only his gambling and smuggling to recommend him."

Her mother sniffed with offense. "We're doing the best we can, under very trying circumstances. There's no need to chastise."

"Isn't there?" Felicia gaped at her mother, wanting to shout at her, wanting to shake her.

The woman was worried about her reputation! Felicia was being forced to wed Mr. Scott, and her mother was complaining about gossip! If that wasn't complete proof of Felicia being a nonessential detail on the fringe of their family, she didn't know what was. Why would she sacrifice herself for such heartless, callous people?

She should have refused to obey, but she had no idea how. If she declined the engagement, what would become of them? No doubt Mr. Scott would immediately foreclose. If that occurred, she would always blame herself for the consequences.

"If Mr. Scott makes me live over his gambling club, I'll kill myself." She paused, then dramatically added, "I take that back. I'll kill *him*, and when they're leading me to the gallows, I'll climb the stairs with a smile on my face."

"Tell us about our parents."

"You don't know? You don't remember anything?"

"Very little."

Evangeline nodded encouragingly at Miss Etherton. The Etherton family was connected to her own, Miss Etherton's uncle front and center when Evangeline and her brothers were torn apart. He'd placed Evangeline at Miss Peabody's School for Girls, having enrolled her under the false name of Evangeline Etherton, when her true name had been Anne Blair.

He'd enrolled Bryce at a boy's boarding school and had tried to give

Bryce a false name too, but Bryce had been older and wouldn't use it.

Over the years, Attorney Thumberton had checked on Evangeline and Bryce for Mr. Etherton, but Thumberton hadn't known who they were or what had transpired. It had all been secretive and mysterious.

Mr. Etherton was deceased, but his niece, Eugenie Etherton, had agreed to meet with them. They were in her cottage, in her parlor. Miss Etherton was a spinster who'd cared for her uncle as he'd aged, then passed away. In her forties, she was plump and plain, but very friendly.

"When you never came to inquire," Miss Etherton said, "and my uncle was convinced you eventually would, I'd begun to imagine you weren't curious—or weren't interested."

"We didn't recollect any of it until recently."

"Well, I'll be..." Miss Etherton mused.

She'd asked what they remembered about their parents, and Bryce said, "Was my mother an actress?"

"Yes, on the stage in London. She was quite remarkable—as an actress and a singer."

"I knew it," Bryce muttered.

He glanced at Evangeline, delighted to have the news confirmed. They both had enormous talent as actors and musicians, and it made Evangeline feel closer to her mother to realize they shared the same traits.

"She was pretty, wasn't she?" Bryce said. "I recollect her being very pretty."

"She was beautiful," Miss Etherton replied. "I have a portrait of her that I'll give you. You can take it with you when you go."

"You have a portrait?" Evangeline was a bit dazed.

"Yes," Miss Etherton answered, "and you look just like her. She had blond hair and blue eyes—like the two of you."

"Was she famous?" Bryce asked.

"She wasn't yet, but people expected her to be." Miss Etherton blushed, as if perhaps she should have kept the information to herself. "I'm sorry. I'm uncertain as to how much I should say."

"Please be blunt," Bryce said, "and don't hold anything back."

"Are you sure?"

"Very sure," Bryce told her.

Evangeline added, "We want to find our brothers, so whatever you can tell us, it will help us in our search."

"Some of it might shock you," Miss Etherton insisted.

"We're unshockable," Bryce claimed, and they all laughed.

"What about our father?" Evangeline inquired.

"You don't know? Seriously?"

"No," Evangeline and Bryce replied together.

Miss Etherton rose and curtsied to Bryce, offering the oddest comment. "Welcome to my humble home, Lord Radcliffe. I'm honored to have you visit."

Evangeline and Bryce scowled, and Bryce said, "What are you talking about?"

"Your grandfather was Earl of Radcliffe, and your father was Julian Blair, the earl's oldest son and heir to the title."

Bryce shook his head, almost with dismay. "No, no, that can't be right."

"It is, I'm afraid," Miss Etherton said.

"How could that be? An earl doesn't lose track of his grandchildren."

"It can happen when the heir marries the wrong girl, when he's disowned and the family refuses to acknowledge his wife or his legitimate children."

"Oh."

Evangeline and Bryce sat in a stunned silence, Bryce appearing too thunderstruck to continue.

"How did it come about?" Evangeline inquired.

"I'm only cognizant of the details my uncle shared with me, and he had to guess at some of it."

"Just tell us what he said," Evangeline urged. "We'll sort through it and decide what we think is true and what is rumor."

"Your father and the earl never got on. The earl was a hard, cruel man, and Julian constantly rebelled. As soon as he was able, he left home."

"Where was home?" Evangeline asked.

"Radcliffe is in Scotland, near the English border."

"It's an estate?"

"Yes. It's small and used to be prosperous. I have no clue as to its current condition."

"My father moved to London?"

"He stayed in London occasionally. It's where he met your mother. They fell madly in love and wed without your grandfather's permission. Your grandfather was livid, and your father was disavowed."

"Was my father a soldier?" Evangeline asked. "Bryce recalls that he wasn't around very much and that when he returned, he had two big pistols he would lock in my mother's closet."

"He wasn't a soldier. He was an explorer and adventurer."

"My goodness."

"He sailed the Nile and traveled across much of Africa and Arabia. He would be gone for lengthy periods, then he'd show up unannounced and surprise your mother."

"So…what happened?" Evangeline said. "Bryce and I were at the docks with our mother. She boarded a ship, and we were separated. Your uncle was there."

"Yes, it was a terrible day that haunted him until he took his last breath."

"Bryce and I are haunted by it too." They still had nightmares.

"It started," Miss Etherton explained, "when your father was killed at Radcliffe."

"Killed!"

"Yes. It was announced as a hunting accident, but my uncle never believed it. Julian was too tough to die in something as boring as an accident. It didn't make sense."

"If it wasn't an accident, are you claiming he was…was…"

"My uncle thought he was murdered."

"By his relatives?" Evangeline nearly slid to the floor in an astonished heap.

Miss Etherton shrugged. "Don't repeat my comment. My uncle never had any proof. He just…suspected."

"What aroused his suspicions?"

"Your grandfather was very stern and unbending. He wouldn't recognize your father's marriage to your mother, and he arranged a different marriage—what he felt was a proper marriage—to a suitable aristocratic girl. Julian had gone to Radcliffe to scold your grandfather about it, and he never came back."

"And my mother? After my father passed, what happened to her?"

"They'd been wed for years by then, and your father had given her money and a house and jewelry. Your father's kin accused her of stealing items that belonged to the family—the jewels and such."

"There was no one to speak on her behalf?"

"Her only friends were other actors and actresses, so she didn't have the power or connections to fight your grandfather. She was convicted of numerous felonies and transported to the penal colonies in Australia."

Evangeline's shoulders slumped, and she sank into her chair. Bryce had insisted their mother was transported, but he had been viewing the event through the eyes of a five-year-old boy. They hadn't been certain, and it was heart-wrenching to have the worst confirmed.

"Was there ever any news of her after she left? Do you know if she survived?"

"We never heard another word about her," Miss Etherton responded.

"She could be alive?"

Miss Etherton's smile was sympathetic and concerned. "I suppose she could be, but you shouldn't hope for it. It was such a long time ago, and the journey around the globe is treacherous. Many never make it to their destination, and many others perish after they arrive. I'm told the conditions are very harsh."

"Of course I can hope for it," Evangeline loyally declared. "Until I learn otherwise, I'll tell myself she made it with no difficulty."

Miss Etherton looked dubious, but nodded in agreement. "I'm sure optimism will serve you well—and give you peace of mind."

Bryce finally managed to emerge from his stupor. "How could my grandfather have hidden all this? How could he have murdered my father, destroyed my mother, disavowed me and my siblings, but there be no accounting? How could there have been no questions asked?"

"Have you had much experience dealing with the aristocracy, Lord Radcliffe?" Miss Etherton inquired.

"Some—and please don't call me Lord Radcliffe. It's sounds so… pretentious."

Bryce glanced at Evangeline who was now a viscountess. They hadn't wanted Miss Etherton to be intimidated, so they hadn't apprised her of Evangeline's elevated status. But the woman had already been aware that Bryce possessed status of his own, and it was much higher than Evangeline's.

"A man like your grandfather can be a formidable foe," Miss Etherton said.

"I understand."

"Your mother was grief-stricken over your father's death and not thinking clearly. By the time she saw the peril barreling down on her, it was too late to jump out of the way."

Bryce asked, "How was your uncle involved in this? Who was he to my parents?"

"He met your father at school when they were boys, and he accompanied your father on some of his adventures. He loved him like a brother."

"So…he helped us after Mother was sent away?"

"As much as he was able. She begged him to watch over you and keep you safe. She had no relatives and couldn't seek assistance from your father's family. They refused to acknowledge your existence, and she was afraid that…ah…"

Miss Etherton's voice trailed off, and Bryce said, "She was afraid of what?"

"That your grandfather might harm you." Miss Etherton blushed bright red. "Oh, dear me, I probably shouldn't have revealed that."

"It's all right," Bryce insisted. "We're anxious to know everything."

"Your father had a brother—George—who was your grandfather's favorite."

"An uncle!"

"Yes. He was the perfect, obedient son as your father could never be. He became the heir after your father died, and his sons moved into the line of succession. The earl wouldn't have let any of you claim your inheritance."

"My parents were lawfully married!" Bryce huffed.

"Your grandfather and uncle contended they weren't, that all of you were illegitimate."

"We could never prove any of this, could we?"

"Well you *could*." Miss Etherton went to a desk in the corner and retrieved a satchel full of papers. "I have a marriage certificate."

"A marriage certificate!"

"You'd have to establish that it wasn't a forgery, and it's been thirty years." Miss Etherton handed the satchel to Bryce. "Here are my uncle's records. They include your birth certificate, as well as your sister's. The marriage certificate is on the bottom."

Bryce pulled out a small journal and showed it to Miss Etherton. "What is this?"

"My uncle kept records of all that transpired, and he jotted down information that Mr. Thumberton sent after he checked on you."

"Why have Thumberton do it?" Evangeline asked. "Why not come himself?"

"He was injured in a carriage accident and lost the use of his legs. After that misfortune, it was difficult for him to travel."

At the simple explanation for Thumberton's visits, Evangeline tamped down a smile. She'd wasted many hours trying to figure out why Thumberton had checked on them, why Etherton hadn't. She'd invented scenarios and plots, when the easiest explanation clarified the mystery. Mr. Etherton hadn't visited because he wasn't able.

"Your uncle paid our tuition?" Bryce asked.

"Yes."

"That was kind of him."

"As I mentioned," Miss Etherton said, "he loved your father and aided you children because of that affection. He merely wished he'd been wealthier. He wanted you at better schools and in better circumstances, but he did what he could with what he had."

"I've been wondering something," Evangeline said. "Why was my name changed?"

"The woman who owned the school…"

"Miss Peabody."

"Yes, that's her. She was a stickler for the proprieties, and when she was pressing my uncle for details about you, he wasn't a very good liar. She was dubious over the story he'd concocted as to how he'd come to be your guardian. She wouldn't let you remain as a student if there was scandal attached to your name."

"So he gave me his name instead."

"Yes, they decided it should be changed."

Again, Evangeline had fretted over plots and scheming as to her name, but there was no mystery involved.

Miss Peabody had been a stern, grumpy taskmaster who'd never liked Evangeline. Evangeline could absolutely see Miss Peabody demanding Evangeline's past be hidden from the other students.

"What of our brothers?" Bryce inquired.

Miss Etherton sighed, looking very sad. "The twins. Michael and Matthew."

"What happened to them?"

"I have no idea."

"We all left the dock that day," Bryce said. "A man carried the twins away—one under each arm."

"Yes, he was my uncle's servant. He and his wife were supposed to take the twins to the school my uncle had arranged."

"Why didn't they simply go with me?"

"My uncle was afraid of your relatives, and matters were hectic. As with your mother, I don't believe he was thinking clearly. He was the only one who'd stood by her through the trial and sentencing, and he felt it would be safer if you were separated. Plus he couldn't find a headmaster who would accept all three of you boys when you were so young."

"They never arrived at their destination?"

"No. They stayed overnight at a coaching inn, but there was a terrible fire."

Evangeline and Bryce gasped, and with a huge amount of dread, Evangeline asked, "They perished in the fire?"

"No. The servant and his wife passed away though."

"And the twins?"

"Vanished off the face of the Earth."

"Your uncle searched for them?"

"Until the day he died, but there was no trace." Miss Etherton pointed to the satchel. "There are notes about the fire and about the leads my uncle pursued."

"They could be alive then, couldn't they?" Evangeline's hope flared again, and she prayed it wasn't misplaced.

"Yes, they could be alive," Miss Etherton replied, "but you should proceed cautiously. I'd hate for this to cause more heartache than it already has."

"I'm grateful for your uncle's assistance," Bryce told her. "He was good to us."

"He tried to be, but he always felt he'd failed you—and your parents. He went to his grave feeling he'd failed."

Miss Etherton sighed again, and they were silent, reflecting on the enormous implications of the news they'd received. Bryce posed a few more questions, and Evangeline posed a few more too. They finished the tea then prepared to depart.

While they waited for a maid to retrieve their cloaks and hats, Miss Etherton said, "Oh, I have one more thing for you. Two things actually."

She hurried out of the room and down the hall. Momentarily she returned, and she'd brought two portraits. She gave one to Bryce and one to Evangeline.

"Our parents?" Evangeline asked.

"Yes. Your father had them painted to celebrate their marriage."

"Can we…have them?"

"Yes, yes, of course. They're yours. I've been keeping them for you all these years."

Bryce had the one of their mother, and he held it out so Evangeline could see. Their mother was blond and blue-eyed and very, very beautiful.

"You look just like her," Bryce said.

"What a precious compliment, my dear brother."

They studied the picture of their father who was tall, fit, handsome, and imposing. He looked like Bryce, and he had their same striking blue eyes, but he had dark hair rather than blond.

"They were so young," Bryce murmured.

"Your mother was twenty when they met," Miss Etherton said. "Your father was twenty-five."

"It was love at first sight, don't you imagine?" Evangeline couldn't help asking.

"I'm sure it was," Miss Etherton agreed.

They made their goodbyes and walked out to their carriage. It was late in the afternoon, and they had booked lodging at a nearby inn. They would leave for London in the morning.

"What do you think of that?" Evangeline queried once they were sequestered inside the carriage.

"I *think* I'm a bloody earl. You can call me *my lord*."

She chuckled. "It suits you."

"When I was a boy, I'd brag that my father was an aristocrat, but I thought it was an orphan's boasting. There were so many wealthy students at my school, many of whom had fathers who were members of the peerage. I was desperate to believe my own father was a man of status and not a fisherman or butcher."

"It doesn't surprise me to learn you're highborn. I've always deemed you to be remarkable."

He froze, then smiled. "I just had a memory."

"What was it?"

"Of Father. He was tossing me in the air and saying, *'how's my little lord today?'*"

They had memories that came on them in bits and pieces. Sometimes they made sense, sometimes not.

"That's lovely, Bryce. Really. It's very lovely."

They beamed with pleasure, and Evangeline asked, "What now?"

"My head's spinning, and I'm bewildered. I suppose I should travel to Scotland and take a peek at Radcliffe. It might be interesting to see what I lost because my grandfather was an obnoxious cur."

"I'll travel with you. Aaron can join us, and we'll—"

"No, I'll go alone the first time. I'll decide if you should eventually visit too."

Evangeline was in the family way, her condition not yet overly visible, and everyone expected her to tiptoe around like an invalid.

"It wouldn't kill me," she scoffed.

"It might."

"I'm not a shrinking violet, you know."

"Yes, I know."

"What is your guess about Mother? Is she still alive?"

"I wouldn't speculate, but you can start investigating while I'm in Scotland."

"What about the twins?"

He lifted the satchel Miss Etherton had given to him. "I'll read Mr. Etherton's notes and figure out how to proceed from there."

"We'll find them, Bryce. We'll find all of them."

"Here's hoping, my eternal optimist. Here's hoping indeed."

CHAPTER THIRTEEN

Ramsey stood in front of the Vicar Sterns Rescue Mission and watched Rebecca's carriage approach. At least he hoped it was her carriage. If it wasn't, he'd slink away and pretend he hadn't been waiting on pins and needles like a besotted idiot.

He had no decent intentions toward her, and if Michael ever learned what Ramsey had set in motion, there'd be hell to pay, so Ramsey had no idea what he was thinking. He blamed it on his rash nature.

As a boy, he'd grown up poor and hungry. Now though he was tough, wealthy, and cocky enough to feel that he should have whatever he wanted. He *took* what he wanted, and for some reason, Rebecca Wells had wound up on the top of his list.

Magdalena Wells had volunteers in charge while she was off with Michael, and it had been easy to lie to them and claim her sister was coming to stay while Miss Magdalena was away. Ramsey was well known in the neighborhood, and none of them had questioned his story.

Rebecca's sister would be gone for a month and perhaps much longer than that if she pleased Michael. Why shouldn't Ramsey take advantage?

By the time Michael brought Miss Magdalena back to London, Ramsey was sure he and Rebecca would be sick of each other. He'd have sent her home, or she'd have left on her own. Why not misbehave while he had the chance?

He'd given her money so she could travel to town. He'd been curious to discover how serious she was, if she was the swooning sort, which she didn't seem to be. Would she actually come? Would she dare? How anxious was she to escape the misery at Cliffside?

The hackney rattled to a stop, and she popped up in the window.

"My goodness, am I glad to see you!" she gushed. "I couldn't decide if you'd be here or not."

"I told you I would be."

"Yes, but I don't exactly know you, and I don't especially suppose you're very reliable."

"I'm reliable as hell."

She glanced up at the mission and wrinkled her nose. "That has to be the dreariest building in the kingdom. I can't believe my sister's lived in it for seven years."

"It's nicer now than it was in the past."

Ramsey had resided there off and on when it was old Mr. Scott's orphanage. When Scott had owned it, it had been an awful, decrepit place. But he'd passed away, and Vicar Sterns had shown up with a fistful of money for remodeling. It was clean. The roof didn't leak. The chimneys worked.

Ramsey walked over and opened the carriage door. She fell into his arms, and he whirled her and set her on her feet.

"You didn't bring a ton of luggage, did you?" he asked.

"You said not to." She pointed to a portmanteau on the floor. "I just have the one bag, so I hope you're not expecting me to attire myself like a society lady."

He expected her to be naked—if he could coax her out of her clothes.

He reached inside and grabbed the portmanteau. "Look around. Does it appear as if you'll be dressing all posh and going to the theater?"

She wrinkled her nose again. "This street is horrid."

"You don't get out much, do you?"

"No. I've lived at Cliffside all my life. I'm afraid I'm a snob."

"It's not so bad after you get used to it."

"What if I never do?"

"I'll send you home. Or you can leave. It's not as if you're my prisoner."

He threw a few coins to the driver, and the fellow clicked the reins and scooted off. It wasn't an area where he'd want to linger.

She sniffed the air. "What's that smell?"

"The docks. The sewer. The rats."

"Ew!"

"Like I said, you'll get used to it."

She leaned nearer and whispered, "Are you certain my sister is gone?"

"For at least a month."

"Where is she again? From your letter, I didn't understand where she was."

"She's in the country with Michael."

Rebecca frowned. "With Michael Scott? What for?"

Ramsey wasn't about to explain the devil's bargain between Michael and Gaylord Farrow. He shrugged and lied. "He has a grand house, and she didn't believe he'd own something so fine. She demanded to see it."

"For a whole month? It must be really big."

"It is." Luckily she didn't press the issue, so he didn't have to invent any further stories.

"If she comes back early and I'm still here, what will I tell her?"

"Tell her the truth. You couldn't abide Farrow another second."

She grinned. "That will work, and it's definitely the truth!"

Ramsey had promised to find her lodging, and he probably would, but he hadn't decided. Was she worth the bother? If she was spoiled and impossible, if she was dull in performing her bedroom duties, he wouldn't want to be saddled with her for very long.

He gestured to the open door of the mission, and she strolled inside. For all that she purportedly cared about her sister, she didn't exhibit much curiosity.

"Where is my bedchamber?" she asked.

"This way."

He went to the stairs and climbed, and she clomped up behind him.

He'd already snooped through Miss Wells's private rooms, and they'd suit for Rebecca and what he intended while her sister was away. He entered and walked straight to the bedchamber, dropping her portmanteau on the bed.

She peered about, taking in the dilapidated furnishings. "Is this my sister's apartment?"

"Yes."

"I suppose it will do." She plopped her bottom on the mattress, her blue eyes alight with mischief. "What now?"

"Are you hungry?"

"No."

"Are you tired?"

"A little."

If she was nervous it didn't show, but then she'd traveled to town specifically to ally herself with him in an illicit fashion. It was too late to fret.

She shed her cloak and bonnet and tossed them on the chair, but her hips were still balanced on the mattress. It was a small room—the whole place was small—and he was a large man, so with one step he was right next to her.

"What did you tell Pamela about coming to the city?" he asked.

"I claimed I'd been invited to watch over things while Maggie is away."

"She didn't try to stop you?"

"She tried, but I told her to stuff it."

"That's my girl."

She flashed a sly look. "Am I your girl, Mr. Scott?"

"We'll see what you turn out to be, but you should call me Ramsey. It'll save us from being confused over whether you mean me or Michael."

"I imagine you'd like to call me Rebecca."

"Don't be a shrew about it or we'll get off on the wrong foot. If you hitch your wagon to mine, you'll need to lower your standards. I don't care for snooty manners or putting on airs."

"I can't have you thinking me a snob, so you may call me whatever you like."

"I will. Now let down your hair."

"Why?"

"Because I want it flowing down your back."

"Then I certainly will. I'm here to make you happy."

"Yes, you are."

"How's that?" she asked as she tugged out a few combs, and the brunette mass tumbled down.

"Perfect."

"Ramsey?"

"Yes?"

"What if I don't make you happy? Will you send me back to Cliffside?"

"It won't be yours to go back to."

"But Gaylord claimed it was settled between him and Mr. Scott, and we don't have to leave."

"I wouldn't take your brother-in-law's word for anything."

"He was lying?"

"Not exactly, but the conclusion he's envisioning won't be the one that actually occurs."

"Why is that?"

"Because he's a vain prick, and Michael loathes him, and that's all I'll say about it. So don't ask me again."

"Yes, sir, as you wish, sir." She gave a jaunty salute—as if she was a private in the army.

She was wearing a pert little jacket, with a row of fussy buttons down the front. He started unbuttoning them, and her first fit of nerves was displayed.

"Are we about to…to…"

She couldn't finish the sentence, and he finished it for her. "No, not this afternoon. I have to get back to work."

She sighed with relief. "I realize you expect some intimate behavior from me."

"In my world, there's a price for everything. You have to pay it to reimburse me for my trouble."

"I understand," she hastily said. "I just don't know what I'm supposed to do."

"I'll show you."

"All right."

"But it will be tonight. I live my life in the dark and sleep the day away, and I have to make sure matters are running smoothly at the club. With Michael away, it's my responsibility."

"That's fine."

"So you should nap, because it will be the wee hours when I arrive, and we'll likely be up into the morning."

He was suffering some qualms over deflowering her on her sister's bed. Typically he wouldn't have worried about it, but he liked Magdalena Wells, and he was preparing to use her sister in awful ways. For an instant, he wondered if maybe he shouldn't, which was ridiculous. He never hesitated, never refused to take what he craved.

He pushed the jacket off her shoulders to reveal a gown with a neckline that was cut very low. Her corset was laced tight, so she was exhibiting a spectacular amount of cleavage.

The sight had him considering a delay in his return to the club. But no! He wouldn't rush this event. He had to ease her into the sexual activity. If he didn't, she'd be unenthused whenever he wanted to fornicate with her, and he suspected he'd want to quite a bit.

Her dress buttoned in the back. He drew her to her feet and quickly undid the fastenings, then he shoved the garment down to her ankles so she was attired in her corset and petticoat.

As he studied her, he had to give her credit. She didn't flinch from his salacious assessment.

"Turn around," he told her.

"Why?"

"I want to unlace your corset."

"I thought you had to get back to work."

"I do, but that doesn't mean I can't have some fun first."

She glowered as if he might have finally pushed her too far, but in the end she spun and let him remove it. She had a faded chemise underneath, and he tugged it off too, so her upper torso was bare and she was clad in just her petticoat and shoes.

He snuggled himself to her back, reached around and grabbed her nipples.

She gasped with surprise and complained, "You might have warned me what you were about."

"Get used to it. I plan to touch you when it suits me, but you'll like it."

"I'd better, or you won't have your way for long."

He snorted and twirled her so she was facing him. Her cheeks were flushed, and she wouldn't look him in the eye.

"What's wrong?" he asked.

"It's too much too soon."

"It will be worse tonight."

She scowled. "Why?"

"I have to train you as if you're a filly learning how to be ridden."

"That doesn't clarify anything."

"I guarantee you'll like it though."

He eased her hips onto the bed and tipped her so her body was lying on the mattress, her feet on the floor. He spread her thighs and stepped in, her petticoat bunched up and providing a fine cushion to cradle his cock against her private parts.

He clasped her hands, shackling her wrists over her head, and he stared down at her breasts. They were just the right size, pert and round, the pink nipples jutting out. He dipped down and sucked on one, then the other, keeping at it until she was squirming and moaning with pleasure.

As he drew away, he realized he was desperately anxious to dawdle in her company, and his heightened interest was frightening.

He never grew attached to women—in his world, they were all doxies—but for some odd reason, he wanted a connection with *her*. He'd already played the role of knight gallant to save her from her dastardly brother-in-law. If he wasn't careful, what insane acts might she spur him to in the future?

He pulled away and she sat up.

"Are we done?" she asked. "Is that it?"

"For now, but I'll be back. You can fall asleep if you like, and I'll wake you after I'm here."

"What should I do in the meantime?"

"Tarry in the apartment. Don't go for a walk. Don't explore the neighborhood."

She pouted. "Why can't I?"

"Because it's dangerous, you naïve ninny. This isn't Cliffside, and you're a green girl from the country. You'd likely get your throat slit."

"What if I'm bored?"

"Then you're bored. Don't go out! If you'd like to see the sights, I'll show you around town."

"Are you always so grouchy?"

"It's your fault I'm testy. I'm riled up and eager to sample your wares."

"You make everything sound so crass."

"If you wanted poetry and sweet-talk, you should have stayed in the country."

"I don't want poetry, but some sweet-talk once in a while would be welcome."

"I'll think on it." He bent down and kissed a nipple, kissed the other one, then stood. "I'll send over some supper."

"Thank you."

"And I'll have some underclothes delivered too."

"What's wrong with what I'm wearing?"

"I like a woman in pretty things, and yours are too plain. A frilly corset makes me frisky."

"Then bring me the frilliest one you can find."

He went out to the door, and as he glanced over his shoulder, she was still seated on the bed. She looked lovely and lonely, and he had to force himself away before he lost the will to go.

"Come over and lock the door," he said, "and don't let anyone in but me."

"What if I don't hear you knocking later tonight?"

"I'll enter through the window."

"Oh."

She walked over, and as she neared, the air fairly sizzled with erotic promise, as if sparks might ignite, and he grinned.

"We'll get on swimmingly, Rebecca."

"I hope so, or I've wasted a lot of energy and effort. I'm pinning my hopes on you, Ramsey. Don't disappoint me."

"Well, I usually disappoint everyone, but I'll try not to this time."

"I appreciate it."

He took a final caress of her breasts, then he yanked away and stepped out. He waited and waited, listening for the key to grate in the lock. When it didn't, he said, "Rebecca, don't forget about the door."

"Oh, oh, yes."

The lock clicked into place, and he rolled his eyes and kept on down the hall.

"Michael?"

"No, no, don't…"

"Michael!"

Maggie leaned over and shook him. They were in the midst of another picnic, which had become an afternoon habit for them.

They spent long hours riding through the countryside. He'd espy a picturesque spot by a stream or on a hill, and they'd plop down a blanket and loaf the day away. They always brought an easel and canvas, and she painted the scenery while he lay next to her and made a pest of himself.

For once, they'd remained home and were lounged under a large elm tree in the garden behind his house. He'd dozed off, and she'd been watching him sleep, thinking he appeared very young, much as he must have as a boy. She felt a stab of sorrow for his mother who had missed seeing him grow up.

But suddenly his peaceful nap had morphed into an awful nightmare.

"Michael!" she said more firmly, and she shook him again.

He lurched up, his hands thrust out as if he was desperately reaching for someone, his motions so violently frantic that she had to jump out of the way. He stared off to the hills in the distance, then gradually his vision cleared, his senses returning.

"Are you all right?" She rested a comforting palm on his back.

"Yes…I'm fine." He didn't look fine.

"You were having a bad dream."

He shuddered, the images rocking him. "Ah…I hate that one."

"You have it often?"

"Not often. Just…occasionally." He was sheepish and embarrassed.

"What's it about?"

He made a waffling gesture. "It's merely some ancient twaddle."

"No, tell me. I want to know."

"It must be something that occurred when I was little."

"Is it the fire you told me about?"

"No, before that."

"It's an old memory, then. You must have been very young."

"Or maybe it's not me at all." He scowled. "It seems to be me though, but there are always two of me."

"Two of you?"

"Yes, I'm two boys."

"What could it indicate? Were you split in half? Have you a twin that you don't recollect?"

She mentioned a twin in jest, but the word shocked him, as if she'd poked him with a pin. He stared off into the distance again, holding very still, then he scoffed.

"How could I have a twin and not remember? That's the sort of detail a fellow would never forget."

"What's happening in the dream?" He simply grinned his devil's grin, and when it became obvious he wouldn't answer, she ordered, "Spill all, you thick oaf."

He considered, then confessed, "I'm at the docks—with some people."

"Children or adults?"

"Both, but I don't understand what's transpiring. It's bad though, with crying and quarreling. There's a man there, and he sends me away."

"My goodness."

"This time, there was a third boy too. He said to the man, *how can I watch over them if they go away?* The man said back, *you'll see them again very soon.*"

"What do you suppose it means?"

"I told you I don't know," he testily replied. "I've never known."

"Then what happens?"

"I'm staring at myself—eye to eye and nose to nose—and I can read the other boy's mind. *We'll get even,* we tell each other in our heads."

"Get even for what?"

He shrugged. "It's a dream, Maggie. It could signify anything—or nothing. A different man picks me up, but he picks up two of me, one under each arm and…" He stopped and thought and thought. "And then you woke me up."

"In your dream, you were reaching out to someone."

"Was I? I don't recall."

A cloud drifted over the sun so the light dimmed and the temperature cooled. It was an eerie moment, almost as if the heavens were peering down and mourning his story. He felt it too. He shivered and pushed himself to his feet.

Off on the horizon, thunderheads were building, an afternoon storm approaching.

"I've had enough picnicking for today," he said.

"The weather wouldn't dare spoil our fun."

"I'm expecting it might." He nodded to the house. "Let's hurry inside. I don't want you to get soaked. You might catch a chill."

"Or *you* might. I'm much too hardy to be sickened by some paltry raindrops."

Though she hated to admit it, their sojourn in the country had become a splendid idyll, and she frequently found herself wishing they never had to return to the city.

They'd already frittered away a whole week, and while he constantly claimed they had to leave, that he had to get back to his many business enterprises, he'd quickly change his mind.

He was folding up the blanket, and she was inordinately pleased to see him involved in such a domestic chore. It seemed as if they were sweethearts or perhaps newlyweds.

Throughout her entire visit, except for that first night when he'd been a beast, he'd been thoroughly charming. He doted on her, spoiled her, listened to her, entertained her, and generally made her more welcome than she'd ever been anywhere.

Though it was ludicrous to assume so, he appeared to have developed fond feelings for her, and she wasn't too sure about her own sentiments.

He kept surprising her. In the evenings, he'd light a fire in the grate, and she'd read to him or they'd talk. On a few occasions, he'd actually sung songs and played the pianoforte to accompany himself. They were bawdy songs with indecent lyrics, such as you'd hear in a saloon, but still, when he finished she'd smile and wildly applaud.

He insisted he'd never had a single lesson, so how could he be so musically inclined? The short, private concerts had her thinking he'd shown her a side of himself he'd never shown to anyone else, and the notion thrilled her.

There was only one detail that bothered her, and it was the fact that he hadn't seduced her again. He was unceasingly polite, and he always gazed warmly, as if there were affectionate words he'd like to speak aloud, but he couldn't voice them.

There were quiet moments too—when he'd escort her into the dining room for supper or when he'd walk her to her room at bedtime—where she thought he might kiss her. But he hadn't tried, and she couldn't decide how she felt about his clear lack of interest.

While she should have been relieved that he'd left her alone, she suspected she'd failed to satisfy him in a carnal fashion she didn't understand. Women had many feminine wiles, and they used them with striking effect, but Maggie had never had the chance to discover what they were. She knew how to kiss a man and that was it.

She often caught herself reflecting on the trollops who filled his world, and she wished she'd learned some of their wicked habits, because she was increasingly overcome by memories of him without his shirt. As a spinster, she hadn't fathomed that a man's body could be so stirring and beautiful, and she was vexed by the recollection.

He'd touched her in exciting ways that had provoked and aggravated her, as if her veins had been scraped raw. She was chafing, anxious for some sort of respite, but she had no idea how to attain it for herself. *He* knew all kinds of devious behaviors that could allay her suffering, but she was too shy to beg him to show them to her.

And she didn't actually want him to. Did she? She was happy with their relaxing holiday. Or maybe she wasn't.

Oh, wasn't she a mess! What was it she truly desired? She couldn't figure it out and was certain that—whatever she chose—she'd regret it later on.

He handed her the blanket, then gathered up her art supplies and their picnic basket, and they headed in. At the rear door, as she reached for the knob, he stole a quick kiss.

"I'm having a wonderful time," he said. "I'm glad you're here with me."

"So am I."

"It's pleasant to be out of the city. Usually I don't like it, but you've made it worth my while to linger."

It was on the tip of her tongue to ask when they'd leave, when he'd determine he'd had enough frivolity, but the prospect of departure caused a wave of anguish to sweep through her. If he declared himself ready to go, their friendship would end, and she might never see him again.

A footman saved them by opening the door from the inside, and he relieved them of their burdens then slipped away so they were alone again.

They stared at each other, and his affection was plainly visible. Would he announce heightened sentiment? If he mentioned burgeoning emotion, how would she reply? Would she admit to growing smitten too? Would she dare? Probably not. There was no benefit to be gained by pursuing a relationship.

Yet no rousing comment was uttered. He stepped away, his evident fondness neatly tucked away as if it had never been there at all.

"Will you be upset if I vanish for a few hours?" he asked.

Since that first morning, he hadn't been off the property without her, and the news that he would abandon her—even if it was just for a bit—was incredibly distressing.

But she forced a wide smile. "I'm sure I can manage."

"I'll tell Cook to fix you a delicious supper."

"I can tell her myself. I could have a tray of bread and cheese sent up to my room. There's no need for anyone to fuss."

"I want them to fuss."

"If you insist," she teased. "I enjoy how everyone spoils me."

"Good."

He surprised her with another quick kiss. Two kisses in a matter of minutes? What did it portend? Perhaps it was an odd sort of farewell.

Since she'd awakened him from his nightmare, he'd been disoriented.

"You seem a tad...lost." She couldn't think of a better word to describe how he looked. "You're coming back, aren't you?"

"Of course I'm coming back."

"Promise?"

"Yes. I need some fresh air. I'll take a long ride and clear my head."

"It might rain, remember?"

"I won't melt. I'm tougher than you."

"I doubt it."

They were grinning, gaping like halfwits. He slipped his hand into hers and gave her fingers a tight squeeze.

"If it storms, you hurry home." She'd scolded him as if she was his wife, as if it was perfectly appropriate for her to chastise.

"Yes, ma'am."

"I'll worry if you don't."

"I'll be fine, Magdalena."

He stole another kiss then sauntered down the hall. She hovered by the rear door, fighting the urge to chase after him, to beseech him not to go. But she refused to embarrass herself with such a blatant display of emotion. She wasn't an adolescent girl in the throes of her first amour, and she wouldn't act like it.

She dawdled, listening as he murmured instructions to a servant in the foyer. Then the front door opened and closed.

Slowly, she walked to the main parlor and she huddled behind the drapes, watching the lane that led out to the road, standing in the shadows until he rode off. She kept watching until he exited through the gate, until he was swallowed up by the trees, then she went over to the sofa and eased herself down.

The house was so quiet with him gone—as if he'd taken all the vitality with him when he left. The only sound was the ticking of the clock on the mantle, and it dawned on her that—without him sitting beside her—she was the loneliest person in the world.

CHAPTER FOURTEEN

Michael tiptoed into Maggie's bedchamber and stood next to the bed.

She was sleeping, looking young and pretty, and the oddest wave of protectiveness surged through him.

She inspired a host of peculiar emotions he'd never supposed he could experience with a woman. She made him laugh, made him relish the hours they'd wasted together.

He shouldn't have tarried with her for a single minute, should have returned her to her brother-in-law, untouched, unsullied, and told Farrow he didn't like her and wasn't interested. But the sorry fact was that he liked her very much and was afraid maybe he *more* than liked her, and now he wasn't sure what to do with her.

He was too disconcerted to decide such an important matter, *and* he was about to marry someone else—a pertinent detail he kept conveniently forgetting.

The bad dream he'd suffered at their picnic had rattled him. Usually he marched through the world without being sidetracked by peripheral issues. He was dispassionate and unsentimental, but old recollections had reared up to plague him, and he often felt as if he was racing toward some kind of violent collision.

The wounds from his past had wreaked significant damage that he hated to acknowledge, and he'd never understood why they'd been inflicted or why they continued to haunt him. Yet when he was around Maggie, the painful memories weren't nearly so excruciating.

As he'd ridden in the rain, as he'd galloped down deserted country roads and let himself be pummeled by the deluge, he'd begun to question whether he shouldn't accept Gaylord Farrow's terms.

If Michael ruined her, he'd have the right to keep her for six months, would be able to fill his days and nights with her. And if he pressed ahead, he refused to think of it as a ruination. A bond had developed between them, and he was certain she'd agree to his proposition—if he posed it correctly.

During their affair he'd shower her with gifts and affection, and when he was finished with her, he'd set her up with a trust fund so she'd always have an allowance, so she'd never have to work again. It was much more than most women could ever hope to receive.

He wondered if she owned the building where the rescue mission was located. If so, he'd buy it from her and give her that money too. If she didn't, he'd find out the identity of the owner, purchase the property and shut it down so she *couldn't* work, so she had to take the allowance.

No, there would be no ruination. There would be joy and companionship and financial reward when it was over.

He eased a hip onto the mattress, and she frowned but didn't awaken.

"Magdalena," he murmured.

Her eyelids fluttered open, and on seeing him, she smiled. "You're back."

"Of course I'm back. I told you I'd be fine."

"I was so worried. I sat by the window for hours, watching for you."

It was the sweetest remark she could have uttered, and the comment had his heart lurching in his chest. He couldn't remember a single time when anyone had waited up for him. Ramsey did occasionally, but he didn't count.

Her fondness had him soaring with elation, and he yearned to cradle her to his chest and offer boons he would never actually deliver. She stirred his manly instincts, but he never made promises because he never kept them. So he bit down on every tantalizing, declarative word that was begging to spill out.

He'd been drenched in the rain, so he'd changed clothes, but his hair was still damp. She ran her fingers through it and scolded, "I warned you not to get wet. I hope you don't catch a chill."

"I'm too tough to catch a chill."

"If you do, I'll feed you chicken soup and stroke your fevered brow until you're better."

"You've convinced me to fall ill merely so you'll have to take care of me."

"I'll be the best nurse you ever had."

She'd be the *only* nurse he'd ever had. In his chaotic orphan's existence there hadn't been any doting females, and as an adult, the women who crossed his path were a rougher sort who weren't known for their nurturing tendencies.

"I missed you," he admitted.

"You were only gone for a few hours."

"Yes, but you're growing on me, and apparently I can't bear to be away from you."

"Should I tell you a secret?"

"Absolutely."

"I missed you too, but you're much too vain already so don't gloat."

"We're a sorry pair, aren't we?"

"We definitely are."

"I've never brought a woman to Orphan's Nest before."

"You'd mentioned that you hadn't. Why was I so lucky? Am I special to you?"

"Yes, you silly girl. Why would you suppose you're here?"

"I *suppose* I'm here because of that ridiculous wager. You dragged me to the country with bad intentions."

"It hasn't all been horrid, has it?"

"No."

"I started off with dastardly plans, but I abandoned them."

"I've appreciated it."

When he was around her, he couldn't help but feel splendid, but since that night when he'd barged in and tried to scare her, he'd avoided even the most minimal dalliance. The intimacy of it had been more than he could abide.

She was like a dangerous drug infecting his blood, which was the real reason for his lengthy ride. In the new blue dress he'd bought her, with her straw bonnet—bow tied under her chin—she'd been so pretty. He hadn't been able to resist and had stolen a few quick kisses as they'd walked in his rear door. There had been such a sense of destiny, of belonging with her, that he'd been disturbed by the powerful emotions and had fled.

But he was back, his mind was clear, and he knew exactly what he wanted from her. He was certain he could persuade her to provide it.

"Are you all right?" she asked.

"Yes, I'm perfect."

"You look sad."

He chuckled. "You always assume there's something wrong with me."

"That's because there always is."

"I've never had anyone worry about me before."

"Then I am thrilled to be the first, and if you'll let me I'll fuss like a doting nanny."

"I didn't think I'd like having a woman fuss, but maybe I'm changing."

"Just wait until you've spent more time with me," she saucily said. "After I'm through with you, there's no telling what you'll be like."

"You'll make me a better man?"

"You don't stand a chance, my poor fellow."

She was correct that she could have an enormous impact on his behavior and attitudes. There was no question he was rough around the edges, that he could be arrogant and stubborn and unbelievably violent. There was definitely room for improvement, and it would be amusing to have her trying to mold him.

"You're so good for me," he confessed. "I'm glad you're here."

"Even if it was under nefarious circumstances?"

"Yes. You don't hate me anymore, do you?"

"No, I don't hate you. In fact, I've decided you're rather grand."

"Grand! Well…" He laughed, contentment washing over him. "I'm incredibly flattered by your high opinion."

She sighed. "I wish we never had to leave."

"Really? Would you forsake your life in the city and stay here with me?"

"If you asked me, I might."

He studied her, then snorted. "You liar. You never would. You'd be bored to death in two seconds. You're too much like me."

"Heaven forbid! I'm nothing like you."

"I just mean we like to be busy."

"I'll agree to that tiny similarity, but that's the only one. I'd be an awful lady of leisure. I've spent too many years working to earn my keep."

"And I've spent too many years being a lout, but we enjoy being active."

"Yes."

For a moment Felicia popped into his mind.

He didn't intend to ever bring her to Orphan's Nest. She was accustomed to ostentatious surroundings, so he'd give her Cliffside, which would suit her.

But he tried to envision her with him at Orphan's Nest as he'd been with Maggie. He tried to imagine what they'd talk about, how they'd get on, but he couldn't picture it.

Perhaps it was because Maggie was seven years older than Felicia, or perhaps it was the broken heart Maggie had suffered at seventeen. The tragedy had taught her that life could crush you, that it could pitch you off into a tempest you never expected. It had forced her to learn how to acclimate and carry on.

Felicia had recently encountered her initial bout with adversity, and as a remedy she would simply trade her father's extravagant mansion for Michael's. She'd had no experiences to mature her, so she'd never understand Michael or care about the strife that had shaped him.

Magdalena cared about those things, and a wave of sadness bubbled up, but he shoved it away. He wasn't marrying Felicia for companionship or solicitude. He was marrying her to enrage her father, to put him in his place, to bluster his way into the circles of the aristocracy.

After the newness of being Felicia's husband wore off—and he was sure it would occur rapidly—he doubted he'd ever see her. He wouldn't ponder Felicia, not when he was lying on a bed with Maggie. He tugged back the blankets and stretched out on top of her.

She scowled. "What are you thinking?"

"I want to misbehave with you."

"Well, *I* don't want to misbehave with you."

"Don't you?"

He pinched her nipple, and her whole body shuddered, right down to the tips of her toes.

"If you're not interested," he said, "you shouldn't let a man into your bedchamber."

She scoffed. "If I remember correctly, I was asleep. I didn't *let* you. You barged in."

"You're glad I did. Admit it."

"I might be a little glad. But just a little."

"I'm dying to know you in a manner I haven't so far," he told her.

"Meaning what?"

"You know *what*."

She was shocked by his suggestion, but then it was his own fault. He'd allowed her to presume he didn't desire her, that he didn't fantasize about fornicating with her every minute of the day.

She induced a constant and strange sort of yearning, and he'd decided to stop fighting it, to let it flourish, to let it lead him wherever it would.

She shook her head. "I can guess what you're contemplating, and I don't want it from you."

"You're a spinster and a virgin, Magdalena. You have no idea what you want."

"It's a sin. It's wrong."

He shrugged. "The preachers claim it is."

"You disagree?"

"Yes."

"You would." She rolled her eyes. "People are supposed to wed first."

"Sometimes they do, but not usually. Not in my world."

"I wouldn't necessarily assume your world is typical."

"Wouldn't you? How many female friends have you had who've had a baby six months after the wedding? The babies look perfectly normal—even though they're three months early."

"Oh."

"And how about your sister and Farrow? Didn't they dally before the wedding?"

"Oh."

"I rest my case."

"Just because others behave badly, there's no reason we should imitate them. When I walk down this road, I plan to have a husband walking with me. Why do I expect you don't have matrimony in mind afterward?"

I can't marry you. I'm about to marry someone else.

He didn't mention Felicia though. She and Maggie occupied two different parts of his life, and those two parts didn't intersect. Besides, Maggie was very moralistic. If she learned of his betrothal, she'd never permit him to join her in her bed again, and the thought of her kicking him out was distressing.

"I might have matrimony in mind," he petulantly insisted.

"Now who's lying? You're a confirmed bachelor. I'm certain of it."

"Maybe you're so wonderful I'm sick of being a bachelor. Maybe I've decided I should be a husband instead."

She laughed and laughed. "You're hilarious."

"Why?"

"Because rumor has it that when a man is suffering from a fit of ardor he'll say anything to persuade a woman to lift her skirt."

"Or her nightgown."

"I'm smart enough to realize I shouldn't proceed unless I have a ring on my finger. Which you would never give me, and which I would never demand. I've sworn off men, remember?"

"You always claim you have, but you're an innocent where physical amour is concerned. You might find you can't live without it."

"I've made it twenty-five years so far."

"What if you dropped over dead this very instant?" he asked. "You'd die without ever discovering what it was like."

"I'll risk it."

"You're a hard woman, Magdalena Wells."

"So I've been told."

"May I kiss you goodnight."

She pretended to consider, then smiled. "I suppose I could allow it. Just the one though! Don't push your luck."

"Haven't you heard? I always push my luck, and I always wind up getting exactly what I want."

As Michael pulled her close, she felt as if she was soaring, as if she was lighter than air. Since the day she'd arrived at Orphan's Nest, she'd been waiting for him to kiss her urgently and frequently, and she couldn't fathom why he'd been so reticent. During that previous carnal foray, he'd goaded her into a wild paroxysm of pleasure, had left her agitated and disturbed, and while she'd kept telling herself she'd rebuff any seduction, she'd been lying.

When he'd mentioned a goodnight kiss, she'd thought he'd bestow a quick peck like the one he'd delivered at the conclusion of their picnic earlier in the afternoon. But clearly he had other ideas.

He was kissing her as if it was their final farewell, as if the world was about to end and he would never see her again. She should have remained stoically detached, but she couldn't ignore what was happening and couldn't fail to participate.

She was tugging at his shirt, desperate to view his sculpted chest again. In her memories, it was delectable, and she was anxious to discern if her recollection was accurate or if her imagination had embellished what she'd witnessed.

She yanked the fabric up and off, with Michael having to help work it over his shoulders, then the offending article was gone. She had a moment to study him and was delighted to report that her memory had been extremely precise.

He was still kissing her and kissing her. He hadn't paused, hadn't slowed, and as the torrid embrace continued, she felt as if they were on a raft careening down a rampaging river. She couldn't halt their forward progress, couldn't temper their frantic pace. She could only hold on and hope she didn't crash on a rocky shore.

Gradually he was removing her nightgown, and she didn't lift a finger to prevent him. The hem glided up her legs, past her thighs, stomach, breasts.

He drew the garment up and over her head, and it was the perfect opportunity to protest, to tell him *no,* but she didn't say it. Apparently she was happy to march down the road to perdition without a word of complaint.

With her nightgown tossed on the floor, she was naked and as he stretched out again, her bared breasts were pressed to his chest. The sensation was so riveting she was amazed she didn't swoon.

He glanced down her body, looking decadent and very, very debauched, providing ample evidence that she had no business being in a bed with him. Nothing good could come from it. Or perhaps she was wrong. Perhaps something very, very good might come from it, but while she might deem it to be *good* in the heat of passion, she was quite sure in the morning she'd be aghast.

"You're so pretty, Maggie," he said.

"No one ever told me that before."

"The men you've known must have all been idiots."

"They were." She sighed and snuggled closer, and the feel of her nipples on his skin was so powerfully arousing that she wasn't certain what to make of it.

"We should probably stop," she stated with a halfhearted resolve.

"Not just yet. I'm not done."

"If you keep on much longer, I'm likely to burst into flames."

"Marvelous. I can't wait."

He started in again, and her meager dissent was over.

She was melting with desire and knew he could end her agony, but he was in no rush. Finally, finally, he abandoned her mouth and nibbled a trail to her bosom. He sucked on her nipple, laving it, biting it until she was writhing beneath him, calling him names, begging him to hurry.

At his instigation, she'd become wanton and loose, and she didn't mind a whit! She was a physical being who had no goal other than pleasure, and she wanted that pleasure to arrive immediately. She didn't care about modesty or decorum or anything else.

He touched her between her legs, and she shattered into a thousand pieces, flying to the heavens, then floating back down. He was preening, laughing, proudly vain that he pitched her into ecstasy.

"You are such a gem," he murmured.

"How do you do that to me?"

"It's easy. You have a very sexual nature, and I'm luring it to the fore."

"You're making me wicked."

"I'm not sorry."

"I can see that you're not."

Her limbs had turned to rubber, and she should have slid away to escape, but if she'd tried to stand she'd have collapsed to the floor in a heap.

Having learned some marital secrets, she wondered how a wife ever finished her daily chores. There was such delight to be had in a husband's arms. Why would a wife ever crawl out of her bed?

It dawned on her that there was a reason young ladies were so vigilantly chaperoned. Clearly there was a level of corporeal enticement that could lead a woman to ruin, that could leave her incapable of restraint.

Her entire life, there had been stories of girls who'd gotten themselves into trouble, and she'd scoffed with derision, deeming them weak of character or morally suspect. She hadn't realized—as other, wiser people obviously did—that carnal amour was devastatingly addicting and made it impossible to behave.

"I want you to do something for me," he said.

"What is it?"

"It's what I asked when we started."

"I couldn't proceed until after we were married."

"We don't have to be married to accomplish it."

"Why not?"

"It's more of this same physical conduct."

"Tell me what it involves."

"It's hard to describe. It's easier if I show you."

"Tell me," she repeated, needing to have some idea.

He cupped her with his palm. "I'd join my body to yours. Here."

"I don't understand what that means."

"That's why it's easier to show you."

She peered into his blue, blue eyes and he peered back, his handsome face open, beseeching.

When he looked at her so intently, she was confused about what was transpiring. How could he gaze at her like that unless he possessed genuine, heightened feelings? Initially they'd traveled to the country due to his despicable bargain with Gaylord, but had fondness blossomed? Had love bloomed? Was it possible?

She didn't imagine it was likely for a man like him, but occasionally she'd catch him staring off at the horizon, and he seemed so lonely. Maggie was lonely too.

Would he consider establishing a bond with her? Could it happen? If she gave herself to him, he'd have to wed her afterward. Morals demanded it. The law required it. The Church insisted on it.

He might fuss and complain, but she suspected that—deep down—he'd like very much to have a wife and a family. She could be that wife. She had no doubt. He'd beguiled her with his beautiful home, with his perfect manners, and if he wasn't in love with her, she was nearly a hundred percent in love with him.

He'd bought her a wardrobe of pretty clothes, had been kind and charming and remarkable, and in return he was asking her to do this one, simple thing. She hadn't ever believed that she would, but perhaps she should, perhaps it was time.

Still though, she hesitated.

"You'd have to wed me," she insisted. "If you say you will, I'll agree."

"Why would you want me for a husband? I'd be awful."

"You might not be. Actually, you might be just what I've always needed."

"I'm nobody's savior, and you shouldn't assume I might be."

"I think you'd make me happy, Michael Scott. And I think I would make *you* happy."

"I don't know if I've ever been happy."

"Then give me your vow that we'll wed after, and you'll be the happiest man in the kingdom."

"I will, will I?"

"Yes. You can't walk this far down an illicit road with me, but change course at the very end."

"No, I suppose I can't." He brushed his lips to hers. "Be careful what you wish for, Magdalena. You might get it."

"Was there a proposal in there somewhere?"

"What the hell? Why not?"

He began kissing her again, driving her up the spiral of desire. She dove into the deluge with him, so she had but a fleeting instant to ponder whether he'd truly promised. It seemed that he had, but it also seemed he hadn't.

Swiftly and without warning, another wave of pleasure swept over her. All thoughts of his pledge to marry later on flew out the window. She could only focus on this moment and this man and this splendid encounter. The past and the future were irrelevant. Only the present mattered.

As her pulse slowed, he was frowning, looking determined, resolved to proceed.

"What's wrong?" she asked.

"Nothing's wrong. Everything is very, very right."

"I'm glad."

"You won't ever regret this, will you?" he said.

"Regret what?"

"That you were here with me like this? That I was able to make you mine?"

"No, I could never regret it. And you're mine now too, remember?"

"Yes, I remember."

He nibbled a path to her breasts and he played with them, licking and sucking, while down below he was fumbling with his trousers. He pulled them down around his haunches and settled himself between her thighs.

He slid a finger into her womanly sheath, then added another. He stroked them in and out in a tantalizing rhythm, and her hips moved to match that rhythm.

Then, something else was there. Something bigger than his fingers. She'd been so distracted by his hand that she hadn't noticed what it was.

"What are you doing?" she inquired.

"I'm preparing to join my body to yours."

"I told you I didn't know what that means."

"We're built differently in our private parts."

"We are?" She was such a naïve ninny that she'd had no idea!

"It's awkward the first time."

"Will it get better?"

"Yes, you'll grow accustomed very quickly. Now relax for me."

"I can't. It feels too odd."

She wasn't convinced she'd made the correct decision. Matters had escalated so rapidly, and she was perplexed over what she'd instigated. It was a little too late to complain. Wasn't it?

"It will be over in a few minutes." He studied her and scowled. "Are you scared?"

"No. I'm simply nervous about what I don't understand."

"It's very easy to accomplish. Every wife in the world does it on a regular basis."

The word *wife* soothed her anxiety, for she recalled that there was a purpose to their actions. When they were through, she'd have him for a husband.

She forced a smile, and he smiled in return, his gaze so warm and affectionate her heart raced with elation. He had to be falling in love with her. She couldn't imagine what other explanation there could be for such evident fondness.

"Put your arms around me," he murmured.

"Like this?"

"Yes, just like that. Hold me tight."

"I will."

"Don't be afraid."

"I never could be—when I'm with you."

He started kissing her, caressing her breasts. At the same time, he was flexing with his hips, pushing himself into her, each plunge bringing him closer to a goal she couldn't fathom but definitely craved.

She raised up and met his thrusts with cautious thrusts of her own, and suddenly he was inside her. They froze, the strangeness of the event rocking her. It didn't hurt precisely. His prior ministrations had left her damp and relaxed, but it felt so peculiar.

Tears welled into her eyes, but they weren't tears of sadness or of joy. She was suffering a different emotion entirely, one she couldn't describe, but she was overwhelmed in a manner she hadn't known to be possible.

He smiled down at her.

"Are you all right?"

"Yes. Is that it? Are we finished?"

"There's a bit more. Don't let go of me."

"I never will."

He commenced his flexing again, and the initial discomfort began to wane. Learning the ropes, she moved with him, and just as she started to relish the bizarre coupling, he gave a particularly deep thrust and groaned as if he was in pain.

He hovered for several seconds, then collapsed onto her, his large torso pressing her down. He should have felt heavy, but he didn't. He felt warm and welcome, and she stroked her palms up and down his back, savoring the quiet intimacy, the extraordinary experience she would never share with another person.

Eventually he rolled off her and snuggled onto his side. She rolled too, so she was facing him. They were nose to nose, grinning, happy with what they'd wrought, as if they were naughty children behaving as they shouldn't.

"Did you survive it?" he asked.

She chuckled. "All in one piece."

"It gets better with practice."

"Does that mean we can try it again someday?"

"We can do it all night if you're not too sore."

Her inner areas were actually quite sore, but she would never admit it. "I'm not sore."

"You arouse me beyond my limit, you scamp. I couldn't slow down or hold back."

"I'm not a virgin anymore, am I?"

"No, and you won't ever be again. So no regrets, remember?"

She wished he'd quit speaking of regrets, for it seemed as if perhaps *he* had a few misgivings, and she couldn't bear for him to have any doubts.

"What now?" she inquired.

"Now…we can take a nap or I can order up some food or a bath."

"You'd bother the servants?"

"For you? Anything."

She shook her head. "I'm fine, and it's very late. We're not waking the servants."

Besides, she'd die of embarrassment if any of the staff realized what she'd allowed. She was certain she was already the source of much kitchen speculation, and she refused to provide more fodder for their cannons.

She gave a very unladylike yawn, and he laughed.

"I didn't know sexual conduct could be so draining," she said.

"It's the best way to fall asleep."

He turned her away from him and spooned himself to her back, his body cradling hers. She could have expired from gladness.

"Everything will work out, won't it?" she asked.

"Everything will be perfect."

"We'll marry."

Did he hesitate? "Whatever you want, Maggie. Just rest."

"Afterward, we have to talk about my sisters. I don't care about Gaylord, but I hope—if I'm your wife—you can be kind to them."

"Sure," he mumbled, and he yawned too.

They were silent, floating along in a languor that was riveting and splendid.

A thrilling notion occurred to her. "Could I be...with child from this?"

"No," he scoffed. "Well, you could be, but it rarely happens from just one time."

"I can't be a woman who has a baby too early. I won't stir gossip."

"I'd kill anyone who gossiped about you."

She elbowed him in the ribs. "You would not."

"I might not kill them, but I'd administer a good thrashing."

She sighed, contentment sweeping through her. With him as her husband, there would never be a dull moment, and she'd like to have pondered how she'd suddenly decided she was eager to be a bride, but she was too exhausted.

She elbowed him again. "You can't doze off. The servants would find you in here in the morning."

"They won't, and even if they did, they wouldn't care."

"*I* would care."

"I'll nap a bit, then I'll go. I don't want to leave yet."

"I don't want you to either."

There were a dozen questions she was desperate to ask him—when they'd marry, where they'd marry, where they'd live—but she drifted off without learning any of the details.

When she woke, the sun was so high in the sky she was afraid it might be approaching the noon hour. Could it be? Had she slept that late? She never had, not since she'd been a pampered girl with a rich father and stable family.

She rolled onto her back and stretched her arms over her head, the move making her private parts ache, reminding her of what they done in the dark of night.

Glancing over, she was positive he wasn't there, but she was lonely and wishing she hadn't been so adamant about his having to depart. She'd love to see his beautiful smile first thing, and she grinned, recognizing that—as his wife—she'd see that smile every morning for the rest of her life.

She dragged herself out of bed, excited to get downstairs and be with him again. How would they interact? Would he tease her for loafing? She had no idea, but she was so happy!

As she spun to walk into her dressing room, she noticed a note had been placed on the nightstand.

She frowned, for some reason being flooded by the worst sense of dread. With trembling hand, she flicked the seal.

Ramsey came for me in the night. Trouble in London. Had to leave. Sorry.

He went on to explain that she should stay in the country, that he'd return as soon as he was able. He'd signed it with his full name, Michael Scott, as if she might not remember who he was.

Rudely, like the snob she apparently was, she mused that he could read and write after all, that he had excellent penmanship and spelled his words correctly. She'd wondered if he'd been educated, and evidently he had been.

She read the message over and over, as if searching for hidden clues, but there weren't any. How could he flit off to London without a goodbye? Had the prior night meant nothing to him? She'd been completely changed. How could he be so indifferent?

Feeling angry and hurt, she sank down on the bed.

He'd charmed her until she'd let down her guard. He'd seduced her until she couldn't resist. He'd deflowered her. He'd promised marriage. Then…he'd left without a goodbye.

What man behaved that way? After what they'd shared, what man would just pick up and go?

She crumpled the note into a ball, tossed it on the floor, and staggered to the dressing room to find her clothes.

CHAPTER FIFTEEN

"Don't move a muscle."

"Why not?"

"I want to look at you."

Rebecca grinned up at Ramsey.

She was in the kitchen at the rescue mission. It was late and quiet, and she had the place to herself. A single candle burned over on one of the tables.

There was a bin behind the stove that heated water, and she'd made it a habit to treat herself by taking a bath in Maggie's bathing tub. Rebecca had mentioned it to Ramsey, hoping to draw him over to the mission with wicked intent, and apparently her ploy had succeeded.

She was naked and sitting in the tub, but it was too small to cover what ought to be covered, so he could see numerous pertinent spots. Yet he was over in the doorway and hadn't moved any closer.

She was beginning to suspect the thick oaf was afraid of her. Or perhaps he was afraid of Michael Scott.

Mr. Scott had commanded that Ramsey stay away from Rebecca, and clearly the warning was vexing Ramsey. Rebecca had to lure him over to her way of thinking.

"I'd given up on you visiting me," she said.

"I've been busy."

"With what?"

"With Michael's business."

"Are you his faithful dog?"

He shrugged off the insult. "You could say that."

"You practically begged me to come to town."

"I never beg women," he scoffed.

"All right then, you *asked* me, but now that I'm here, you've hardly spent any time with me."

"We're not all rich and idle like you. Some of us have to work to earn our keep."

"I could entertain myself, but you ordered me not to go outside."

"I meant it too. If you got yourself in a jam, I'd have to murder the idiot who harmed you."

"Would you really kill somebody for me?"

"Yes."

"How about Gaylord? If I asked, would you kill him?"

"I'd enjoy it too much."

He pushed away from the door and approached so he was next to the tub. The water lapped at her waist, but her breasts and arms were on full display. She leaned toward him, eager to drive him wild with lust.

She'd been in London for five days, but there'd been no progress. He rarely stopped by, and when he bothered, he'd quickly leave. She was growing alarmed that he'd changed his mind and was wishing he hadn't brought her to the city.

She was an accomplished flirt who'd nearly compromised herself with several different men. She'd been that desperate to escape Gaylord and Cliffside, and with her dowry squandered, seduction and ruination had been her only option.

Yet the potential swains had turned out to be cowards who'd backed out before things went too far, so she hadn't managed to stumble into marriage that way.

She'd been so sure of Ramsey Scott, sure he wouldn't be able to resist her, and sure that—after she was despoiled—he'd feel compelled to tender an offer of support and who could guess what else. But he remained aloof and disinterested.

Nudity and a steamy bath had seemed the best choice. Had she finally ensnared him? From the look in his eye, she was supposing she might have.

With him so close, she noticed his knuckles were red and swollen, and there was a bruise on his cheek.

"Have you been fighting?" she asked.

"Not fighting. Teaching a lesson to a stupid fool."

"Did he learn it?"

He smirked. "Definitely."

"I like that you're tough."

"Little lady, you have no idea." He nodded, indicating her naked torso. "Stand up."

"Why?"

"Because it's time for us to finish what we started at Cliffside."

"You're always saying that, but you're too afraid of Michael Scott to follow through."

"He gets to tell me some things, but on other things he gets to mind his own business. Stand up."

She rose slowly, inch by inch, flaunting herself as she unfolded from the tub. Water sluiced down her body, lapping at her knees.

It was the bravest act she'd ever committed, allowing him to assess her. She stretched and preened, pretending strange men constantly ogled her. In reality she was terrified, but she refused to cower. No doubt he consorted with all sorts of loose women. They would know how to entice him, and she wanted him to believe she possessed the same wicked aplomb.

"Will I do?" she saucily inquired.

"You're not bad. Turn around. Let me see your ass."

She spun, being careful not to slip and tamping down a squeal when he grabbed the curvaceous globes of her bottom and gave them a squeeze.

"I like a shapely ass," he said, "and you're too skinny. I figured it wouldn't be much to look at, but it's fine. You're probably worth the trouble you'll cause me."

She snorted. "I'll be worth every speck of trouble I cause."

There was a towel on a nearby stool, and he held it for her.

"Climb out."

"And then what?"

"You get out, and I'll show you."

"Tough talk, Ramsey."

"Climb out," he said again.

She clutched his arm to steady herself and stepped to the floor. He draped the towel over her shoulders and dried her, swiping it down her back, then her front.

As he reached her thighs, he knelt down so he was eye to eye with her private parts. Stunning her, he sniffed the intimate spot, then ran his thumb through the curly hairs. His touch was so electric, she felt that he'd scalded her.

"Real pretty," he said. "You ever think of shaving it?"

"What?" she gasped.

"Shave it. Lots of doxies do. I like it when it's shaved clean."

It dawned on her that she might have bitten off more man than she could chew.

"Isn't that a tad…perverted?"

"Not to me," he claimed.

He flung the towel away and gestured to the large table where Maggie's volunteers kneaded bread in the mornings.

"Get yourself over there."

"Why?"

"I'm about to give you what you've been dying to receive."

"On a table?"

"Yes, but I promise you'll like it."

She walked over hesitantly, and even though the room was warm from the earlier cooking and her hot bath, she shivered. She wasn't cold though. It was from excitement and a flood of anxiety.

Clearly her wish was about to be granted, but she was no longer certain she wanted it. However, it was too late to complain.

He walked over too, until they were toe to toe, until the nap of his clothes rubbed against her nipples. They tightened and began to throb.

"Are you still a virgin?" he abruptly asked.

"More or less."

"More or less? What kind of answer is that? In my experience, a woman either is or isn't. It's cut and dried. There's no in between. Which is it with you?"

She'd had a few fellows touch her where they shouldn't, but she didn't know if that qualified as an official deflowering. She didn't think so, so she corrected herself.

"I'm still a virgin."

"We'll see, I guess. I'll try not to ram myself in too hard."

He gripped her thighs and lifted her onto the table so her buttocks were balanced on the edge. Without warning, without wooing, he stuck two fingers inside her and stroked them in and out. She moaned with delight but with dismay too, and struggled to squirm away, but he wouldn't let her escape.

"Are we going to…?"

"Yup."

"Can't you at least kiss me first?"

"Never saw much point in it."

"Give it another shot. Just for me?"

He studied her then grinned, reminding her that she was always knocked off her pedestal by that grin. He was very handsome, but in a rugged, manly way that ignited her feminine sensibilities.

He leaned in so she thought he'd kiss her after all, but at the last second he dipped down and kissed one of her breasts instead.

He was very rough, very forceful, allowing no chance for her to acclimate, but again she didn't suppose she should complain. This was the conclusion she'd sought.

Gradually he eased her down, and once she was lying flat, he left her bosom and nuzzled a trail down her stomach. He widened her nether lips and substituted his tongue for his fingers. The feeling he produced was so shocking and so unexpected that her body was jolted into a powerful wave of pleasure.

She'd previously suffered the wild agitation, usually at night when she'd have an erotic dream. She'd awaken drenched with sweat, her heart pounding, so she knew it could happen. But she hadn't understood that it could happen with a man being present. She hadn't understood a man could *make* it happen.

My goodness! What was she to think?

"Just as I suspected," he muttered as he straightened.

"What?"

"You have the soul of a harlot."

"I do not!" she huffed, then she considered his remark. "Well, maybe a little. I've always wanted to try wicked things."

"You've come to the right place, because there's no one who enjoys a bit of wickedness more than me." He pushed her down so she was on her back again. "Let's see if you were telling the truth about that virginity you're so proud of."

"I'm not proud of it. I've worked to be shed of it for years."

"Then it's your lucky day."

"Why?"

"You've finally found the man who's happy to take it from you. Now be quiet and quit fussing."

Down below, he was unbuttoning his trousers, and she stared at the ceiling, suddenly alarmed and wondering if she'd like it or hate it.

She'd heard women titter over the marital act, but factual information was difficult to obtain, the common opinion being that a maiden shouldn't learn the details in advance. The wives' attitudes varied, with some deeming the experience to be grand, others finding it a duty and a chore, and still others finding it revolting. Occasionally it sounded as if violence was thrown in too.

How would it be with Ramsey? If she loathed it—after waiting so long to try it—she'd be so disappointed!

"Do you know what's about to occur?" he asked. "Has anybody explained it?"

"I have a general idea."

"It's physical."

"I know, Ramsey," she retorted with no small amount of exasperation.

"I'm just saying. I don't want you to swoon."

"I'm not the swooning type."

"It's messy and sweaty. You might muss your hair."

"Oh, for pity's sake. Get on with it, would you? If you keep babbling like that, I'll fall asleep from boredom."

"It will hurt the first time, but only the first time, so let's get it out of the way."

He stepped in, pushing her thighs very wide, and momentarily she could feel his manly rod probing at her center. She braced, certain he would scale her chaste walls with a vicious thrust. To her amazement, he was very careful, very gentle.

He wedged himself in, then wedged himself in a bit more, and while she'd meant to act nonchalant, as if she was deflowered every day, the whole episode was too bizarre. She simply couldn't relax.

"Ready?" he asked.

"As ready as I'll ever be."

"Here goes. Don't you dare complain when it's over."

"I won't complain, you lout!"

"Swear it."

"I swear."

He paused—looking at her naked body, at the decadent area where their privates were intimately joined—and he was absolutely brimming with masculine vanity.

"You're the only real lady I ever fucked," he crudely said.

"I'll be the last—if you don't hurry up."

"You're always in a rush. Live a little, would you? Enjoy the ride. We won't ever be able to do this precise thing ever again."

"I can't understand why you're moving as slow as a snail. Aren't you excited to learn what it will be like?"

"Oh, I know what it will be like. You're the one who's in for a surprise."

He lifted her bottom and dipped down to suck hard at her nipple. As she arched up, he gave a fierce shove.

Just that quick, just that easily, he was buried to the hilt.

She whooshed out a breath of astonishment, and she held very still, assessing the swings of emotion coursing through her. She was happy and sad and eager and aghast all at once.

Primarily though, she was so bloody glad they'd proceeded. There was no going back, and he couldn't return her to Cliffside. Not after this.

I've got you now!

She'd dealt her hand, made her wager, and won the bet, and she was vastly relieved to have maneuvered him into the exact spot where she'd wanted him to be.

"What do you think?" he asked.

"It's...interesting."

"I guess you were telling the truth."

"About what?"

"You were a virgin after all."

"I told you I was."

"I didn't believe you."

He grabbed her legs and showed her how to wrap them around his waist, then he started to flex with deliberate motions, his male member penetrating as far as it would go, then he'd pull it out, only to plunge it in again.

Initially it was awkward, but she rapidly adapted to his steady rhythm, and she merrily joined in. While she hadn't known what to expect, she was delighted to discover that it was wild and raucous and definitely worth trying.

His movements grew more profound, until finally—with a loud shout—he emptied himself in her womb. She wasn't worried about any consequences. If a babe caught, she'd fret about it once it became a problem. That was her typical mode of staggering through life, and she saw no reason to change.

His hips ground to a halt, and he kissed her on the mouth then drew away and stood. She sat up, and she'd had her hair piled on her head, but the combs had fallen out so the brunette curls tumbled down her back. Her thighs were bruised, her inner parts raw and sore.

All in all, she felt quite grand.

"You're no longer a virgin, Rebecca, but you don't look very pleased."

"It was…fine." She couldn't locate the appropriate words to describe her sentiment. She was too thunderstruck.

"It was better than fine. Admit it."

"Yes, it was," she said, and to her horror, she burst into tears.

He was aghast. "Are you crying?"

"Yes."

"Why? Are you hurt? Didn't you like it? What?"

"I'm so happy."

"You have a funny way of showing it."

"Trust me, I'm bowled over by you."

"Of course you are."

She'd hoped maybe they'd hug or cuddle, but then he wasn't a romantic sort. The notion had probably never occurred to him, but she was desperate for a display of tenderness. When next they dallied, she intended that it would be in a bed so they could lie down and take their time.

She'd cast her lot with him and planned to keep him for as long as he'd have her. If she'd known how to cook, she'd have wound her path through his belly, but women of her station were never taught how to perform such menial tasks. Carnal tricks seemed the best alternative, and she'd be the premier student in his class of debauched lessons. He'd never be sorry.

He grabbed her robe and draped it over her shoulders, stuffing her arms in the sleeves, then he dragged her off the table, easing her feet to the floor.

"We're leaving tomorrow," he said.

It was the last comment she'd expected, and she scowled. "To go where?"

"Scotland."

"Scotland! Why?"

"We have to hightail it up there and get ourselves leg-shackled."

"We agreed there'd be no strings attached."

"Yes, well, I've thought about it, and if I don't marry you, Michael will murder me when he finds out. You'll be a widow before you're ever a bride."

She shook her head. "You don't want to wed, Ramsey."

"It won't kill me."

"It won't *kill* you? That makes me eager to proceed."

He bent down and kissed her. "It won't kill you either."

"But...*married.*"

She actually shuddered with dread.

What would it be like to wed such a tough, violent individual? He was an orphan who'd grown up on the streets of London, and as far as she was aware he had no kin, no past worth mentioning, and only dissolute, reckless Michael Scott as a friend.

How could she marry him? What would people say?

As quickly as the frantic questions arose, she chased them away. Who cared what people would say? After Gaylord's financial collapse became common knowledge, after he surrendered Cliffside and was publicly beggared, none of her acquaintances would maintain a relationship.

She'd be a pariah. She'd be a laughingstock. For years, she'd been foundering on Gaylord's sinking ship. Ramsey would be the port in her personal storm.

"I never asked," she said, "but have you any money? You work for Mr. Scott, so I'm assuming you have an income."

"Honey, I'm rich as Croesus."

Her brows shot up. "Really?"

"Yes, really, and I bought you a house. We'll move in after we're back from Scotland."

"A house? Seriously, Ramsey?"

"Yes. Were you afraid I'd make you sleep in a ditch?"

"Well…"

"Don't answer that. I told you I needed to figure out a plan, and I have."

"Wife, home, and family? That seems like quite a jump all at once."

He shrugged. "I've never had any of those things, but it's about time I did. Besides, what else would I do with all my money?"

"What else indeed? You might as well spend it on me."

"That's what I was thinking." He swooped in and took another kiss. "We'll ride out in the morning. Pack a small bag so we can travel fast."

"All right."

"Leave your sister a note so she won't worry."

"What should I tell her? I'm not sure she'll be happy that I'm eloping with you."

"Tell her anyway. Tell her I have honorable intentions, and she shouldn't fret. I'll bring you back safe and sound."

"And married."

He nodded. "And married."

He spun and walked to the door. At the last second, he glanced over. "Give that table a good scrubbing. They cook food on it."

Then he was gone, and she staggered over to a chair and collapsed down onto it.

Would she traipse off to Scotland with him? She'd wanted to be rescued. Was that the best decision?

She had no idea.

"Magdalena, what are you doing here?"

Pamela gaped at Maggie, having found her sitting quietly in the front parlor. There had been no indication that a guest had arrived. No carriage had rolled up the drive, no one had banged the knocker.

Not that her sister needed to knock. But Maggie was supposed to be off with Michael Scott, securing Pamela's future and saving Cliffside. Gaylord had heard she'd succeeded. Mr. Scott had been effusive in his praise, declaring himself delighted with Maggie.

"I'm on my way to London," Maggie said. "I popped in to say hello. May I stay the night?"

"Certainly, but why are you on your way *to* London? Where have you been?"

"I've been visiting."

Pamela knew Maggie had been visiting—and with whom—but Pamela was positive she should pretend to have no knowledge of Maggie's acquiescence or her downfall at Mr. Scott's hands.

To Pamela's dismay though, Maggie appeared very glum, a likely sign that she hadn't enjoyed her ruination as much as Mr. Scott had. Pamela tried to muster some sympathy for her sister, but honestly!

Maggie was twenty-five, and her virginity had been going to waste. Why shouldn't she have used it to save her family? As Gaylord frequently mentioned, it was unnatural for a female to remain chaste. By Maggie giving herself to Mr. Scott, she was merely following the normal and accepted path for a woman.

Mr. Scott had written to Gaylord claiming he'd keep her for the whole six months. Pamela's home would be safe for that entire period, and at that very moment Gaylord was in the city, talking to lenders and creditors, furiously attempting to get Cliffside back in their possession where it belonged.

If Gaylord played his cards right—which he hadn't so far—at the end of the six months, Pamela wouldn't have to move.

Yet from how Maggie was moping, it seemed something had happened that might destroy the arrangement. Why was Maggie traveling to town alone? Where was Mr. Scott? Why wasn't he with her?

If Maggie had reneged at the last minute, Pamela would throttle her.

"I went away with Mr. Scott—as you begged me to do," Maggie explained.

"You did?" Pamela feigned surprise.

"Yes."

"Thank you. I'm grateful for your help."

"We've decided to marry."

Pamela frowned, confused by the news. "You and Mr. Scott?"

"Yes, and since I'm about to be his wife I've pleaded with him to be kind to you with regard to Cliffside."

"What was his reply?"

"He's agreed to be merciful, but I don't believe any assistance will be given to Gaylord. Just to you and Rebecca. That's it. That's the only guarantee I could wring out of him. It's why I stopped by on my way to the city—so you'd know his opinion."

Pamela was enraged. Of course assistance would have to flow to Gaylord. He was Pamela's husband and the head of the family. She would never leave him in the lurch—not when she'd risked so much to make him her own. How could Maggie imagine he wouldn't be included?

"I'm curious about your engagement," Pamela said.

"Why would you be? Will it gall you if I wind up with a husband? Were you hoping I'd simply end up ruined and in trouble?"

"I never wanted that!"

"Didn't you?" Maggie scoffed. "I'm delighted to report that, during our holiday, Mr. Scott and I grew very close."

"And…he proposed to you?"

"Yes. Could we have the ceremony at Cliffside? I'd like to hold it here if you don't mind."

"No, no, I don't mind. Ah…where is Mr. Scott? Why isn't he with you?"

"He was called to London on an emergency."

"I see," Pamela murmured, not actually *seeing* at all. "Would you excuse me? I need to inform the housekeeper you'll join us for supper and overnight. Must you leave in the morning? You're welcome to stay longer."

"I have to get back to work."

"Fine, then. Go if you must."

Pamela strolled out, exuding calm and composure, but the instant she was in the hall and out of Maggie's sight, she collapsed against the wall, a palm clapped over her mouth to stifle her gasp of astonishment.

Michael Scott was betrothed to Lord Stone's daughter. Gaylord had told Pamela as much, but even if he hadn't, the announcement had been in all the newspapers. There had been several grand parties hosted by her parents, and a betrothal ball was scheduled.

What was Mr. Scott thinking by lying to Maggie? And what would become of her when she learned the truth?

CHAPTER SIXTEEN

Maggie stood in the front drive at Cliffside, dawdling as a footman brought out her luggage. A carriage had been harnessed for her, and she would take it into the village then ride the mail coach into town.

She had more bags now than when she'd departed the city. Michael had been extremely generous, providing her with several dresses, plus the shawls, shoes, and other accoutrements that went with a new wardrobe.

Considering how he'd abandoned her at Orphan's Nest, how she'd fled his residence in a fit of pique, she'd nearly left it all behind, but in the end she hadn't. It had been so long since she'd had any new clothes that she'd kept every item.

No matter what ultimately occurred between her and Michael, she figured she deserved what she'd been given. She viewed it as payment for the aggravation he'd caused her.

She was eager to leave Cliffside, eager to return to her job and life in London, and she was feeling very uncertain about what she'd find once she was there.

A visit to Pamela was always distressing. Luckily Gaylord had been away, but Rebecca was gone too, claiming Maggie had asked her to watch over the mission while Maggie was away.

Maggie didn't admit as much to Pamela, but Rebecca was the very last person who would be suitable to watch over the rescue mission or any other endeavor. Maggie had issued no invitation, so what was her sister doing in London? Maggie was almost too alarmed to learn the truth.

On top of all her other troubles, she was incredibly confused over Michael and his treatment of her.

She'd waited four days to hear from him, four grueling, humiliating days that had ticked by in a slow sort of torture. Like a ninny, she'd assumed he'd write or send a messenger who would apprise her of his plans. But the selfish oaf hadn't come back, hadn't contacted her, hadn't penned a letter.

She'd paced and fretted and fumed, and finally her temper had gotten the better of her. She wasn't a doxy who could be used for illicit purposes then discarded when he was finished. Nor was she stupid or foolish. She could handle her own problems, and she wouldn't sit twiddling her thumbs for any man. She'd packed her bags and headed to town.

During the protracted journey, she'd pondered their ardent night of amour. When she'd been immersed in their tryst, it had seemed as if he'd proposed. It was the reason she'd surrendered her virginity. She wouldn't have otherwise. At least she didn't expect she would have.

With how passionate it had been, she wasn't sure of anything. Were they engaged? She definitely felt they were, but she couldn't guess what he was thinking.

Well she had news for Michael Scott, and she'd deliver it in the most brusque, curt way she could manage. She might not have a ring on her finger, but as far as she was concerned they were betrothed and would wed right away. She wouldn't risk that a babe had caught in her womb, and she wouldn't listen to any nonsense from him that might delay the inevitable.

They were marrying, and that was that.

She took a final look at the house, wondering when she'd be back, wondering—as she always did when she departed—if she'd ever see it again.

As usual, she suffered no nostalgia and had no regrets. Cliffside might have been her home as a girl, but too many awful events had transpired under her father's roof, and the terrible had wiped out the good.

There was motion out on the road, and as she glanced over, a carriage turned up the lane, a man on a horse riding alongside it. She stared, trying to discover who it might be.

Guests would delay her, which was irritating. Their arrival meant she couldn't hurry off, so she tarried, not wanting to seem rude if it was a neighbor or acquaintance.

For a minute, vehicle and rider were swallowed up by the trees. Shortly they came into view again, much closer now, and to her stunned surprise the rider was Michael Scott.

The carriage had a fancy crest on the side, indicating an exalted family, and a pretty blond woman leaned out the window. She was peering up at him, and they were chatting amiably. He pointed at the orchards, at the park, at the hills beyond. He appeared very proud, as if he was giving her a personal tour.

Maggie's pulse began to pound. What was happening?

He'd been called away to London by an emergency, one that had been so dire Ramsey Scott had rushed to the country to fetch him. She'd exhaustively imagined what it could have been—a fire at his club, the death of an employee, a horrid accident—but she knew so little about the day-to-day facts of his life that she couldn't speculate with any accuracy.

But in none of her frantic imaginings had she envisioned him on a pleasure jaunt with a beautiful girl.

She hovered behind her own carriage, peeking out, spying on them. Up until that very moment, she'd truly expected everything would be fine. She'd pictured a tempestuous meeting in London where they'd spat and quarrel, but where they would realize it had all been a hideous misunderstanding. They'd kiss and apologize, and Michael would be sorry and would spoil her with gifts and pamper her like a queen.

Yet with how the blond woman gazed up at him—her expression a mix of awe and infatuation—Maggie was forced to accept that every detail she'd believed about Michael Scott was a lie.

They had no future together. The proposal she was positive she'd heard hadn't been a proposal at all. What had it been?

"What do you think?" Michael asked the woman.

"It's lovely, Mr. Scott. I'd say it's nicer than Stone Manor."

"I thought you'd like it." He smiled at the woman in much the same way he'd smiled at Maggie during their lazy afternoon picnics. She'd presumed it was a special smile, showered on her out of fondness and regard, but apparently he displayed it for every female he encountered.

"When will the tenants be out?" the woman inquired.

"Six months," he said. "I recently negotiated the end of their lease."

"Perfect," the woman gushed. "It leaves me just the right amount of time to arrange the ceremony."

Six months!

Maggie sagged against the side of her carriage, out of sight from Michael and the woman. The tenants to whom he'd blithely referred were Maggie's family. Was he giving Cliffside to his companion? He'd promised Maggie he'd be merciful about Cliffside. He couldn't give it away! Not before she'd had a chance to speak with him about it!

And what about the six months he'd mentioned?

It was the length of Gaylord's illicit bargain. Was that the period Michael was talking about? Could it be?

Maggie listened as the other carriage halted, as the door was opened, the step lowered, and the woman helped to the ground. Had Michael helped her? He must have. There were no servants about.

"Shall we go in?" Michael inquired.

"Yes, by all means," the woman replied. "I'm eager to see every room. I'm so pleased."

"I'm delighted to hear it," he said.

Maggie took a deep breath, then walked toward them. When the pair headed for the stairs to climb to the front door, she was standing in their path.

The woman was younger than Maggie by several years, perhaps still in her adolescence. She was pretty and plump, attired in a striking lavender gown that highlighted the blue of her eyes, the gold in her hair. Every detail, down to the tiniest stitch on her bonnet, bespoke wealth and privilege.

"Hello, Michael." Maggie glared at him, refusing to cower or look away.

On observing her, he scowled, but evinced no other reaction. "Maggie, what are you doing here?"

"I could ask you the same."

"I told you to wait for me."

"Well, I didn't." She yanked her attention to the woman. "Who is your friend? May we be introduced?"

"Ah…"

Michael was visibly flummoxed. Two slashes of red darkened his cheeks, and he'd been rendered speechless.

Silence reigned. Birds stopped flying. The wind stopped blowing. The Earth seemed to have stopped spinning on its axis.

Maggie couldn't bear the awkwardness, and she stepped to the woman. "Mr. Scott's manners have fled. I am Magdalena Wells, and this has always been my family's home. I am Mr. Scott's fiancée."

The woman blanched, then her gaze became insolent and rude. She let it travel down Maggie's body, assessing Maggie's dress, scuffed shoes, and messy chignon. Her disdain was overt and insulting, and she clearly deemed Maggie beneath her notice.

"You're his fiancée?" The woman scoffed. "That's not possible."

"What do you mean?" Maggie asked.

"I mean that I am Lady Felicia Gilroy, and *I* am his fiancée. I have been for ages." She slipped a proprietary arm into Michael's, and she grinned up at him. "Let's go in, darling. Show me my new home."

Without another word, they swept by Maggie, and she was frozen in her spot. If Lady Felicia had pulled out a pistol and shot Maggie, she couldn't have been more viciously wounded.

"Michael!" she called, desperate to receive some sort of explanation.

He glanced over his shoulder.

"We'll talk later," he said, but that was all.

They went up the stairs and vanished into the house.

Maggie's knees gave out, and she collapsed to the ground and huddled in the dirt in a stunned heap. She wanted to leap up and chase after them, but she felt as if the bones in her legs had melted. She couldn't rise, couldn't speak, couldn't think.

No one rushed to her aid, although the driver of Lady Felicia's carriage—who'd heard all—leaned over and frowned down at her.

"Are you all right, Miss?" he asked like an idiot.

"Oh, yes, I'm just dandy." A mad hysteria bubbled up.

"Would you...ah...like me to fetch someone?"

"No. You go on."

He hesitated, then clicked the reins and his horses kept on to the barn.

Maggie stayed where she was, and she couldn't have guessed how much time passed.

The term *broken heart* had often been bandied in her presence. People assumed it was a romantic expression, utilized to describe intense emotion. They didn't comprehend that it was a real physical condition that was deadly and devastating.

Eventually a footman came out. He was the one who'd loaded her luggage, who was driving her into the village. He saw her and ran over.

"Miss Maggie! What happened? What is it? Shall I get your sister?"

Maggie stared at the house where she'd been such a happy girl, but she could no longer remember when anything good had occurred in it.

If she told him to bring Pamela, her sister would fuss and flutter and drag Maggie inside. Maggie would have to dawdle in the parlor, listening as Mr. Scott showed his fiancée around.

If Lady Felicia was his betrothed, what was Maggie? His consort? His concubine? Was she his prize to use and abuse so Pamela and Gaylord could remain at Cliffside a few more months?

In the period years earlier, after Pamela had announced that Gaylord had seduced her and they would marry, Maggie had always thought it the most wrenching time. She'd presumed that naught else could ever transpire that would hurt her quite so much. But she'd been wrong.

She peered up at the footman.

"No, don't get my sister. I...tripped and fell. That's all. Help me up."

He looked dubious, but she extended her hand, and he drew her to her feet.

"Are all my bags in the coach?" she asked.

"Yes."

"We should be off then. I've delayed so long, if I'm not careful, I'll miss the mail coach when it stops in the village."

"If you're sure...?"

"I'm sure."

Her knees were still very weak, so she let him lead her to the carriage door, let him steady her as she stumbled in. She flashed a tepid smile, trying to appear half-sane so he wouldn't race inside to find Pamela.

He hovered for a moment, his concern visible, and she waved to the box.

"I'm fine, really. Let's hurry, so I'm not late."

He climbed up, called to the horses, and they pulled Maggie away.

CHAPTER SEVENTEEN

"You have a guest, Miss Wells."

The cook's helper had knocked on her apartment door, and Maggie peered over and asked, "Who is it?"

"He wouldn't provide his name, but he'd like to speak with you down in the common room."

Maggie bristled. It had to be Michael Scott, and she couldn't bear the notion of sitting down to chat with him. She'd been back in London for three days and had been waiting for him to slink in like the cur he was.

He was so vain. He'd want to hash out every humiliating detail, would want to *explain*, but he could never make her understand, could never earn her forgiveness.

She blew out a heavy breath. "Tell him I'm busy."

And she actually was busy. She was folding all the pretty clothes he'd given her and planned to donate them to her church's next charity fundraiser.

The volunteer was nervously hovering, and Maggie inquired, "What is it?"

"He said he'd come up here—if you didn't come down. He seemed quite determined about it."

"He did, did he?"

Maggie's temper boiled over, and she had to admit it was refreshing to feel an emotion other than bewildered shock. Since her return, she'd been staggering around like a blind person, unable to concentrate or focus on any task. She was so discombobulated that she couldn't even muster any worry about her sister.

Rebecca had stayed in Maggie's apartment as she'd advised Pamela she would. Several people had seen her arrive, but none of them had seen her leave. For her entire time, she'd remained in Maggie's room and had never ventured out. No one had visited her, and she'd gone to visit no one.

Yet there was no sign that she'd been present a single minute. Whatever her ploy had been by traveling to London, it was over and she'd departed. She'd left no letter of explanation. She'd simply drifted in and out as if she were a ghost.

Maggie had forced herself to write a one-sentence note to Pamela, asking if Rebecca was at Cliffside, but Maggie had received no reply and that paltry query was all Maggie could do. She couldn't do any more than that.

She felt feverish and ill, her mind wandering aimlessly as if she was elderly and growing senile. Was it possible to die of heartbreak? Of shame or regret?

Agonizing questions tormented her: Why was she so gullible? Where men were concerned, why was she so naïve? Was she so desperate to be loved that she'd believe any lie a man told? Was she so desperate to be loved that she couldn't discern truth from reality?

Due to Gaylord's perfidy, she'd resolved to never succumb to affection ever again. It had been the foundation of every decision she'd made as an adult. Why then had she stumbled off the path she'd chosen for herself? Why had she let Michael Scott mean anything to her?

"I'll take care of this," she muttered, and she marched out and headed to the stairs.

She was so angry. She'd intended to storm down, to order Mr. Scott out of her building and out of her life, but as she began to descend, her strides slowed. She had no idea how to have this conversation. She'd once had a similar one with Gaylord, and it had been horrid and pointless.

How dare Michael Scott put her through such agony? How dare he show his face where he was so unwelcome?

Trudging to the bottom, she glanced over. To her stunned surprise, it wasn't Mr. Scott. It was Gaylord!

She was astonished to see him. In all the years since she'd fled Cliffside, he'd never visited, and for an anxious instant she wondered if Rebecca had suffered a mishap and he was there to inform her. But no. There was no sign of distress about him. If Rebecca was imperiled, even a man as jaded as Gaylord would have to evince some unease, wouldn't he?

He was seated on a bench at a dining table. In his expensive suit and hat, his gold-tipped walking stick, he looked distinctly out of place, and he nervously studied the dreary surroundings as if the poverty might rub off.

When he observed Maggie, his expression changed so he appeared smug and superior, as if he had a secret or as if he'd played a sneaky trick on her. There was an awkward silence, and Maggie went over and slid onto the bench across from him.

"Why are you here?" she asked. "Is it about Rebecca?"

"Rebecca? No."

"Is she all right?"

He shrugged. "As far as I know."

"Then if this is not about one of my sisters, I'd rather not talk to you. Get out."

Gaylord smirked and raised an arrogant brow. "We have numerous topics to address, namely my contract with Mr. Scott."

Maggie was so irate that red dots formed in the corners of her vision. If she opened her mouth, flames of rage might shoot out.

"You mention that lewd pact to my face, Gaylord? To my face?"

"Mr. Scott is *very* happy with the trial period."

"Shut up."

"Why did you leave his country house? I guess he told you to stay there, but you left."

Maggie was aghast. "You've spoken to him?"

"Of course. We have a deal, and you're front and center for all the terms."

"The two of you had the gall to discuss me as if I was a…a…sow at the fair?"

"No one's bartering over you," he scoffed. "We're merely confused about what's occurring. Are you going back to the country or what?"

"No, I'm not going back."

"But he's so pleased! He's agreed to let us remain at Cliffside for the whole six months."

"Bully for him."

"You can't renege. Everything is arranged to the satisfaction of all parties."

"Which parties are satisfied?" Maggie hissed. "I assume you're referring to yourself and Mr. Scott, for I must tell you that I'm not satisfied at all, and from my vantage point I'm the only one who matters."

"You have to continue doing your part."

"With Mr. Scott?"

"Yes." Gaylord's voice became cajoling. "You have to help the family, Maggie. We're all counting on you."

"Mr. Scott is engaged!"

"So?"

"I can't be his mistress! He's about to marry an aristocrat's daughter. They were at Cliffside, and it sounds as if they plan to live there after their wedding."

"They just *think* they will. You're aware that I'm working to retrieve the property from him. Lady Felicia and Mr. Scott will never make it their home."

Maggie studied his deceitful eyes. "When you bargained with him, you knew he was engaged, didn't you?"

"Well…"

"You knew, and you proceeded anyway."

"I offered marriage, and he declined, so I offered a different option, and he jumped on it. He was extremely eager to have you."

"Meaning he informed you that he was betrothed and couldn't marry me, but he'd be happy to have me as his mistress."

"Yes, but don't get your petticoat in a wad over it. His betrothal has naught to do with you."

"How can you say that? Call me foolish and naïve, but I thought he would wed *me*."

"You!" Gaylord snorted with amusement. "Why would you believe that? Mr. Scott is a wealthy, imperious brigand, and you're poor as a church mouse. He can have any girl he wants, and Lady Felicia is giving him land and ships as a dowry, plus entry into the highest circles of society. If she can provide him with all that, why would he ever have picked a poverty-stricken spinster like you?"

There was no crueler comment Gaylord could have uttered. She wasn't an aristocrat's daughter, but once in her life, she'd had a fat, rich dowry and would have been a fabulous bride for an affluent man like Michael Scott.

But Gaylord had taken all of it away, and he'd never exhibited an ounce of remorse about any of the catastrophes he'd perpetrated.

She'd never understood how a person could be driven to commit murder, but at the moment, if she'd had a knife she'd have stabbed him in the center of his cold, black heart.

"Go away," she quietly, stoically stated. "Go away, and don't ever come back here."

"I won't depart until I have your promise that you're heading to Mr. Scott's country house to complete your six-month sojourn."

"You disgrace yourself by suggesting it, but then I would expect nothing less from you."

"Listen to me, you little shrew," he said.

"No. I've been listening to you for seven years. I'm *done* listening to you."

He wagged an angry finger under her nose. "If you don't carry on with the bargain, what will happen to your sisters? I don't care what you think about me, but what about them?"

"Don't throw them in my face. Whatever happens to them is all your fault, and you never get to make me feel guilty ever again."

She rose to her feet, and he leapt up too. His cheeks were red, the veins bulging in his neck. "You will heed me and do as I bid you," he warned, "or by God, you'll rue the day you crossed me."

"You've already shown how you can hurt me. You proved it when you seduced my sister. I survived that calamity, so I figure I can survive any other disaster you toss at me."

She spun and walked to the stairs, and he began shouting at her, threatening her, his booming voice echoing off the rafters. The cook and two male helpers were in the kitchen, and they rushed in to see what was transpiring.

Gaylord noticed them and his bellowing immediately ceased. He always hid what he was really like so others wouldn't witness his true demeanor.

"This is my brother-in-law," Maggie told the trio. "He's leaving, and if he doesn't, please find some men out on the street to drag him away. Then lock the door behind him so he can't slither in when we're not paying attention."

Their eyes widened with surprise, but they nodded, and she kept on.

She was trembling, not crying precisely, but tears were falling down her cheeks. They were tears of rage and regret, of fury and shame, and she swiped at them with her hand.

What now? What now?

The words rang through her mind.

Her family was destroyed, her home frittered way, her trust fund squandered, and without it, how would the rescue mission endure?

She supposed she could visit Evangeline Drake and plead for financial assistance, but it was mortifying to envision begging her old friend. In their prior relationship, Maggie had been rich and Evangeline the orphan and charity case. With Maggie's humiliations piling up, she couldn't imagine such a meeting.

Her pride was the only thing she had left, and her plight was likely to shred even that. But who could she ask besides Evangeline?

There was a general sentiment among the wealthy that the poor deserved their fate, that aiding them encouraged them in their poverty, so she'd never raised sufficient funds to achieve fiscal security.

If the mission was shut down—the benevolent venture Vicar Sterns had personally entrusted to her—what would she do? Cliffside was lost, so she couldn't even trudge home like the failure she was.

She staggered into her apartment and continued on to the bedchamber. The window looked down on the alley rather than the street, so she couldn't see Gaylord, but she stared out anyway, pretending she could watch him mounting his horse and riding away.

She rested a palm on the glass of the window and sent a thousand wishes out into the sky, that something good would happen, that she wouldn't have to go on all alone, that she might actually be loved someday.

She drew her palm away and rubbed it over the center of her chest where her heart was aching so painfully she suspected it might simply quit beating. People suffered heartbreak and survived. *She* had suffered it and survived, but she didn't know if she'd survive this.

Behind her, the door to the hall opened as someone entered the apartment. Footsteps started toward her, and she frowned, wondering who it could be. If it was the cook or a volunteer, she couldn't abide any sympathy, and if it was Gaylord...well...

"Maggie?"

She scowled and whipped around to find Michael Scott in her doorway. For the briefest second, her entire being soared with pleasure. She yearned to run over and throw herself into his arms, to tell him how sad she was, to have him soothe and comfort her. But as rapidly as the feeling arose she shoved it away. She was aghast at her weakness, appalled at her reaction.

He was betrothed to another and about to be wed. How dare he visit! How dare he barge in and assume he'd be welcome!

"Who let you in?" she fumed.

"There was no one downstairs. I came up on my own."

"Was my brother-in-law still in the common room?"

"I didn't see him."

"What do you want?"

"I thought we should talk."

"You thought we should *talk*? About what? I can't think of a single topic we need to address. I'm quite sure we've said everything that ever needs to be said."

He hovered, appearing abashed and a bit shy, as if he was nervous about approaching her. Could it be? Could arrogant, imperious Michael Scott be embarrassed by his conduct?

Why would he be? He blustered through life, ruining families, destroying lives. Why would a simple woman who'd merely had her hopes dashed bother him at all?

"I wanted to tell you about Felicia," he claimed, "but I didn't know how."

"Don't mention her name in my presence."

"Why shouldn't I? You seem upset about her."

"I *seem* upset? Mr. Scott you have no idea. You're lucky I'm not holding a pistol. If I was, I'd shoot you right between the eyes."

"You would not," he scoffed as if her fury was an irksome bout of feminine hysterics.

He saw the box on her bed where she'd been packing the clothes he'd bought her. He hurried over and riffled through the neatly-folded pile.

"What are you doing with your clothes?" he snapped.

"I'm donating them to my church."

"You can't give them away. They were a gift from me."

"Mr. Scott, I realize this will come as a great shock to you, but you don't own me. You're not my brother or my father or my husband, so you enjoy no position of authority. If I wish to donate these clothes or rip them to shreds or dump them in the street and light them on fire, it's none of your business."

He grabbed the box, stomped over to the wardrobe, and tossed it in. Then he spun and gaped at her as if she were a lunatic.

"Why are you so angry?" He sounded surprised and looked sincerely confused.

She shook her head with disgust. "You have the gall to ask me why?"

"Yes. I don't understand any of this. I took you to Orphan's Nest—a spot where I've never taken another female. We trifled and played and became friends. We were happy there, weren't we?"

"*You* were happy. I wasn't."

"No, you're lying. We established an amazing bond. I'm not wrong about that."

He marched over to her and she braced, as if for an assault, and it was an assault of sorts.

She couldn't bear to be so close to him. It was as if he emitted a secret signal or aroma that only she could detect, one that was too riveting for her to resist. It made her want to act in any brazen way he suggested.

She leaned away, needing to put a few inches of space between them, but the wall was behind her and she banged into it.

"Why didn't you stay in the country?" he asked. "I told you to, and I told you I'd be back. Why didn't you wait?"

"Again, Mr. Scott, you're laboring under the mistaken impression that you have some authority over me. You don't."

"Stop calling me *Mr. Scott.*"

"I no longer deem it appropriate to address you in a familiar fashion."

A muscle ticked in his cheek, his temper flaring. He was such a bully that it had to be a rare occasion when his commands were ignored. No doubt he hadn't any idea how to respond to insubordination.

He had a reputation in the neighborhood for violent reprisals, but what could he do if she refused to obey? Spank her? Send her to bed without supper?

The conceited oaf was too absurd for words.

"It seems to be my day to suffer unpleasant visitors," she said. "First Gaylord, now you. I have no desire to entertain either of you, so go away and don't come back."

"You're mine," he declared. "You know that. For six whole months."

"Don't you dare bring up that insulting bargain."

"But...*you* agreed to abide by the terms. No one forced you. You consented of your own free will."

"I did not."

"You did! I tried to dissuade you, but you insisted we proceed. When we left for Orphan's Nest, you were aware that I had wicked designs on you. You were aware of what you'd sworn to do for Farrow and your sister. Don't pretend that you were tricked or inveigled into behaving in a manner you never intended."

She glared at him, hating that he was correct. Yes, she had traveled with him of her own accord. Yes, she'd agreed to the terms, but she hadn't meant it!

She'd believed him to have a different character than the one he exhibited to the world, that—rather than cruel and horrid—he was actually kind and generous and merciful. She'd assumed she could lure those honorable traits to the surface and obtain a conclusion that didn't involve her ruination.

In the end she'd succumbed because she'd been so smitten, and she'd...*loved* him. There! She'd admitted it. She'd fallen madly in love, but clearly he'd possessed no heightened affection.

It had all been fake, every sordid bit of it, and she would never forgive herself for her gullibility. She would never forgive *him* for not being the man she'd hoped.

"I never planned to give myself to you," she fiercely retorted.

"No, you didn't, but you changed your mind and I'm glad. It was grand."

"It was grand for you maybe, but from where I'm standing, it looks like something else entirely."

"What does it look like?"

"You used me to get what you wanted, then you trotted off to London without a goodbye."

"I was on my way back!"

"You were at Cliffside! Showing it to your bride!"

"You're being ridiculous." He waved away the meeting, as if it was of no consequence.

"*I* am being ridiculous?" she seethed.

"Yes. According to my deal with Farrow, I now have the right to keep you for six months, but I'd be delighted to keep you much longer than that after the initial period expires. We could be together for a year. Perhaps more than that. You can't tell me it wouldn't be wonderful."

"With each sentence you utter, I am more humiliated."

"What are you talking about? I've spoiled you and showered you with gifts. I've shared my home and my life. How could any of that be humiliating?"

"You're engaged to be married!" she shouted, and she shoved him.

He stepped away—because he felt like it, not because she'd been strong enough to push him—so she was able to slip by him and storm out to the sitting room. She huddled behind the sofa, using it as a barrier so he couldn't come so close again.

"Yes, I'm engaged." He burst through the door after her. "What of it?"

"What of it?" she angrily repeated.

Gaylord had made a similar comment. Where had the two men acquired such convoluted logic? Where were their morals? Was this how gaming altered a person? Or was it the huge sums of money over which they dickered? Had they been corrupted by the pursuit of wealth and status?

"You don't want to discuss Lady Felicia," he said, "but it definitely sounds as if we should."

"Fine. Let's discuss her."

"Fine. Let's do."

"When you took me to the country, were you already betrothed to her?"

"Yes."

"Was your wedding approaching?"

His cheeks reddened as if with chagrin. "Well, we hadn't set the date yet."

"I spent the night in a bed with you."

"Yes, and it was spectacular, so I can't understand why you're raising this fuss."

"Does any of that evening ring a bell with you? While I was sprawled there, naked and deflowered, do you happen to remember our conversation?"

"I remember every word."

"Really? Then explain this to me, because I can't fathom how you could have forgotten."

"Forgotten what?"

"You proposed marriage."

"I never did!" he hotly retorted. "I couldn't!"

"You proposed!" she responded just as hotly. "Don't tell me you didn't. You said we'd be together forever."

"And we can be, you little fool, for as long as we're happy! We don't need some stupid piece of paper—a marriage license—to seal our fate."

"No license?"

"No."

"We'd live in sin, outside the bounds of civilized society?"

"We'd be happy!" He was shouting too, as if an increase in volume would make her comprehend what she couldn't quite seem to grasp.

"I wouldn't be your wife! You have another one in line ahead of me. Didn't you notice? There's another woman in this line, and it's not me."

They stared and stared, an expanse as vast as the ocean separating them, and a thousand doubts assailed her. While he claimed to vividly recall that inglorious night, and she claimed to have vivid recollections too, she was lying.

She'd been so overwhelmed that her memory was hazy, but two remarks stood out. As she'd insisted she wouldn't proceed unless they wed, he'd said, *Why would you want me? I'd be an awful husband.* As she'd pressed him for the answer she'd sought, he'd said, *What the hell? Why not?*

He'd never actually proposed, had never declared heightened feelings. He'd never asked her to be his bride. He'd muttered *why not*, as if she was a leftover item that could be discarded after he grew bored with it.

"You didn't mean marriage, did you?" she glumly mumbled. "When you said we'd be together, you meant I could be your mistress."

He shrugged. "It was all I could offer you."

There was no statement that would have wounded her more.

"What were the new clothes supposed to be? Payment for services rendered?"

"They were *supposed* to be a gift. So you'd look pretty. So I'd smile whenever I saw you walking in my garden. I can't bear to think of how hard your life has been. I'd like to make it easier."

"By giving me *things*? By buying me clothes and coaxing me to surrender my virginity? Perhaps you've given me a babe too. Is that one of the little gifts I should be watching for?"

"You're not increasing."

"Are you God now? How can you say that?"

"You're not increasing!" He announced it like an edict, like a universal decree. He was so notorious and exalted, maybe he thought he was a deity.

"What if I am with child?" she nagged. "What will I do?"

"You'll come to me and I'll…help you."

It took him so long to produce the word *help* that she nearly marched around the sofa and shook him until his teeth rattled.

"Yes," she sneered, "that's a conversation I'm dying to have. I'll slither over to your gambling club where I will beg your servants to let me in so I can climb to your private office and plead with you on behalf of my unborn child." She waved to the door. "Would you go?"

He was the most obstinate man who'd ever lived, so of course he didn't heed her request.

"Why are you acting like this?" he inquired. "Why are you making this so difficult?"

"Because my heart is broken," she raged. "I am absolutely devastated, and your presence here is killing me. Why are *you* making this so difficult?"

He huffed out a frustrated breath. "It's just a marriage, Maggie. It's irrelevant to you and me."

"Shut up, Michael."

"*She* doesn't mean anything to me."

"Shut up! You're embarrassing both of us."

"You're the woman I care about."

"You have a funny way of showing it."

"I've treated you better than any female I've ever known."

"Aren't I special?" she facetiously spat. "If I'm so important to you, cry off from your betrothal."

He scowled. "I can't."

"Why can't you? It's simple. You ride over to her father's house and tell him you love another and you're marrying her instead." She paused, waiting for him to say that he would, but his scowl only deepened, and bleakly she said, "Unless you don't love me and never have."

She waited for him to disagree, to assert that—just that very moment—he'd had an emotional epiphany, but he couldn't.

"I don't love anyone," he insisted. "I never have. It's not in me to suffer such a maudlin sentiment."

"*Love* is a maudlin sentiment? Is that what you think?"

"It's what I know."

"Then I feel very sorry for you—and your fiancée."

"There's no need to feel sorry. We're going into it with our eyes wide open."

"If she'll get no fondness from you, why would she proceed? What's she expecting to achieve?"

"She's saving her family."

"From what?"

"From financial ruin."

"Ah…" Maggie mused. "I see now."

"You see what?"

"Her father gambled away his estate to you."

"Yes. I thought you knew. It's common knowledge here in the city." He made a waffling gesture with his hand, as if his destruction of yet another family was of no consequence.

"And Gaylord gambled away Cliffside to you."

"He certainly did."

"Her father and Gaylord both offered you female relatives to square their debts."

"Not to square them, but to lessen them."

"This is what's vexing me, Mr. Scott. Lady Felicia gets a ring and a husband and fiscal security. What am I supposed to get besides a few pretty gowns and a bastard babe in my belly?"

"Stop saying that," he fumed.

"Please comment on my assessment of the situation as it compares to Lady Felicia. She gets everything—including the home that's been in my family for two centuries—and what do I get?"

He was visibly flummoxed by her question, and for quite a lengthy interval, he considered an answer. Ultimately he responded with, "You get me—for as long as you like. Why can't that be enough?"

"It can't be *enough*, Mr. Scott, because I'm a very normal, ordinary female. I too want the wedding ring and the husband and the fiscal security a spouse can provide."

"Maggie, we could be so happy." For some reason, *happiness* seemed the key to him, the main issue, as if—should he be happy—nothing else mattered.

"*You* could be happy in a sordid arrangement," she said, "but I wouldn't be at all."

"So…just like that it's over between us?"

"Yes, just like that, although I must tell you that it ended a tad sooner for me. I believe the break was final in the driveway at Cliffside when your fiancée introduced herself."

She went over to the door and yanked it open. "Now then, it's almost time to serve supper downstairs, so I'm very busy. Would you go?"

He tarried, trying to figure out how to sway her, but he never could.

He'd been raised on the streets, in a world filled with the violence and immorality of reckless, negligent men. Clearly he couldn't understand a woman such as herself who yearned for esteem and respectability and propriety.

Lady Felicia could have those boons from him, but when Maggie demanded the same he scoffed with derision.

Eventually he headed toward her, and he halted and stepped in, standing so close that the toes of his boots slipped under the hem of her skirt. She could have backed away, but she suspected he was deliberately intimidating her, reminding her how tough he was, how domineering and dictatorial. But his days of overwhelming and coercing her were over.

"If you won't finish out the six months," he warned, "Pamela and Gaylord will have to move right away. That's the terms of the deal. Can you do that to your sister?"

"As I told Gaylord, I have no desire to rescue them."

"I could force you to comply. He and I have a written contract."

"You could *force* me?" The sly threat was so insulting, she was surprised she didn't faint. "How dare you speak to me so despicably!"

She slapped him as hard as she could, and he could have prevented the blow but he didn't budge. He let her have her petty outburst, so perhaps he thought he deserved a bit of censure. Her palm stung, and she could see its imprint on his cheek.

He gazed at her, his eyes very sad, his expression distressing to witness.

"I shouldn't have said that," he murmured.

"No, you shouldn't have."

"I would never force you into anything."

"You couldn't. Not after this."

"I'm sorry," he claimed. "I'll be sorry forever."

He waited, then waited some more for her to accept his apology, but she refused to accept it. For a painful second it occurred to her that this was the last time she'd ever stare into his handsome face. It was a wrenching realization, but she didn't know why it would be.

He appeared as if he might offer a profound parting remark, and she steeled herself to fend off whatever it might be. In the end, though, he turned on his heel and left.

She shut and locked the door, then went into her bedchamber to peer out into the alley again so she wouldn't hear his boots clomping down the stairs.

CHAPTER EIGHTEEN

"What was it like? I want to hear every detail."

Bryce Blair smiled at his sister, Evangeline, and he sighed.

After they'd chatted with Eugenie Etherton, after she'd filled their heads with her stories about their lost heritage and betrayed parents, Bryce had been excited by the notion that he had an elevated lineage.

Throughout his life, he'd boasted that his father had been a prince, that he was secretly a prince too. People had always insisted he looked like royalty. Why not claim aristocratic ancestry? Who could disprove it?

For a brief period, it had been thrilling to suppose his orphan's fantasies had a basis in truth, and he'd rushed to Scotland to chase after that possibility. On the journey north, he'd chafed with purpose, determined to bluster into Radcliffe, to make himself known and demand explanations. But as he'd ridden south again to return to London, his initial burst of enthusiasm had vanished.

What precisely could he achieve by coming forward and announcing he was Lord Radcliffe?

If he believed Miss Etherton's tale about his parents—and he guessed he did—what could he do about it? His father's relatives were present at the estate, fully accepted as the lawful occupants.

If Bryce had blundered in and asserted ownership, he'd have been tarred and feathered and chased off with sticks.

"It wasn't that large or grand," he told Evangeline.

"Don't say so!" she protested. "I've had a thousand visions painted in my mind of it being the finest place in the world."

"It was a castle."

"A castle! My goodness."

"It was quite ancient, but folks at the tavern in the village said it had been remodeled with modern amenities."

"Did you go inside?" Evangeline asked. "Were there public visiting hours?"

"No. It's surrounded by a pretty lake though. I studied it from the far shore."

"Oh, you coward," she scolded. "You were afraid to introduce yourself."

"I wasn't…afraid, exactly."

She scrutinized him and laughed. "You were. Don't deny it. I should have gone with you. I'd have barreled through the front gate and bellowed out our names. What's the entrance called in a castle? A portcullis?"

"Something like that."

"Did you meet any of the family?"

"No."

He sighed again. They were at her London town house. Well, her husband's town house, having tea in the parlor.

Bryce had been back for three days and had just mustered the courage to face her. When he'd left for Scotland, he'd been certain they could wrest a fair ending for themselves. But subsequent reflection had quelled his fervor.

The theft of their heritage—if that's what it had been—had happened thirty years earlier. How could they establish their identities? Yes, they had a few pieces of paper that showed a marriage, that showed legitimate births for himself and his siblings, but who could verify that the documents weren't forgeries?

They had old paperwork and the word of Miss Etherton, but her uncle—who'd kept track of the details—was dead. Who would listen to Bryce's braying? Who would care? It was too fantastic, and if *he* was having difficulty accepting the truth, how could he convince others?

"What's wrong?" she asked. "You've been to Radcliffe, which should have been exhilarating for you, but you're not very happy."

He shrugged. "The entire trip upset me."

"In what way?"

"The farther I traveled from London, the more it seemed a fool's errand."

"You didn't think you'd be believed?"

"I didn't try to make anyone believe me. I could picture the reaction of the current residents of Radcliffe if I'd blustered in. I'd likely have been taken up as a lunatic. It's all too implausible."

"Not to me," she staunchly declared. "Look what I found while you were away."

She went to her writing desk and returned with a very old newspaper, the pages yellowed with age. She pointed to an advertisement regarding a new theatrical comedy that had opened in London.

Bryce read the title of the play. "*The Widow's Merry Chase*. Should it mean something to me?"

"Yes. Look toward the bottom, where the actors are listed."

"*Renowned Thespian, Mrs. Anne Blair*. Mother…" Bryce murmured.

"Yes."

It was the first evidence he'd had as an adult that she'd actually existed, and her ghost suddenly seemed to be hovering. A rumble of her merry laughter drifted by, her voice deep and husky, perfect for elocution on the stage.

A memory intruded. She was seated at a harpsichord, and she patted the empty space next to her on the bench.

Sit with me, my little lord, she said to him. *Sing a song with your mother...*

He gasped, and Evangeline asked, "What is it?"

"I just had a...vision of her. She wanted me to sing with her."

"Did you?"

He struggled to focus, to bring the memory back again, but it had vanished. "I'm sure I must have." Feeling stunned, he asked, "How did you find this advertisement?"

"I've been searching while you were away. I told you I would."

"I didn't expect you to have any success."

"I've been visiting the newspaper offices, snooping in their archives. It's so easy to garner assistance when I have the very public title of *Lady* attached to my name. Everyone is helpful."

"I figured there had to be a benefit in marrying Aaron, *Lady* Run."

"You don't know the half of it."

"Have you stumbled on any mention of Father or his passing?"

"Not yet."

"How about Mother's trial or conviction?"

"Nothing so far, but I've learned there are ship manifests of the prisoners who were transported. I've hired some clerks to go through the records to see if we can locate her name or the name of the ship upon which she sailed."

"It must be nice to have money to waste on clerks and research."

"I wouldn't call it a *waste* of money, but yes, it's very nice to be rich. If I have to pick between being rich and being poor—as I was for most of my life—I pick *rich*."

He chuckled, charmed by her as he always was. She'd grown up at a girl's boarding school, and her flamboyant allure had been tamped down by the stern, stuffy headmistress. Evangeline had had to constantly hide and ignore the natural abilities she'd inherited from their beautiful, gifted mother.

Luckily her husband, Aaron, reveled in her flare and beguiling personality. She was now free to behave as extravagantly as she liked. Under Aaron's adoring eye she was blossoming, utilizing her full potential in ways few women were ever allowed.

"Even if you're being a grump about it," she said, "I won't stop searching."

"No, you shouldn't ever stop."

"But *you* have lost your enthusiasm."

"For some of it."

"Oh, Bryce…"

"I can't imagine how we'd get the property or title restored to us."

"You might be surprised what I can accomplish."

"No, I wouldn't, you scamp," he teased. "I saw how you worked your wiles on Aaron. The bloody man didn't stand a chance."

"No, he didn't."

She grinned, appearing wicked and dangerous to a fellow's equilibrium.

She was near the same age their mother had been when she'd been shipped off to Australia, and in Bryce's fleeting recollections of their glamorous, exotic mother, Evangeline was exactly like her. No wonder their father hadn't been able to resist. No wonder he'd wed their mother despite his family's insistence that he not.

"I want to find out about Mother," he said, "and our two brothers. I want to keep on with that."

"So do I. Very much."

"But the rest of it, the title and such…"

His voice trailed off, and she finished the sentence for him. "You don't think we could succeed, so you can't bear to try."

"No."

"What an absolute fusspot you've become."

He flushed with embarrassment. "It's humiliating. I admit it."

She studied him, her blue eyes digging deep. "What else is this about? You are my daring, dashing big brother. You'd never let a bit of difficulty dissuade you."

He shrugged again, vexed by his low mood. "Since I learned about all of this, I'm at loose ends. I don't know who I am anymore."

"You never did. You were an orphan with no past or connections."

"I had those…memories though, of our parents. They haunted me."

"And now that they're not just memories? Now that there is some heft behind them?"

"I'm very sad for all that was lost, but for what might have been too."

She reached over and patted his hand. "That's certainly understandable, Bryce."

"I don't fit in the life I built for myself."

He was a gambler and occasional actor who performed when he could, wagered when he assumed he could win, and constantly scrounged for money. Since discovering his true history he was adrift, as if his current activities were too frivolous to pursue.

"What do you mean?" she asked.

"I feel as if I should do more or *be* more than what I am."

"Too right, my dear brother!" she fumed. "You're Earl of Radcliffe. You shouldn't have to sing for your supper."

"I'm good at it though."

"Yes, you are. We both are—thanks to our magnificent mother."

"I won't sing again," he announced more abruptly than he'd intended. "I'm through with it—for the foreseeable future."

"Why?"

"I'm leaving London."

"Leaving?"

"Yes. It's all decided so don't try to discourage me."

"Of course I'll *try*. I've only just found you. I'm not too eager to have you dash off."

"It won't be a dash," he claimed. "It will be more of a slow trip into the sunset."

"You're departing the country?"

"Yes."

"To go where?"

"To follow in my father's footsteps."

She gaped in horror. "Adventuring?"

"Yes. Down the Nile in Africa."

"You're joking."

"No. We sail in two weeks."

"So soon? You've never previously mentioned an interest in such a dangerous endeavor. Who put this insane idea into your head?"

"Some acquaintances are financing a venture, and when I heard about it my blood raced."

"Our father's blood perhaps?"

"Perhaps. Chase Hubbard had already signed on. He asked me to join him."

"Chase Hubbard! I'll kill him, and if I can't get my fingers around his slender throat, I'll have his sister do it for me."

Chase Hubbard was a childhood friend of Bryce's. His sister, Amelia, had taught school with Evangeline in the years before she was ever Lady Run.

Chase's life resembled Bryce's in nearly every way. His father had been a French count, his mother the man's mistress. When his father had died, he'd received no monetary settlement, no inheritance, no recognition at all. He was adrift in the world as Bryce had always been adrift—with only his sister, Amelia, at his center.

As far as a companion on an African adventure, Chase was likely the very best and very worst choice. He was carefree enough to step up and participate, but wild enough to land himself in enormous trouble after he was there.

"What brought this on?" she ultimately inquired.

"I have to try something different—for if I remain here I'll go mad."

"I want you to stay."

"I can't."

"What about Mother? What about our brothers?"

"Find them for me while I'm away. Let me come home to learn that you've located them and they are all safe and sound."

"We agreed to marry."

"You agreed. I didn't. Not exactly."

Ramsey glared at Rebecca. Suddenly she was balking over their plans to wed, and if she continued to refuse, what would he do with her? They'd left London in a fast attempt to elope, but she'd gotten cold feet, which he viewed as a hilarious development.

He was the consummate bachelor, so it seemed that he was the one who should have been fussing. But she was spoiled and foolish and starting to wonder if she couldn't arrange a better ending. And she probably could have—in the past.

They were beyond the day when she could have found a wealthy nob for a husband. She was very pretty, but with her dowry squandered she wasn't much of a catch. He was rich enough for both of them, so it didn't matter to him that she was poor.

"What if you're increasing?" he asked.

She scowled, perplexed by his query. "Why would I be?"

"Rebecca, we've been fucking like rabbits," he crudely reminded her.

"Oh. How would I know if I was?"

"If you were what? Increasing?"

"Yes."

"Do I look like a midwife to you? How would *I* know? That's information a woman is supposed to possess, not a man."

"I thought there were signs."

"There are." He considered for a minute. "Your monthlies stop."

Her cheeks flushed bright red. "I can't believe I'm in the middle of a conversation where a man voiced the word *monthlies* to me."

"It goes with the carnal territory, sweetheart. If you want to misbehave, you should be able to talk about your bodily parts."

They were in a bedchamber in Michael's country house. They were naked, with him stretched out on the bed and Rebecca pacing. He was waiting for her to calm down so something interesting could happen, but she was more intent on fretting and stewing.

They'd been passing through the area on their journey north when Rebecca had suffered a fit of nerves. Michael and her sister, Magdalena, were back in the city, so the place was empty, and Ramsey figured they might as well stop and regroup. The added benefit was that Michael wouldn't expect Ramsey to be at Orphan's Nest, so his friend would never come there should he feel compelled to mount a search.

The servants knew Ramsey. He'd previously stayed with Michael, so they hadn't been overly curious when he'd blustered in with an unidentified female. He hadn't clarified her presence—or his—but clearly the staff understood Ramsey was engaging in an illicit affair.

"My monthlies aren't ever regular," she said.

"Then I haven't a clue what to tell you, but are you willing to risk having a babe without a husband? How would you support yourself? How would you explain it to the neighbors?"

"I could claim I'm a widow and that my husband was a soldier who was killed in the war."

He rolled his eyes. "Are you imagining you'll be the first person to peddle that malarkey?"

"Aren't there ways to prevent a babe from catching? I heard some women whispering. They insisted it was possible."

"There are some *ways* to prevent it, but normally you have to practice them before you spill yourself against a womb on a dozen different occasions."

"Oh."

"You're being ridiculous about this," he scolded.

"Am I? I don't know you at all, and I've realized I'm a tad afraid of you."

"It's a hell of a time for you to discover you're afraid."

"What if you're not rich? You told me you are, but what if you're not?"

It was a fair question. He was a renowned liar who'd grown up on London's mean streets. A boy in that seedy environment quickly learned how to survive, and lying was the least of his transgressions.

"It's a little late for you to complain or worry," he said.

"Better late than never."

"If I'm not wealthy I guess you're screwed, but aren't you screwed anyway? If you don't hitch yourself to my wagon, what will you do?"

"I have no idea."

"It's not as if you have any options left after me. I could take you to Michael's club and convince him to hire you as a whore. I could vouch for your abilities."

"Michael Scott employs whores?"

She was so shocked that he laughed. "It's a squalid, disreputable gambling club, Rebecca, where men wager and pretend they're not married to their nagging, frumpy wives. Of course he employs whores."

"Have you met some of them?"

"Met them? Honey, I'm the one who gives them a ride to see if they're worth hiring."

She stopped pacing and glared at him. "I can't ever decide if you're telling the truth."

"Then you'll never be bored with me, will you?"

He studied her, thinking her body was so fine, like a sculpture that might be displayed in a museum. She was slender, but rounded in all the right spots, her breasts pert and full, her ass the perfect size to fill a man's questing hands. And she was so beautiful.

He'd never planned to wed, but once he'd settled on the prospect, he'd swiftly gotten used to it, and he couldn't fathom not having her as his bride.

If he couldn't persuade her he was beginning to suspect he'd regret it forever, but he couldn't figure out why he would. She was flighty as a mockingbird, fussy and spoiled and hard to please, but damn, didn't he yearn to try!

"Come over here, Rebecca." He patted the mattress.

"I don't like that gleam in your eye. When you look at me that way, you always coerce me into doing things I shouldn't."

"Good, now come here."

"Why?"

He put his fingers on his cock, stroked it a few times, and it grew to an impressive length. She was loose and immoral, possessed of every doxy's best traits, and her interest was immediately piqued.

"I want to show you an interesting trick," he said.

"What is it?"

"You can do it with that mouth of yours instead of talking."

"What do you mean?"

He gestured for her to approach, and slut that she was, she obeyed. With her having such rampant sexual curiosity, he couldn't believe she hadn't already birthed a dozen babes.

"Climb up on the bed."

"I might—if you tell me what's in it for me."

"Lick me with your tongue."

"With my tongue!"

"From the root to the tip. When you get to the top, you suck the whole darn rod into your mouth."

She stared him down with a sort of horrid, fascinated excitement. Eventually she mused, "I've heard about this."

He snorted. "For a girl who's never been wed, you've been privy to an awful lot of gossip that you shouldn't have."

"If I hadn't eavesdropped, how else could I find out? It's not as if I could ask my sisters."

"Too true."

She slid onto the mattress, perched over him, and finally she leaned down and flicked her tongue as he'd instructed. He clasped her neck and held her in place until she did it several times. Then she sucked him between those ruby lips of hers, and he took a few slow, deep thrusts. She drew away, and he let her sit up.

"That was very…wicked," she murmured.

"It's a whore's tactic, so I thought it would tickle your fancy."

His lazy gaze wandered down her torso, and his heart seemed to swell in his chest. It dawned on him that—besotted fool he apparently was—he'd do anything to stay by her side.

"We don't have to marry," he told her. "Not if you don't want to."

"We'd keep on as we are?"

He shrugged. "Why not? It's not as if there's anyone to complain. And if we ever raise suspicions, we can lie and claim we've been wed for years."

"I'd feel more comfortable that way—for now."

He realized she was anxious over what she'd set in motion. Often he noted her pondering whether she should flee when he wasn't watching. On the one hand, she grasped the safety of a connection with him, but on the other, if he turned out to be dangerous or untrustworthy, she was plotting her escape.

But there was no going back. He'd warned her, but it was difficult to explain facts to a female who wouldn't listen.

He pictured her staggering to Cliffside, ruined, with child. Gaylord Farrow would understand instantly what had happened to her, and he'd likely toss her out on the road and lock the door behind her.

The only path Ramsey could devise was to fornicate with her as frequently as he could. Sooner or later a babe would catch, and she'd be caught too.

"Put your mouth on me again," he said.

"You like it?"

"Of course I like it. It's a man's favorite treat in the world."

"Then I'd best practice until I can do it correctly."

She bent down and applied herself to the task. He grinned up at the ceiling, thinking his life could never get any better than it was at that very moment.

"Mr. Farrow!"

At hearing his name, Gaylord nearly didn't glance around. He was stomping down the busy city street, in a temper and in no mood to chat. As usual, Maggie's stubbornness was wrecking his plans. Still though, his manners won out, and he spun to see who had summoned him.

It was a lady's maid, dawdling next to an ornate coach. To his surprise, the maid's employer—Lady Felicia Gilroy, Lord Stone's daughter and Michael Scott's fiancée—was waving at him out the window.

They hadn't previously been introduced, so he wasn't sure how she knew who he was, but his pride was stroked by her recognition, and his mind was already calculating furiously, trying to ascertain how he could use it to his advantage.

"Lady Felicia." He smiled his most charming smile and went over to her. "I haven't had the pleasure, and I am extremely flattered by your regard."

"I hope you don't find me too forward," she said.

"Not at all. What can I do for you?"

"Could you spare a minute of your time?"

"Certainly."

A footman jumped to assist, and Gaylord climbed in the carriage and seated himself across from her. The maid huddled outside, giving them some privacy, which piqued Gaylord's curiosity.

What on Earth could Lady Felicia want?

"I made some inquiries," she told him, "and I've been informed that you are the current tenant at Cliffside."

"Well...yes, I am."

"I visited the other day. I believe I met your wife, Mrs. Farrow?"

"Yes, she mentioned it. We were honored to have you call on us."

"My betrothed is Michael Scott."

Gaylord beamed with false delight. "He's an old and very close friend."

A frown creased her brow, and he could see that—whatever she'd sought—she was having second thoughts. After all, a woman of her status never lowered herself to accosting a stranger.

He flashed a kind, commiserating look. "I was shocked by your hailing me. What is it you need? I beg you to confide what it might be. I'm at your service, milady."

"I must ask you a question," she tentatively ventured.

"Anything." His tone was obsequious, cajoling.

"Can I rely on your discretion, Mr. Farrow? I'd like to discuss a rather delicate situation, and I can't have anyone learn that I had. For example, I couldn't have it getting back to...ah..."

"I'm the very soul of discretion, milady, and I would never reveal your query." He took a gamble, rolled the dice. "Is it about Mr. Scott? He and I are so intimately acquainted. How may I allay your concerns?"

"It's not about him. It's about...well...an odd encounter we had at Cliffside."

If Pamela said something stupid, I'll kill her!

"What sort of encounter?"

"When we arrived, there was a woman in the drive. Her name was Magdalena Wells."

Maggie! Dammit! What had she done now?

"Maggie is my sister-in-law. Has she upset you?"

"Yes."

"How?"

"She introduced herself to me as Mr. Scott's fiancée."

"His fiancée?" Gaylord scoffed. "Everyone knows Mr. Scott is engaged to *you*. Maggie is mad as a hatter. She always has been."

"I must admit that—when it happened—I couldn't decide what to think. And I was too embarrassed to ask Mr. Scott about her."

"I completely understand."

She gnawed on her bottom lip. "So…she has no hold on him?"

Gaylord reflected on Maggie, on her ceaseless condescension and disdain. She blamed him for every little misstep, and he was so sick of dealing with her. Her refusal to follow through with Michael Scott was galling, and Gaylord had warned her he'd get even, but he hadn't expected the opportunity to arise so soon.

"May I be frank, Lady Felicia?" he softly inquired.

"Yes, please."

"Maggie moved to the city some years ago."

"Moved…on her own?"

"She was evicted, actually, by her father." He leaned nearer and whispered. "She has very loose morals."

"My goodness."

"She runs a charity mission."

"She helps the…less fortunate?"

"Yes—along with a few other, more dubious enterprises."

"How absurd."

"I've always thought so. She's brought great shame to our family." His expression grew sympathetic. "You asked if she has a *hold* on Mr. Scott."

"If she's not engaged to him as she claimed, what is their connection?"

"I'm sorry, but it's too disreputable to describe for your maidenly ears."

She pondered for an eternity, struggling to discern what type of disreputable relationship a woman would have with a man. Finally she gasped with affront.

"She's his mistress?"

"Yes." As if in pain, he blurted out, "Oh, it's all so shocking. She had such a decent, honorable upbringing. Her transformation is inexplicable, but then Mr. Scott is quite dashing. It's easy to see why she'd be bowled over."

"What about Mr. Scott? Does he…love her?"

"Madly, my dear. Passionately." Gaylord pursed his lips. "I shouldn't have told you, but isn't it better to know? Wouldn't you rather hear that you have significant competition? It would eat away at you to harbor suspicions."

"He loves her!" she repeated, sounding stunned and very angry.

"And you about to be his bride. You poor thing! You'll have to battle so valiantly for his attention." He sighed. "I've wanted to tell you. Many people have wanted to tell you, but none of us could figure out how."

"How long have they pursued their affair?"

"For ages. Her establishment is down the street from his gambling club. She stays in the neighborhood so they can be together all the time."

"Together? They live openly in sin?"

He shrugged. "As I mentioned, we've all been anxious to tell you. What new bride should have to begin her wedded life in such a muddle?"

"What bride indeed?" She stared at her lap.

He sighed again. "I wish there was some way to shut her down and move her out of the area. She won't take herself out of Mr. Scott's clutches, but if her establishment was shuttered, she'd have to go away. Our family's disgrace would end, but I simply don't have the authority to close the place."

"If only there was something *I* could do…" she murmured.

"Yes, or maybe someone powerful like your father who has a bone to pick with Mr. Scott." Slyly, as if an afterthought, he added, "It's appalling how she procures girls for him. She must be stopped."

Lady Felicia's gaze whipped to his. "She what?"

"I'd hate to have you swept up in it. If you're his wife, won't it make you complicit?"

"In some sort of…pandering?"

"Yes, that's certainly how I view it."

"That's…that's…despicable."

"Her charity mission is merely a pretense for aiding the downtrodden. Whenever a pretty girl comes in, she informs Mr. Scott, and the girl winds up employed at his club."

"Employed…how?"

"Again, milady, I oughtn't to discuss such dissolute business with an unmarried maiden such as yourself."

"I suppose not."

She appeared sufficiently wretched, and he could barely keep from smirking.

My work here is done!

"Perhaps I shouldn't have shared such horrid tidings," he said.

"No, no, I'm glad we talked. I'm glad to know."

"I can't imagine how hard it will be for you to wed a man of Mr. Scott's…low reputation."

"It will be very difficult," she baldly confessed, and tears had flooded her eyes.

"Magdalena could ruin things for you before you have a chance to be happy with Mr. Scott. But then Maggie is vain and spoiled. She takes what she wants without regard to the damage she inflicts on others. She'll show you no mercy. That I can guarantee."

"Unless she was forced from his life," she mused. "If she was eliminated as a temptation for Mr. Scott, she couldn't harm me."

"Too right, milady."

He reached for the door, and an alert footman noticed and opened it.

"If I can be of further assistance," Gaylord gushed, "don't hesitate to contact me."

"I won't. Thank you."

With a flourish, Gaylord offered her his calling card, then he stepped to the street and sauntered off, whistling as he went.

CHAPTER NINETEEN

THE SENSATION—WHEN IT OCCURRED—WAS always very strange.

Michael would be in the middle of a perfectly ordinary conversation, then he'd lapse into a dreamlike state, very much as if he'd been rendered unconscious. Except he didn't enter a black void.

The place where he went was filled with color, light, and sound. He'd view everything as if he was looking through another man's eyes. And it was always the same man. It had happened all of Michael's life, and in fact when he'd been a small boy, they had communicated in an odd, made-up language that only the two of them could understand.

Was the other person an angel? A ghost? Why was Michael connected to him—or it—in such a strange way? When the visions faded, he was confused and bereft and wondered if he wasn't insane. If he wasn't suffering from a touch of lunacy, how could he explain it?

This time was no different.

He was inside the other man—a soldier, apparently—and studying his surroundings. Riding a fine horse, he could see the red of a uniform coat sleeve where a hand gripped the reins. The man had been in the army for years and was comfortable on the animal's back. It was a summer day, the sky blue, the temperature warm and balmy, the trees a green canopy that shadowed a pretty lane.

There were orchards on either side, and in front of them, a grand house was perched on a hill.

There it is, a second soldier said from off on his left. *What do you think?*

Michael felt his shoulders shrug. *It'll do, I suppose.*

Bloody right, you lucky bastard.

Michael was aware of numerous emotions. Vanity. Amazement. Worry. Exhaustion.

They'd been traveling for weeks, the journey almost over, but there was no peace awaiting them. There would be fighting and quarrels, and the man loathed bickering and wouldn't allow it. A ripple of temper brushed by, but he tamped it down.

Sweet Jesu…

How could you have ever thought to refuse all of this, Matthew? Are you sure we're in the right place?

Matthew…

The name rang in Michael's mind like a loud bell, and he tried to squirm out of his chair, but he was paralyzed and unable to breathe.

Matthew, Matthew, Matthew…

"Mr. Scott? Mr. Scott!"

Michael shook his head, reality returning with a vengeance.

He was at his club, seated at a card table, a very fetching and mostly naked trollop on his lap. Three other men were seated around the table with him and they were staring, assessing him nervously—as if they'd just realized he was mad.

Ramsey was the only one who knew about the peculiar apparitions, and that was because Michael had experienced so many of them when they were growing up. Ramsey believed Michael was some sort of phantom who could inhabit other bodies, but if he was a phantom, he wasn't very effective. He had no ability to talk or influence the other man's actions.

"What?" he snapped, hating to have them watching him in his moment of befuddlement.

Had he spoken aloud during the episode? Ramsey claimed he did sometimes. If Michael had cried out in his catatonic state, what might he have said?

"Are you all right, sir?" the doxy cautiously asked.

"I'm fine."

"Were you planning to bet?" She gestured to the pile of coins. "It's your turn."

He didn't even peek at his cards, but tossed them away. "I'm out."

The other men anxiously peeked at each other, not certain if they should continue or stop too. There was so much money at stake. Michael had wagered upwards of five hundred pounds, which was a shocking development.

He rarely gambled, and when he did, it was for small amounts. If he risked more, it was because his partner was an asshole, and Michael intended to cheat the prick out of all he owned.

But Michael was in a foul mood, drinking and wagering and generally making a fool of himself. Ramsey was gone to Dover and wasn't present to rein in Michael's worst tendencies.

"You can keep on," he insisted to the other players.

Still, they didn't begin, and one of them asked, "Are you sure?"

"It's just money," he replied. "It's naught to me if I lose some of it."

They started in then, but with his temper festering, it was like having an elephant sitting at the table. He was impossible to ignore. He hadn't shaved, hadn't eaten. His clothes were unkempt, his condition messy.

Because he rubbed elbows with the premier rogues in society, he always dressed better, looked better, behaved better, and acted smarter than any of them. But for the foreseeable future, he simply didn't care. People were aware that something had happened to disorient him, and they were speculating over what it could have been, but none of them dared to pry.

Only Ramsey could have inquired. Only Ramsey could have fixed what was wrong, or at least calmed Michael's fury, but Ramsey was away just when Michael needed him the most.

A servant tapped him on the shoulder, and Michael scowled. "What is it?"

The man leaned nearer and murmured, "There's a woman to see you."

He glanced to the door, surprised to find Magdalena huddled in the foyer. She was attired in one of her frumpy gray gowns, her hair in a tidy, unflattering chignon. She might have been a fussy governess, a nun without her hood. Her eyes were cool and hurt as she tried not to notice the slattern on his lap.

"What does she want?"

"She'd like to speak with you. She claims it's urgent."

"Urgent?" he scoffed.

"Isn't that the lady from the charity mission?" the doxy said.

"It is. She's probably here to read a couple of Bible passages about sin and damnation."

The doxy laughed, and the servant asked, "Shall I tell her you're busy?"

Michael let his bored gaze meander across the room to her, his disdain oozing out. She wasn't interested in a relationship? She'd discounted what had blossomed between them? Well, to hell with her!

Yet he was curious as to why she'd come. During their last meeting, she'd been very clear as to her opinion of him. Other men, weaker men, might have mourned and raged over her rejection, but not Michael. His whole life had been one of heartache and loss. He never grieved. He never lamented his fate.

For a fleeting instant he wondered if she was about to inform him that she was increasing with his child, but he suspected it was too early for her to know, and he hoped it wasn't the case. She'd declined his help and support, and he was perfectly happy to leave her alone. A babe would complicate the picture, would force them into further contact.

"I'll see her," he grumbled. "Take her up to my office. Tell her I'll join her when I'm damn good and ready."

He glared at her, watching as the servant escorted her to the stairs. As she passed by Michael's table, he laid a hand on the slattern's breast and trained trollop that she was, she thrust out her bosom for greater access. He began kissing her, and he kept on kissing her until Maggie was out of sight, then he drew away and eased the doxy to her feet.

She pouted and tried to slip an arm around his waist, but he stepped away and headed to the bar to down a few glasses of whiskey. He dawdled until he was certain Maggie would be furious, then he went to the stairs and climbed.

He entered his office without knocking, annoyed to realize that he was pondering whether he *should* have knocked, if he should have been more courteous.

To hell with her, he fumed again. He didn't want her on the premises and thought she possessed an incredible amount of gall to have visited.

She was seated in a chair in front of his desk, and he walked by her and plopped down in his own chair. There was a whiskey decanter next to his elbow. He poured himself another glass, then—rudely staring at her over the rim—he insolently slouched down, legs crossed at the ankles.

"What can I do for you, Miss Wells? The man guarding the door said your matter was urgent, so I agreed to meet with you. But I must confess that I can't think of a single topic we need to discuss."

Instead of replying, she asked, "What's wrong with you?"

"What's *wrong*? Nothing. What do you want? Get on with it and, for pity's sake, be brief."

"Are you ill? Has something happened? What?"

"Are you deaf, Miss Wells? I'm fine. Now speak your piece and go."

She gestured to his shirt that was unbuttoned and most of his chest showing. "You're...slovenly."

"I definitely am, though why you'd notice or assume you're welcome to comment is beyond me."

"And you're intoxicated."

"So?"

"I've never seen you drunk before."

"As you don't know me very well and haven't spent much time with me, you wouldn't have had many chances to witness me in a state of inebriation, which I assure you is frequent and enjoyable."

He was being a prick. He recognized that he was, but what did she expect?

Their sojourn at Orphan's Nest had meant nothing to her. So...it hadn't meant anything to him either. He could be a cold, cruel asshole. He was used to it. He was good at it, and he was exasperated that she'd feel free to pop in and criticize.

"You're upset with me," she said.

"Me, upset? Why would you think so?" He tossed his glass toward the corner, and it shattered quite effectively against the coal stove that heated the room in winter.

She frowned, but didn't cringe or jump. "Don't act like this. We're friends, aren't we? I hate that you're so angry."

"Miss Wells, you are laboring under the mistaken and misguided impression that you have the right to barge in and pester me. You don't. You've found me in a condition you don't condone, but if you don't like it, you can leave."

Her cheeks flushed a pretty shade of pink. Obviously he'd hurt her feelings, but he refused to be moved. She wanted no liaison and that's what she'd receive. She'd suffered no heightened fondness, and if *he* had, so what? He wasn't some green lad who'd had his heart broken by his first girl.

Women were a penny a dozen. He'd get over her. He already had.

A silence festered and grew awkward, and finally she murmured, "I need your help."

"I'm not inclined to provide any assistance to you."

"I have nowhere else to turn."

Those beautiful blue eyes of hers had always been his undoing. He'd never been able to gaze into them and remain indifferent.

"What is it?" he was disgusted to hear himself ask.

"My sister, Rebecca, has run off with Ramsey Scott."

He was positive he'd misunderstood. "She what?"

"She ran off with Ramsey Scott."

"What do you mean by *ran off*?"

"Apparently they've eloped."

"To where? Scotland?"

"Yes."

She pulled out a letter and placed it on the desk so he could read the words her sister had penned. He was floored by the news, and he scowled, his fury bubbling up.

Ramsey had claimed he was riding to Dover to deal with a shipment of liquor they'd smuggled in from France, but he'd lied about his destination, and Michael couldn't believe it.

Ramsey had left England with Miss Rebecca? Ramsey had married her without a peep to Michael? Ramsey had forged ahead without seeking Michael's opinion or blessing? Ramsey had proceeded even though Michael had specifically warned him to stay away from Rebecca Wells?

Michael couldn't decide which sin was the greatest, and he was practically dizzy with trying to sort through his various outrages.

"Rebecca came to town while I was in the country with you," Maggie explained. "She was at the mission without my knowledge or consent. When I got back she'd already departed, with no one having any information as to where she was. I was hoping she was at Cliffside."

"Clearly she wasn't," he griped with more venom than was necessary.

"She wrote me this note, but it had fallen under the bed. I just found it."

"What exactly is it that you expect me to do?" He checked the date at the top. "It's been over a week since they sneaked off."

"Would you…go after them for me?"

"No."

"Please?" Tears swarmed into her eyes.

"If you assume some tears will sway me, you're dead wrong."

"I have so little left in my life. Rebecca and my sister, Pamela, are all I have. We've lost Cliffside, and I'm not certain I'll be able to keep the mission open."

"Why wouldn't you?"

"I had a trust fund to cover my costs but…"

She couldn't finish the sentence, so he finished it for her. "Gaylord squandered it."

"Yes."

She glanced down at her lap as if she was embarrassed, as if Farrow's despicable behavior was her fault.

In the days since he'd returned to the city, since he'd gone to her with his heart in his hand and she'd stomped on it and sent him away, he'd been reeling with dismay.

Her disdain had rocked him in ways he didn't comprehend, but he liked to picture her just down the street, liked to suppose that he could pass by her building and see her walking to the market or talking to a waif. The thought of her *not* being there, of the mission being closed and her moving away was extremely alarming.

He was about to tell her she couldn't leave, that *he* would personally finance her bloody charity if it would guarantee she'd stay in the neighborhood, when she said, "Ramsey Scott can't have any good intentions toward Rebecca."

Michael shrugged. "Probably not."

"Would he actually take her to Scotland? Would he marry her?"

Michael shrugged again. "Probably not."

"Will you ride after them? Will you stop them for me?"

"It's too late, don't you think? I can't imagine there's much of her chastity or reputation remaining."

She pushed herself up from her chair and rounded the desk, falling to her knees and clasping his hand as she had during a prior visit. He sighed with aggravation. It was all too much.

"I'm begging you, Michael. I know you can find your friend, that you can make him see reason."

"I likely could find him," he grudgingly admitted, not sure that he could.

"If I ever meant anything to you at all, if I ever—"

He couldn't bear to hear how she might conclude the remark, and he groused, "Get up, Maggie. Get up. There's no need to beg."

He gripped her wrist and pulled her to her feet, reluctantly advising her, "I'll look for them. I'll bring them back."

"Thank you."

"When I locate her, I can't guess what you'll do with her afterward. What if they're married? What if they're not and he's simply ruined her? Which situation would be worse?"

"I'll deal with it when she's home where she belongs."

"All right." He hated to have her so near, and he grabbed her arms and set her away. "Go now, and please don't come here again." She was about to argue the point, and hastily he added, "I'll send word when I have news."

"I appreciate it."

"You'll be at the mission?"

"Yes, I'll be at the mission."

He nodded, but was suddenly overwhelmed by the terrifying notion that he might rush to Scotland, then hurry back only to discover the mission shuttered and Maggie vanished.

A thousand panicked scenarios raced in his mind, and he absurdly yearned to clutch her to his chest and shout, *Don't leave me! Stay with me forever!*

He swallowed down the wildly inappropriate sentiments he longed to utter, and relief swept through him as she walked away, for once behaving precisely as he'd requested.

MAGGIE REACHED THE DOOR, and though she ordered herself to depart, she couldn't. Feeling naïve and ridiculous, she whirled to face him. But why linger? Why extend her anguish? It was torture being in his presence. Why tarry and make it worse?

Since she'd learned of his engagement, since they'd quarreled so viciously, her world was askew. She felt feverish and ill, confused and off balance, as if the floor had shifted and she couldn't stand up straight.

The previous night, as she'd tossed and turned in her lonely bed, it had gradually dawned on her that she was waiting for him to sneak in, to tell her he was sorry, that he hadn't meant any of it. She'd been listening for his tread on the stairs, for his hand on the doorknob. But of course he hadn't arrived, and she'd been crushed by his lack of regard, which was silly.

Evidently deep down she possessed a morsel of doubt as to whether she should have parted with him, so clearly she was insane. There was no other explanation, but she truly believed that if she never saw him again her life would not be worth living.

She couldn't fathom why he wouldn't cry off from his betrothal to Lady Felicia and marry Maggie instead. He was so stubborn. Why would he persist with Lady Felicia when the match was so insignificant to him? He was very rich, so he didn't need the wealth Lady Felicia would bring.

He'd stated over and over that *happiness* was his goal. Why then would he cast Maggie aside over a few ships and a bit of land? If he sought contentment and Maggie provided it, why not stay with her? Why not choose Maggie over Lady Felicia?

Maggie recognized that her vanity was in play. Once prior, she'd been smitten beyond reason, then jilted. The exact same thing had happened again, and she simply couldn't wrap her head around it.

Why was she so unlovable? She seemed determined to prove him wrong, to demonstrate her value, to demonstrate his error in selecting another over her. Yet what if she could convince him to wed? After all the harm he'd inflicted on her and her family, why would she want him? Was she mad?

"What?" he asked, on seeing her hesitate.

"I...don't know."

"I said I'd help you with your sister."

"And I'm grateful."

"Fine. You're grateful. Now go away."

"Don't you wish…"

Her voice trailed off as she realized she had no idea what she *wished*, and if she wasn't certain, how could she expect him to have an answer?

"Wish what?" he snapped.

"That...we could have found a different ending?"

"No. I gave you every chance, but you refused to take them."

"I thought you cared about me," she shamed herself by mentioning, as if she was begging for a crumb of affection.

"I did, but it didn't matter to you, and I'm not the type to rue or regret. I offered you what I could, and you tossed it back in my face. I'm over you."

How could he blithely move on? She was drowning with remorse, trying to figure out how to manage the remnants of fondness he'd stirred in her, but he didn't seem bothered to have had it collapse.

His eyes were cold and hard, his expression stony, supplying no hint that he'd ever been the funny, charming swain who had reveled with her in the country.

"I'm sure it's for the best if we part," she tepidly claimed.

"I'm sure it is too."

He came toward her, and for just a moment she braced, thinking he might pull her into his arms, that he might share some words of comfort or sympathy. Her mind was awhirl with debating whether she'd like it to occur or not.

Before she could decide, he stepped by her and opened the door, yanking it wide. He motioned for her to exit, indicating that she'd been dismissed, so it was pointless to dawdle, but despite all that had transpired, she was frozen in place.

The servant who'd initially escorted her was hovering in the hall, and when he saw them he leapt to attention, almost as if he was a soldier.

"Miss Wells is leaving," Mr. Scott said. "Show her out."

The man gestured to the stairs. Maggie dithered, feeling as if so much had been left unsaid, but it hadn't been really. They'd hashed it out to the bitter end.

"What will happen to my sister, Pamela, now?"

"Her circumstances are none of my concern. I suggest you ask your brother-in-law."

"Will she have to move at once?"

"Yes."

It was on the tip of Maggie's tongue to tell him he could have his affair, that she'd proceed with it, that she'd rescue Gaylord and Pamela one last time, but she simply couldn't. Not again. And when they'd always been so awful to her, why would she consider it for a single second?

She had to toughen up, had to grow a spine, had to stop letting the entire world walk all over her as if she was a rug in a parlor.

"Goodbye," she told him.

He could have told her goodbye too, but he merely nodded. He pushed her into the hall and closed the door. Swine that he was, he turned the key in the lock. It was a particularly snippy act that was rude and unwarranted, and she was a hairsbreadth away from pounding on the wood, from informing him he was the biggest horse's ass she'd ever met.

But if she responded in kind, she'd only be lowering herself to his level, would only embarrass herself further, so why engage in an untoward display? He likely wouldn't even notice.

The servant said, "Miss Wells? If you'll come with me, please?"

She spun and marched away.

CHAPTER TWENTY

"What do you think of her husband being so accommodating?"

Michael hadn't been listening to Felicia, and as he noticed she'd asked a question, he scowled. She was scowling too, glaring at him as if he were a barbarian who'd wandered in by mistake, or perhaps a burglar about to sneak off with the silver.

They were in Lord Stone's music room, which was packed elbow to elbow as people squeezed in for a concert that was about to start.

Michael didn't want to be at Lord Stone's house again, didn't want to be socializing with Felicia. The fete was another betrothal gala her mother had arranged—as if frequent interaction with Michael would make him more palatable to her snooty friends.

He should have left London already in search of Ramsey and Rebecca Wells. But after his most recent encounter with Maggie, he was more of a mess than ever. He hadn't been able to focus or concentrate, so leaving the city to chase after her reckless sister had been impossible.

He'd ride out in the morning—if he could get his head on straight—and he was in no hurry to locate Rebecca Wells. He'd known Ramsey for more than twenty-five years, and there was no way in hell Miss Wells was still a virgin. Why rush around, trying to find her. The damage was done and couldn't be repaired.

"What did you say?" he asked Felicia.

"Mother invited Lady Run to perform, and she agreed without first consulting her husband."

Michael's scowl deepened. "You're shocked because she'll perform without her husband telling her she can?"

"Yes."

"I'm sure the world will keep spinning."

"If I wanted to sing, I wouldn't have to seek your permission?"

"Why are you curious? Are you about to sing? I didn't realize it was one of your talents."

"It's not, but I'm curious as to how lenient you'll be with me."

"I won't be your nanny, Lady Felicia. As long as you don't shop until you beggar me, you can behave however you like—unless I see you fraternizing with scurvy characters."

"What are you talking about?"

"When I arrived, you were out in the garden whispering with a brigand named James Blaylock."

She blinked and held very still, claiming, "I have no idea who you mean."

"Nice try, Felicia, but he's a snake in the grass. Be careful you don't get bit."

"Are you bossing me?" she huffed.

"In this matter? Absolutely."

His reply incensed her and they might have erupted in a full-blown quarrel, but the entertainment was about to begin.

He was taller than most men in the room, so he could peer over the crowd to where Lady Run was standing next to a harpsichord. A blond man was seated at the instrument to accompany her.

Most of London seemed to be in attendance, so there was a crush of guests, and of course Michael had come late so he hadn't been aware that Lady Run was present. He studied her, assessing her beautiful blond hair, her big blue eyes.

"Is she a renowned singer?" he asked.

"Very renowned. You haven't heard her?"

"No. I don't spend many evenings at musical soirees."

"Your loss then, Mr. Scott." Her lips were puckered, as if she'd been sucking on sour pickles. "She's taken London by storm."

"Who has? Lady Run?"

"Yes, Mr. Scott, and please pay attention." She was exhibiting an unusual animosity. "It's annoying when you ignore me."

They were on the verge of a quarrel again, but he wasn't interested enough to learn why she was upset. If she grew too snippy, he'd depart. He couldn't figure out why he'd bothered to show up at all, but Lady Stone had sent him a dozen reminders, and he'd been too exhausted to flout her adamant summonses.

"Who is the man at the harpsichord?" he inquired. "Is that Bryce Blair?"

"Yes, he's her brother. They were separated as young children, though no one knows why."

Felicia continued speaking, but her words were just a loud buzzing in his ears. For some reason he was so dizzy he could barely remain on his feet. He felt as if he'd been poked with a pin. An old vision clouded his sight, and a query rang in his head.

How's my little lord? How's my little lord?

He saw a large, vibrant man laughing and tossing a blond boy up into the air. Michael was tiny too, watching the happy spectacle, grinning and holding hands with another boy. Was he holding hands with himself? Was he staring into a mirror? He and the other boy were whispering in their secret language.

He's home! He's home!

Michael was yanked from his disturbing hallucination by Bryce Blair's fingers whisking across the keys of the harpsichord. Lady Run began to sing, her vibrant, robust alto echoing off the rafters.

Michael's disorientation surged alarmingly, and his viewpoint narrowed as if he was observing Lady Run through a dark tunnel. She was standing at the end, surrounded by a halo of light. He couldn't catch his breath and was very afraid he was about to collapse to the floor in a stunned heap.

"Mother…?" His voice was strange, as if he was a toddler rather than an adult, and his arm was extended out to Lady Run in a beseeching way.

"Mother!" Lady Felicia cruelly snickered. "She's not your mother, Mr. Scott. It's Evangeline Drake. It's Lady Run. What's wrong with you? Are you ill?"

Lest he faint where everyone could see, he staggered out, reeling down the hall in a blind panic. After a bit of stumbling and groping, he found a door that led onto the rear verandah. He lurched out, feeling like a drowning man who'd heaved to the surface.

He listed over to the balustrade and leaned against it, peering up at the stars. Was he ill? Felicia had asked if he was, and he thought it might be worse than that. He thought he might be deranged.

He dawdled, terrified that he belonged in an asylum. People were locked away for much less. Should he put himself out of his misery and have himself committed? Was that the answer?

Suddenly Felicia was there beside him, and he nearly snapped at her to leave him be. Couldn't the bloody girl sense that he was desperate to be alone?

He had to compose himself, then sneak out and go home. He needed to drink copious amounts of liquor, imbibe until he was numb, then fall into a dead slumber so he could arise at dawn and rush to Scotland.

Why was he at another of Lady Stone's ridiculous betrothal parties? He'd hated every one so far, and if he spent much more time around Felicia, he'd start to hate her too. He kept coming by simply to be civil, to let her become accustomed to him, but he didn't care if she grew accustomed.

"When I mentioned that you looked ill," she said, "I was joking. But you seem unwell, and I decided I should check on you. Are you all right?"

"I'm fine."

"Are you sure? You're shaking like a leaf."

"I'm fine!" he repeated more curtly.

"Didn't you like Lady Run's singing?"

"She was grand, Felicia. Stop prattling at me."

She snorted with offense. "You don't have to be rude."

Lord, help me.

Struggling for calm, he forced a smile. "You needn't tarry out here with me. Go back in. I'll join you in a few minutes."

She was incredibly aggravated and appeared much too young to be a bride. What was he thinking attaching himself to her? When they fornicated, it would be like fornicating with a child.

"I haven't seen you since we visited Cliffside," she said.

He shrugged. "I've been busy."

"Yes, you're always busy, aren't you?"

"It's why I'm rich, Felicia. I *work* for a living, as opposed to some men I know." His disdain obvious, he nodded to her father's mansion.

"I need you to explain something to me," she said.

"What is it?"

Instead of clarifying, she added, "I don't suppose I should pursue the matter, but I'm anxious to have an answer."

"Well, ask away. I can't guarantee I'll reply to your satisfaction, but I'll certainly try."

"This is difficult for me."

"What is? Asking me questions?"

"No. Marrying you. I didn't want to."

"I realize that."

"My father ordered me to proceed, and I'm trying to be a good sport."

"You've been terrific."

"So…" She took a deep breath, looking as if she was about to jump off a high cliff. "Tell me about Magdalena Wells."

He frowned so hard his face hurt. "Miss Wells? Why would you be worried about her?"

"She was waiting for you that day at Cliffside."

"She wasn't *waiting* for me. I have no idea why she was there."

"Is she a friend of yours?"

He dithered, wondering how to describe Maggie, and finally chose, "I don't have female friends."

"She's convinced she's your fiancée. I heard her very clearly."

"She's insane."

"Is she?"

"How could I be engaged to two women at the same time? Why would I embroil myself in such a morass?"

"I agree. Why would you?"

He studied her angry expression, her clenched fists and squared shoulders. She was braced for battle, but he didn't have the patience to bicker. He was too befuddled by Lady Run and her brother.

"What's this about?" he asked. "Why are you fretting over her?"

"I talked to Gaylord Farrow."

Michael's blood boiled. "Did you?"

"I assume you know Mr. Farrow? You don't deny it?"

"No, I don't deny it, but whatever he told you, you shouldn't believe him."

"Oh, really?" she sneered. "And why is that?"

"Because he's a cad and liar. First James Blaylock, now Gaylord Farrow. You're mad to confer with men of such low repute, and I hope to God you weren't off alone with Farrow. Do it again, and I'll have a word with your father."

"Don't try to bully me, Mr. Scott. You're not my husband. Yet."

"No, I'm not, but I recognize a scoundrel when I meet one—as you obviously don't."

She pulled herself up to her full height, which was very short. "I forbid you to consort with Miss Wells ever again."

He snorted out a laugh. "You forbid me?"

"I may have to wed you. I may not have a choice, but I will not begin my marriage with your…concubine attached to your side."

"My concubine?"

"Yes."

It was on the tip of his tongue to tell her to sod off, but she was young and very inexperienced. Still though, he wasn't about to have her commanding him.

"Lady Felicia—" he started.

"Don't patronize me. When you use that tone, you're about to treat me as if I'm a child. I'm eighteen, I am your fiancée, and I'm about to be your wife. Speak to me with the respect and deference I am due or don't speak to me at all."

He hadn't previously seen this aspect of her character, but he should have expected it. She'd been raised with a silver spoon in her mouth, and apparently she viewed him as being on a level with her servants. Was it because of his low blood? Was she presuming he'd meekly acquiesce to being scolded? And by a woman no less!

"As you wish, Lady Felicia. I shall speak to you as the adult female you are."

Regally, she dipped her head. "I appreciate it."

"Let me be clear on one very important fact."

"What is it?"

"My personal life will never be any of your business."

She was feistier than he'd given her credit for being.

"I'm not poking into your private concerns. I'm simply informing you what I will tolerate and what I won't. You will *not* have mistresses. Another woman might put up with such a humiliation, but I won't."

He ignored her comment and kept on. "I have no affectionate relationship with Miss Wells."

Felicia scoffed. "I have it on excellent authority that you've been intimately connected to her for years, and you still are. I insist you cease your affair. I ask it as my bride gift from you."

At hearing her question his word, his temper flared, but he tamped it down.

"Believe what you will, but Miss Wells is an acquaintance."

"An *acquaintance* who thinks she's your fiancée."

"I told you she's deranged."

"She lives on your street, and she operates her charity there. I want her gone—from your neighborhood and your life."

"She's nothing to me," he firmly stated, and he nervously glanced up at the sky.

If he'd been a religious fellow—which he wasn't—he might have been struck by lightning for spewing such a bald-faced lie.

"If you don't remove her from your world, *I* shall have her removed. I swear it."

"Are you threatening me or Miss Wells?"

"I am not threatening anyone. I'm advising you of the consequences if you refuse to heed me. I'm very aggrieved, and I won't abide cheating or betrayal."

She was a veritable ball of umbrage, and he pondered how she could have mustered such indignation and bravado. It was shocking for her to have raised such a scandalous topic with him, and he was impressed.

Unfortunately for her though, no one bossed him or attempted to control his conduct, and most assuredly no one threatened him. Especially not a mere girl of eighteen.

"Let's go inside," he said, and he clasped her arm.

"We're not finished discussing this."

"We *are* finished. This subject is entirely inappropriate, and we're not pursuing it any further."

"I'm doing what my father ordered me to do!" She clutched a fist over her heart. "I've taken every action demanded of me by my family. So I think—on this small issue—I should get my way."

"There is no issue. Despite what Mr. Farrow claimed, I barely know Miss Wells."

"Liar."

"Let's go in," he said again. "You're overwrought, and I am in no mood to deal with a fit of hysterics. Nor will I listen to any slurs on my character."

He tightened his grip, and though she tried to wrestle away she couldn't. He escorted her in and pushed her into the music room where Lady Run was concluding her song to rousing applause. As the last notes rang out, he felt faint again.

Lady Felicia tossed a remark at him that was angry and insulting, but over the whoops and cheering of the audience, he couldn't decipher what it was. He clicked his heels, gave a polite bow, and walked out the front door.

Would he ever return? She was bringing him a few ships and a plantation in Jamaica, but their value wasn't equal to this sort of discord. If she could grow this incensed over rumors of Magdalena, just imagine how furious she'd be in the future when real matters arose to plague them.

Suddenly his marriage to an aristocrat's daughter didn't seem worth the exorbitant price.

RAMSEY SCOWLED AND SNIFFED at the air.

He could smell smoke, but had been slumbering so deeply that he couldn't bestir himself to jump up and check Michael's house for a fire. With Rebecca snuggled beside him, her curvaceous ass pressed to his thigh, wild horses couldn't have dragged him away.

He sniffed again, hearing a cork pulled from a liquor decanter, the rim of the bottle clinking on a glass, liquid pouring with a glug, glug sound.

He glanced to the window, wondering what time it was and how many hours until dawn.

"Shit!" he muttered and he sprang up, the blankets falling to his lap.

Michael was seated in a chair, slouched down, his coat off, giving every indication that he'd been there for quite awhile. He was smoking a cheroot, sipping a whiskey, and from the diminished amount in the decanter, it wasn't his first helping. How long had he been watching them?

"You're in my bed," he complained.

"Shit," Ramsey said again. "Sorry."

"Sorry you're in my bed? Or sorry I caught you in it?"

Rebecca drowsily rolled over, an arm across Ramsey's waist as she groggily mumbled, "What did you say?"

Michael answered for him. "I said, you two are in *my* fucking bed, and you've made a bloody mess of it too. I'll have to buy a new mattress. I won't sleep on that one again."

Rebecca lurched up on an elbow and shrieked, "Mr. Scott! What are you doing here?"

"I could ask you the same damn question, Miss Wells."

"Ah!"

She skittered away from Ramsey as if he was too hot to touch, and she scooted down and yanked the covers over her head, acting like a child who assumed she could render herself invisible.

"I can explain," Ramsey feebly insisted.

"I should hope to shout."

"It's just that—"

Michael held up a hand. "I'm not about to discuss this when you're naked—and in my bed. Have I mentioned that you're in my bed?"

"Yes, yes, I can see that you're upset about it."

"Put on some clothes," Michael snapped, "and haul your ass down to the front parlor."

He downed the dregs of his glass and stomped out.

"Shit," Ramsey muttered a third time.

He slid to the floor and was tugging his trousers on as Rebecca peeked out.

"Why would he look for us here?"

"I don't know."

"You didn't tell anyone where we were, did you?"

"No, did you?"

"No."

"A servant might have written to him," Ramsey said. "The butler corresponds regularly."

"The butler is a tattle? Why didn't you apprise me? If the servants gossip, we should have been more discreet."

He found her robe and tossed it at her. "Get dressed. He has a temper. Let's not keep him waiting."

"I can't talk to him! I won't!" She appeared horrified, as if Michael might tie her to the rack and torture her.

Ramsey sighed. "It's probably best if I speak with him alone."

In their raucous sexual foray, they'd pretty much destroyed the room, with chairs tipped over and furniture upended. He riffled through a pile and located his shirt and drew it on as she sat up, the blankets clutched to her bosom.

"What will he do to us?" she asked.

"To you? Nothing. To me? I couldn't begin to guess."

"What does that mean? Will he fire you? Will he beat you to a pulp? Will he shoot you? What?"

"He'll pick a spot somewhere between firing me and murdering me."

She gasped. "He wouldn't murder you. You're joking, right?"

"Yes, I'm joking. Get dressed for me though. He might kick us out, so we should be ready to go."

"Why would he kick us out? It's the middle of the night."

"But dawn's coming. He might order us back to the city."

"He's not my father," she sniffed. "He can't tell me what to do."

"Well, he can tell *me* so while I'm downstairs, prepare for us to depart."

Ramsey leaned over the bed and stole a quick kiss, hating to have the erotic interval conclude so abruptly. He'd wanted to wake up with her, to learn what outrageous act he could convince her to perform next. For a girl who'd been a virgin a few days prior, she was incredibly creative.

He hurried down the hall, wearing just his shirt and trousers, not bothering with shoes or coat. He was dizzy and disoriented and in no condition to spar with Michael.

When he'd left London with Rebecca he'd lied to Michael, claiming he was on his way to Dover to check on their liquor smugglers. Michael demanded absolute loyalty from people, so Ramsey couldn't predict Michael's response. Michael dealt with large sums of money and had to be certain that those around him were reliable. There was always too much at stake, so he didn't allow second chances. He couldn't.

Had Ramsey squandered Michael's trust? In all their years together, Ramsey had never deceived Michael on any topic. Had Rebecca been worth it? He couldn't decide.

Michael was in the parlor, in a chair by the fire, still drinking, still smoking. He motioned for Ramsey to sit, and Ramsey slinked over like the cur he was.

"Sorry," he mumbled yet again.

"You keep repeating that, and I heard you every time. You can stop now."

"All right."

"You said you could explain."

"And I can!"

"Give it your best shot."

"I like her. You know that."

"I could have sworn I told you to leave her be."

"I tried!" Ramsey declared.

"Not very hard."

"No, not very hard at all. I guess I couldn't resist."

Michael sipped his whiskey, his blue eyes like daggers boring a hole in Ramsey's gut.

"Why are you at Orphan's Nest?"

"We...ah...were traveling to Scotland to marry."

"You were going to marry her? Seriously?"

"I was." Ramsey nodded vigorously.

"But...?"

"She got cold feet and didn't want to."

"*She* got cold feet."

"Yes."

"Not you. Her."

Michael was dubious, and Ramsey shrugged. "Originally she thought it was a good idea. She was desperate to escape her brother-in-law's trouble, but she's reconsidered. I expect she's hoping she can find somebody better than me."

Michael snorted at that. "I expect she can too."

"So...we've just been passing the time."

"I already talked to the butler."

"Oh."

"He informs me that you two are disgusting."

Ramsey and Rebecca had used the house in sordid ways, eating and imbibing and generally making fools of themselves.

Rebecca was wild and loose, and since she'd always lived with her fussy older sister, she'd never had a chance to misbehave. But she'd definitely reveled in Michael's home.

They'd fornicated in every room—except Michael's bedchamber—

but in the end, there hadn't seemed any reason not to try it. Yet with Michael on the premises and his being extremely irate, Ramsey felt awful.

"How did you know we were here?" Ramsey asked.

"I didn't. I was riding north, hunting for you. I simply stopped to sleep for the night."

"Why were you searching?"

"Miss Wells left a note for Magdalena about your eloping. Maggie was worried. She thinks you're a bad influence."

"*I* am a bad influence? Obviously she doesn't know Rebecca very well."

"You're blaming this on Rebecca?"

"Damn straight." Ramsey studied Michael, gauging his dour mood. "Am I fired or what?"

"I couldn't fire someone who's been the friend you've always been to me."

Relief swept through Ramsey. "Thank you."

"But I wouldn't deem it amiss if I beat the crap out of you for being an idiot."

"Would you like to?"

"Not really. Your head's so hard, I'd likely break my hand. You'll have to work to worm yourself back into my good graces though."

"I will. I'll do anything, Michael. You know that."

"I *thought* I knew that. I'm not so sure anymore."

"I'll make it up to you. I promise."

Michael scoffed, his gaze irked and angry.

"What now?" Ramsey inquired.

"Now…you're about to get married."

"What do you mean?"

"We're saddling some horses, and we'll keep on for Scotland. You're not coming back to London unless it's with a leg-shackle on your ankle."

"I don't believe Rebecca wishes to wed."

"When have you or I ever listened to a woman?"

"Never?"

"Never," Michael agreed. "We're not about to start with an annoying tart like Rebecca Wells."

Michael rose and marched out.

"Where are you going?" Ramsey asked.

"To explain the facts of life to your fiancée."

"Maybe...ah...you should let me speak to her. She can be stubborn."

Michael glared over his shoulder. "That vixen has your prick wrapped around her little finger. I'm not about to waste time letting you tell her anything."

Michael reached the stairs and climbed to his bedchamber, Ramsey tagging after him like the faithful dog Rebecca accused him of being. As he arrived at his room, he didn't bother knocking, but then it was his house, and Ramsey and Rebecca had blatantly intruded.

Luckily she'd dressed—at least as much as she could without a maid to help. Her anxiety evident, she was sitting on the bed, her hips balanced on the edge of the mattress, her feet on the floor.

On seeing Michael, she scowled and demanded, "What's happening?"

"The minute the sun crests the horizon, we're riding for Scotland," Michael told her.

"Scotland! What for?"

"The two of you are marrying, just as quickly as I can accomplish it."

"I don't want to marry Ramsey."

"That horse is out of the barn, Miss Wells. You're about to be a bride, and I can't deliver you back to your sister without a ring on your finger."

"What if I refuse to accompany you?"

"You don't have a choice, so I suggest you get used to the idea that you're about to be a wife—with Ramsey Scott as your husband." Michael peered at Ramsey and, his derision clear, he muttered, "Poor girl."

CHAPTER TWENTY-ONE

Felicia huddled in her carriage, the curtain tugged back so she could peek out at the proceedings down the block. Magdalena Wells had returned to her establishment to find a heavy chain barricading the door, the windows being boarded up.

"I don't understand," Miss Wells complained.

"Which part is confusing you?" James Blaylock asked her.

He was acting in an overbearing manner, pretending to be a government official, and from Miss Wells's deferential attitude, he'd definitely succeeded in fooling her.

When Felicia had decided to put her foot down about Miss Wells, she hadn't been able to glean any sympathy from her mother, so she'd taken matters into her own hands. Mr. Blaylock seemed to be the only person in the world sensitive to her plight, so she'd sought his assistance.

Apparently, he and Mr. Scott were old enemies, though Mr. Blaylock wouldn't confide the root of their quarrel. But his dislike was potent and unwavering. He'd been practically gleeful over the chance to inflict secret harm on Mr. Scott, with that *harm* being perpetrated against Miss Wells.

When he'd suggested his ruse to Felicia, she'd been more than happy to follow his advice. Miss Wells wouldn't realize it was a sham until it was much too late.

"This is my building," Miss Wells said. "I've owned it for years."

"The prior owner was a Mr. Sterns? Is that correct?"

"Yes, but he was Vicar Sterns. He was a preacher."

"You bought it from him?"

"No, I inherited it when he died."

"He was behind in his taxes."

"What has that to do with me?" Miss Wells inquired.

"They are due and owing." Blaylock smiled a grim smile. "Can you pay them? It's quite a substantial sum."

He was holding a sheaf of papers, and he shoved them under her nose, pointing to the number at the bottom. She gasped with astonishment.

"Of course I can't pay that much, and I'm sure you're mistaken about this."

"I'm not."

"What is your name again?"

"Mr. Blaylock."

"What is your function in this situation? I don't believe you ever made it clear."

"I work for the tax assessor," he lied.

"Oh."

Felicia snorted with amusement.

She had to wed Mr. Scott, had to comply with her father's edict but if Mr. Scott was in love with another woman, she would not go forward. It was beyond the pale of what she could abide.

Felicia had grown up imagining the handsome swain she'd eventually marry, but as she'd stepped into adulthood, she'd had to accept that none of her dreams would come true. In her union with Mr. Scott, she would have the sort of tedious, unsatisfying life that her friends and her sisters were forced to endure. Their husbands all had mistresses and illegitimate children from their many affairs. They spent their money on trollops as well as on homes, clothes, and food for their second, alternate families.

Felicia would not live that way!

Mr. Scott was out of town, so it was the perfect time to act. She'd begged him to send Miss Wells away, but he'd refused, and his disregard had incensed her as nothing had in ages.

She didn't have control over much, but she intended to have control over *this*. Miss Wells would not remain in close proximity to Mr. Scott where she would cloud Felicia's existence with her scandalous presence.

"How can I rectify the dilemma?" Miss Wells asked Mr. Blaylock. "Whom should I contact?"

"There's no one, really—unless you're prepared to tender the whole amount."

"But...but...how would I?"

"That's not my problem, Miss Wells."

"You're being ridiculous. You can't simply confiscate my property and board up the windows without my permission."

"I can and I have," Blaylock pompously retorted, "and since the taxes are in arrears, the place isn't actually yours anymore."

"Stop, please," Miss Wells fumed. "I must write a letter to...to..."

"To whom, Miss Wells? Is there someone who could pay for you?"

Miss Wells gnawed on her cheek, and Felicia wondered if she was pondering Mr. Scott. Would the Jezebel dare mention him? If she named Mr. Scott as an ally, Felicia couldn't predict how she'd react.

Miss Wells's shoulders slumped. "No, there's no one who could help."

"And there's the other matter too," Mr. Blaylock continued. "You'll have to answer for it in court."

"What other matter?"

"The charges of pandering."

"Pandering?" Miss Wells asked. "What is pandering?"

"Do you deny that you supply girls to work in Mr. Scott's bordello?"

Miss Wells scowled. "That I what?"

"Don't pretend, Miss Wells. Mr. Scott has already been questioned, and he's admitted your scheme."

"My scheme?"

"When a pretty girl eats at your purported charity mission"—Blaylock imbued the word *mission* with an enormous quantity of disdain—"you steer her to Mr. Scott."

"I most certainly do not. He's a menace to society. I try to keep people away from him."

"A likely story, Miss Wells, and we have too many witnesses who say otherwise."

"What witnesses?"

"Mr. Scott for one."

"I demand to speak with him at once."

"I'm afraid that won't be possible."

"I demand it!" Miss Wells tried again.

"Now then, if you'll come with me?"

Blaylock clasped her arm and urged her toward his carriage, and though Miss Wells protested and dragged her feet, she was much too small to halt Blaylock's forward momentum.

Felicia let the curtain drop. There was nothing more to see. Blaylock would stop by to chat with Felicia after he was shed of Miss Wells, and no doubt, the rest would conclude without a hitch.

Poor Miss Wells...

Mr. Blaylock was extremely competent, and he had Miss Wells's downfall planned to the last detail. She would be dumped into London's convoluted and chaotic prison system. In the official records, her name would be misspelled so that—even if a person thought to search for her there—she wouldn't be listed on any prisoner manifest.

If she survived her incarceration—many didn't—and her case ever came to trial, Blaylock would bribe witnesses to testify against her. She'd be convicted and transported with no trouble at all.

Mr. Scott would return to the city to find the mission shuttered and Miss Wells vanished into thin air. No one would be able to inform him where she was or who had taken her. She'd disappear as if she'd never lived in the paltry neighborhood, as if she'd never known Mr. Scott. She would be gone forever, and Mr. Scott would swiftly forget her.

Felicia sighed. She hadn't realized she could be so cruel, that she had such a malicious streak buried deep inside. But honestly, when faced with such an outrage, how could she be expected to look the other way?

She knocked on the roof of her carriage and ordered her driver to pull away, and she didn't glance back. Not once.

MICHAEL SLOWED HIS HORSE and proceeded down the street to Maggie's charity mission.

If he'd had an ounce of his wits remaining, he'd have continued on past her building and kept on to his club, which had been sorely neglected of late. Considering the shady characters who patronized his establishment, and the rough brigands with whom he did business, there was no telling what shape the accounts were in.

He'd escorted Rebecca and Ramsey to Scotland, had stood with them as they'd recited their vows. Though he hadn't been rude enough to carry a pistol into the church, he might have been holding a gun on one member of the bridal party—and it hadn't been Ramsey.

His friend had been perfectly delighted to wed Rebecca Wells, but Rebecca hadn't wanted to, even though she was good and thoroughly ruined. Despite how Michael had scolded her and chastised, he couldn't make her feel guilty. During the ceremony, he'd guarded the door lest she try to sneak out when he wasn't watching.

Michael had never been the most moral man, but he'd been shocked by Rebecca's attitude. She'd been particularly blunt in explaining how she'd used Ramsey to escape her brother-in-law, and she insisted that matrimony had never been on the table between them. Ramsey had offered to help her, and she'd accepted with no strings attached.

She appeared to like Ramsey and they certainly got on well, but she didn't trust him, and Michael couldn't blame her. Even though Michael had vouched for Ramsey a dozen times over, he hadn't been able to convince her that Ramsey wasn't such a bad catch.

Michael sympathized over her reservations but for pity's sake, she had shred every ounce of reputation she'd ever possessed, and in the rules of her world—which she seemed to think no longer applied to her—she had to wed. Besides, if they hadn't, what would Michael have said to Maggie when he returned to London?

Michael had fixed the mess by forcing a marriage. Rebecca had been furious, but to hell with her. He didn't know what Maggie's opinion would be, but he hoped she'd be glad, and since the union was an accomplished fact, it was too late to complain.

On the trip south he'd left the dissolute pair at Orphan's Nest with instructions to enjoy a short honeymoon, but after that, he expected Ramsey to get back to work.

Ramsey had promised he would, but the poor oaf was so besotted that Michael had no idea if he'd ever see the man again or not. He might just keep on and on with Rebecca until his cock fell off.

After riding away without the newlyweds, he'd had a lengthy opportunity to deliberate his own future. What was it he wanted out of life? What direction should he take?

He'd never been prone to reflection or regret. He picked a path and blustered down it, but recently he was careening from one horrid decision to the next.

He'd relished the chance to poke Lord Stone—and his peers—in the eye by marrying into the *ton*, but Michael didn't actually care about a grand match. He didn't care about Felicia or her father. As her husband, he'd never experience anything but misery.

Felicia would never forgive Michael for pushing himself on her, so the whole arrangement was a hideous folly. His secret wish was to wed and replace the family he'd lost somewhere on the way. Marriage to Felicia wouldn't bring him any of the boons he sought. She'd be wretched forever, so why torment her?

The question had vexed him throughout the journey. Vanity was driving him, and it would stick in his craw to cry off, but if he did he'd no longer be engaged to Felicia. And if he was no longer engaged to Felicia, he could become engaged to someone else, that *someone* being Magdalena Wells.

Once he'd reached that realization, the rest had been easy.

Maggie was tough and smart and funny and resilient. She wasn't afraid of Michael, wasn't alarmed by his past or overly concerned about his status or ancestry. She understood him better than anyone—better even than Ramsey who'd been around in Michael's earliest memories.

When he'd quarreled with her about Felicia, he'd kept claiming that he wanted to be happy, and Maggie made him happy, *so* happy that he wondered if he hadn't fallen in love with her. He'd never been in love and had always assumed he couldn't suffer such a ridiculous sentiment, but if it wasn't love, how could he explain what was occurring?

He thought about her constantly, worried over where she was, if she was all right. Her rejection had pitched him into a gambling, drinking frenzy, but after he'd staggered back to sobriety and sanity his course was instantly clear.

He was mourning the loss of her and what she could have brought to his life. Why accept the ending she'd set in motion? Would he let her go without a fight?

To hell with Lady Felicia. To hell with Lord Stone and his debt. To hell with Michael's enormous pride.

He would extricate himself from the debacle with Lord Stone, then spend every second convincing Maggie she had to be his, and he wouldn't give her a minute's peace until he had the answer he needed.

Her building was in the middle of the next block, and suddenly he was in a glorious, ecstatic hurry to speak with her. He spurred his horse into a trot, but as he reined in, the sight that greeted him was so bizarre that he glanced around, certain—in his distracted state—he'd wandered down the wrong street by mistake.

The mission was shuttered, the windows boarded up, a chain with a padlock barring the door. Even the ragtag sign Vicar Sterns had hung when he'd first bought the place had been removed.

What could have transpired? The worst feeling of dread swept through him. Had she been injured? Had she passed away?

When she'd stopped by the club and begged him to chase after her sister, she'd specifically said she'd wait for news. She'd been definite. There'd been no mention of her leaving, of her selling out or sneaking off.

To his chagrin, he couldn't remember if she'd ever revealed who owned the property. Was it hers? If not, had she been evicted? He knew she was having financial trouble. Had she failed to pay the rent?

The prospect—that she might have been kicked out for being unable to pay—left him speechless and furious.

He would have helped her! He would have given her any amount of money. If a landlord had been bothering her, a quick visit from Ramsey would have fixed the entire situation.

But had she bothered to confide in him?

No, she had not!

He jumped down from his horse as a dozen street urchins rushed up, pleading to tend the animal for him. He tossed the reins to an older boy.

"What happened to Miss Wells?" he asked them. "Who saw?"

All of their hands went up, and the boy holding the reins said, "Some men took her away."

"In a carriage?"

"Yes. They tied her wrists with a rope!"

"Was she under arrest?" Michael asked.

"She seemed to be."

So...it wasn't an injury or illness, but it might have been an eviction. She might have been adjudged a debtor. Was she in that much of a fiscal mess? Was she in prison? Was she so proud that she'd let herself be arrested for penury rather than seek his assistance?

"When was this?"

"Two days ago."

"Who were the men? Did any of you know them?"

The children shook their heads, and the boy said, "Hadn't seen them in the neighborhood before."

Strangers, then. Strangers—who weren't aware of the rules. Anyone living in the area wouldn't have dared engage in mischief without obtaining Michael's permission.

He walked to the door and kicked at the rotted wood. It fell away, the chain and lock dropping to the floor with a dull clinking sound.

Like a berserker, he burst in, mentally understanding that she wasn't present, but determined to check anyway. He marched around the empty rooms, thinking the place seemed abandoned, as if it had been boarded up for years instead of days.

He climbed the stairs to her apartment and strolled through, but it didn't appear as if anything was missing. He opened the wardrobe and riffled in her pitiful collection of clothes. Her gray dresses were there and, folded in a box in the corner, were the garments he'd purchased for their sojourn in the country.

He picked up the box, deciding to keep it for later, to have a few pretty items for her to wear once he found her. And he *would* locate her. He made a silent promise to her and to himself, and the idiots who'd taken her had better beware. If she'd been harmed in even the slightest way, they'd pay forever.

He stomped down the stairs, box tucked under his arm, and as he stepped into the common room a flurry of activity erupted outside. A coach had stopped out front, but he couldn't imagine who would visit. The children moved away, clearing a path so a woman could approach, and his heart lurched in his chest.

"Maggie?" he said, but as the woman walked over the threshold, he said instead, "Lady Run?"

"Mr. Scott? What are you doing here?"

"Looking for Maggie Wells."

"So am I. What on Earth happened?"

"I have no idea," he replied, "but I intend to find out."

CHAPTER TWENTY-TWO

Evangeline stared at the empty dining room in what had been Maggie's charity mission. The place was decrepit and in need of a coat of paint, but during her prior visit, it had been thriving with activity and moral purpose.

Now, the windows were boarded over, and there was a general air of abandonment. The front door was demolished, and Mr. Scott the only one on the premises.

"Was it a break in?" she asked him.

"No. Some of the children outside saw her taken away two days ago."

"Taken to where?"

"It sounds as if she's been arrested."

"Arrested!" Evangeline huffed.

"Her hands were tied with a rope, and she was whisked away in a carriage."

"I've known Maggie Wells since I was seven years old, and I can assure you she'd never commit a crime."

"I'm wondering if she'd been swept up for penury."

"Oh, no..."

People were incarcerated for being poor. It was a shame and a scandal, but it was the law. A debtor had to pay his bills, and it wasn't a defense to say he had no money. The common feeling was that a person shouldn't spend more than he had, and it was wrong to defraud a shopkeeper or landlord.

She staggered over to a bench and sank down. "Was her situation that dire?"

"She was having financial trouble, but I don't know how bad it was."

"I wish I'd stopped by sooner. She wrote to me, but I was out of town. The moment I returned, I came over." She gestured around. "I can't believe this."

"Neither can I."

"We have to locate her. If she's having legal difficulty, I'll be able to get her out of it. If no one will listen to me, they'll certainly listen to my husband."

Mr. Scott was still standing, and he was swaying, appearing dazed.

"Sit, would you?" she said. "I realize it's horrid to mention this to a manly fellow such as yourself, but you look as if you might faint."

"I'm fine. I'm...I'm..."

The sentence trailed off, and he pulled out the bench across from her and dropped onto it. His gaze was unfocused, as if he'd been rendered comatose or was suffering a malady. Was he ill? Was he prone to seizures?

In the stories she'd heard about him, he was considered tough as nails, and there'd never been the slightest hint of his having any weaknesses.

"Mr. Scott," she quietly murmured, and when he didn't respond, she repeated it more firmly. "Mr. Scott!"

As if he'd been in a stupor, he physically shook himself, embarrassment coloring his cheeks.

"Where were you?" she asked. "For a minute there, you were completely absent."

"I'm sorry. Did I...ah...say anything?"

"No."

He mumbled, "Thank God."

"May I inquire as to your...*interest* in Maggie Wells? I've visited twice now, and you were here both times."

"She's a...friend."

"A good friend?"

"I suppose you could describe it that way."

The enigmatic reply concerned Evangeline. There were a hundred awful rumors swirling about Mr. Scott, each worse than the last. The members of the *ton* were agog over Felicia Gilroy having to marry him. Evidently he was a very shady, very notorious character with no honorable intentions toward anyone.

Why was he sniffing around Maggie?

"Are the two of you romantically involved? Is that it?" His eyes narrowed as if he'd scold her for her rude query, and she hastily added, "I apologize if I'm prying, but she seems to be all alone in the world. It would be easy for a dishonorable person to take advantage of her."

He chuckled. "They don't come anymore dishonorable than me."

"You're engaged to Lady Felicia. I was present at the party when your betrothal was announced. We met there."

"Yes, I remember."

"Should I worry about Maggie? Or should I worry about Lady Felicia?"

He didn't answer, but leaned forward, his elbows on the table. He studied her, and she returned his stare, studying him just as meticulously.

Though he enjoyed a very low reputation, and she probably should have been afraid of him, she wasn't. There was a familiar aspect to him, as if they'd been closely acquainted forever, which was extremely peculiar. She didn't really know much about him other than what she'd gleaned from gossip.

Her husband, Aaron, had pointed out that Mr. Scott looked just like Bryce. Mr. Scott was tall, handsome, and masculine as Bryce was tall, handsome, and masculine. Their facial features were exactly the same, the only difference being that Bryce had Evangeline's blond hair, and Mr. Scott's hair was dark.

But those blue eyes…

There weren't many people who had eyes like that. Could they be related in some fashion?

"Where are you from, Mr. Scott?" She leaned on her elbows too, so they were nose to nose. "I was told you're an orphan, but have you any information about your kin?"

Again, he didn't respond, but continued to assess her. Finally he posed the oddest question. "Have you found your brother?"

"My brother?"

"Yes, you and your brother, Bryce, have another sibling, and you were separated from him when you were young. Aren't you trying to locate him?"

"I am trying to locate him—them."

"Them?"

"My twin brothers, Michael and Matthew Blair."

"Matthew…Blair."

"Yes."

At her speaking the name *Matthew*, he seemed to fall into a trance, and he cocked his head as though he was hearing voices. For a nervous second, she glanced at the door, wondering if he was a lunatic, if he might be dangerous, but he exuded no impression of menace or peril.

"Mr. Scott!"

She snapped her fingers, the noise yanking him out of his spell.

"I beg your pardon." He physically shook himself again. "I'm not myself today."

"You have some unusual quirks, Mr. Scott. Is Lady Felicia aware of this…affliction of yours? Does it plague you often?"

But his reply was, "How were your brothers lost?"

"It's a tragic tale, actually. I'm not sure I have time to tell it."

"I want to know."

She smiled a sad smile. It was difficult to confide that her mother had been a convicted felon, but her only crime had been loving a man who was too far above her. With Evangeline up-jumping into her own marriage, her character and motives in wedding Aaron were suspect. It wouldn't burnish her halo to confess such a horrid event.

Yet she wasn't ashamed of what had happened to her mother. She was angry about it, enraged by the unfairness and—despite Bryce not pursuing the matter—determined to obtain justice on her parents' behalf. And Mr. Scott was genuinely curious. Considering his own past, he wouldn't judge or condemn.

"My mother was an actress and singer," she said.

"Ah…of course." He added the oddest comment. "I remember now."

"Remember what?"

He made a *hurry up* motion with his hand. "Go on."

"My father should have been Earl of Radcliffe."

Mr. Scott gasped. "Radcliffe, yes."

"You've heard of it?"

"No."

She could see why he was reputed to be such a successful gambler. He could hide every bit of his emotions, providing no clue what he was thinking. She scowled, deeming him more peculiar by the moment.

"They were madly in love, but his family didn't approve."

"They married, didn't they?"

"Mr. Scott, do you know more about me than you're telling?"

"No, but what happened to your parents? They're not still alive, are they?"

"Well, my father is not. He passed away, but my mother was transported to Australia."

"As a felon?"

"Yes."

"On what charge?"

"My father had showered her with gifts and money. After he died, his relatives claimed she stole it."

"Bastards." Quickly, he muttered, "My apologies, Lady Run."

"No, no, it's all right. You've stated my opinion exactly."

"And your mother? Have you learned any information about her?"

"No, but I've just started investigating."

He frowned. "Might she be alive?"

"The chances are slim, but I'm hoping." She gave a self-deprecating laugh. "My husband says I'm the eternal optimist."

"What about your siblings? The twin brothers? How were you separated from them? Was it when your mother was transported?"

"Yes. A friend of my father's, a Mr. Etherton, took custody of us for her. He arranged for us to attend different boarding schools. My brother, Bryce, and I arrived at ours, but the twins didn't."

"Why?"

"They were traveling with Mr. Etherton's servants, and they spent the night at a coaching inn. There was a terrible fire, with a great deal of confusion. We're certain they didn't perish in the fire—"

"But the servants minding them died."

"Yes. How did you know?"

He studied her as if he actually had the answer, then he shrugged. "I just guessed."

"They vanished without a trace—even though Mr. Etherton searched for years. Again, I'm hopeful we'll find them."

She couldn't bear to think of her brothers, those little lost lords cast to the winds of fate. She didn't remember them, but Bryce said they'd been rambunctious, sturdy boys, devoted to each other, as if they were one person instead of two.

They'd resembled their handsome, dashing father rather than their mother, and they'd just celebrated their third birthday. Evangeline liked to imagine a happy ending for them, that a kindly, childless couple had found them wandering and taken them in. The more likely scenario was that they'd starved on the streets, or were murdered, or sent to a parish poorhouse where they'd passed away from lung fever.

A wave of anguish crept in, tears flooding her eyes, and she opened her reticule to retrieve a kerchief. As she yanked it out some of the contents plopped onto the table, among them a small statuette carved from ivory that had belonged to her mother. It had always set on her mother's harpsichord.

Mr. Scott froze again, in that bizarre manner he had. He gaped at the statue, then reached out as if he might trace his finger over it, but he didn't. His hand hovered, almost as if the statue had magical powers and he was afraid to touch it.

"I have to go," he suddenly said, and he rose so hastily that the bench he'd been sitting on toppled over behind him.

She gazed up at him, feeling inordinately glum that he would leave so abruptly, that their conversation was over. Though she couldn't explain it, she was drawn to him as if they possessed a deep, potent bond.

"What about Maggie?" she asked.

"I'll find her. I swear it to you."

"And your *friendship*? What will become of it?"

"If I have my way, she and I will get a lot closer."

"Have you honorable intentions?"

"Plenty of honorable ones and no dishonorable ones."

She couldn't decide if that would be a blessing or not, but then Maggie had many problems in her life, and Michael Scott didn't look as if he had any problems at all. No one would dare trouble him, which meant Maggie would always be safe under his protection.

"What of Lady Felicia?"

He didn't reply. Instead he asked, "Your brother, Bryce, should he be the Earl of Radcliffe now?"

"Why…yes, he should be," she hesitantly admitted. "But he's not. Our cousins inherited."

She hadn't divulged the more scurrilous details to others, and she'd already told Mr. Scott much more than she'd told anyone else. But it seemed a moment for sharing confidences, and he had an ability to draw out what she hadn't planned to reveal.

"Will he fight to regain his birthright?" he asked.

"I don't believe so. He was overwhelmed to learn the truth, and it would be so difficult to assert a claim all these years later."

"Won't he revenge himself on those who harmed your mother?"

"No," she scoffed.

"*I* would."

"Bryce isn't a vengeful individual. He's a singer and an actor—as our mother was. Mostly he's a happy fellow. It would be out of character for him to be cruel or spiteful."

"Would he like someone to do it for him?"

"Do what?"

"Kill the people who ruined your lives."

"Kill…my father's relatives?"

"Yes."

She stared into his blue eyes—eyes that were so much like Bryce's, so much like her own—and she felt as if she could read his mind. He was offering to murder her grandfather and uncle, and the realization was astonishing.

She'd never previously met a person with such vicious tendencies, and it was tempting to say *yes, make them pay*. But she wasn't cruel or spiteful either.

"No one's killing anyone, Mr. Scott. Bryce has decided to go adventuring in Africa."

"Why?"

"My father was an adventurer who sailed the Nile several times."

"An adventurer…" Mr. Scott murmured the word and added another of his completely incongruous comments. "That explains it."

"Bryce wants to follow in my father's footsteps. Perhaps the journey will toughen him, and when he returns he'll be bent on retribution."

Mr. Scott took a deep breath and held it, as if swallowing down remarks he couldn't or shouldn't speak aloud.

"There were twins?" he asked. "You're positive?"

"Yes, Matthew and Michael. Two dark-haired scalawags—from what Bryce tells me. I don't recollect, but they called me Sissy."

"Sissy…"

"Apparently they were so close, they had their own secret language."

He blanched with a sort of bewildered surprise, and again he looked on the verge of a profound statement, but he simply nodded. "I'll contact you when I have news of Maggie."

"Do you know how to locate me?"

"Yes, I'm acquainted with your husband. You introduced us."

She scowled. "He doesn't gamble at your establishment, does he?"

"He doesn't."

Mr. Scott smiled a smile so like Bryce's that she was stunned by it. He was so familiar to her, their connection so riveting.

"Mr. Scott, have you any information about your past or your parents?"

"No, none."

"You don't suppose—"

"I have to be going, and you should go too. Let me walk you to your carriage."

It seemed wrong to leave. They'd likely never have another quiet interlude where they could chat without a dozen people hovering and listening in. The notion left her very sad, but she rose to her feet, gathering up the items that had been in her reticule.

"That's an interesting carving," he said as she stuffed the ivory statuette inside with everything else.

"It was my mother's."

He peered at her and appeared to say, *I know.*

But again he didn't speak his thoughts aloud. He was the most infuriatingly taciturn fellow!

"What about the front door?" she asked. "Did you kick it in?"

"Yes, I'll send someone to repair it."

"How will you start hunting for Maggie?"

"My men will scour the neighborhood. We'll find out what happened. Don't worry."

He seemed so competent, and his calm attitude made her feel better, made her feel that—if anyone could learn Maggie's situation—Mr. Scott certainly could.

She went to the door, and he followed her out. Instantly they were surrounded by street urchins. They were in awe of him as if he was a deity, and in their world maybe he was.

MICHAEL WAS SURE OF it now. There was no question, could be no doubt.

Evangeline Drake, Lady Run, was his sister, although he didn't recall having a sister, and he most definitely didn't recall having a female named Evangeline in his life.

As he urged her through the crowd of milling children, he pondered Fate, how the universe worked in strange ways. They'd crossed paths because Lord Stone had a gambling problem, because Michael had become engaged to Felicia. If he hadn't, would he have ever met Lady Run?

He was the brother for whom she was searching. He hadn't admitted it though. His head was spinning over the news she'd imparted. She'd given him a dozen openings to blurt it out, but he hadn't. He'd been afraid she wouldn't believe him, and if she hadn't he'd have been incredibly distressed.

He'd tell her. Eventually. He'd show her his birth certificate and the other papers that had been shoved in his coat during the fire at the coaching inn.

A fire! A damned fire that had left him alone in the street like the neediest orphan, and his father in line to inherit an earldom! It clarified so much about the terrifying nightmares he always had, why the smell of smoke alarmed him, why he always felt as if he'd lost something important.

He wasn't mad! He wanted to shake his fist at the heavens and celebrate. His family hadn't simply dumped him on the side of the road and forgotten him. He'd been loved and cherished. He'd belonged somewhere vital and special.

Matthew...

It all made sense, his visions of the little boy who was exactly the same, the one who had been so close that it had seemed Michael was missing a piece of his body. Often he'd awaken in the dark, certain a cruel devil had sawed off his leg. Frantically he'd reach down and pat under the covers to guarantee it was still there.

Yet it hadn't been a limb. It had been a twin brother.

Michael stared into the void where his mind occasionally led him, and he saw Matthew standing in a thick forest, attired in his red soldier's coat. For once, Michael let the truth settle in. His *brother*.

Matthew evidently perceived Michael rattling around in his head, and he frowned, noting Michael's arrival and wondering who the hell Michael was—just as Michael had ceaselessly wondered.

I'm coming for you, Michael told him. *I'll find you—if it takes the rest of my life...*

He tried to picture that night at the coaching inn. Where had Matthew been? Had they been together? Were they separated in the chaos? If so, who had separated them? Where had Matthew gone? What had happened to him? What had happened to Michael?

He'd never been able to recollect. In his next clear memory, he'd been living at old Mr. Scott's orphanage.

He shook himself out of his trance. In his sister's presence he'd already drifted off numerous times. Very likely she thought he was insane. He was escorting her to her carriage, a footman waiting to open the door, when a boy pushed out of the crowd.

"Mr. Scott?"

"Tim, isn't it?" Tim was the boy who had originally brought Maggie to Michael's office. Michael explained to his sister, "He works for me."

Luckily she didn't ask in what capacity. She simply smiled. "Hello, Tim."

"Make your bows to Lady Run, Tim," Michael said.

"Milady."

Tim surprised her by bowing courteously, displaying perfect manners as if he'd been raised at an expensive boarding school. But then he was being trained how to dress, act, and talk so he could walk around rich men and pick their pockets without their suspecting he didn't belong in their midst.

Tim turned to Michael. "Beggin' your pardon, Mr. Scott, but you needed information about Miss Wells."

"Yes, what have you heard?"

"That brigand, Blaylock, was here."

"Blaylock? On our street? You're sure?"

"I saw him with my own two eyes. He claimed he was a tax collector and Miss Wells owed money for taxes."

"What was Miss Wells's response?"

"She couldn't pay, so he bound her hands and forced her to leave with him."

His sister scowled. "She was arrested for not paying her taxes?"

"No," Michael replied, "it was a scam perpetrated by a con artist, though why he'd pick on Maggie I can't begin to guess."

Tim looked worried. "Should I have stopped him, Mr. Scott? He had four men with him. I didn't think I could help her."

"You did fine, Tim, to watch and tell me what occurred. I wouldn't have wanted you to be hurt."

"What can all this mean?" Lady Run inquired. "Maggie doesn't have much but this decrepit old building. Why torment her?"

"I haven't a clue, but believe me, Blaylock will be sorry."

Tim interrupted to say, "There was another carriage."

"What?"

"Down the block, there was a carriage with a pretty blond woman in it. She kept peeking out the curtain at Miss Wells."

Michael frowned. "Did you recognize her?"

"No, but there was a fancy crest on the side—a falcon, with a gold braid wound in its feathers."

Michael was so stunned he nearly fell over. "A falcon with gold braid," he repeated. "You're positive?"

"Yes, and her outriders were wearing red livery with gold braid."

"Do you know who it is?" his sister asked.

"Oh, yes," Michael said.

"Is it good news or bad?"

He shrugged. "It depends whose perspective you're considering."

"You're an interesting man, Mr. Scott."

"You're the only one who's ever thought so, Lady Run. Now let's get you out of here so I can find Maggie."

"You know where she is?"

"No, but I know who does."

CHAPTER TWENTY-THREE

MICHAEL REINED IN AND dismounted in front of Lord Stone's town house. A stable boy rushed up to take his horse to the mews, but Michael waved him away.

"I won't be here long," he explained.

He assumed Lady Felicia was still in London, but if she'd had any genuine understanding of his temper and power she'd have skittered away to hide.

Farrow had filled her head with nonsense about Maggie, and Michael would deal with Farrow later. As to Felicia, though she'd nagged and complained about Maggie, it had never occurred to him that Felicia might harm her.

And to use that cretin, James Blaylock! It boggled the mind. On two separate occasions, Michael had suspected her of secretly conferring with Blaylock. How long had their mischief been percolating? Why hadn't Michael put a stop to it?

He approached the door just as it was being opened from the inside, and when he saw who was exiting, he muttered, "Speak of the devil."

James Blaylock!

Blaylock had his back to the driveway, so the fool wasn't watching his surroundings—when he definitely should have been. As he turned to walk out, Michael rushed up and hit him so hard that he flew into the doorframe.

He grabbed for the wood to steady himself, but Michael hit him again, even harder, and he collapsed to his knees. Blood gushed from his nose and mouth.

The butler peeked out, looking alarmed, and Michael snapped, "Get inside. This is none of your business."

On realizing it was Michael inflicting the damage, the butler couldn't decide the best course. Michael was Felicia's fiancé, but Blaylock had just been a guest. In such a seedy scenario, what was the appropriate reaction?

Without a word, the butler closed the door and spun the key in the lock.

Michael was left alone with a dazed and battered Blaylock who—very stupidly—tried to rise again. Michael kicked him in the ribs, probably breaking a few, and Blaylock gave up the fight, slumping down with a woof of air exploding from his lungs.

Michael reached down, found a knife in Blaylock's coat, and stuffed it in the waistband of his own trousers. Then he gripped Blaylock by his shirt, lifting him up so they were nose to nose.

"Michael Scott?" Blaylock mumbled, barely able to focus. "Where the hell did you come from? You're supposed to be out of town."

"The interesting thing about a person leaving is that he eventually returns."

"You've always had a smart mouth."

"You must remember our last meeting, Blaylock. I told you I'd kill you if I saw your sorry face in my neighborhood again."

"I remember, asshole."

"Did you think I wasn't serious? Did you think I'd forget?"

"Prick."

Blaylock spat at Michael, blood peppering Michael's shirt.

"You meddled in my affairs," Michael seethed, "and you've ruined a perfectly good shirt in the process."

"Bastard."

"I'm not a bastard," Michael said. "I have it on excellent authority that my parents were married. So *don't* insult my mother."

He hit Blaylock again, merely because he felt like it, and he demanded, "Where is Maggie Wells?"

"Maggie who?" Blaylock snidely said.

"I'm going to ask you once more, and if you pretend you don't know her you're about to draw your last breath."

"You wouldn't murder me on Lord Stone's doorstep."

"Wouldn't I? Are you willing to take that chance?"

Michael retrieved the knife he'd found in Blaylock's coat and stuck the tip into Blaylock's cheek, right under his eye.

"You're as crazy as everyone says you are," Blaylock complained.

"I've never denied it. Now where is she?"

Blaylock was mulishly silent, and Michael dug the tip in a little deeper as Blaylock moaned and acted as if he wasn't terrified.

Ultimately he admitted, "Newgate Prison."

"She's in prison," Michael repeated. "At Newgate."

"Yes."

"Under what name?"

"Her own," Blaylock answered. "What would you suppose?"

But he glanced away, giving clear evidence he was lying, and Michael was better at reading a facial expression than any man alive. It was the main reason he'd grown so rich.

"If you tell me the truth," he casually said, "I won't start breaking your fingers."

"You wouldn't dare."

"You're really an idiot, Blaylock. On the one hand you claim I'm crazy, but on the other you claim I won't behave in a crazy way."

He seized Blaylock's wrist, pressed it to the ground, and stomped on his index finger. There was a loud crack as the bone shattered, and Blaylock howled with misery.

"Under what name is she being held?" Michael calmly asked again, after Blaylock had stopped his bellowing.

"Margaret Wesley."

Michael studied his eyes then—satisfied with the reply—let go of Blaylock's shirt, and the man curled into a ball, his maimed appendage clutched to his chest.

"Whose idea was it? Yours or Felicia's?"

Blaylock responded without hesitation. "She begged me to help her make Miss Wells disappear. The ruse was mine, but Lady Felicia was happy with everything I suggested."

"She watched from her carriage?"

"Yes."

"You never wondered if I'd mind if you harmed Miss Wells?"

"Why would you have minded? She was naught but a—"

He never finished his derogatory comment. Michael kicked him in the balls, and Blaylock turned a horrid shade of puce and vomited the contents of this stomach.

Michael stood and straightened. "You were correct about one detail."

"What was it?" Blaylock had to force out the words.

"I won't kill you on Lord Stone's stoop, but you'd best keep peeking over your shoulder. Next time I see you, you're dead."

He looked to the corner of the house, and the stable boy and two footmen were observing the altercation with a sort of appalled fascination.

Michael motioned to them. "Take Mr. Blaylock to the mews and let him rest a bit. When you feel he can stay on his horse, put him on it and get him off the property. Be sure he's gone before I'm ready to leave myself. I'd hate to have to murder him in Lord Stone's barn."

Michael went to the front door, which was still locked. Apparently it was a day for wrecking doors. He gave the wood a hard kick. Then another. The latch fell away, and Michael stormed inside.

The butler and several housemaids were huddled in the hall, but Michael ignored them. Felicia was up on the stairs, just starting down, and when she saw Michael entering like a deranged maniac, she paused for a brief second then squealed with alarm and ran up the steps.

Michael flew up after her and grabbed her by the arm.

"Where is Lord Stone?" he shouted to the butler, and the butler pointed at the hall behind him.

Michael dragged Felicia down as she hissed and fought and tried not to accompany him, but he was too strong and too angry.

Michael marched past the butler and the housemaids as a squirming, pleading Felicia said to them, "Help me. Get my mother. Please!"

Yet none of the servants moved. They were all too stunned by Michael's behavior.

He continued down the hall, finding Lord Stone in the library at the end. He was over in a corner, seated on a chair by the window, and enjoying a quiet brandy.

"What is the meaning of this?" He rose, attempting to appear grand and imperious, but failing in the effort.

Michael was taller than Lord Stone, younger and tougher and much more physically fit. He towered over the older man who was disheveled and scruffy and smelled as if he was intoxicated even though it was just after two in the afternoon.

"Tell him what you did," Michael fumed at Felicia.

She had the temerity to claim, "I did nothing. Mr. Scott is insane."

Michael tossed her to her father, but Lord Stone refused to catch her. She staggered by, latching on to his chair, or she would have toppled to the floor.

"Your daughter has interfered in my personal affairs," he advised Lord Stone, "and deliberately harmed my close friend, Magdalena Wells."

Lord Stone scowled. "Felicia couldn't have. She isn't smart enough to figure out how."

Felicia had the gall to say, "Miss Wells is his mistress!"

Lord Stone glared at his daughter and rolled his eyes. "Why would you feel it's your business to complain about him having a mistress?"

"I told him to send her away," she said, "and he wouldn't. So *I* sent her away."

"Bloody hell." Lord Stone grumbled. "What were you thinking? His private relationships are none of your concern."

"Precisely," Michael agreed, "so I'm crying off. I won't have this wretched, immature girl as my wife."

"Well, I hardly want you," Felicia spat, but he and Lord Stone ignored her.

Lord Stone cut to the chase. "You're crying off? But…where does that leave me?"

"Your daughter has had Miss Wells arrested."

"She deserved it!" Felicia seethed.

"Shut up, Felicia!" Lord Stone hissed. "Let the man talk."

"Oh, I hate you both!" she hurled, and she stomped out.

Michael didn't bother watching her go. His attention was locked on Lord Stone.

"Miss Wells is incarcerated in Newgate."

"Felicia accomplished that?"

"With a bit of assistance from James Blaylock."

"Dammit. I'm sorry, Scott. I had no idea what she was up to. I didn't realize she was even acquainted with Blaylock."

"I intend to locate Miss Wells and bring her home," Michael said.

"Good, good…"

"You can have your daughter back, but I'm keeping the plantation and the ships as damages. I'll sell them and give Miss Wells the money to compensate her for the trouble Felicia caused."

"Now, see here, Scott, you can't just—"

"Do you have a problem with that decision?"

"I…I…"

"If you don't tell me I can keep them, I'll make you and your idiotic daughter pay forever. What's it to be?"

Michael loomed over Lord Stone, looking as fierce and dangerous as he'd always been described to be.

Lord Stone stepped away and hastily said, "No, no, I don't have a problem with it. I get everything else though, don't I? I get the rest back?"

Lord Stone's beady gaze flitted around the room as if cataloguing his possessions, as if Michael might pilfer some of them when he walked out.

Michael scoffed with disgust. "Yes, you can have it all—so you can gamble it away in another drunken rout. Come by my club some night, and I'll be happy to take it from you again."

He spun on his heel and marched out, and from behind him, Lord Stone called, "I'll want it in writing. To be sure of the terms, you know?"

"I'll have my lawyer speak with you."

He started for the foyer, pushing by the servants who were hovering so they could hear every juicy word of the quarrel. They were brimming with speculation and would have weeks of gossip in the kitchen.

Felicia was up on the stairs, and when she saw him she straightened, as if bracing to rudely insult him. His fury soared.

He'd been lost as a toddler, had risen from nothing to become one of the richest, most powerful men in the kingdom. People such as her father quailed when Michael went by.

How dare she scorn him! What was there about her that was so bloody grand? Naught that he could discern.

"I realize," he told her, "that—with me being so lowborn and all—you thought your life was ruined by being engaged to me."

"It was!"

"My father was a Scottish aristocrat. I am an earl's brother."

"You liar. You are not."

"I am, and in the future I'll probably bump into you on occasion at social events. Please pretend you don't know me—for I shall certainly pretend I don't know *you*."

"I'd never pursue an acquaintance after this!"

"And good luck finding another fiancé." He wasn't usually cruel to women, but he just really didn't like her, and he couldn't help adding, "I fear you may have a lengthy spinsterhood, for I can't imagine who'll want you after I've had you."

As a parting shot it wasn't half bad, and he had to admit that it was better than taking a switch to her. She shrieked with offense, and he kept on out the door, being delighted to see the stable boy holding his horse's reins.

Michael leapt onto the animal and rode away without a backward glance.

"You wished to speak with me?"

"Sit, Miss Wesley."

"It's Wells," Maggie tersely said. "Magdalena Wells, and I demand that I be permitted to contact my sister."

She glared at the portly, obnoxious man seated across from her. He'd introduced himself as Mr. Turner, and they were in his office in the prison. He had a role of authority, but she hadn't cared enough to have his position clarified. She simply needed a quill, ink pot, and paper so she could write to Pamela.

She wasn't sure her sister was still at Cliffside or that Pamela would assist her, but other than Pamela, there were only two others who might actually be able to help her. One was Evangeline, and Maggie would die rather than let Evangeline learn she was in such a squalid place. The other was Michael Scott, and Maggie would hack off her arm with a dull blade before she communicated with him on any topic.

He'd told that brigand, Mr. Blaylock, that Maggie conspired with him to ruin pretty, young girls. He'd lied about her sending them to work at his gambling club. After all the altruistic work she'd performed on his street over the years! After all the mercy and charity she'd extended to the less fortunate! And this was her reward?

"My records say your name is Margaret Wesley," Mr. Turner informed her.

"Your records are wrong. I'm in complete control of my faculties, and I know my own name."

Mr. Turner scowled, looking as if he never allowed a prisoner to sass him. That's what Maggie was—a prisoner. The very idea stirred such a virulent wave of fury that she could barely remain in her chair. She was dizzy with ire, almost too enraged to talk.

"It doesn't matter," he muttered.

"Why not?"

"Your bail has been posted."

"My bail?"

"Yes."

"Who paid it?"

He didn't enlighten her, but said, "The charges will be dropped too."

"Why would they be dropped?"

"I'm not a lawyer, Miss. I couldn't begin to guess."

"Am I to be released?"

"Yes, absolutely."

He flashed a dodgy smile that only heightened her unease. What was happening now? Obviously he didn't have her best interests at heart. Had he orchestrated some other, worse fiasco?

He shoved a paper across the desk. "Would you sign this, please?"

"What is it?"

"It states that you absolve me and the other guards of any erroneous behavior."

"*Erroneous* behavior?"

Her fury spiked to a whole new level, one that she hadn't realized she could attain.

She had been in the jail for two days and two nights. Since she hadn't understood she was to be incarcerated, she hadn't brought money, blankets, a coat, or any other personal items that were necessary to survive in the ghastly facility. Nothing was free beyond the most meager sustenance.

She still couldn't fathom why she'd been arrested, why Mr. Scott had so cruelly lied about her. But she had a sneaking suspicion of why the catastrophe had developed. As Blaylock had watched the prison gates clang shut behind her, she'd asked him, "Why would you do this to me? Why?"

He'd grinned and said, "Lady Felicia sends her regards."

Maggie couldn't comprehend why Lady Felicia hated her, and any animosity was ridiculously misplaced. Maggie had been a trifle to Michael Scott and posed no challenge to Lady Felicia's betrothal. Maggie had begged Michael Scott to cry off from his engagement, but he'd refused.

She pointed to Mr. Turner's paper. "If I don't sign, will I still be allowed to leave?"

"Well…ah…yes."

"Then take your document and stuff it."

If circumstances had been different, if her bail hadn't been paid by an unknown benefactor, she couldn't predict what reprimand her sarcasm might have produced.

Mr. Turner glowered with such evil dislike that she was alarmed by it. She leaned away in her chair, wishing she could put more space between them. He seemed ready to storm around the desk and strike her.

If he did, it would simply be one more degradation in a lengthy line of degradations that hadn't stopped since the day Gaylord Farrow had crossed her path.

Why was life so hard? Why was she constantly punished?

She spent all her time helping others. Her only moral lapse had been her affair with Mr. Scott, but she'd *loved* him, and she'd proceeded because she'd thought he loved her too. She'd been horridly wrong, but she'd believed it nonetheless.

Couldn't there be a bit of forgiveness? Of redemption?

Luckily Mr. Turner never had his chance to lash out. Footsteps sounded in the hall. They were heavy, male boots marching toward her so…not Pamela. And not Gaylord; he walked like a dandy.

"Ah, here he is now," Mr. Turner said.

"Here is *who*?" Maggie glanced over to see Michael Scott enter the room. She gasped and demanded, "What are you doing here?"

"I've come to fetch you. Let's go."

"If I was dead and dying and you were the sole person in the kingdom who could save me, I wouldn't leave with you."

"Don't be absurd," he scoffed. "Come. I won't linger in this rat hole one second longer than I have to."

He reached for her, but she leapt up and skittered behind the desk to stand by Mr. Turner. She couldn't figure out why she'd feel Mr. Turner was the better option, but she wasn't thinking clearly.

She'd been tricked and deceived and kidnapped and arrested and incarcerated. She was filthy and hungry and terrified. She'd had her family ruined, her heart broken, her life destroyed. Michael Scott had been front and center for most of it.

She couldn't imagine departing with him, and he was no woman's savior.

She peered beseechingly at Mr. Turner, who glared at her as if she'd lost her mind.

"Don't make me go with him," she said to Turner.

"Of course you will," Turner replied. "It's all arranged."

"I'm afraid of him."

"Aren't we all?" Mr. Turner muttered, and he stood and turned his sleazy smile on Mr. Scott. "She's all yours, Mr. Scott, and the warden wanted me to tell you that he hopes there are no hard feelings."

"Not yet," Mr. Scott said, "but if I learn later that any of your guards had a hand in her mistreatment, there will have to be consequences."

He looked very regal, very imposing, as if he could carry out any threat of violence, and Mr. Turner certainly deemed that to be the case. At the overt warning, he blanched with dismay.

"I'm sure there will be naught to learn about the guards," Turner said.

"I'm told it was all Mr. Blaylock's scheme."

"Blaylock has already paid some of the price, but he still owes me more." Mr. Scott's stony gaze shifted to Maggie. "Let's go, Maggie, and I won't ask again."

"How dare you come for me," she raged.

"If I hadn't, who would have?"

Exactly so, Mr. Scott.

It was the saddest comment ever, and to her horror she burst into tears.

In the entire world, who cared about her? No one. Not a single, solitary soul.

"Are you crying?" he said like a complaint. "Stop it. You know it wounds me when you do."

"I'll cry if I want to. If I'm upset, it's none of your business."

He held out his hand, appearing apprehensive, as if she was a wild animal that might bolt, and that's precisely how she felt. Alone. Scared. Abused. Neglected. Unloved.

The events of the past few days were too awful to describe or endure. She was just an ordinary woman. How was she to survive such an ordeal? How was she to muddle through it in a sane manner? She had no idea.

She pushed away from Turner and brushed by Mr. Scott, ignoring his outstretched hand. She marched into the hall, momentarily confused about which direction she should go.

A guard was there, and he gestured to her right. "This way, Miss."

"Thank you."

She hurried off at a brisk pace, and behind her Mr. Scott called, "Maggie, slow down. Wait for me."

"I won't wait for you, Mr. Scott. Not ever again. So I suggest you walk a tad faster if you mean to keep up."

CHAPTER TWENTY-FOUR

"A little gratitude wouldn't be amiss."

"Gratitude!"

Michael scowled at Maggie, finding himself inordinately hurt by her temper and disregard. Wasn't that just like a woman? He'd finally found himself smitten, had finally admitted he might be in love, and she couldn't care less.

"I could have left your shapely ass in there to rot," he told her.

"Why didn't you?"

"If you'd rather, I can give you back to Mr. Turner."

They were in his carriage and headed for their rundown, tumbledown neighborhood. He'd tried to sit next to her so he might have held her hand or put a comforting arm over her shoulders, but she was having none of it. She'd slid onto the seat across, making it perfectly clear she had no desire to have him anywhere near.

He wasn't sure what to do with her now. He'd have liked to take her somewhere else besides their decrepit street, to his country house perhaps, or out to Cliffside, but they were both too far away.

Her sister, Rebecca, was an option, but with her and Ramsey being newlyweds—and considering how disgustingly they carried on—he didn't suppose Maggie would enjoy being a guest.

He had his bachelor's apartment, but she'd never agree to stay there. The only other place was her charity mission, and he was vehemently opposed to that idea.

Yet, if not there, where? A hotel? A coaching inn?

She was nestled against the squab, her eyes shut as if she was extremely weary. He studied her, thinking she appeared so young and defenseless. Though she'd been incarcerated for just two days, she seemed to have lost weight. Had they starved her? She was skin and bones.

He looked closer and was upset to see she was crying again. Or maybe she hadn't stopped.

"Maggie," he murmured, wishing he could calm her.

"Leave me alone."

"It will be all right."

"How will it be?"

"We'll figure it out."

He patted her knee, but she yanked away, her eyes flying open.

"How dare you have me locked away!" she absurdly charged. "How dare you tell lies about me."

"What?"

"I've spent every minute of the past seven years helping other people. I've been kind to every downtrodden person I've met. I've *never* sent a girl to work in your despicable club." She glared with an enormous amount of animosity. "I never would."

"Of course you wouldn't."

"You've destroyed my family, seized my home for your own, and stolen my virginity. But was that enough for you? No! You had to ruin my reputation too."

"What are you talking about?"

"As if you didn't know," she fumed.

"I don't. I swear."

"The fiend who arrested me, Mr. Blaylock? He explained everything."

"What did he explain?"

"He said there were witnesses who accused me of pandering. He said he questioned you about it and you admitted the whole scheme."

Another sin for which Blaylock will pay…

A muscle ticked in Michael's cheek. "It never occurred to you that he might have been lying?"

"Not for a second."

"You don't know me better than that?"

"I only assumed I knew you, but I don't. You're a disloyal, pompous bully—as you've proved to me over and over."

"That's not true," he mumbled, feeling incredibly wounded by her scathing opinion.

Obviously she was tired and afraid, and she'd just endured more than any woman should ever have to endure. But he'd always believed people were more likely to be candid when they were distressed, and he couldn't abide that she thought so poorly of him.

Typically he would have lashed out and ordered her to be silent, but for once he swallowed down the angry words. She needed to eat and bathe, to rest and be pampered. He decided he *would* whisk her off to Orphan's Nest, and he'd remain there with her until she was hale and happy again.

The carriage rattled to a halt, and she pulled on the curtain and gazed out. They were in front of his club, and she frowned.

"Why have we stopped?"

"I'm taking you to the country in the morning. We'll stay here tonight."

She gaped at him as if he was insane. "In your den of iniquity?"

"If you'd rather, we can rent a room at a coaching inn, but still, I have to make arrangements before we depart."

"Mr. Scott, you're laboring under the delusion that I would accompany you."

"You'll recover faster in the clean, country air. It's the best place to recuperate."

"I don't need to…recuperate. I'm perfectly fine."

"You're not fine, Magdalena. You're a mess."

"It's Miss Wells to you. Now take me home."

"To where? Cliffside?"

"No, to my charity mission, you thick oaf. Where would you suppose?"

"It's not safe for you there."

"According to whom? I've lived there for seven blasted years, and I never had any trouble until I met you."

"It's not safe!"

He was scared to let her out of his sight. She was prone to landing herself in jams. If he wasn't around to keep any eye on her, what might happen?

She leaned out the window and called up to the driver. "Would you drop me at the Vicar Sterns Rescue Mission? It's just up the street."

Michael's temper flared, but he tamped it down. How could he make her see reason? How could he make her understand how afraid he'd been, how he wanted to watch over her forever?

"Why won't you listen to me?" he asked.

"Because I don't wish to hear anything you have to say."

"You're being foolish."

"No, I'm leery and I don't trust anyone. You. My family. Every person in the world. I don't trust any of you." She leaned out farther and complained to the driver. "Will you take me home? If you can't, I'll walk the rest of the way."

"You're not walking," Michael scolded.

"Don't boss me, Mr. Scott. You can't."

Michael leaned out too, and ordered, "Take her to the mission."

The carriage rolled on, and they plopped into their seats. Furtively he observed her, struggling to figure out how to calm her, but it seemed impossible.

"Blaylock is leaving London shortly," he said. "He won't ever hurt you again."

"Good."

"I have no idea what he told you about me, but I wasn't complicit in your arrest. I haven't spoken to him in nearly a year, and I've certainly never discussed you with him."

"A likely story."

"Lady Felicia was responsible—at Gaylord Farrow's urging."

"It doesn't surprise me that Lady Felicia was involved. But Gaylord?"

"Yes."

"Why would he have harmed me in such an evil fashion?"

Michael shrugged. "Why does Farrow do anything? He's a menace, and he won't ever hurt you again either. I'll see to it."

"You'll *see* to it. What do you mean?"

"He's done inflicting himself on you and your sisters."

She scrutinized him, trying to decipher what he was actually confiding, but he'd never confess his plan for Farrow. He knew women. If he revealed Farrow's approaching fate, she'd tell her sister, and Michael was determined that Pamela Farrow never learn what had occurred.

The carriage halted again, this time outside her mission. She glanced out and scowled. "I have a new door. What happened to the old one?"

"I kicked it in."

"Why?"

"Because you'd disappeared, and I was terrified. I went in to be sure you weren't dead on the floor."

"Aren't you special?" she sarcastically seethed.

"I repeat, a bit of gratitude would be nice."

She scoffed. "Who repaired it?"

"I did. The back door too, with sturdier wood and better locks."

"You have the new key?"

"Yes."

"Give it to me."

She held out her hand, and though he had the blasted key in his pocket, he couldn't bear to relinquish it. It represented his connection to her, his being in charge of her so he could watch over her properly.

"Please don't stay here," he said. "I'll be so worried about you."

"Why would you worry? I'm none of your concern, Mr. Scott. You really needn't trouble yourself. Now give me the accursed key."

He sighed and pulled it out. She snatched it away, and as she reached for the carriage door, he suffered an instant of panic. Would he ever see her again? What if he didn't? What if this was the very last time?

She was so angry, and he hadn't uttered a single comment that hadn't sounded idiotic, and she'd misconstrued every remark.

He had to hope that—eventually—she'd forgive him, that she'd remember she'd loved him once. That sort of potent emotion couldn't just evaporate.

"I've cried off from my betrothal," he said.

"Bully for you."

"I couldn't keep on with Felicia, not after I discovered what she did to you."

She snorted with disgust. "She had to have me kidnapped, arrested, and incarcerated before you decided she wasn't right for you? You're mad, Mr. Scott. You are absolutely stark raving mad."

"Maggie…I…"

For a minute she hovered, her body tilted toward him as she awaited his next words.

"What?" she demanded when he couldn't spit it out.

"I…love you."

It was the first and only time he'd ever spoken the phrase aloud, so it was a significant occasion in his life. He didn't know what reply he'd expected in return, but it wasn't the one he received.

"You do not love me. You don't love anyone. You practically bragged about it."

"I do love you!"

"You're being ridiculous, and I need a bath."

The footman took that moment to open the door. He hadn't yet lowered the step, but she jumped out anyway.

"Maggie!"

"What!" She was growing ever more exasperated.

"Will you marry me?"

She gasped as if he'd hurled an epithet. "Marry you?"

"Yes. Will you?"

"I'd rather be boiled in hot oil."

She stomped over to her new door, rammed the key in the lock, and found that it worked perfectly. In a trice, she vanished as if she'd never been there at all.

"You own this place? Truly?"

Ramsey grinned at his wife and said, "Yes, *Mrs.* Scott. I own it."

He emphasized *missus*, liking the way it sounded.

Rebecca cocked an elegant brow. "So…when you kept boasting about how rich you are, you weren't lying."

"No, I wasn't lying. I'm so bloody rich, you couldn't beggar me if you tried for a hundred years."

She grinned too. "I'm delighted to hear it. For a while there, you had me worried."

"I realize that you were."

She breathed a sigh of relief. "After living with Gaylord, I can't imagine how refreshing it will feel to have a bit of stability floating around."

Ramsey puffed himself up. "I rescued your shapely ass, and don't you forget it."

"It's not as if you'll let me. It's all you talk about."

"Well, you have a short attention span."

They were back in London and standing in front of the house he'd bought her. Initially he'd planned to bring her to it as his mistress. That had been their agreement, but thanks to Michael insisting on a wedding, Ramsey had ended up with much more than he'd ever expected to have.

Over the past decade he could have married any number of girls, but they'd all been raised in his same sort of rough and tumble existence, and he hadn't been interested in any of the lowborn females.

He couldn't have explained why though. Michael was the one who had some blue blood running in his veins, but maybe Ramsey had a few drops too. He'd always wanted to latch on to a real lady and now he had. Fate had dumped her in his lap.

In the beginning she'd been reluctant and hadn't figured he'd be much of a husband. She still didn't, but he'd show her. With how flighty she was, she needed a strong man at her side, one who could protect her, who would keep her out of trouble—because she was the type who'd land herself in plenty of it.

He'd always lived with Michael, and for many years had stayed in a room over the gambling club. As a bachelor it had suited his purposes, but he was thirty or thereabouts—he'd never been certain of his age—so it was time he carried on like a normal person.

A wife. A house. Furniture. Servants. If he wasn't careful, he'd wind up being halfway respectable. Perish the thought!

"Shall we go in?" he asked.

"Yes, we should."

Suddenly he suffered the worst wave of anxiety. What if she didn't like it?

It wasn't Cliffside by any means, but it was a fine residence all the same. Constructed of red brick, with black shudders and white trim, it was three stories high with a stable for a carriage and a garden in the back.

The area was quiet and safe, and the neighbors went to their jobs in the day in crisp gray suits such as lawyers and businessmen might wear. Ramsey didn't belong in such a tepid, cultured group, and he was richer than all of them put together, but he liked the idea of pretending he fit in.

Rebecca would, but Ramsey? Never. If folks got too annoying, they'd just move. He'd find another quiet street, in another safe neighborhood, and try to make Rebecca happy.

From here on out, that would be his goal: to keep Rebecca happy. Well, other than working for Michael and keeping *him* happy. Rebecca would come directly after Michael, but considering all the ways Michael had constantly helped Ramsey, it wasn't such a bad spot for Rebecca to occupy.

Everything they had, everything they would accumulate in the future, would be because of Michael, because of his wits, cunning, and generosity.

"The furniture came with it," he said, "but if you don't like it, we can toss it out and buy new."

"All new?"

"Yes."

"I'm sure what's already here will be fine."

"I hired two footmen and two maids to start out. You can use them or not. It's up to you."

"I'm sure they'll be fine too."

"I didn't hire a cook yet. I thought you'd know more about what kind of person you'd like."

"Could we hire someone French?"

"Absolutely. And if you think you need a dozen more servants, bring them in. The more the merrier."

"You're being awfully accommodating."

"I want you to like it, but if you don't we'll sell it and purchase something else."

He was babbling like an idiot, but couldn't shut up. He was so nervous! He'd convinced himself he didn't care if she liked what he'd selected, but he'd been lying. He was desperate for her to like it.

He walked her over to the door. The servants were expecting them, and a footman snapped it open and greeted them at just the right moment. Ramsey eased her over the threshold, but she peeked up at him from under those long dark lashes that drove him wild.

"You're supposed to carry me inside," she said.

"Am I?"

"It's good luck."

"Then by all means, let me carry you."

She was light as a feather, and he scooped her off her feet and marched into the foyer, pleased as punch with her and what he'd wrangled for himself.

He put her down and introduced the servants, then he stepped back and shyly watched—when had he gotten shy?—as she studied her surroundings.

She pushed by him and went into the parlor, and she strolled about, touching things, sniffing things, peering in drawers, and tugging on drapes to check the view out the windows.

He couldn't stand it and asked, "What do you think, Mrs. Scott?"

"I think…" She looked sly, crafty, and so darn beautiful.

Her lengthy pause terrified him. "Just say it!"

"It's perfect."

"You're sure?"

"Yes, Ramsey, I'm very, very sure. Stop worrying so much."

"I can't help it."

"I'm so relieved to be here with you."

"But if you don't feel it's grand enough or wish I'd—"

"Ramsey?" She stamped her foot, cutting him off. "It's one-hundred percent perfect, and I can't believe I managed to snag you for my own."

She skipped over and flung herself into his arms. He picked her up and twirled her around, kissing her and kissing her until he was too dizzy to continue.

"I guess you're staying," he said as he drew away.

"I guess I am."

"With me, it's forever."

"It better be."

He took her hand and headed for the stairs.

"Where are we going?" she asked.

"We should try out our bed to see if the mattress is comfortable."

They were hurrying by the servants, and he didn't notice any of them reacting to his lewd suggestion—servants weren't supposed to react—but she must have.

She grinned at them and said, "We're newlyweds. It's allowed."

He swooped her up again and rushed up the stairs.

"Sorry, Mr. Farrow, but I can't permit it."

"Please?"

Gaylord smiled his most charming smile, but the servant guarding the door was unmoved.

They were at the entrance to a gambling club he'd joined a few weeks earlier. He'd owed a membership fee, and with his excellent verbal skill he'd persuaded the owner that he had money coming and would pay once it arrived.

Of course he had no money coming, and when the owner found out, his membership had been promptly cancelled. There was no greater shame a gentleman could suffer than to be told he was too poor to socialize with his friends. It was the ultimate humiliation.

If only he were an aristocrat! Those accursed men were blessed with a title, so no one ever insisted they cough up funds when they fell a little behind.

"Your privileges have been revoked," the servant informed him.

As if he didn't know! "I don't need to gamble. Just let me sneak out the back."

"I can't. The boss would have my head."

If Gaylord had had two pennies to rub together he'd have bribed the fellow, but his financial situation had worsened considerably.

Though he couldn't fathom why, creditors were suddenly following him around the city, his lines of credit having collapsed like a house of cards. Every trivial idiot who'd ever loaned Gaylord a farthing was demanding immediate imbursement.

He'd been accosted on the street by process servers who had warrants for his arrest. They claimed he'd been adjudged a delinquent debtor and was to be incarcerated.

As they'd reached for him he'd raced away, and the crowd of passersby had ensured they couldn't catch him. They were close on his heels though.

"Look, mate." He gazed soulfully.

"I'm not your *mate*, Mr. Farrow."

"There are some cretins chasing me." Gaylord chuckled as if it was of no consequence. "They say I owe them money."

"Do you?" the servant had the audacity to inquire.

Oh, how the mighty had fallen!

"It's all a minor misunderstanding," Gaylord scoffed.

"I'll just bet it is."

"You wouldn't be so heartless as to let them find me, would you?"

The man studied Gaylord, and Gaylord had to admit he was a pathetic sight. Typically he was dapper and well-groomed, but wagering, drinking, and lack of sleep had left him in less than pristine condition.

He smelled.

A flurry of activity erupted on the sidewalk, and the servant peered outside. Gaylord peered out too. The process servers were there, asking if anyone had seen him!

Gaylord blanched with alarm.

"Please!" he wheezed.

"Go ahead"—the servant tossed a thumb toward the gaming room—"but you march straight to the back door. You don't linger."

If the man said anything else, Gaylord didn't hear it. He dashed through the club, ignoring the intoxicating clink of the dice, the strong odor of alcohol that invited him to sit down and imbibe.

Men glanced at him as he ran by, but fortunately no one hailed him. He kept on and staggered into the dark alley.

It was very quiet, though it stank of garbage, and rats skittered away. He tarried for a few minutes, calming his breathing and figuring out which direction was best for an escape. Finally he tiptoed over and peeked out to the street.

Hoping he appeared more composed than he felt, he riffled his fingers in his hair and tugged on his vest. He intended to slip out and walk away unobserved, but before he could a male behind him said, "Hello, Farrow."

He yelped with fright and spun around to find Michael Scott had crept up on him. The large, violent fiend, Ramsey Scott, was with him.

"Michael Scott!" He forced a smile. "Fancy meeting you here."

"Yes, fancy that."

"You scared the life out of me."

Michael Scott assessed Gaylord's rumpled suit, his disheveled state, and he smirked. "You look as if you're having a spot of trouble."

"No, no, I'm fine. If you'll excuse me?"

He turned to go, but Ramsey Scott blocked Gaylord's way.

"You seem to be in a hurry, Mr. Farrow." Ramsey Scott, brute that he was, wouldn't budge.

"Yes, I'm in a hurry."

"Why is that?" Michael Scott inquired.

"I'm a busy man," Gaylord claimed.

"So I hear," Michael Scott amiably agreed. "Do you know what else I hear?"

"No, what?"

"Someone has been all over town buying up your markers."

"A vicious rumor," Gaylord blithely said.

"Is it?"

"Why would anyone buy my debt? My fiscal situation is very sound."

Both Scotts chuckled, and Michael Scott said, "I should probably be clearer. *I* have purchased your debt."

Gaylord's mind raced as he tried to make sense of Scott's announcement. The bloody oaf already owned Cliffside. How much more did the greedy bastard need?

Gaylord scowled. "Why would you bother with my paltry obligations?"

"Oh, they're not paltry," Michael Scott insisted. "In fact, they're sufficient to get you jailed for penury—and for a very long time too."

"What are you saying?" Gaylord asked.

"You shouldn't have hurt Maggie."

"Maggie!" Gaylord huffed. "I haven't seen her in weeks. How could I have hurt her?"

Michael Scott grabbed Gaylord by his shirt, lifting him until his toes brushed the ground. The seams in Gaylord's coat started to pop and tear.

"You have the gall to pretend you didn't hurt her?" Mr. Scott asked.

"I haven't done anything lately."

At Gaylord's retort, Mr. Scott was so irate that Gaylord lurched away but simply bumped into Ramsey Scott. He was trapped between the two men.

Michael Scott lifted Gaylord again. "Have you—by any chance—

talked to Lady Felicia recently?"

"Why would I have spoken to Lady Felicia? She and I hardly run in the same circles."

"It doesn't matter if you lie or not," Mr. Scott replied. "I know the truth."

"As I've never met your fiancée, I can't imagine what truth you assume you *know*."

"Shut up, Farrow." Ramsey Scott loomed over Gaylord's shoulder and peered at his friend. "This prick is too stupid to live. Let me kill him."

"What!" Gaylord shrieked.

"Let me put the Wells sisters out of their misery," Ramsey Scott begged.

"Help!" Gaylord called.

The street was swarming with people. Surely someone would stop to assist, or would at least get a good look at Michael and Ramsey Scott so the two brigands could be identified when Gaylord's body washed up on the shores of the Thames.

But before Gaylord could generate enough of a ruckus to be noticed, Ramsey Scott whisked him farther into the alley. Michael Scott stepped in again.

"I don't want him dead," Mr. Scott told Ramsey Scott.

Gaylord gulped. "What do you want?"

"I want you to pay me the money you owe me. Immediately. Can you?"

"Of course not."

"Then I'll have you jailed for fraud."

"Jailed! Are you insane?"

"Yes." Mr. Scott grinned a wicked, evil grin. "Everyone has always thought so, and I never deny it."

Gaylord remembered how Michael Scott had doted on Maggie, how smitten he'd seemed, and he said, "Maggie would be very angry if you were cruel to me."

"Maggie will never know."

"She will!" Gaylord warned. "She'll find out."

"Not from where you're going."

"What do you mean?"

"Have you heard what Lady Felicia did to Maggie?"

"No."

"You weren't a conspirator? You didn't participate?"

"Heavens no," Gaylord insisted. "The wretched girl and I haven't… *conspired* on any subject."

"She had Maggie arrested on a false pretense. Maggie was ordered to pay a substantial sum of money—that she didn't have. She was jailed, but booked under a fake name so if anyone ever searched for her, there would be no record." Mr. Scott's smile grew even more ghastly. "Since you set the whole thing in motion, I decided *you* should suffer a similar fate."

"What *fate?* You're being absurd."

"Your name is Gaylord Farrow, but Gregory Fishburn will suit you in prison."

"Now see here!" Gaylord was absolutely alarmed. "You can't just… just snatch a fellow off the street and have him carted off to gaol."

"I'm not snatching you anywhere. I have a hundred judgments against you. As opposed to what happened to Maggie, I actually have a reason to have you detained."

"Lady Felicia is the guilty party. You're mad to blame me."

"Yes, we've already established that I am." Mr. Scott turned to Ramsey Scott. "The debt collectors are nearby. Take him to them."

"It would be my pleasure," Ramsey Scott said.

"Make sure he's bound and gagged."

"Bound *and* gagged?" Ramsey Scott asked.

"Yes, I'm sick of listening to his excuses."

Ramsey Scott grabbed Gaylord's arm and dragged him away. Gaylord wrestled and fought, but couldn't halt their forward progress.

"Mr. Scott! Mr. Scott!" he pleaded, and he glanced over his shoulder.

Michael Scott was stoically watching him from the dark shadows of the alley.

"What?"

"Don't do this. You can't want to."

"Yes, I do. I want to very, very much."

"But…when will I be released? When will I be able to go home?"

"How about never?"

Mr. Scott shrugged and laughed, and when Gaylord cried out to him again, the wicked beast, Ramsey Scott, stuffed a kerchief into Gaylord's mouth so he could only mumble and groan from that point on.

CHAPTER TWENTY-FIVE

Maggie and Rebecca sat in the front parlor in Rebecca's new house. It was a fine residence, with big glass windows, bright, airy rooms, and comfortable furniture. Apparently Ramsey Scott had picked it out himself with no help from Rebecca, and Maggie was stunned by his good choice.

Rebecca appeared happily married, and Maggie couldn't fathom why her sister would be. If anyone had sought Maggie's opinion, she would have pronounced Ramsey to be an awful matrimonial prospect. But in light of Maggie's experiences with men, she had to admit she probably wasn't the best judge.

"My head is still spinning over my decision to sell," Maggie said.

"It will pass, and once it does you'll realize you're lucky. An opportunity arose and you seized it."

"I suppose I'll eventually look at it that way, but if I don't own a rescue mission anymore, what will I do with myself? I'm not exactly a lady of leisure. I have no idea how to be idle."

Rebecca shrugged. "You'll find something that interests you."

"You make it sound easy."

A few days after Maggie had arrived home from her ordeal at Newgate Prison, an attorney had shown up at the mission. He represented a consortium that was buying property in the area, and he'd wanted to purchase Maggie's building.

Her initial reaction had been to decline, but when she was apprised of the amount he was offering for the decrepit place, it would have been silly to refuse. She'd spent an agonizing evening fretting and stewing, and it had dawned on her that there was no reason to stay in the neighborhood. Why not sell?

Vicar Sterns had started the charity with high hopes and grand expectations, but they hadn't improved the lives of the downtrodden they served. The task seemed fruitless, and with her recent trials and tribulations, she'd been altered and no longer viewed the effort as personally fulfilling.

And if she was honest, she'd been afraid to remain where she was. Mr. Blaylock, Gaylord, and Lady Felicia were all aware of where the mission was located. Any one of them could abuse Maggie again, and as had been proved in their initial attempt, she had no ability to protect herself.

Every time she heard a noise, she'd jump and peek over her shoulder, wondering if Blaylock might have arrived to finish the job he'd begun at Lady Felicia's behest. Gradually her nerves would calm, but for the moment she was a mess.

Michael Scott had rescued her the first time, but in the future she couldn't count on his assistance. In fact, she knew she couldn't. After how bitterly they'd parted, she was sure she'd never see him again.

His commanding presence on her street was another reason she'd agreed to the sale. People were acquainted with him. People talked about him and discussed his antics. Carriages loaded with his notorious customers generated a steady stream of traffic as rich gamblers traveled to his disreputable establishment.

With how deeply she'd loved him, each mention of his name was like the prick of a knife in her heart. She couldn't bear the constant reminders of him and what he'd once meant to her. She'd been so foolish, so pointlessly naïve.

She'd visited the lawyer, and in a matter of hours the deal had been complete. Yet it had transpired so rapidly, her prior life ending so abruptly that she was still convincing herself she'd made the correct choice.

Wasn't it better to move away? To move on? But to where? And to what? After so many years of being poor, she couldn't wrap her head around the notion that she *wasn't* in dire fiscal straits.

She didn't possess a fortune, but the sale had provided a small nest egg. It was a relief to have options, but she had too *many* options. When she could live anywhere and try her hand at any venture, she was having trouble whittling it down.

"Pamela wrote me." Rebecca yanked Maggie out of her morose reverie.

"What did she say?" Maggie asked, not really caring.

"There's been no word as to Gaylord's whereabouts."

"I can understand why Pamela would worry, but if you want my opinion, he probably fled to America with creditors at his heels."

"Probably. Or maybe he found a wealthy heiress and glommed on to her. He'll bleed some other family dry instead of ours."

"They have my greatest sympathies." Maggie snorted with disgust. "Where is Pamela? Is she at Cliffside?"

"Yes, she's there, but she's moved to the old dowager house."

"Why?"

"Mr. Scott opened it for her and forced her over there."

"She can't be happy about it."

"No. He's letting her stay there for six months, then she has to be out."

"Where will she go after six months?"

"If she can locate Gaylord she'll live with him, but if not, I can't guess."

"Watch out, Rebecca, or she'll show up here and beg you to take her in."

"As if I would!" Rebecca scoffed. "Once you're settled, you'd better not send her your new address either. She'll show up at *your* house rather than mine. You're much more of a pushover than I am."

Maggie scowled. Was she a pushover? Was she malleable and easily manipulated?

Ultimately she had to accept there was validity to the remark, so she had to make some changes. She was finished with being used and abused by everyone she'd ever loved. It wouldn't happen again.

"Do you suppose Mr. Scott did something to Gaylord," Rebecca asked, "and that's why he's missing?"

"It's entirely possible. That last day when I spoke to him, he swore Gaylord would never bother us again. I wouldn't be surprised at all if he paid someone to…"

Maggie's voice trailed off as she envisioned what sort of heinous act Mr. Scott might have perpetrated. Surely he wouldn't have murdered Gaylord. Would he have?

"You wouldn't be surprised if he…what?" Rebecca pressed.

"Don't listen to me. I haven't a clue how Mr. Scott might behave."

"You may have a low view of Mr. Scott, but I'm growing to love him."

"Which one?" Maggie inquired. "As far as I'm concerned, there are too many Scotts in this family now. You. Ramsey. Michael Scott. Are you talking about Ramsey or Michael?"

"Michael. If it wasn't for him and how he's looked after Ramsey, I can't imagine where I'd be."

"You're giving him more credit than he deserves," Maggie sourly retorted, refusing to imbue Michael Scott with any positive traits.

"Everything Ramsey has is because of Mr. Scott."

"Seriously?"

"Yes. They met in that orphanage, and according to Ramsey, Mr. Scott took Ramsey under his wing and taught him all he knows."

"About what? Crime? Theft? Violence? Intimidation?"

"Don't disparage their skills. It's made them obscenely rich."

"They may be rich, but I wouldn't brag about the source of their income."

"Well, I'm certainly not protesting. Not when I've ended up with so much more than I ever thought I'd have. Ramsey saved me from Gaylord and Pamela, so I didn't go down with their sinking ship. I'll always be grateful."

Maggie forced a smile and told herself she should be grateful for her sister too. She'd been at Rebecca's for several days, her apartment at the charity mission lost when she'd sold the building. So she'd had a chance to closely observe Rebecca and her husband, and evidently Maggie was very petty and envious.

Rebecca—who'd grown up cosseted and spoiled—was becoming even more pampered. Ramsey Scott doted on her, and Maggie could barely stand to watch them together. When she saw how much Rebecca suddenly seemed to have in her life, it only underscored how little Maggie had. Would she ever be happy?

"By the way," Rebecca continued, "as to your complaint that there are too many Scotts in the family—"

"It wasn't a complaint. I was just stating the facts."

"There's about to be one less."

"What do you mean?"

"Michael Scott plans to change his surname to Blair, so he'll be Michael Blair from this point on."

"But...why?"

"He and Ramsey used Scott, because it was given to them at that orphanage. But he's always had some papers that list his true identity."

"And it's Michael Blair?"

"Yes."

Maggie was inordinately hurt by the news. During her many intimate conversations with Michael Scott, he'd claimed he hadn't had any information about his past or his parents, and it wounded her to learn that Rebecca had discovered details about him that Maggie hadn't.

Her upset was ridiculous and absurd. What did it matter how Michael Scott chose to be addressed? She *didn't* care about him and would never cross paths with him again. His name—and every other aspect—was irrelevant.

A knock sounded on the front door and Rebecca rose to answer it, which was odd. She had a dozen servants who waited on her hand and foot. She never answered her own door.

"Are you expecting someone important?" Maggie asked.

"No, I'm not expecting anyone," Rebecca said, but she hurried out.

Maggie dawdled and was finishing a cup of tea when Rebecca returned.

"Maggie, you have a visitor."

"*I* have a visitor?"

Maggie frowned. She'd moved out of the mission in such a rush that very few people knew where she'd gone. Who would have bothered to track her down?

Rebecca stepped aside, and Maggie was aghast to see Michael Scott enter the room.

"Why is he here?" Maggie demanded of her sister. "Did you tell him where I was?"

"Ramsey told him."

"Traitor," Maggie muttered, not having the slightest idea why Mr. Scott would show his sorry face in Rebecca's parlor. Maggie was quite sure they'd said everything that needed to be said. What could be left?

"I'll just give you two some privacy." Rebecca slipped out and shut the door, leaving Maggie alone with him.

He remained where he was, and he looked around, taking in the furnishings and décor. With him studying his surroundings she had her own opportunity to study him, and she was aggravated to note that he appeared hale and fit and very, very grand.

His color was high as if he'd been out riding, and his long hair was untied and brushing his shoulders. Dressed in a flowing white shirt, tan breeches, and knee-high black boots, he exuded vigor and good health, and his obvious vitality irked her immensely.

She felt wan and exhausted, pummeled and worn down by events, and he'd caused much of her woe. Yet he didn't seem affected in the least by what had occurred, and it wasn't fair that she should be suffering so horridly while he was more wonderful and imposing by the second.

There was a sideboard in the corner, and he went over and poured himself a tall glass of liquor. She was seated on a sofa, and he came over and eased into the chair across. He sipped his drink, grinning as if he had a secret, as if he might share it if she begged prettily enough.

"I'm so amazed by this house," he said.

She hadn't intended to comment, but caught herself asking, "Why would you be?"

"I've been acquainted with Ramsey for maybe twenty-five years, and he never once mentioned that he'd like to live like this. I didn't even realize he hoped to marry someday. I assumed he was happy with his life the way it was."

"I suppose that's what love will do to a person," she facetiously retorted.

"I suppose it is," he amiably agreed. "I heard you had a bit of financial good luck."

"I'd tell you about it—if I thought it was any of your business."

"Can you actually imagine an incident could happen on my street and I wouldn't know?"

"You talk as if you rule that part of the world."

"It's my own little kingdom."

"Are you aware that Gaylord is missing?"

"Yes."

He flashed such a wily smile that she was certain he was guilty of something.

"What did you do to him?"

"Me? What makes you think *I* did anything?"

"Where is he?"

"I don't have any idea, and that's the God's honest truth."

"Don't bring the Lord into this. You might get struck by lightning."

"I might."

"My sister, Pamela, hasn't seen him. She's worried."

"I predict that—after awhile—she'll be glad to have him gone. She's set at the dowager house for as long as she'd like to stay there."

"Not six months?"

"No, she can live there forever if she wants—just not with her husband."

"You seem awfully sure he's not coming back."

"He might come back. Who knows?"

He shrugged and downed his liquor. Then he went to the sideboard and poured himself another. He opened a decanter of wine and poured a glass. He carried them over, and as he sat down again, he offered her the wine.

She refused to grab it, and he placed the glass on the table between them.

"Why are you drinking?" she said. "And why would you expect me to drink with you?"

"We're celebrating."

"Celebrating what?"

"My cancelled betrothal and you selling your building."

"Yes, last time we spoke you told me you'd cried off. How did your fiancée take the news?"

"She was ecstatic."

"I'll just bet she was," Maggie grumbled.

Lady Felicia had been raised in the loftiest echelons of society, and he'd been keen to move into the circles that Lady Felicia inhabited. He was vain and proud and should have been chafing, but he didn't look disconcerted. He looked more proud and vain than ever.

"Aren't you disappointed over losing your aristocratic bride?" she asked. "Or have you already found another one? Have you ruined some other father or brother who handed over his female relative?"

"You have such a sharp tongue. I can't decide why I keep bothering with you."

"Neither can I."

"I've never won anything those rich idiots didn't intentionally and eagerly gamble away, but I suppose it would be a waste of breath to mention it."

"It would," she concurred. "Since you're not giving Cliffside to Lady Felicia, what is your plan for it?"

"I have some other tenants in mind."

"Do you?" she fumed.

She'd been angry enough to picture him living at Cliffside with Lady Felicia. But now he'd blithely give it to someone else? The prospect enraged her, but before she could vent her fury, he slyly said, "Guess who bought your mission?"

"The lawyer wouldn't provide me with their names."

"*I* bought it."

"You?"

Her shoulders sagged with defeat. She was so stupid. The notion had never occurred to her, and if it had she would never have sold it.

"Why would you buy it?"

"I wanted you out of that horrid neighborhood, and you were too stubborn to leave on your own."

"So you yanked it out from under me."

"Yes, and I coughed up an exorbitant amount too, so don't you dare complain."

"I don't want the money. Give me my property back."

"No."

"I won't take charity from you."

"It wasn't charity, you little fool. It was money, lots and lots of money too. Take it and be glad."

She would have liked to protest, but in reality she *was* glad and wouldn't pretend otherwise. If she was cautious with her expenditures, the windfall would last a few years, so she had plenty of time to reorganize a life that was currently in shambles.

Besides, after all the harm he'd inflicted on her and her family, didn't she deserve some compensation?

"I am glad," she forced out. "Thank you."

"See? That wasn't so hard, was it?"

"It was pretty hard."

He laughed, which made her wish she could go back in time and retract the statement.

"I have another surprise too," he said.

"I hate surprises."

"No, you don't. Be quiet and listen."

Upon his arrival she hadn't noticed he was carrying a satchel filled with papers. He laid it on the table, opened the flap, and pulled out what appeared to be legal documents.

"What are those?" she asked.

He didn't explain, saying instead, "Once I agreed to wed Lady Felicia, I was to receive a dowry from Lord Stone of a plantation in Jamaica and a couple of ships."

"Lucky you." She oozed false cheer.

"When I jilted her, I should have lost them, but then—with Lady Felicia behaving so despicably toward you—I decided *you* should have them as damages."

"Damages?"

"Yes, damages, so the plantation and ships are yours."

"They're…what?"

"They're yours, free and clear. You can sell them if you like, but I've reviewed the accounts and they're very profitable. I'd keep them if I were you."

She felt as if she'd gone deaf. "I own a plantation? I own ships?"

"Yes. The past month, I've been negotiating with Lord Stone's lawyers. That's why I didn't stop by earlier. I couldn't bear to get your hopes up until it was finalized."

"You've been meeting with lawyers on my behalf?"

"Among other things, but it took forever. They thought they could cheat me, but they weren't cunning enough to figure out how." He picked up the glass of wine he'd poured and held it out to her. "Now would you drink with me to celebrate?"

She was trembling, and she reached for it and downed a hefty swallow. She hated it when he was charming and kind! When he was marvelous, she forgot that she loathed him.

"Why do all this?" She was so very, very confused.

"Because I don't want you to ever be poor again. From here on out, you'll always be wealthy and settled. You're not working again either—unless it's to volunteer on some rich woman's fussy project."

"I don't understand you."

"What's to understand?"

"Why would you bother?"

"Why would I…*bother?* I swear, Magdalena, your recent difficulties have addled your wits. I told you I love you. Did you assume I was joking?"

At his declaring himself, her heart flip-flopped with joy, but she ignored it. "Not…joking exactly, but you can't expect me to believe you were serious."

"Have I ever *not* been serious? Don't claim you don't know me well enough to have an opinion. You know me better than anyone. Don't deny it. If you try, I'll call you a liar."

Suddenly he stood and shoved the table aside. To her shock and dismay, he dropped to one knee and clasped her hand. She panicked and struggled to pull away, but of course he wouldn't let her.

It was overwhelming, having him so close. He had broad shoulders, the type a woman could lean on in times of trouble, and she yearned to fall into his arms, to weep against his chest and tell him how much he'd hurt her, how much she'd missed him.

Had she no pride? No shame? After all he'd perpetrated, what was she thinking?

But even as she posed the questions, a voice in her head was shouting for her to remember the good things he'd done, the inflated price he'd paid for her property, the negotiations with Lord Stone.

Because of his efforts, she'd never have to worry about money, would never have to fret about the future. The financial independence he'd provided was a gift without compare, a gift she'd always treasure.

"I asked you this before," he said, "that day in the carriage."

Her pulse started to race. "Asked me what?"

"I asked you to marry me, but I didn't do it very well. You were upset, and I was being vain and obnoxious."

"You were obnoxious. I heartily agree."

"So…I want to try again, and I'm begging you to let me. I plan to keep talking until I get it right."

He was so near, his mesmerizing blue eyes only inches from her own. She'd never been able to resist those eyes. When he gazed at her—as if she was special and amazing—she couldn't stand firm. Despite all that had occurred, she was anxious to hear his comments.

"I've always been alone," he murmured.

"I realize that you have."

"When I was younger, my life was very hard. I had to toughen up to survive. I told myself I was happy on my own, that I didn't need anyone."

"Everybody needs someone."

"I know that now. I learned it after I met you."

She blew out a heavy breath. "Don't be charming. If you are, I can't remain angry with you."

"You shouldn't be angry." For a moment he seemed to consider their recent history. "Well, perhaps you can be a little angry, but do you suppose you could forgive me?"

"Why should I?"

"Because I love you so much, I'm dying with it."

"You don't mean that."

"If you send me away, how will my life be worth living?"

It was such a pretty speech, and he was speaking the words she'd once been desperate to hear. Yet wasn't it too late for him to voice them?

Previously, when she'd been so madly in love with him, when she'd waited on tenterhooks for a similar statement, he'd been secretly engaged and had had no intention of ever binding himself to Maggie.

Couldn't he change his mind? Yes, but it was all too fast, too convenient. How did a man cry off from one betrothal and immediately pitch himself into a different one? She didn't trust the sudden change. She didn't trust *him*.

"I have no idea what to say," she told him.

"Say *yes*. Say you'll have me."

Overcome by his proximity, she leaned away. "Sit, would you, Michael?"

"You look like you're about to refuse me, so *no*, I won't sit."

"You are so stubborn."

"You don't know the half of it." He lifted her hands and kissed her palms. "What's troubling you?"

"Let it go, Michael. There's no point in my being cruel."

"Tell me," he pressed.

"I don't trust you."

"Why don't you? Except for my engagement, when have I ever been dishonest?"

"Well, let's see. How about when you gambled with Gaylord? How about when you came to Cliffside, but you didn't reveal why you were there? How about—"

"All right, all right," he hastily grumbled. "I've made some mistakes."

"You certainly have."

"In my defense, I didn't know you then. I only knew Gaylord, and he was such a horse's ass that I didn't care about anything but ruining him. But I care now."

"Do you really?"

She eased away, stood and went over to the window to stare into the garden at the rear of the house. It was a beautiful summer day, the flowers in bloom, big puffy clouds drifting by.

Behind her, he rose to his feet.

"No matter what ultimately happens between us," he said, "you can keep the ships and the plantation and the money. I have accountants and clerks who can manage your affairs if you require assistance. You wouldn't need me by your side."

She didn't glance at him. "No, it doesn't sound as if I would."

"But don't you ever think about how awful it is to be alone? Wouldn't you like to have a family, to have a place where you belong?"

"I might have thought about it occasionally," she grudgingly admitted.

"My most secret wish has always been that I would come home late at night and there would be a candle burning in the window just for me." He paused, emotion rocking him. "I've never had that type of existence, but I crave it so badly."

"Oh, Michael…"

He walked up and snuggled himself to her back. She elbowed him in the ribs, trying to force him away, but the arrogant beast wouldn't oblige her.

"Don't send me away, Maggie."

"I don't know what to do. I don't know what's best."

"Well, *I* know—even if you don't seem to." He spun her so she was facing him. "Be mine, Magdalena. Be mine forever. Please?"

"I doubt you'd be much of a husband."

"What if you're wrong? What if I turn out to be the greatest husband in history?"

She chuckled miserably and was disgusted to hear herself ask, "Where would we live?"

"Anywhere you wanted."

"How would we carry on?"

"I imagine we'd stumble through. I swear, if Ramsey and Rebecca can figure it out, I'm sure we can."

Her chuckle became a full-blown laugh.

Was she truly considering his proposal? Apparently yes. He was wearing her down, as he'd clearly understood he could. She was putty in his hands.

"Could we live at Cliffside? Would you apprise your new tenants that they can't have the property? Could we have it instead? Would you do that for me?"

"Those *new* tenants I was talking about? It's us, you silly girl. I was talking about us residing there as man and wife."

"You'd give me my home?"

"Yes. I'll sign the whole damn place over to you if that's what it will take to get you to have me."

She peered into his blue eyes, and a wave of visions raced in her mind. She remembered the first time she'd met him, how handsome and dashing he'd been. She recalled his slow seduction, her gradual relenting, her pathetic, inescapable glide to being in love.

They'd shared those splendid days at Orphan's Nest, a blissful sojourn that should never have ended.

He was infuriating and exasperating and impossibly conceited. He made her angrier than she'd ever been, but he made her feel so alive too. For so long, she'd been drifting, stuck at the rescue mission with no hope and no future that appealed. He'd brought her laughter and joy and passion. The few brief weeks she'd spent with him had been the most frustratingly wonderful period.

Could she refuse him? Could she send him away? What if she never saw him again? Could she bear it? The resounding answer was *no*.

He'd asked her, what if he was the best husband ever? What if he was?

He could be cruel and tough and merciless and domineering, but he could also be generous, kind, helpful, and supportive. Would she toss it all away? For what? To remain a spinster?

"I need to hear your reply," he said, "and then, depending on what it is, I have to tell you something important."

She blanched. With his penchant for mischief, it could be any ghastly tidings.

"Tell me what it is first."

"No. I can't have it influence your decision."

She studied him, but of course his expression gave nothing away.

He dropped to one knee again, and he gazed up at her, his affection washing over her like a cool rain.

"Will you marry me, Magdalena? Will you make me the happiest man in the world?"

She was conflicted and confused, but ultimately she forced out, "Yes,

Michael, I will marry you. I must have gone mad, but I believe I will."

She pulled him to his feet as he grinned and preened.

"I knew I could convince you."

"Vain oaf," she scolded. "You've pressured me horridly, so what's your news? If it's dreadful, I rescind every word I just uttered."

"You are a hard woman, Magdalena Wells."

"I'm learning from the master."

"So you are. So you are." He rested his hands on her waist, looking very much as if he was on a high cliff and about to jump off. "I have some information about my past, about my parents."

"Rebecca mentioned it. She said you're changing your surname."

"Actually, I was never Michael *Scott*. Very soon, I will announce that I'm Michael Blair."

"How did you discover this?"

"I've always known. I have some old papers someone stuck in my coat when I was tiny."

"But why now?"

"Because...my sister is searching for me."

"Your sister? My goodness. Who is she?"

"It's Evangeline Drake, Maggie. It's Lady Run."

"Evangeline!"

"Yes, although if memory serves, her name is Annie. We used to call her Sissy. I can't guess how she became Evangeline."

"You're certain of this?"

"Yes. I haven't spoken to her yet, but I'm about to."

"Why keep it a secret until after I agreed to wed you? This isn't bad news. This is wonderful."

"I didn't want to unduly sway you. I wanted you to accept me for *me*, and not because of who my brother is—or who my father was."

"Who is your brother? Who was your father?"

"My father should have been Earl of Radcliffe, and my brother, Bryce, will be someday—if I have my way in the affair."

"Did you say *Earl* of Radcliffe?"

"Yes, the title is connected to a small estate in Scotland."

"You're not joking?"

"Let's review, Maggie. Do I ever joke?"

"No."

"I was a little lost lord, but—"

"You've been found."

"I've been found," he said, appearing amazed.

She shook her head, as stunned as he appeared to be. "It's so bizarre. I have to hear every detail."

Michael grinned his wickedest grin. "You should call me *Lord* Michael."

"Never."

Rebecca poked her nose into the room. "It's awfully quiet in here. You two haven't killed each other, have you?"

"Not yet," Michael told her.

"Maggie," her sister teased, "you're glowering—as if he fed you a sour pickle. What's wrong?"

"He proposed."

Rebecca raised her hands to the heavens as if in prayer. "Hallelujah! Please tell me you said *yes*."

"She said *yes*," Michael answered. "I would have harangued until she did. She knew that. She gave in merely to shut me up."

"You're a lot like my husband," Rebecca said.

"I'll take that as a compliment," Michael replied.

"Rebecca," Maggie stammered, "he's…from an aristocratic family.

He claims Lady Run is his sister. If I marry him, I'll be marrying an aristocrat."

"Why are you so shocked?" Rebecca asked. "Look at the bloody man. Why would you have ever thought he was anything *but* an aristocrat?"

Michael puffed himself up. "I think she should call me Lord Michael, don't you? Or just My Lord Husband."

"Absolutely," Rebecca concurred. "So…it's all settled? It's fine?"

Michael turned to Maggie. "What do you say, Maggie? It was easy enough to tell me when we were alone."

"It wasn't easy at all!"

"Can you say it in front of your sister? Can you say it to the whole world?"

She gazed over at Rebecca, then gazed at Michael. He had been—and always would be—her heart's delight. He was smiling at her, appearing so deliciously magnificent that her pulse raced again. Maybe it would never slow down.

"Yes, Rebecca," she admitted, "I'm suddenly engaged."

"Told you," Michael muttered, preening again.

"If he plays his cards right," Maggie said, "I might call him my *lord* every now and then."

"If I play my *cards* right?" he scoffed. "My dear, Magdalena, since you've agreed to be my bride, it's obvious I've won every blasted hand."

EPILOGUE

"I'd like to speak with Lady Run."

"Who shall I tell her is calling?"

Michael almost said *her brother*, but he didn't suppose it was the sort of news he should divulge to the woman's butler.

"Tell her it's Michael Scott. We're acquainted."

"Please come in."

The butler stepped back so Michael could enter the house, and he was escorted to a front parlor and seated on a sofa.

"It may be a few minutes before she can see you."

"That's all right," Michael said. "She wasn't expecting me, and I'm in no hurry."

"While you wait, may I bring you a refreshment?"

There were liquor decanters over on a sideboard, and he thought it was absolutely the moment for a stiff glass of whiskey. Then again, if he planned to introduce himself to his sister, perhaps he shouldn't have the odor of alcohol on his breath.

He dithered, then pointed to one of the decanters.

"Is that whiskey?"

"Yes."

"Pour me a tall glass." The butler couldn't quite hide his surprise, and Michael added, "She and I are about to have a difficult discussion. I should probably fortify myself."

"Very good, sir."

The man prepared the beverage and left Michael alone, promising to return as soon as Lady Run was free. Michael dawdled, the silence settling in. He gazed around, assessing the furniture, the paintings on the walls, the rugs on the floor.

From her humble orphan's existence, she'd risen so high, had landed herself an amazing spot in the world. Her husband, Aaron Drake, Lord Run, was a fine man, his greatest asset in Michael's view being that he didn't gamble. Most of Lord Run's peers were addicted to wagering, and it took a challenging level of restraint to decline to join in.

Maggie and Evangeline had attended the same boarding school, had been friends throughout the years, losing touch after they'd graduated and Maggie had gotten engaged to Gaylord Farrow.

Michael had made Maggie cough up every detail she remembered about his sister, peppering her with questions until she'd finally thrown up her hands and claimed she couldn't recall another fact.

She'd begged to accompany him to Evangeline's home, but Michael had refused to let her. This was a conversation that should be private, that should be special and participated in by only the two of them. There would be plenty of time later on for Maggie and Evangeline to chatter about it like hens in a henhouse.

In his mind, he reached out to his twin brother. Now that he'd been told about Matthew, now that his memories had been jarred, he was recollecting scattered tidbits.

They'd been toddlers when they were separated, and Michael still distinctly felt the loss, the heartbreak and grief having never completely faded.

Matthew, are you there? It's me, Michael. It's your brother.

It was becoming easier to reach out, easier to mentally connect. He could sense that Matthew heard him, that Matthew was aware of Michael digging around in his head, but clearly Matthew was as confused and bewildered as Michael had always been.

No doubt Matthew wondered if he was insane—just as Michael had wondered.

I'm about to talk to Sissy. She's so pretty. She's all grown up, and she looks just like Mother. She sings just like Mother too.

"Ha!" Michael smirked to himself. "Stew on that for a while, little brother."

Somehow Michael knew he was the older twin, that he'd always been the older brother.

He tarried in the quiet, thinking, reviewing what he wanted to say, but no matter how often he'd rehearsed his speech it never seemed exactly right. Should he blurt it out? Should he work up to it slowly? What if she didn't believe him? What if she accused him of lying?

Even as the dreadful notion roiled him, he pushed it away. He had the birth certificate, but even if he didn't he was certain she'd instantly grasp he was speaking the truth. She could simply peer into his eyes and she'd *know*.

He sipped his drink, his anxiety spiraling to the point that he considered leaving without seeing her. Which was absurd. Why be afraid? Why fret?

The tragic secret was about to be revealed. He didn't have to hold it in anymore, and he suspected—once he shared his story with Evangeline—

the anguish that had constantly consumed him would vanish.

Gradually he realized that the house wasn't as deserted as he imagined. It dawned on him that a woman was singing. The sound drifted by, and he cocked his head, listening, and he was positive it was Evangeline.

Was there a music room? He'd bet there was. Every rich man's mansion he'd ever entered had a music room.

The butler hadn't appeared to fetch Michael, and it would be incredibly rude to wander about and find her on his own. Her butler was very competent, and there was no reason to suppose that he wouldn't bring Michael to her the minute she was available.

But Michael was so keen to get it over with.

He stood, listened again, and started off. After a few twists and turns, he stumbled on her in a small salon.

She was seated at a harpsichord over by the window, the yellow sun reflecting off her hair so it glowed like a halo. As he focused on the words of her song, another memory stirred.

It was a lullaby their mother had sung to them every night. It had silly lyrics that had made them giggle and sing with her. An impression of…joy, of happy children and doting parents swept through him. He didn't remember actual, physical events with his family, but he remembered those feelings of joy.

Oh, how wrenching it was to be confronted with all that they had lost.

Someone would have to pay for taking it from them. Michael wasn't the type of man who could sit idly by and let such an injustice go unremarked. Had his father been the same way? Had Michael inherited his father's stubbornness and cunning, his sense of right and wrong? He hoped so.

She came to the end of the tune, her fingers playing the last chord, and she was very still, her eyes closed. Suddenly their mother seemed to be hovering, her presence so tangible Michael was surprised he couldn't observe her over Evangeline's shoulder.

"Sissy?" he murmured.

She scowled and tensed as if unsure she'd really heard him, as if it might have been a ghost from their past.

"Sissy. It's me. It's Michael."

Her eyes flew open and she gasped. They stared, their identical blue gazes locked together, a thousand unvoiced questions flitting between them.

"Michael Scott..." she said.

"No, Michael Blair. It's always been Michael Blair."

"I've been searching for you."

"I know."

"Why didn't you tell me, you scoundrel?"

"I couldn't figure out how."

"But I should have guessed who you were, shouldn't I? I should have guessed."

"I think you knew all along."

Her smile lit up the room. "I think I knew too."

She jumped up from the harpsichord so fast the stool fell over behind her. She raced over to him and leapt into his arms, and he hugged her as tightly as he could. He twirled her in circles until they were both dizzy and out of breath.

"Call me Sissy again," she told him as she laughed and cried. "Call me Sissy and never, ever stop."

THE END

Don't Miss the Second Novel in
Cheryl Holt's "LOST LORDS" Trilogy!

Heart's Desire

The Story of Matthew (Blair) Harlow and Clarissa Merrick

Coming in July, 2015!

CHAPTER ONE

"Wake up!"

Matthew Harlow heard the curt summons, but he was dreaming fitfully and couldn't rouse himself.

It was a beautiful summer day in August, and he was napping on the ground, the grass providing a welcome cushion. The prior evening, he'd over imbibed in a manner he normally never would, so he had a ghastly hangover. As they'd galloped down the country road, his head had been pounding so fiercely he'd finally had to stop.

He'd found a shady spot under the bows of a huge oak tree and dozed off.

"Wake up!"

The voice came again, and he swatted with his hand and sank back into his dream. Or perhaps he should call it a nightmare. When he was a little boy, he'd nearly died in a fire at a coaching inn, and the memory had plagued him all his life. It seemed to represent a great loss, the final time he'd been truly happy—though why that would be so, he couldn't imagine.

He was trying, as usual, to escape the flames. The halls were chaotic, people running and crying. He reached out to someone who was hidden from view, and he stretched farther and farther, never quite able to grasp the person who was waiting for him out there in the dark.

His nostrils filled with smoke. He couldn't see, couldn't breathe. He couldn't…

"Matthew!"

He jolted to a sitting position, the details vivid enough that he expected to be three years old again and racing down the burning stairs.

But no, he was nestled under the oak. His annoying, dashing younger brother, Rafe Harlow, was seated next to him, their horses hobbled down by the creek and munching on the grass.

"What time is it?" Matthew asked.

"I'm not a clock," Rafe replied. "How would I know?"

"How long was I asleep?"

"Too bloody long, and I'm sick of dawdling here, listening to you wail like a baby. Was it the fire dream or the ship dream?"

"The fire."

Matthew had always had bad dreams, but they generally alternated between two subjects: a fire and a departing ship. He and Rafe had shared a bed when they were children, so Rafe had had plenty of opportunities to witness Matthew moaning with dismay and thrashing around.

"Let's get going," Rafe said. "I want this over with."

"I don't."

"So you've claimed on a hundred different occasions. You're the most ungrateful lout."

"I'm not ungrateful," Matthew said. "I'm…exhausted."

"Whose fault is that? You've been reveling like a man on his way to the gallows."

"This will be difficult—the whole affair. Our arrival. The transfer of ownership. I don't have the energy, and with this hangover, I'll probably make a mash of it."

"You always make a mash of it. You're too stubborn and inflexible, so you simply bluster in and piss everyone off."

"I wish I'd never saved a single soul."

"You'd have rather they all drowned?"

"No," Matthew groused, "but if I'd been a tad less noble, we'd still be in Europe, tending to the sort of business we understand."

"Soldiering…" Rafe uttered the term like an endearment, like a caress.

They were soldiers, with Rafe a lowly private and Matthew a tough, hardened captain. He had years of valorous combat under his belt. He wasn't afraid of anything, never quailed or dithered, never cowered or retreated, and Rafe was learning his worst habits.

Soldiering they comprehended. Soldiering was where they excelled. They'd been raised in a world of men, thrived in a world of men. It's what they knew, what they enjoyed. Diplomacy and tact were what eluded Matthew. He said what he thought, spoke his mind, and deftly carried out every order and promise.

People who assumed he wouldn't, who misjudged or underestimated him, did so at their peril. He was too used to having his own way.

He had all the traits necessary to be a good leader, to convince men to follow him. With his bold strength and unfailing courage, men yearned to imitate him, to be like him, but none of them could ever hope to muster his brave daring.

As to women…?

He had limited experience with women, other than the rough and tumble types in army camps and port towns. He'd never spent much time around females, unless it was to have them perform salacious services.

His only variation had been his recent decision to keep a mistress.

Penelope Bernard was British, and he'd met her in Belgium at an officers' soiree. She was the daughter of an important government official, but he couldn't see that her behavior was much different from any other trollop.

She had several scandals in her past, which was why she'd been hiding in Belgium, having been banished there by her father. Her illicit path was widely recognized, so marriage for her wasn't likely, and she was happy to find an idiot like Matthew to pay her bills.

He'd involved himself in a manner he'd never intended, and already he was wondering what had possessed him. But then, she was extremely proficient on a mattress, and a man could never discount such a boon.

"How far is it to Greystone?" he asked.

"I'm not a map either," Rafe snapped.

"You're a ray of sunshine today, aren't you?"

"My hangover is worse than yours, but you don't hear me complaining every two seconds."

"No, you just bite my head off at every turn."

"Well, I'm tired of you."

"I'm tired of me too."

Rafe pushed himself to his feet. "Get a move on, you bloody hero."

"Don't call me that."

"What, hero?"

"Yes. You know I hate all the fuss."

"You didn't seem to when we were standing in that cocked-up salon at the palace and everyone was cheering your name."

Matthew rolled his eyes. "It was pointless folderol."

"You had every beauty in the room hanging on your arm."

"There is that."

"It put Penelope's nose out of joint to see that gaggle drooling over you."

"She needs to have her nose tweaked every so often."

"That she does," Rafe agreed.

For all of the life Matthew remembered, it had been just him and Rafe. Matthew was thirty and Rafe twenty-two, with Matthew the older, wiser, tougher brother who'd watched over Rafe, protected him, and never left him behind.

With them being the only siblings in the Harlow family, Rafe had never had to share Matthew with anyone or compete for Matthew's attention. Rafe loathed Penelope and was jealous of Matthew's relationship with her, but it was silly for him to fret.

She was stunningly pretty, but acted like a whore. She was also vain and greedy, so there was much about her that was unlikable. He suspected—if Greystone turned out to be magnificent—she'd attempt to finagle a marriage proposal out of him.

But Matthew wasn't a fool and—should he ever wed—he'd never pick such a spoiled, immoral brat. He'd marry for love and affection, which were things he thought he might have once had, but had lost somewhere along the way.

Rafe oozed appeal and charisma, his bravery and boldness indisputable, but he was a child at heart, and Matthew would never choose Penelope over Rafe. Matthew's bond with Rafe was unbreakable and eternal.

"Let's go," Rafe urged again. "Since we're unsure of how far we still have to travel, I'd rather not arrive in the dark."

"Neither would I."

Head pounding, Matthew stood and brushed off his clothes while Rafe readied the horses. They mounted and rode on, the name of his new estate—Greystone—echoing with each clop of hooves.

After another hour or so, they found the front gate, a pretentious arch over the entrance, with *Greystone* chiseled into the stone. They reined in and studied the lane that wound into the woods, the house not yet visible.

"Ready?" Rafe asked.

"As ready as I'll ever be."

"I'll race you."

"We're not racing," Matthew scolded. "I have no desire to gallop in like a pair of bandits bent on robbery."

"Do you think the servants know we're coming?"

"The place is empty. It's what I was told, anyway."

"What will we do for help?"

"Rafe, we've lived in army camps for…what? Fifteen years? Twenty years?"

"Yes."

"We can fend for ourselves for a few days."

"I guess we'll survive."

"Plus, I imagine they're all in the village, waiting to hear if I'll keep them on."

"Will you?"

"It depends if I like their looks or not."

"That's what you say about soldiers under your command."

"It's the same animal." He nodded up the lane. "You first."

"No, *you* first," Rafe insisted. "It's your property. You should lead us."

Matthew might have presumed Rafe was being courteous, except that his words dripped with sarcasm.

Ever since the night of his alleged heroics, they'd viewed the entire brouhaha as a hilarious nuisance. He'd been on that deserted beach by accident, watching as a ship had foundered in heavy seas, then been impaled on the sharp rocks of the coastline. It sank quickly, water sweeping over the deck.

Passengers had started jumping into the surf and almost all of them had been women and children. He'd always been a strong swimmer and had the courage of a lion, so he'd dove in and begun rescuing people. He'd done a fine job of it too, saving nearly everyone, with only a handful of the crew and some toddlers lost to the tempest.

Later, he learned that the ship was filled with the families of high-ranking British officers. They'd been on their way to visit their husbands and fathers in Belgium. And of course, three of them had turned out to be favored royal cousins. After that discovery, Matthew's intention to ignore the incident had evaporated.

He'd been decorated and praised and lauded until the clamor had grown embarrassing. The last straw had been his receipt of Greystone as a reward for his valor to the Crown and the citizens of Britain. It all seemed too much, and he'd planned to decline the gesture, but Rafe had yanked Matthew to his senses before he could make such a recklessly stupid decision.

Though no one would listen, Matthew kept insisting he'd simply behaved as any other man would have, but the honors had been foisted on him despite his protests. His acclaim had become so pronounced that he'd finally shrugged and opted to revel in the moment. It was interesting to have something different happen for a change, something that didn't involve fighting and maiming and killing.

They rode into the woods, Matthew's eyes alert, checking out the trees, the blue sky above. The woods opened to orchards, then meadows of grass where horses grazed and frolicked.

Eventually they rounded a bend, and it loomed in front of them. Greystone Abbey. It was huge, solid, constructed of grey brick and shaped like an ancient castle, with turrets—turrets!—on the corners, ivy clinging to the walls.

"There it is," Rafe said. "What do you think?"

Matthew struggled to exhibit nonchalance. "It'll do, I suppose."

"Bloody right, you lucky bastard."

Jaws agape, they stared and stared, taken aback by the grandeur, by the majesty. He'd expected a sturdy house, perhaps a few fields and a manicured garden. Not a castle fit for a king. Not orchards and herds of cattle and horses running in the pasture.

Matthew whistled and shook his head. "Sweet Jesu…"

"How could you have ever thought to refuse all this, Matthew?" Rafe asked. "Are you sure this is the correct place?"

"I'm pretty sure. We can both read. The sign at the entrance said Greystone. I doubt there are two such estates in this part of the country."

"Probably not." Rafe glanced over at him, his impish grin infectious. "Are you ready for this?"

"Give me a minute." Matthew studied the Abbey, the barns behind, the rolling hills beyond. Clearly the servants were still in residence. He could see people going about their chores.

Rafe noticed the same. "Nobody's left."

"No, it doesn't appear they have."

"If the servants are here, the Merricks are likely here too. If they are, this could get tricky."

"It definitely could," Matthew agreed.

Greystone Abbey had previously been owned by a man named Harold Merrick who'd concocted a massive financial swindle. The deceit had ultimately defrauded several of the kingdom's most notable aristocrats, as well as the Prince Regent and Duke of York.

As a result, Mr. Merrick had forfeited everything and been jailed, having had the good sense to hang himself in his cell before he could be shipped off to the penal colonies in Australia. His downfall had provided Matthew's rise to prosperity, and while Matthew hated to consider Mr. Merrick's loss, Merrick had obviously been an idiot, so no sympathy was warranted.

Yet…what about his family? If they were skulking about, feeling aggrieved and robbed of their heritage, they wouldn't be happy to have Matthew riding in.

"Let's switch coats." Matthew said.

"What?"

"For the moment, you'll be Captain Harlow."

"A promotion! Wonderful! Will I receive an increase in wages?"

"No."

"But I'm to be your superior?"

"You'll never be my superior, you wise buck. We'll just play a game on the occupants until we learn the lay of the land."

"They'll think I'm you, but who will you be?"

"I'll be Private Rafe Harlow, your trusted advisor and friend."

"If we're using the same surname, we have to admit we're brothers."

"All right, but no one ever believes we are."

And they weren't, actually. Matthew had been raised by Rafe's parents, taken in by them after the fire when Matthew was a little boy. Matthew's parents had died in the tragedy, and in the chaotic aftermath, Rafe's mother—who'd also been staying at the inn—had brought him home for what was to have been a short hiatus.

Yet no kin had ever searched for Matthew, and Mrs. Harlow had never been able to find a relative to claim him. Or so she'd said. She'd assumed herself to be barren, so she'd kept Matthew and reared him as her own. Then Rafe had come along and killed her during the birthing.

Matters had gone downhill from there.

But they declared themselves to be brothers, though they were nothing alike. They were both six feet tall, with the tough, honed stature of soldiers, but Rafe was golden blond, charming, and dashing. Women studied him with keen interest whenever he passed by.

Matthew was handsome too, but his looks were more mature, more rough and tumble. His hair was dark, his eyes very, very blue, and with his dangerous air of menace and daring, he was more highwayman than gentleman. When he and Rafe stood side by side, they might have been an angel and a devil, the perfect pair for an artist to paint on a church ceiling.

"How long do I get to be a captain?" Rafe inquired.

"Probably for a day or two. I'll have a better feel for the place if no one's certain of my status."

"Can I act all arrogant and officious?"

"Yes, but if you grow too obnoxious, I'll let you know."

"I could never be *too* obnoxious. I'm marvelous. Ask any of the ladies."

Matthew snorted with disgust. "Give me your coat."

Rafe grinned. "Once I have, can I order you around—as you've always ordered me?"

"No. Now shut up and give me your coat."

Heart's Desire

Matthew and Clarissa

Book #2 of the Lost Lords Trilogy

Coming in July, 2015!

ABOUT THE AUTHOR

CHERYL HOLT IS A *New York Times, USA Today,* and Amazon "Top 100" bestselling author of thirty-nine novels.

She's also a lawyer and mom, and at age forty, with two babies at home, she started a new career as a commercial fiction writer. She'd hoped to be a suspense novelist, but couldn't sell any of her manuscripts, so she ended up taking a detour into romance where she was stunned to discover that she has a knack for writing some of the world's greatest love stories.

Her books have been released to wide acclaim, and she has won or been nominated for many national awards. She has been hailed as "The Queen of Erotic Romance" as well as "The International Queen of Villains." She is particularly proud to have been named "Best Storyteller of the Year" by the trade magazine Romantic Times BOOK Reviews.

She lives and writes in Hollywood, California, and she loves to hear from fans. Visit her website at www.cherylholt.com.

Printed in Great Britain
by Amazon